I0565337

INSIDE
Part 1

by Kyra Anderson

THE
AMIVERSE

www.the-amiverse.com

Website: www.kjamidon.com

Published by K.J. Amidon

ISBN: 978-0-9832280-6-6

1st Edition © 2014
2nd Edition © 2024

Cover Art by K.J. Amidon

Printed in the United States

Dedicated to:

My friends and family who inspire me every day

R&D&Z, who put up with brainstorming sessions until the wee hours of the morning. You guys are awesome!

Beckers, for listening to me talk about this book incessantly!

Cheryl, you are my rock. You helped me through this darkness. I'll never be able to thank you enough.

Table of Contents

Author's Note

Welcome, Reader!

Inside is a very long novel that has been broken into three parts in order to be easily digestible and affordable to you.

This novel is not for the faint of heart or easily-offended. The story elements of this novel are meant to provoke intense and often unpleasant emotions. This is not a warning to try and sound edgy—this is to cover my bases in case some readers do not heed all the other warnings before purchasing this book.

Like all authors I ask that you suspend your knowledge of reality and step into the world created in these pages. Please remember that this is a work of fiction! Any similarities to people, places, or situations are not intentional. None of these events are meant to push political agendas, nor should anything in this book be taken as politically accurate. The politics, laws, and scenarios in Inside are 100% fiction.

This book has been broken into three (almost) equal parts. This book gets progressively darker, and due to the dark themes of this book, there are two endings. If you find that the first two parts of this novel are testing your mental limits, please read the *Alternate* Part Three. Please remember that this is not a series, but one continuous novel. Parts Two and Three will not recap everything that occurs in this book other than a quick synopsis in the Author's Note at the beginning. Part Two picks up on Chapter Thirty-Six and continues where this book leaves off.

Prepare yourself to enter the dark and twisted world inside the Commission of the People and follow Lily Sandover as she fights to keep her freedom and her sanity from the clutches of Dana Christenson.

Chapter One

Things could always be worse.

There were worse things in life than having to move away from the city I had always called home. For instance, our country could still be locked in civil war, and we could still be wrapped up in foreign politics at the expense of our country's stability. The crime in our country could also be at the high rate seen just before the Second Revolutionary War.

But none of that was the case.

So having to move away from everything I had ever known was devastating.

My father was running for the position of Official Regulator of America's Western Region. It had been obvious from the start of the running that he had the people's favor. Three months travelling the region and making connections with those who would be working under him if he was appointed practically secured his victory.

I came from a long line of politicians. My paternal grandfather had even run for Leader of America decades previous. Despite the fact that the Second Revolution had ended two decades before he ran, and he had seen the carnage of the revolts first-hand, he did not have what it took to keep the former United States on the mend from the bloody revolution and lost the running, though remained in politics until the year of his death.

Having been raised in the political arena, it only made sense that my father followed the same path. As with most government officials, he started on the Regulation Force, keeping the peace in the Western Region by enforcing the codes set by Central and the Commission of the People—the government branches founded on the tail of the Second Revolution. During his years in the Regulation Force he met my mother, a filing secretary at his office. They married and had me after obtaining their Child Rearing Permit—which was granted after the allotted five-year waiting period.

Seventeen years later, I, Lily Sandover, was filled with dread at knowing my father was going to become Official Regulator of the Western Region and, consequently, the reason my family would uproot.

On the day of the decision I went to school as usual, thinking of the friends I would leave behind when our family moved to the new American capital, Central.

Diane and Marcie were waiting for me outside the front gate of our school, knowing I was dreading the events of the day and prepared to do what they could to cheer me up.

"Think about it this way, at least you can get away from Mrs. Crane now," Marcie laughed, referring to our brutal and foul-smelling biology teacher.

"The silver lining." I rolled my eyes. "But with my luck, she has a twin in Central."

There was a sense of foreboding about leaving my old life. I had absolutely no interest in politics. Politics made things overly-complicated and filled the population with fear and anger. But with my family so heavily involved in the tiers of Central, it was expected that I would also become an active member of Central society.

The Second Revolution had ended seven decades previous but the country was still caught up in the glory of the reform. Everywhere I turned there were reminders of the revolution. People would regale tales of the conflict, demonizing the corruption of the Washington System while simultaneously managing to make me feel like my generation was charged with keeping the legacy of our Central forefathers alive.

It was a societal expectation I could barely stomach.

As I ate lunch with my friends, trying not to panic about my father's appointment, another friend, Mary, clamored to our table, terrified about her history test in thirty short minutes.

"Quick, help me," she said breathlessly. "Thomas Ankell led the Purging of Washington with the Children of America after the government massacred which university rally?"

"Reform or Rebel Rally, which marched down the west coast and were massacred on their way to Stanford University, which officially started the Second Revolution and led to Washington being burned to the ground," I answered. My father had drilled me on major events of the Second Revolution before I could even pronounce most of the words correctly, making me the go-to study aide for most of my class on the history of the Second Revolution.

"And Ankell went into hiding…when?"

"When the True New World group attacked Central to try and overthrow him," Diane answered. "The True New World group was crushed when the Commission of the People was first established."

"Right," Mary said with a nod. "And the Commission was started by Ankell's right hand man, Bryant…Matthews?"

"Morris," I corrected.

"Why do I keep wanting to say Matthews?" Mary groaned, rolling her eyes. "Okay, Bryant *Morris*. Also, the study guide says know the first three courses the Commission of the People started in their first twenty days..." Her eyes scanned the table pleadingly. "...help?"

"Did you study at all?"

"No. I tried, but I had a huge chemistry project and I totally forgot about this test!"

"That's what you get for slipping out of class to go to the lab," I teased.

"I want to go into pharmaceutical research," Mary defended. "My grade in Advanced Chem could impact which university I get into."

"Are you sure this has nothing to do with Mr. Hyatt?" Diane leered, causing everyone to chuckle at the thought of our serious, but decently-attractive, chemistry teacher.

"No!" Mary defended. "Please, just help me."

"Okay," I started, grabbing her attention, "remember it this way. What is the motto of the Commission of the People?"

"To preserve the rights, humanity, and well-being of the people of America."

"Exactly. First, The Preservation of the American Life, where the Commission purged the country of all non-citizens and all whose family had been brought here as slaves, illegal immigrants, or expatriates, as well as any others that the Commission deemed 'undesirable.' Second, the Humanities Course. What did that one do?"

"That was when the Commission dissolved the state lines and determined the region boundaries. That way they could rebuild whatever had been destroyed during the Second Revolution region by region."

"Good, and the third? Think back to the motto."

"The...Well-Being and...Country Conservation Course?" Mary said, scrunching her face in thought.

"You got it."

"And that was when they started construction on the north and south border walls and the American Foreigners Regulations were enacted," Mary completed. "Okay, I think I can remember that. And just to be sure I got this right, Ankell stepped down from leading the country *before* he died, right? Leader Hank Fannen was the first Leader after Ankell, but Ankell was still around."

"Yeah, Ankell died from a heart attack years after he stepped down," Marcie concluded.

"Okay, and the last part says our essay question is going to be to give a brief summary of the role of the Commission of the People."

"That should be easy. The Commission of the People monitors the Regulation Forces of the regions," I answered. "They ensure the well-being of everyone in the country and act as the active intermediary between the American people and Central. The Commission keeps the country running smoothly. Currently, the Commission of the People is headed by Dana Christenson."

"The most powerful man in the entire country other than Leader Simon," Marcie added, "and no one has seen his face."

"Makes you wonder, doesn't it?" Diane said, raising her eyebrows. "Why is he in hiding?"

"Maybe he's really smart and powerful and everything, but he's hideous," Mary suggested with a laugh.

Quizzing Mary, unfortunately, brought my attention back to my family situation with laser focus. I was happy for my father's growing achievements and success, of course. He had worked very hard, trying to balance his ambitions for advancement while being available to his family. He had never made me feel that his job was more important than me—even though I knew he was responsible for the well-being of thousands. I knew it was selfish to be so upset about the move.

Even though I lived in the biggest city on the coast of the Western Region, my school felt very small that day as everyone wished me luck, as if *I* was the one running for the position. Teachers caught me after class and encouraged me, saying that my father would most certainly get the appointment.

Marcie, Mary, Diane, Sonya, and I walked home together after school, as we had since being trusted to leave school without parental supervision. We lived in the same neighborhood and even though it was a thirty-minute walk, none of us could drive—the driving age was twenty-one, four long years away.

"Mary, how did the test go?" Diane asked. "Did you remember Bryant Matthews?"

"I remembered Bryant *Morris*," Mary said with a playful glare. She turned to me. "Thanks, Lily. I would have been dead without you."

"You're welcome." Mary's face dropped, seeing my forced expression.

"Worried about your dad?"

"No, not really," I said. "I just don't want to leave. I don't want to go to Central and go to school with the children of other politicians."

"It won't be so bad," Sonya said. "Maybe you'll even find a boyfriend."

I groaned. "It's so nice to know I have to move away completely to find a boyfriend."

"Well, I think everyone in the city remembers that you broke Tommy Barker's nose two years ago."

"He grabbed my ass," I defended, "what was I supposed to do?"

"Oh, no doubt he deserved it," Diane agreed. "But now everyone is afraid of you. Tommy was a *big* guy. He changed schools because of you!"

Gossip about other students entertained us on the walk home, including the rumors about a pregnant classmate who was facing the sentence of abortion and a three-thousand dollar fine for conceiving a child not permitted by a Child Rearing License.

The pregnancy laws were put in place by the Commission of the People in the Family Preservation Act, which defined the ideal American family. Marriage was only allowed after the age of twenty-five and after a required two-year engagement, lowering divorce rates dramatically. Divorces were looked down upon, and the children of broken homes were often heavily-bullied and put on watch as being "unstable." That led to high suicide rates among broken-home children. The Child Rearing License was meant to eliminate the possibility of children living in such undesirable environments. The five-year waiting period for children demanded that the couple prove economic stability, proper upstanding moral codes, and mental acuity for acceptable American parenting.

Unfortunately for me, nothing in those child rearing laws prevented parents from moving their children away from their home towns.

When I stepped through my front door I was greeted by my cat, Dexter, a routine that had been repeated for nearly five years.

"Hey, Dex." I stooped to pick him up. "Did you behave today?"

"Lily?"

"Hi, Mom!" I replied, following her voice to the dining room. I stopped in the doorway, shocked to see papers spread over the table's surface, cascading around my mother and her laptop. "What's all this?"

"Most of it is for the campaign," she answered. "Funding papers, mostly." I glanced over the stacks, overwhelmed by the mere sight of so much paperwork. "Lily," my mother beckoned, motioning me closer, "what do you think of this house?"

"Mom..." I groaned. "You're looking for houses already?"

"We have to be prepared."

"Dad hasn't even won, yet."

"You don't think he'll win?" she said in a tone that sounded condescending. I forced a smile, placing my hands on her shoulders and leaning down to kiss her cheek.

"Of course he'll win."

Once I was able to escape from house hunting in Central, I disappeared into my room, Dex happily curled in my arms. I couldn't tell my parents how much I dreaded Dad's victory. I could never tell them how much I hated politics and the constant reminders of the Second Revolution that plagued everyday life. I understood the significance of the war, but the way it was discussed made it sound like a religion rather than a historical event.

I flopped onto my bed, snuggling with Dex, pondering the rapidly-changing direction of my life with my stomach in angry knots.

My father had always said if I did not want to work for Central he was not going to force the issue—but he said it with the parental tone that suggested he would be "disappointed" if I did not continue the family tradition of political careers. It was such an important part of his life that he wanted his only child to share in his passion. I felt guilty for wanting no part in Central, but even the thought of participating in the circus of the government made me feel sick.

I pulled Dex closer, trying to make myself as small as possible on my bed.

I did not realize I had fallen asleep until the sound of the front door woke me.

"Karen? Lily? I'm home!" my father called. I took a few deep breaths, blinking the sleep from my eyes and mentally preparing to share my parents' enthusiasm for Dad's campaign.

I made my way downstairs, the sinking feeling in my gut consuming me with each step. My father was happy. *Very* happy.

"There's my beautiful little girl!" he greeted, hugging me tightly and kissing my cheek.

"I'm not so little anymore, Dad."

"I know," he said. "But you'll always be my little girl." He looked between my mother and me. Mom looked expectant, trying not to grin *too* broadly.

"Alright, alright." He raised his hands. "I spoke with Cynthia earlier and she says that, so far, I'm in the lead."

"That's wonderful! Tom, that's *wonderful!*" my mother gasped, ecstatic. She rushed forward, kissing him. I forced my smile wider, feeling my face pale a few shades.

I understood that there was no logical reason to feel such anxiety at moving away. True, I would be away from my friends and everything I considered comfortable, and I knew our new city would be entirely focused on politics. Yet those were not at the core of my fears. There was something deep in the pit of my stomach screaming at me that

Central was dangerous. It was a feeling I could not explain, nor completely ignore.

Our family spent the rest of the evening camping around the living room. I sat in a chair with Dex, reading a book while my parents actively watched the news coverage on the new appointments in the Regulation Force.

I had never had a problem concentrating on a book over my surroundings before. Living in a house where there were constant visitors, whether political advisors or other members of the Regulation Force, had honed my ability to focus on my homework when there were forty other people talking in the same room. But even as I moved my eyes over the screen of my e-reader, I could not absorb the words of the story.

My worry was making it impossible to drown out the noise on the television.

"And, still holding a strong lead from the Regulators in the Western Region, Thomas Sandover appears to be the one who will take the position of Official Regulator for the Western Region. There is still one hour before we will be able to call the race, but with the difference between Sandover and his competitors, it's going to be difficult for anyone to catch up," the news anchor explained.

I had already known that my father was going to win, but hearing the possibility of the *official* announcement caused cold dread to pierce my chest.

I set my e-reader aside and curled up tighter in the chair, watching the television, disinterested, waiting for the final, official word on my fate.

* **** *

It was cold. I shivered and huddled closer to Dexter, my eyes fluttering open in confusion at the sudden change in temperature. Startled, I straightened immediately, my cat giving an angry mewl and bounding away. The living room was dark, illuminated only by the ambient street lights outside. Everything appeared in proper place, but the room was devoid of my parents.

It was impossible to ignore the icy feeling enveloping the house. I slowly stood, my breath forming a cloud in front of my face. The heat of summer was already a constant as the end of the school term drew near—there was no logical explanation for the chill.

I entered the kitchen, my feet sliding over the hardwood, my hand on the counter guiding me through the dark. I jumped at every creak in the floorboards, my heart in my throat.

"Lily..."

I halted, a shiver running down my spine.

"Who's there?"

My eyes scanned every shadow, but there was no one with me. Trying to still my shivering, I tiptoed to the dining room.

"Mom?" I called, my voice hushed, unable to rise above a whisper. "Dad?"

I slipped into every room downstairs cautiously, searching for my parents, feeling as though I was being watched.

"Lily..."

The voice floated to me once again. I did not recognize it. It was dark, sinister...*cold.* I wrapped my arms around myself, my eyes searching every nook and cranny for the owner of the voice. I could feel his eyes on me, observing my every action as I searched my darkened home.

My brain jumped to the horrible conclusion that my parents had left, that they had gone to Central without me, leaving me alone in our old house with the owner of the ominous voice.

I crept to the stairs, holding my breath, terrified any stray noise would give away my location.

"Lily..."

While being cold and terrifying, the voice was also alluring and seductive, almost demanding to be found. I stared into the dark shadows at the top of the staircase, searching for any sign of my parents or the owner of the voice tantalizingly calling my name.

"Mom? Dad?" I placed my foot on the first step, transferring my weight as slowly as possible to avoid making noise.

As I ascended the stairs, I could feel his eyes on me...following me...

"Little Lily..." the voice whispered. It was closer, drawing nearer as I climbed the stairs. I could almost feel his breath on my neck, whispering the endearing name, causing my hair to stand on end.

I turned at the top of the stairs, starting toward my parents' bedroom, my eyes passing over displayed family portraits. Framed pictures extending through generations of my family broke the boring tan paint on the wall. In the center of the collection of photographs was one that my father had always said was his favorite. It was a picture taken when my grandfather first took him fishing. The young face of my father was smiling triumphantly, holding his prized trout with a look of unbridled pride as my grandfather pointed at the fish with a broad grin of his own.

My father often teased about how my grandmother had trimmed the picture down to squeeze it into the only frame she had at the time, slicing off one of my father's ears, the tail of the trout, and the top of my grandfather's head just to hang it on the wall that much sooner.

Despite the small picture, it was one that my father adored and stared at often, so it caught my attention. For some reason, in the darkened hallway, it looked as though all the other photos on the wall had moved away from my father's favorite, causing it to stand out in the circle of framed pictures.

"Look, Lily..."

The picture was different. As I drew closer, I could see it was the entire picture—before it had been cut to fit the frame. There was a third person, leaning his head leaning against my father's with a brilliant smile. I stepped closer, trying to discern the stranger's features.

"Lily."

"Lily! Look!"

I snapped awake, my heart pounding. It took me several moments to realize I was in the living room once more, the lights on and my parents seated on the couch next to my chair. My startled jump disturbed Dexter and he hissed, jumping from my lap and slinking off irritably. My parents were laughing boisterously, adding to my groggy confusion as I turned my attention to the reason my parents were making a fuss.

"The new Official Regulator for the Western Region is Thomas Sandover. The incumbent Official Regulator for the North-Midwest Region..." the reporter named off who had won methodically, drowned out by the celebration taking place in our living room.

"I'm so proud of you!" my mother exclaimed, kissing my father passionately, her arms wrapping around him, nearly causing them to fall clumsily off the couch.

I could not share in their elation. I felt as though my throat had closed up, making it impossible to breathe. I stared at the floor, my heart thundering in my chest.

If my dream was any indication, I was already lost in the dark shadow my father's victory had cast over my life.

Chapter Two

It was the last day of school and the last day before our move to Central. I was on the verge of tears all day—my close friends *were* in tears as we said our goodbyes. We hugged and tried to stay together as long as possible outside my house before they went home to prepare for the school's summer trip to Europe. I was too upset about having to move to the capital to be disappointed that I would miss the annual summer trip. My friends would return and go back to the school they knew with the friends they knew, and I would have to start again in a new city that I already disliked.

I kept asking my friends if one of their families would adopt me—they did not realize the question was serious.

We hugged once again before they departed and I felt a part of me leave with them as they disappeared from view.

I stepped through our front door, barely recognizing the house without the furniture that had barely moved or changed since we had moved into the house ten years previous. The moving men would get the beds and final large furniture items the following morning for the last truck load to our new house in Central.

Everything I had ever known had been stripped away with each packed box. I wanted to be excited and happy for my father and his accomplishment, but the reality of our move hurt too much for me to feign elation.

Dex had become agitated as we progressively packed the house and had taken to clinging to me whenever I was home. He trailed close behind as I trudged to the living room, staring at the bare walls, feeling like a stranger in the house.

My mother poked her head out of the kitchen.

"Good talk with the girls?"

"Yeah…"

"Don't worry. You'll stay in touch with them."

I could tell from her tone that even she did not believe the statement—she was just saying what she thought I needed to hear. She had been going on and on about the new life waiting for us in Central for weeks, making it painfully obvious she had no qualms leaving behind the life we had already built.

"Dinner is just about ready. Can you help me?"

I set aside the glasses and plates for that night's dinner before pulling the rest of the dishes out of the cabinets to be packed.

My father came downstairs and helped, trying to cheer me up by explaining that things were going to be great in Central. He said that I would be exposed to different kinds of people and I would grow even more as a young lady. I nodded, unable to force a smile, and told him "I know" quietly. Both of my parents had clearly not figured out that their tactics at reassuring me were making my anxiety far worse.

As we ate dinner, my mother took my father's hand.

"This is so exciting, Tom."

"It's not like we haven't been to Central before," I mumbled, recalling various trips we had taken to the new capital city for one reason or another.

"I know," my mom said. "But this is different. We'll be a part of the people. We are going to be part of something *big*…something…" She ran out of words, letting out a breath and smiling, giddy. "It's going to be *wonderful*."

"I hope so," my father said. "And Lily, I know you'll enjoy it once we get settled. It will take some adjustment, but you'll love it in time."

I could only nod, not nearly as confident.

I continued staring at the blank walls of my room late into the night, Dex fast asleep beside me. I felt the tears overwhelm me like a wave, rolling down my face as I tried to stifle my sobbing.

The emotions stirring in my chest were a sickening storm of anger and sadness, but those feelings were paltry compared to the terror that wracked my body. I could not understand my fear, but it was potent. The move was not only ripping me away from the life I had always known. It was also deciding my future for me, as though I was signing over my life and walking into a cage I could never escape.

* *** *

It was a three-day drive to Central. My parents had chosen a house they loved from a virtual tour. Most of our furniture and boxed belongings had already arrived, which felt disconcerting, since I had not seen the virtual tour and had no idea what the house looked like, let alone how it would look with our belongings in it.

My mother was the most excited, saying over and over again that life in Central would be like a dream.

It was already starting to feel like my nightmare.

Dex and I were silent in the backseat as we drove across the land to our new life.

I would start at a new school when the next semester began in three weeks—since the school in Central was on an intensive-track program and had shorter summer breaks—so I had less time to settle in the new house and get to know the layout of the city, adding to my anxiety.

I had to admit, though, after three days trapped in the car with my giddy parents, I was *very* grateful to arrive in Central.

The city was alive with activity and intense energy. The last time I had been in the capital I had been fourteen and the Central I saw out the car window seemed different from the city of my memories. When I was fourteen the city was steeped in history, filled with old museums and statues of the heroes of the Second Revolution. Now three years older I realized the city was far more modern and hummed with vibrant activity.

"Is it like you remember, Lily?" my dad asked.

"Not really…"

"Let's get to the house and then we can go out for dinner," my mother said. "We'll celebrate being here and your impressive achievement!"

"Alright, stop," my father chuckled, taking her hand tenderly. "You're going to give me a big ego."

Our new neighborhood was so clean and spacious I could not help but stare. The houses looked more like estates, and there were children playing on the front lawns with pets as parents watched from seats on the front porch or watered their manicured flowerbeds. The neighborhood seemed so stereotypically perfect it was unsettling.

It felt fake.

"This is beautiful!" my mother gasped, her face glued to the car window.

We slowed as we turned onto the street of our new house.

"Here it is!" my mother exclaimed, pointing. "Thirteen, forty-three. Right here! Right here!"

"Yep, that's it," my father affirmed, turning the car into the driveway.

I stared at the house, holding Dexter in my arms as I climbed out of the car. The huge house stood proudly, accented by its perfect front lawn, blooming flowers, and tall fence, trees shading the area with big green leaves that contrasted the tan stucco and clay-red roof.

"Come on," my mom said, hurrying to the door and urging my father to follow with the keys.

When my father opened the front door, we were greeted with the sight of our boxes stacked within. The house smelled new. The drapes were open, allowing in beams of light that did not reveal a hint of dust in the air.

"Oh, it's *perfect!*" my mother gasped, her hands to her mouth as her wide eyes took in everything about our new home.

"Take a look around," my father urged me. "You didn't get to see the virtual tour. This house is quite spectacular."

I stepped out of the foyer, more hesitant than my parents. A large, sweeping staircase stood in front of me leading to the second floor. To my right was the dining area, which had enough room to fit the immense table that my parents used to entertain colleagues. On the left was the living room, which had enormous bay windows looking over the front lawn on one end and a glass door at the other, leading to the biggest backyard I had ever seen in a large, metropolitan city.

The kitchen could be accessed by the living room or dining room and had a connected breakfast nook. The kitchen was fully equipped with state-of-the art appliances that nearly glowed against the dark granite counter tops.

Through the kitchen was another living area, also with access to the backyard. On the far left side of the second living room was a door that led to the three-car garage and next to the door was a smaller staircase.

Dex looked around curiously but made no moves to leap out of my arms and explore. I was unsure if he was uncomfortable with the new house or if he was reacting to my own apprehension.

I climbed the narrow stairs and turned left to see a bedroom. Considering how large it was and the windows looking over the driveway, as well as the lavish attached bathroom, I assumed it was the master bedroom. I pouted.

"I want this room…"

Stepping out of the bedroom, I turned the other way and walked the short hallway to another door, which led to another bedroom. It was smaller but had an amazing view of the backyard. Curiously, I walked through the room, peering into the closet and finally opening the other door to see another short hallway with a door directly in front of me open to another bedroom while the open door to my right led to a bathroom to be shared between the two bedrooms. Walking through the third bedroom, I found myself at the top of the main staircase. The hallway at the top of the stairs was dark due to lack of windows, light only coming from the gaping mouth of the main staircase arch.

Feeling a little lost in the mammoth house, I looked both ways at the top of the stairs and decided to open the door to my right.

My jaw dropped.

It was the largest bedroom I had ever seen, expanding to the front of the house with windows looking over both the front and back yards. The two walk-in closets informed me I had found the master bedroom.

"I guess the other one is ours, Dex."

I walked through the expansive room, marveling at the space before turning at the end of the room, where an archway brought me into an octagonal room with floor-to-ceiling windows.

The archway across the sunroom led to the master bathroom. It had a roman bathtub, a large, double-headed shower with glass doors and a double vanity. The front window was etched with a calming beach scene, obstructing the view from both sides.

"And I thought our other house was nice…"

I managed to find my way back downstairs, taking the main stairs to familiarize myself with the layout, though I knew it would take me time to feel comfortable with all the extra space. Every room moved easily into another, and another, making the whole house accessible from many different areas, with the exception of the room I had chosen—admittedly, that was probably the reason I liked it so much.

I found my parents in the small living room by the office, talking about how they were going to arrange the furniture. When they saw me they stopped talking, both smiling with expectant expressions.

"What do you think?" my mother asked.

"This has to be at least twice the size of our last house."

"I know, isn't it beautiful?"

"How did we ever manage to get it?" I asked. "Seems like a house this nice should have been sold a long time ago. It doesn't look like anyone's ever lived here."

"The agent said it came on the market the day before we asked about the neighborhood," my father explained. "Apparently this was an empty lot for a long time and the contractors just finished this house last month." He smiled and hugged me. "It was fate."

"Have you chosen your room?" my mom asked.

"That one." I pointed to the small staircase.

"I thought that would be the one you wanted."

"Have you seen the master bedroom?" I gaped. "It's *massive*!"

"No, let's go look. I sort of remember what it looks like from the tour," my father said. He turned to me. "You can go get your things out of the car and start thinking about how you want to set up your room. The truck should be here in about an hour."

I returned to the car, leaning in to grab my bag of sketchbooks and Dexter's bed. When I maneuvered the items out of the car with the cat still in my arms, I was startled by a bark behind our car. Dex jumped, his claws digging into my arms as he hissed at the large, black dog.

"Jake, stop it!" the dog's owner scolded. Looking at the other end of the leash, I saw a woman in workout sweats, yanking her dog back. "So sorry," she said, laughing apologetically. "He won't hurt anything. He just wants to play."

I nodded, trying to soothe the still-agitated Dexter. The woman with light blonde hair and wrinkles around the corners of her mouth and eyes looked me over before glancing at the house behind me.

"Is your family moving into this house?"

"Yes."

"Welcome to the neighborhood, and congratulations on your family's appointment. I'm Susan Vance, your neighbor," she introduced herself, pointing to the house left of ours. "And, you've met Jake," she gently pat the Labrador.

"Nice to meet you," I greeted. "I'm Lily Sandover and this is Dexter."

"Very nice to meet you, Lily."

"How did you know my family had been appointed?" I asked curiously.

"Well, because you're moving into this neighborhood." Her tone suggested that the answer to my question should have been obvious. "This area is specifically for people who have been appointed into Central. And I'll let you in on a little secret. Your family must have done something right."

"Why do you say that?"

"Because this area in particular is for those Leader and the Commission think will go far and do well," Susan explained with a wink.

"Leader? And the Commission...you mean the Commission of the People?" When she nodded, my eyes widened even further. "You mean to say that Leader Simon and the Commission decided that my father could go far in Central and that's why they led us to this neighborhood?"

"Absolutely." Susan grinned. "This is where they put the hopefuls. It's the perfect distance between the Leadership District to allow a little space, but close enough to make it to work if there is an emergency of some sort." She looked up at the house, which was fortunate because she did not see how much the statement had disturbed me. I was already worried about how much politics would become ingrained in my life, but now the political hooks were evident. It was surreal to think that the leader of our country and the Commission of the People had looked over my father's work and decided he was qualified to become part of an even higher class of politician in Central.

"Such a beautiful house," Susan mused, breaking me out of my trance. "Have you looked through it, yet?"

"Yes. We're just waiting for the moving truck."

"It's so nice to see someone move in," she continued. "It's been sitting empty for a long time."

"...what do you mean?"

"No one has lived in that house since they built it three years ago."

"*Three years?*"

"Yeah..." She looked over the house again as my chest began to tighten. "I didn't think it was finished yet because I never saw anyone, but I guess they were just waiting for the next hopeful." Finally turning her attention away from the house, her grinning expression fell to me. "Well, I need to take Jake for a walk, but I'll stop by later tonight to meet your parents."

"They'd love that."

"Have a great day and enjoy!" she called, pulling her dog toward the sidewalk. "This is the best place to be."

She continued on her way, the dog padding along beside her. I watched her leave and then slowly turned to the house, wondering why the real estate agent had lied to my father.

The dread that had been choking me loomed darkly over the grand house, causing my fear about our move to Central to swell angrily.

Chapter Three

My room was unpacked and sorted in three short days, so I spent the following two helping my parents organize the rest of the house. Neighbors stopped by to greet us and immediately set to helping. The extra hands were appreciated but I felt uneasy about the smiling neighbors, particularly after Susan had said our home had been vacant for so long. In many ways, it was flattering that so many influential people believed my father could do well in the political arena. But the praise also increased the weight on my shoulders. A world that I wanted no part of was rapidly devouring what little hope I had of a non-political life.

Neighbors invited us to dinners, enveloping us into the community as if we had been there for years. I met kids in the neighborhood but none were my age. The parents of my future classmates explained that the Third Tier Education students were on an end-of-term trip and would be back just before the beginning of the next term—apparently, the end-of-year trip to Europe was not unique to my old school.

During my second week in Central, I ventured out to explore the city. I picked up maps for the bus and train routes, blending in with the tourists as I attempted to find my way downtown.

I explored the city center, taking note of restaurants, shops, and cafés I found interesting, trying to remember the bus routes so I could revisit the spots. I stumbled on an enormous bookstore and decided to look for my school books as an excuse to get out of the summer sun. When I walked in, one of the employees approached me immediately, startling me.

"May I help you find something?"

"Um…" I said, fumbling as if I had been asked to answer in a foreign language. "No, I don't know what classes I'm taking, yet. I'm supposed to get my schedule soon. I just wanted to see where the store was."

"Oh, that's okay," she assured with a brilliantly-white grin. "The school sends your required books here and pays for them. All you need to do is pick them up."

"…the school pays for the books?"

"They do," she affirmed. "Follow me." I obediently joined her at the customer service desk.

"What's your name?" she asked, typing into her computer.

"Lily Sandover."

As her fingers clicked on the keyboard, another girl my age stepped up beside me. She had straight brown hair, dark brown eyes, and was wearing a black tank top that left a sliver of her abdomen exposed above her dark green cargo pants. She was built with lean muscles and, while she looked tough, she had an air of warmth around her.

"Hello, Becca." The store clerk smiled when she glanced up to see who had approached the customer service desk.

"Hey, Hannah," the girl named Becca greeted. "Is it too early to pick up books?"

"No. I'm just about to get Lily's books for her." The store clerk nodded to me. Becca turned.

"Hey, Lily," she said, extending her hand, which I nervously took. "I'm Rebecca Davis," she introduced. "But everyone calls me Becca."

"Nice to meet you," I mumbled, trying to stop the nervous tremor in my voice.

"New to Central?"

"That obvious?"

"A little," she said. "Don't worry, you'll feel more comfortable when you fall into routine."

"I hope so…"

"Here you are, ladies." Hannah returned with two stacks of books bound together with our names taped to the top. Becca glanced at my last name and gasped.

"*Sandover*? You're the daughter of the new Western Region Regulator!"

"That's me…"

"Wow!" She smiled broadly. "My mom is Samantha Davis, Regulator of the North-Midwest Region. Our parents are going to be working together."

I blinked, stunned. "This is the first."

"What?"

"I have never had someone say that their parent was another Regulator."

"Oh, yeah," Becca giggled. "I felt the same way when I first moved here. You get used to it. Particularly with Jessica Daniels' constant reminder that her father is the Chair of Finance for Leader Simon." She rolled her eyes. "You *have* to get used to it just to keep your sanity."

She pulled her stack of books off the counter.

"Want to get some coffee?"

The shy part of me wanted to make up an excuse or false appointment, but Becca's warm smile was inviting and I knew I would need friends if I was going to survive being trapped in Central.

"That would be great."

We went to a nearby café that Becca said was her favorite, sitting at a table near the windows with our drinks. I was desperately trying to act at-ease, though I was sure my nerves were obvious with the way I constantly avoided eye contact.

"How do you like Central so far?" Becca started.

"It's nice," I said mechanically.

She laughed. "I'm not your parents. You don't have to lie."

"No, really. It's nice…"

"*But?*"

"Well, I just…I didn't really want to come here."

"Have you ever moved before?"

"Not out of my hometown."

"Oh, that makes more sense," she said. "Your father must have been born into a political family in the Western Region."

"Yeah. We've always lived in the same city."

"My mom started out as a law clerk," Becca explained. "As she moved higher, we started moving a lot from bigger city to bigger city, but that first move was the hardest."

"It wasn't so much the move or changing houses," I told her. "I just…I don't want anything to do with Central. I felt as though, if I moved here, I would *have* to go into politics. This city is like a factory to manufacture politicians."

"Don't want to follow the family tradition of government employment?" Becca smirked. When I shook my head emphatically, she leaned forward. "Me, neither."

"Really? I thought everyone wanted to work for Central."

"Well, everyone can." She leaned back in her chair. "Not me. I want to work with animals."

"You don't call that wanting to work for the government?" I grumbled, hoping that by lifting my cup to my mouth, she would not hear the quip. Her hearty laugh told me otherwise.

"I like you," she said. "You have a sense of humor."

"You mean because I called everyone in the government animals? You should be careful, you could be pegged a traitor for finding that funny."

"Oh, come on," Becca laughed. "That kind of stuff doesn't happen anymore."

I took a drink, feeling more relaxed knowing that she appreciated my cynical humor.

"So how am I going to survive here with everyone talking politics all the time?" I asked lightly. "How many political kids am I going to run into around here?"

"Well, you're out of luck if you want to avoid them," she said with an exaggerated pained expression. "All children of Central employees, like you and me, go to the same Third Tier school."

"*All* of them?" I blinked in shock. "How big is the school?"

"About one thousand students, give or take. Are you in your third year?" When I nodded, she smiled. "Great! We're in the same year. Are you a social person?"

"No, not really," I conceded.

"Neither am I. However, in order to survive here, you're going to have to become one…or at least pretend. This school is a collective body and if you *don't* know what's going on, you will get destroyed."

"How so?" I asked, trying to conceal my horror at the statement and hoping she was exaggerating.

"Because it's your job to report things to your father."

"*Report*?"

"The children all go to the same school and they talk about what their parents are doing. It keeps everyone in the loop. If there is any chance of something illegal happening in the government, someone needs to tell their parent. That way it can be brought to attention and action can be taken. It's all about being on the inside track and trying to keep Central corruption-free."

"People just talk about their parents' work at school? Like lunchtime gossip?"

"Well, not everyone," Becca said. "Not the Commish Kids."

"Is that what you call kids who have parents in the Commission of the People?" I laughed, choking on my coffee.

"Oh, no." She shook her head. "The *whole* family gets pulled into the Commission, not just the parents. Everyone will tell you if they are part of the Commission, but they won't tell you what happens during the Commission meetings. That's top secret."

"That's not suspicious at all," I grumbled.

"It's a security measure," she said with a shrug. "Since the Commission is the one who deals with the dirty politicians in Central. They have to keep things pretty under-wraps."

"Good point…" I took another sip of my coffee. "So, by being 'social,' what do you mean?"

"The entire school goes to a club at the end of each week. You are considered an outcast if you aren't there unless there is a legitimate excuse."

"A *club*? Really?"

"It's a dance club," she elaborated. "It's actually a lot of fun, and it's where *all* the gossip happens. Club Archangel is a den of secrets."

"And do all the parents *know* that their kids go to this club?" I asked skeptically.

"Oh, of course," she assured. "Then again, there are some things that go on in the club that they *don't* know. But, by the looks of you, you're not into drugs or one-night stands in back alleys."

"No, definitely not me."

"Yeah, I didn't think so," Becca laughed. "Other than the club, there are the trips at the end of the term that you're supposed to take."

"I thought there was one right now."

"There is."

"Why aren't *you* there?"

"I got really sick as soon as school was over," she said, making a face. "Mom says it was the release of stress from a hectic term."

"Are the classes at this school that hard?"

Becca sipped her coffee, taking her time to formulate an answer.

"They're not necessarily difficult, but they're work intensive," she said. "Especially this coming term. We're supposed to read J.A.N.E. and know it forward, backward, and sideways and be able to recite it...or something."

"J.A.N.E.?" I said slowly. "You mean *An Angel Without Wings*?'"

Becca nodded, tapping her pile of books.

"For years we have been hearing about the magnificent work of anonymous writer J.A.N.E. and the unforgettable accounts of the revolutionary Thomas Ankell as he overthrew the corrupt government of the Washington System."

"The first classic of neo-American literature," I added, mirroring her cynical tone.

"I don't know..." She sighed, undoing the binding on her books and picking up the novel we had heard so much about. We had never been allowed to read the book before because, according to the adults, we were not old enough. Becca flipped through the pages. "Seems a little anti-climactic to me."

"You haven't read it, yet."

"I thought it would be heavier, or...I don't know, encrusted with gold," she joked. "Particularly if we're supposed to have the hardcopy. I mean, who reads hardcopies anymore?"

While I wanted very little to do with the government started by Thomas Ankell, I had heard so much about him and about the book that I had an undeniable urge to read it.

"Anyway," Becca continued, setting the book back on the stack, "what kind of grades did you get at your last school?"

"I have a three-point-eight."

"Oh, yeah, you won't have any problems here, smarty-pants."

"I just didn't have a social life at my old school," I disagreed.

"Well, don't let your obligatory social life make your grades suffer," Becca scolded playfully, wagging her finger at me.

Once we grew tired of sitting in the coffee shop, we began walking home. Having just met, we were still slightly awkward around one another as new friends and conversation was harder to maintain.

"Where do you live?" I asked.

"Balkan Street, in the northwest," Becca answered. "You?"

"Capo Avenue."

She stopped and blinked in surprise, her eyebrows raising.

"Really? Your family is in *that* neighborhood?" When I nodded, she whistled. "Your father must be one hell of a politician."

"Does *everyone* know about this placement system?" I tried to laugh off my annoyance.

"There's no system," she corrected. "Just an understanding."

"Which house is closer, yours or mine?"

"Mine," Becca answered. "Want to come over?"

I tried not to show my excitement at the invitation. I was worried that my enthusiasm at making my first friend in Central would scare her away.

"Could I?"

"Sure," she said. "You can meet Davey, my dog."

Becca's house was big but still somehow warm and inviting. Her room was covered in pictures and posters, including some of her best friends—which she claimed were my new friends, too. She pointed to pictures of Jill, a blonde with dark blue eyes, and Taylor, a larger girl who did not have one picture where she sported a straight face. Becca assured me they would help my transition into Central and make sure I did not fall in with a bad crowd.

I was thrilled when Becca invited me over to her house the following day to go over old yearbooks and learn about the school and my other classmates. I accepted quickly, knowing my parents would be too happy I was being social to complain about me not helping unpack the house.

When I got home, my mom asked me what I had found around town, and I told her that I had made my first friend in Central.

Chapter Four

The following day, I went to Becca's house to learn about those who would soon be my classmates, both excited and nervous about acting awkward around my new friend. When I arrived at ten o'clock the door was answered by Becca's father, a tall man with broad shoulders, a kind face, and even kinder eyes surrounded by smile lines.

"Hello," I greeted, extending my hand, "my name is Lily Sandover. I'm a friend of Becca's."

"Oh, yes, Lily, daughter of Thomas Sandover," the man said, stepping aside. "I'm Bradly Davis, Becca's father. Becca!"

A few moments later, Becca came downstairs to collect me, her little dog Davey in tow.

"Lily, it was very nice to meet you, and please send my best to your father," Mr. Davis said as Becca reached the bottom of the stairs. "Now, you two go off and do…whatever it is you girls do when your parents aren't around."

Becca kissed her dad on the cheek.

"It's best that you don't know, Dad."

"I agree," he said quickly.

I laughed when I saw a box of doughnuts on Becca's bed and two mugs of coffee on the nightstand.

"Wow, does it take you a lot to get going in the morning or something?"

"No," she laughed. "*You* have a lot of studying to do." She pat a stack of thick yearbooks on her bed. "I have provided you with the necessary materials—books, doughnuts, and coffee." She shoved one mug in my hands and sat on the bed.

"I really want to thank you for all of this," I said sincerely, joining her on the bed. She snorted, waving the statement away.

"Please, it's no big deal. I was the new kid once, too, and I had Jill. It's my turn to help someone new." Becca took a deep breath. "Okay! So, we have a very short window before school starts and you will need to know a lot by then." She grabbed the first yearbook. "So, we begin," she said ominously with a devious smile.

The first yearbook was from her first year of Third Tier—the year Becca had arrived in Central.

"You don't really need to know the history of the building other than it was built shortly after the Second Revolution like…every other building in this city." Becca rolled her eyes. "What you *do* need to know is where everyone hangs out. That *never* changes. *Ever*."

"So the school is full of cliques," I grumbled.

"Yeah," she confirmed. "And unless you know what clique you belong to, you will be scouted by the one that finds you the most interesting." She snaked an arm around my shoulders. "Lucky for you, you have me."

Becca flipped through the pages, coming across the art students' winning shots of the school, which allowed me to see the basic layout of the building.

"We hang out in this area," she said, pointing to a specific intersection of hallways. "Most of the studious kids hang out inside. The more social ones go outside."

She flipped through the pages, looking for something particular. I caught glimpses of other pictures in the fluttering pages, ranging from school dances to sporting events. There were pictures of students accepting awards and meeting important political figures, though it was difficult to discern exactly who the students were meeting. Being in Central, it could have been anyone.

"Here we go!" Becca readjusted the book on her lap. The pictures of the freshmen class were spread in alphabetical order before me. I leaned in closer, my eyes moving over the faces.

"I'll just point out the really important people you need to know and steer clear of," Becca explained. She pointed to the picture of a girl named Jessica Daniels, the Student Body Leader. She then showed me the child of the Chair of Justice and who she was dating.

She pointed out three girls who were known to be the worst in the school.

"Why?"

"Because they're bitches," Becca stated shortly. "No, it's not just that. They're Commish Kids, and they're dating three of the smartest and best-looking boys in the school—all brothers. Because of that, these girls think that they're royalty, or something."

"They're pretty," I conceded.

"Yeah, they're alright," she agreed. "But their personalities are so bad that they are actually really ugly." She scanned the faces in front of her, contemplating who to talk about next. "This is Todd Douglas, he's part of our group and if you ever need help on anything relating to math or science, talk to him. The rest of us are all idiots in math and science. He's super smart."

"He's cute." I always had a thing for boys with blonde hair and blue eyes.

"Yeah, he's okay."

"Do you have a boyfriend?"

"Nope," Becca said. "I dated Luke Telton and Parker Sampson," she pointed to the two boys' pictures and laughed. "But that was back in sophomore year. I've been living the single life ever since, thankfully."

"At least you've had two boyfriends..."

"What?" she gasped, her eyes wide. "A hot little number like you hasn't had a boyfriend, yet?"

"*Who* are you looking at?"

"Are you kidding me? You are *hot*!" Becca exclaimed, looking me over. "Well, if no one was willing to date you where you came from, that's their loss. Here in Central, you'll be beating them away with a stick."

"I'm so sure," I snorted, rolling my eyes.

She motioned to other pictures in the yearbook, telling me the kids to stay away from and everyone's connection to Central's workforce. There were many kids with parents in close connection to Leader Simon, which made me feel like I was going to school with celebrities, since I recognized so many names.

Becca also pointed out the Commish Kids. She told me it was very important to know who they were before I went to school, because the kids that were part of the Commission of the People were very exclusive and secretive. To approach one of them would be considered inappropriate. She also told me that, if I could avoid Commish Kids, I should.

After she taught me about the students, Becca turned to the faculty page. She pointed out good teachers and those who were particularly difficult to tolerate. I grabbed the schedule I had received that morning and found my teachers. I was relieved to discover that I shared three classes with Becca.

"You are going to be so sick of me," I joked. "I'm going to be sticking to you like glue."

"Hey, nothing wrong with that," she said. "And I doubt I'll get sick of you."

We both had the teacher Becca said was the best in the school. His name was Darrel McDermott and he would teach our Historic Literature class—the class in which we would read *An Angel Without Wings*. Becca assured me that he was lenient and he made class fun, which made me feel a little better after she had told me that the math teacher we shared was a pain in the ass.

In the second yearbook, she showed me some of the new students I needed to know. After two hours, we had both drank two cups of coffee and eaten half of the doughnuts in the box. High on sugar and caffeine, Becca started telling me embarrassing school stories and silly escapades with some of my other classmates. It was nice to be able to laugh and realize that the students of my new school could be just as immature and silly as in my former school. I had been worried I would be swallowed by my loneliness from leaving my old friends, but Becca made me feel as though I'd known her for years.

She was so carefree and happy, like nothing could faze her, and it helped me anchor myself in what would, otherwise, be an overwhelming anxiety of my new reality.

It was close to four in the afternoon when we finally ran out of things to talk about. We remained on her bed, staring at the pictures littering the walls.

"You know something, Lily?"

"Hm?"

"You're really a fun person. I mean, once you loosen up a little!" she teased, poking me playfully in the stomach. I giggled, worming away.

"What are you talking about? I am *always* fun."

Becca glanced at me out of the corner of her eye and I laughed louder. Then I turned to the clock, reading the time with a heavy sigh.

"Okay," I admitted, "I should probably head home."

"Yeah..." she begrudgingly agreed. She sat up and pat the yearbooks again. "Tomorrow, I'll come over to your house and quiz you on everything you learned."

"I didn't know I was going to be tested!"

* *** *

I was excited to have my first friend in Central over to our new house. I was helping my mom unpack, trying to pass the time quickly before Becca arrived, glancing at the clock every two minutes.

"You seem excited about your friend coming over," my mom noted, unwrapping another glass and placing it in its appropriate spot with the other fine china.

"I am."

"You two have really hit it off," she continued, reaching for another glass as I closed the cupboard doors on the fancier plates.

"Yeah, I guess." I was trying to act casual, though I was counting my lucky stars with how well I was able to get along with Becca after knowing her for such a short amount of time.

"Is she a nice girl?"

"Of course she is. She's been telling me about the school and everything I need to know so I don't feel like an outsider on the first day."

"Good. It should make the transition a little easier. Soon, you'll feel right at home."

Becca rang the doorbell around ten in the morning. When I answered the door, she was staring around our front steps with wide eyes.

"This is one amazing house."

"Thanks," I said awkwardly. "Come in."

I introduced Becca to my mom, who greeted her warmly and, thankfully, said nothing embarrassing. After a short conversation with my mom—she would have met my dad but he had already left for work—Becca and I scurried to my room, where she met Dexter. With Dex curled up next to her, Becca began quizzing me on what I remembered from the previous day. She corrected me on things I missed, teasing that the knowledge was more important than anything we would learn in class.

Once we had reviewed the information, even though we were not very serious about the quiz, Becca sat through an hour of me showing her pictures of my friends and adventures back home. Soon, we were laughing at silly pictures and memories as I relayed stories about the antics of my friends.

When we came across one picture, she asked me where it was taken, seeing the paintings hanging on the wall in the background.

"Oh, that's at an art show the students put on at my school," I explained.

"Are you an artist?"

"…I wouldn't call myself an *artist*…"

"You draw, though?" When I nodded, her smile broadened. "I wanna see!" she gasped. "I can't draw to save my life."

I collected the sketchbooks from my desk, including the newest one. I was always a little nervous letting new people look at my work. I constantly got good responses but that never stopped my worries that someone would hate my art. I did not take criticism well.

Her eyes continued to widen, her jaw dropping as she flipped through the pages.

"These are amazing! You should join the art club at our school!"

Feeling more at ease than I had a week before, I enjoyed the afternoon, feeling better able to handle the transition into Central with Becca accepting me with open arms.

Chapter Five

It was the day every student dreaded—the first day at a new school.

Even though Becca had agreed to meet me before our first class, thereby ensuring I was not alone, I was in a state of high anxiety.

I sat on the school bus with nervous butterflies eating my stomach. I fiddled with the straps of my school bag, feeling as though I was walking into a battlefield. Of course, every student would say that Third Tier *was* a warzone.

Finally, the façade of the massive school pictured in Becca's yearbooks came into view. The apprehension inside me grew. At my old school, I was one of three students with connections to Central and I had been able to pretend that there was no difference between my family and my friends' families. Now, I was going to a school full of children connected to the government, and even though my family was now like all the others, I was even more terrified of interacting with my classmates.

The bus approached far too fast for my liking. I took a deep breath and, as the rows in front of me cleared, I stood and left the bus.

I quickly took in my surroundings, trying to remember where Becca said she would meet me. The sea of students out front was much larger than I anticipated. I became lost in the flow of teenagers heading into the building. Rather than stop and point myself out as the obvious new girl, I followed the flow of traffic.

Entering the main doors, I tried to remember the school layout from Becca's yearbooks, discreetly glancing around, pretending I knew where I was going.

Thankfully, I did not flounder for long.

"Lily!" Becca called, weaving her way through the students.

"Hey! I was worried I wouldn't find you."

"I'd never leave you alone," Becca assured, placing a protective arm around my shoulders. "Let's go to the office and find your locker and ID and everything like that."

"Ah, formalities," I groaned.

Becca took me to the main office where I was given the normal paperwork—a map of the school, my locker number and combination, and my ID that was to be displayed on my uniform blazer while inside the building.

She helped me find my locker in the crowded hallways and, as I was placing textbooks inside, a girl I recognized as Becca's best friend Jill greeted us excitedly.

"Hey, you," she said, sneaking up behind Becca. Becca whirled around, throwing her arms around Jill.

"Hey!" she squealed. "I missed you *so much!*"

"I *know!*" Jill agreed. "God, it was *so* weird not having you on the trip. It's the only year that's happened."

"I know…" Becca groaned, rolling her eyes. "Stupid body. It hates me."

"That's alright, we'll just take a trip ourselves!" Jill declared. She turned to me. "Who's this?"

"This is Lily Sandover," Becca introduced. "She's new here, so we're adopting her."

"Great!" Jill said, extending her hand. "Nice to meet you. I'm Jill."

"Hi, Jill."

"What's your first class?" Becca asked.

"Economics…" Jill whined.

"Aw, I hoped we were going to be in the same first class."

"Who do you have for Lit?" Jill asked, her gaze expectant on Becca.

"McDermott."

"Yes!" Jill cheered. "Me too! Third period?"

"*Yes!*" Becca cried loudly, hugging Jill again. "We all have the same Lit class!" Becca said, motioning to me.

"So does Taylor!" Jill added.

"It's fate!"

I watched silently, not sure what to say and feeling very out of place. The two were obviously very close, and with how little I knew about Jill I felt awkward trying to add to their revelry.

Jill must have sensed my nerves because she turned to me.

"Sorry," she laughed. "We're a little crazy. Seriously, if you want, just jump in. Be crazy with us. It's more fun in a group."

"I think she's just a little nervous about the whole first day thing," Becca said. "But we have to go to biology," she said, turning to me. "You remember how the first day of school goes, right?"

"All rules and syllabus-reading?"

"Yep," she affirmed. "We'll meet up again in Lit, and then again at lunch, so we'll have time to get you completely integrated into the gang."

"Like riding a bike," Jill said, nudging me gently with her elbow. "You'll fall right into place. It won't be an issue. It's just school."

Becca bid Jill goodbye and led me to our first class together. Biology was going to be simple for me. I had taken Honors Biology at my previous school but had not passed the test well enough to avoid taking it again. Looking over the syllabus, it was clear I already had a firm understanding of the course material.

When I told Becca, she declared that she was going to be borrowing my brain for the class, since science was one of her weakest subjects.

After the first class, I did fall into the routine easily. Becca told me where my next class was after looking at my schedule and pointing out the classroom on the map. She also told me where the third period Lit class was going to be before sending me on my way.

My nervousness ebbed away as I realized the school was really no different than my old one. Since I did not have the map glued to my face, the other students could not immediately tell that I was new. I was sure that not everyone knew one another in the large student body, so I was temporarily safe from scrutiny.

My second class was English, another subject in which I had always done well. My teacher, Mrs. Booth, was a small, soft-spoken woman, which made me glad that I had chosen to sit close to the front of the room.

After I left Mrs. Booth's class, I made my way to the room Becca had pointed out earlier. I was excited for that class, mostly because I was going to be in it with my new friends, but also because the teacher was said to be one of the best in the school.

I saw Becca waving to me from one side of the classroom as I walked in the door. I sat down next to her and diagonal to Jill, offering a tired smile to them.

"How's it been so far?" Jill asked.

"I'm still alive." I shrugged. "And…for the most part, sane."

"That's the spirit!"

"I am so happy we all have this class together!" Becca said with a beaming grin. "It will make things *so* much easier."

"No kidding," Jill agreed. "We're reading J.A.N.E., too, which is supposed to be pretty difficult."

"That's the only book we're reading, though," Becca pointed out. "So homework shouldn't take as long."

"Yeah, but that means the tests and quizzes are going to be about every minute detail," Jill groaned. "And Mr. Garth has at least twenty books for us to read in his English class," she whined, flopping back in her chair, dramatically lamenting her fate.

"There's Taylor!" Becca announced as she waved the other girl toward us.

Taylor looked exactly the same as she had in the pictures I had seen at Becca's house, albeit a little heavier than I expected.

"Hey there," Taylor greeted, sitting in front of me and smiling at Jill and Becca. She reached over and placed her hand on Becca's. "How are you, girl? I missed you on the trip."

"I know, I missed you, too," Becca pouted, clasping her hand. "I'm alright now, though. How about you?"

"Ah, same old, same old."

"Taylor, this is Lily," Jill introduced me. "She's our adopted child."

"Oh, hey, nice to meet you," she greeted. "Are you Lily *Sandover*?" When I nodded, her smile broadened. "I thought so. My mom's been talking about your dad. She came over and helped you guys move in, or something like that," Taylor explained. "She said that you were really nice but kinda quiet."

"Nah," Becca disagreed, winking at me. "You just gotta get her loosened up."

"Good morning, class," the teacher started at the front of the room. I blinked in shock, not expecting Mr. McDermott to be so young. I had passed him off as a student or assistant at first glance. But when I saw that he was the only one at the front of the room, I realized he was the famous Mr. McDermott. "How was the trip?"

The class answered with a chorus of stories and cheers.

"Good, good, glad to hear it," he said. "How many of you got sunburned?"

Several members of the class raised their hands enthusiastically. Mr. McDermott laughed. "Yeah…I went to Fiji this summer and got pretty sunburned myself, but…I can't show you where because I could lose my job."

I laughed with the rest of the class.

"Yeah, that's what happens when you go to Fiji and your friends insist on going to a nudist beach," Mr. McDermott said with a nod, turning to grab a tablet off his desk. "Learn from my mistakes, don't give in to peer pressure. It causes skin irritation and a whole slew of other problems."

We laughed again.

"Alright, I know a lot of you, but I have to take roll anyway…" He tapped the tablet screen to life and scrolled through the list with his finger, calling out the names on the attendance sheet as we affirmed our presence. He then grabbed a stack of papers off his desk.

"Alright, everyone, let's do it together and get it out of our systems," he said with an exaggerated sigh. "We have to read over the syllabus now. Everyone groan on three. One, two, three."

The class groaned and griped for the fun of it. Mr. McDermott gave a strong, approving nod.

"Perfect," he complimented. "Okay, pass these around."

We went over the syllabus as we had in my other classes, even though Mr. McDermott would crack jokes about the things we had to do and what should have been common knowledge by that point in our schooling.

When he got to the schedule, he told us to look up from the syllabus and focus on him.

"Okay, as you have all heard, we are reading *only* J.A.N.E., so I want you to really pay attention to what I am going to tell you right now. There is only one book to read for this entire year and I know you're celebrating internally, but that means that if you don't do the reading *once*, I *will* know…and I will mock you in front of the class," he teased. We chuckled until he motioned us quiet. "However, in all seriousness, it is very important that you follow the reading schedule. *Do not* read ahead. This is a complicated book, and we need to go over it as I have broken it up. This is extremely important. Do you all understand?" We nodded obediently, though Mr. McDermott's gaze turned suspicious. "Do we need to make an oath?"

"Everyone raise your right hand," he instructed, demonstrating. We laughed and followed the orders, rolling our eyes. "Repeat after me. We, as Mr. McDermott's third period class…"

"We, as Mr. McDermott's third period class…"

"Do solemnly swear…"

"Do solemnly swear…"

"To do the assigned reading, and *only* the assigned reading…"

"To do the assigned reading, and *only* the assigned reading…"

"With the knowledge that my punishment will be to act out the chapter as a mime in front of class if I stray from the schedule."

The entire class broke into disbelieving laughter, demanding to know if the threat was real.

"Finish the oath," he said, avoiding answering directly.

We finished the recitation, giggling the entire time.

Chapter Six

It did not take long to get into the swing of school, but I was concerned that, as the term continued, darker side of the school would make itself known. Once I felt comfortable navigating the building without drawing attention to myself, I started studying my classmates, trying to recall the individuals Becca had warned me to avoid. I became paranoid that my transition to the school in Central was going *too* smoothly.

By the middle of the week, some students sought me out and introduced themselves. There were a few that I recognized from my study sessions with Becca, but fortunately, I was often with Becca, who would fix me with a serious stare to remind me to be careful with my associations. I was always polite to those who introduced themselves, but I was sure to stay close with the three girls I had come to trust.

Even though I was becoming more confident in my ability to navigate the school's student body, my anxiety found a new focus—the Welcome Back party at Club Archangel that Friday.

"Hey, about the party this Friday, do you want us to pick you up or do you want to meet us there?" Jill asked me at lunch. "You know you have to go, right?"

"Yeah…" I grumbled. "I don't know…I mean…I've never been to a club before."

"It's really not that big of a deal. Most of the time, these parties are kinda boring after the first hour or so," Taylor admitted. "I mean, there are certain rules you *absolutely* have to follow, but—"

"*Rules?*"

"She means that there are some things you are expected to do," Jill clarified. "You kinda-sorta-in-secret circle the room and pick up on the gossip. Then you compare what you heard with your group of friends," she motioned to the group, "and try to figure out if the rumors are true."

"That sounds complicated…and a little creepy, honestly."

"Don't worry," Becca assured. "It's hard to explain. You'll understand when you get there."

"Do you want us to pick you up or do you want to meet us there?" Jill asked again.

"*Please* pick me up," I pled. "I don't want to go alone."

For the first time in a very long time I had plans for Friday night, which dumbfounded my parents.

"Do you mind if I go out with my friends on Friday night?" I asked over dinner on Wednesday. Both of my parents froze, blinking at me in surprise, my father's mouth open, his fork suspended in the air.

"You don't have to act as if I just asked you if I could get married on Friday," I groaned.

"No, honey, sorry, it's not that," my father assured quickly. "It's just…you've never had plans on a Friday night to go out with friends, even back at your old school."

"I know…" I groaned, rolling my eyes. I decided not to tell them how much I did not want to go because I did not want to explain why I *had* to attend the Welcome Back party.

"I think it's a good idea," my mother said. "You need to get out and enjoy your youth. You're young. You need to have some fun."

"I have fun," I protested.

"It'll be good for you to make some friends that you can go out with. Get you out of your comfort zone," my mother continued. Then, she nudged me with her elbow. "Maybe you'll even find a boyfriend."

"Yeah, somehow, I doubt that."

"Where, exactly, would you be going?" my father asked.

"There is a club that my entire school goes to called Club Archangel," I explained. "They're holding some kind of party for the new term. A welcome-back-to-school party."

"I heard about that club from Mrs. Grayson," my mother interjected, turning to my father. "Apparently, all the kids go there at the end of each week to unwind and relax. It's completely safe. Very student-centric."

"It does sound like fun," my father admitted, though he seemed reluctant to say so. The thought of his seventeen-year-old daughter going to a club, even a safe one, was not easy for him to process.

"The club closes at ten. I'll be back by curfew."

Even though I had insisted I would be alright and finally got him to agree to letting me go with my friends, I still did *not* want to go. Throughout Thursday I was quiet and brooding, my thoughts consumed with dread about attending.

I entertained the idea of saying that I did not feel well so I could stay at home and draw, or finish my homework, or the things I had always done on my non-social Friday nights. By the end of Thursday, I had worked myself into a ball of nervous energy that was desperate to find a reason *not* to go to Club Archangel.

After school, when Jill and Taylor had run off to catch their buses, I caught Becca's arm and pulled her back.

"Wait, Becca." She turned back to me. Judging by her concerned expression, it was obvious my anxiety was etched into my face.

"Are you okay?"

"Listen…I-I am *really* nervous about the club tomorrow."

"Why?"

"I don't know…"

"There's nothing to be nervous about," she assured. "Really. It's just a gathering like school, only with loud music and flashing lights and dancing." Her words did nothing to ease my nerves. "It's alright," she insisted at my continued hesitation. "I'll be right there with you. We all will. You're not going to be alone."

"But…" I shook my head, not sure what I was going to say or even what I *could* say for her to understand my apprehension.

"Step out of your comfort zone. It's alright to be nervous, but don't let it stop you. You might actually have some fun. You'll meet some of our other friends, too. They'll help you feel more comfortable."

"You mean there's more?"

"Yep. The boys. Taylor's boyfriend and two of his friends. They're all in advanced courses, so they're too busy to hang out with us during a normal day. Friday is when we all get together and unwind."

I drew in a deep, shaky breath.

"Okay, how about this?" she started. "Try it out a couple times and if you *really* hate it, we can think of something to get you out of it without making you the root of rumors."

"Really?"

"Really," Becca confirmed with one of her brilliant smiles. "But I think once we get you there, you'll see it's no big deal. I bet you'll even have fun."

I took another deep breath, nodding even though I remained unconvinced.

"I'll see you tomorrow morning," Becca said.

"Wait, Becca, one more thing."

"What?"

"I don't have anything to wear."

Becca's face lit up. "Oh, this is going to be *fun!*"

* *** *

Friday morning I awoke nervous and tense. I went through my morning routine by muscle memory, my mind distracted with anticipations of the party. It was only as I was heading outside to catch the bus that I realized just how deep my antisocial behavior ran.

I recalled the club scenes I had seen in movies, which only made my fear worse. I had always thought of clubs as places where people had sex or did drug deals, and even though I knew Club Archangel would not be the movie stereotype, it was difficult to get the image out of my head that I was going somewhere I wasn't supposed to be.

I hoped I could get to school and focus on my classes to forget about the party, but as soon as I took my seat on the bus, I was surrounded by conversations about Club Archangel and what everyone was planning to wear, who they were going with, and all other manner of details that made my stomach twist. The party was already surrounding me and it was only eight in the morning.

I met up with Taylor, Jill, and Becca at Jill's locker, as had become routine before classes started. The three girls were far more enthusiastic about Archangel than I had hoped.

"Are you excited for the party tonight?" Taylor asked, shimmying in an excited half-dance.

I could only smile nervously in response.

"Hey, let's kinda stick together this time," Becca suggested. "We want to make sure that Lily isn't completely overwhelmed. It'll be her first time in Archangel."

"Good idea," Jill agreed. She turned to Taylor. "Are the boys going to be there?"

"Yep, they're meeting us at six at the tables."

"Great. They'll be another layer of protection for you," Jill said, placing a hand on my shoulder. "They're great guys. You'll like them."

"One more thing," Becca said, flashing a devilish smile. "Lily doesn't have any clubbing clothes. So, let's meet at her house at five and get her ready. We'll all bring something and see what fits her."

"*Yes*!" Jill exclaimed.

"I'll just bring makeup." Taylor shrugged. "I would bring my clothes, but none of my stuff will be small enough for your hot little body."

"What?" I barked a laugh.

"When we're done with you, you are going to look *so* sexy we'll have to beat the boys away from you," Jill seconded.

As I went through my classes, hearing more and more about the upcoming party, my concerns swelled to a nearly unbearable magnitude. I was thankful that my new friends were going to be with me, but the fact that I was also going to be their dress-up doll was not so comforting.

In Lit class we discussed America's history before the Second Revolution, as we had for the past four days. I was still unable to pay attention, even with our teacher's enthusiastic manner, already knowing most of the information and too busy conjuring up wild scenarios about what I would experience at Club Archangel.

When class was over, Mr. McDermott spoke over the din of scraping chairs and opening book bags.

"Okay, okay, hold on!" he called. "I know you all have a party at Archangel tonight but *do not forget* to read the first chapter of J.A.N.E. this weekend. Alright? It's really short. It won't take you long. Be sure you read it so that we can discuss it in class!" As his students filed out of the room, he shouted the last sentence. "Remember your oath!"

The entire day was about the party. In every class, someone was talking about it. When the students left class, the teachers would tell everyone to be careful that night and be sure to do our weekend homework. Lunch was spent explaining where my house was and what bus we were catching back home—apparently, there was a free shuttle service for the students once the club closed, surprising me further about how accommodating everything was for the students in Central.

Once home, I hid in my room to agonize for two hours before my friends arrived. I tried to do my math homework but could not concentrate, fear tangling my stomach and stunting all productivity.

Around four-thirty, my mom returned home and came to my room.

"Hey, honey," she said gently. I was on my bed, pretending to read a book. "Nervous about the party?"

I groaned, placing the book over my face. "*Yes.*"

"Oh, come on, now," she laughed, slightly exasperated. "It won't be bad, I promise. You'll probably even have some fun."

"Is it bad that I don't want to go?" I peeked at her from under the book. "That I'm so horribly antisocial the mere idea of this party brings me dread?"

"No," she assured. "You're just a different kind of person, Lily. You don't need all the noise and shiny things to amuse you. You are a quiet soul."

"You mean horribly antisocial."

"I did not say that," she corrected with a smile, taking the book off my face. "But it won't hurt you to get out and experience something different. And, even if you don't like it, at least you can say that you tried."

"It's not that simple," I said, sitting upright.

"Why not?"

"Because I'm *supposed* to go to these parties, otherwise everyone thinks there is something wrong with me," I explained. "It's required of us to go."

"If you don't want to go again, you don't have to," my mom chuckled. "That is *your* choice. Don't let anyone force you to do something you don't want to do."

"How long has it been since you were in school? Don't you remember that it's a game of survival?"

My mom laughed and pat my hand.

"I remember that I thought every little thing was so important. But as I got older, I look back and go, 'wow, that really wasn't that big of a deal.' One day, you'll do the same."

* *** *

As promised, my friends arrived at my front door at five o'clock. My mom ushered them inside as I walked nervously to the foyer.

All three girls dressed for the party. Becca was in a tight black halter top with skinny jeans, wedge heels, and a decorative belt, her hair pulled back, emphasizing her dark makeup. Jill was in a short, tight dress with a sheer panel across her belly and high boots. Taylor was in jeans and heeled boots with a halter top that glittered with several long necklaces. Seeing their effort, I became more concerned about how I would look once they were done with me.

A wobbly smile came to my face as my mother turned to me.

"Well, there she is. Are you girls going to make her up for the party?"

"Yes, we are," Jill said, lifting her two bags.

"Good," my mother said with an approving nod. "She's never been one to doll herself up unless she absolutely has to."

"Thanks, Mom."

"Have fun with her." My mother winked at the three girls.

"Oh, we will," Taylor sang.

Becca grabbed my arm, dragging me toward the stairs.

"Come on, you."

Taylor and Jill followed eagerly, giggling maniacally. They closed my bedroom door and Jill smiled evilly, leaning against it to block my only means of escape.

"Let us begin…"

"Put everything out on the bed and let's see what we've got," Becca instructed.

"Don't I get to decide?" I whined.

"No!" Taylor snapped, placing her makeup on the bed.

"Why not?"

"Because there is how you want to look, how you should look, and how you *can* look," she elaborated. "We're going to show you how hot you *can* look."

"Oh, yes," Becca gasped, grabbing a top Jill had thrown onto my bed.

"*No!*" I yelped. The black halter top had nothing covering the belly with a drape floating down the back, connected to the neck by a golden chain up the center of the back.

"Hell yes!" Taylor agreed.

"Okay, wear this," Becca shoved the garment into my hands, "and I have some pants..." She rifled through her own bag and pulled out a pair of simple black pants. "Then we'll use this belt." She pulled out a chain belt with dangling ornaments from the loops.

"Perfect!" Jill declared, handing me the other objects. "Change into those. Where are your shoes?"

"Hold on a second," I said, staring at the jumbled clothes in my arms. "Look, I appreciate what you're doing, but—"

"Nope. No buts," Jill interrupted.

"Girl, trust me, you're going to look *great*," Taylor assured. "You need to loosen up a bit. Everything will be fine. We're watching out for you."

"I agree," Becca concurred. "Besides, I'm excited to see that hot little bod you've been hiding."

"Oh, me too," Jill leered.

I groaned.

"My shoes are in the closet on the bottom shelf." I nodded to the door as I turned to my bathroom. "I'll go change."

"No!" Jill barked, snapping her fingers at me. "You are not allowed to see yourself in the mirror until we are completely finished."

"*What?*" I gaped. "Oh, come on!"

"Nope! Strip!" Taylor ordered.

I groaned yet again, annoyed, nervous, and extremely self-conscious. I turned my back to them and slowly pulled my shirt over my shoulders, keeping my arms close to my chest as I scrambled to put on the other top.

Once I had it over my head, I heard Taylor's voice again.

"Bra needs to come off, hun."

I carefully maneuvered my arms and unhooked my bra, extracting it from under the clothes. Once I had the top on, I took the pants and unfolded them before backing myself in a corner to shimmy out of my jeans. Taylor laughed at my nervousness.

"Why're you embarrassed? We've all got the same equipment."

I still kept myself in the corner, watching Jill and Becca rifle through my shoes. I hastily pulled the black slacks up my legs only to realize the outer seam had a large slit from the bottom hem to the knee, leaving my entire calf exposed.

"I *cannot* pull this off."

"Are you kidding me? They fit you like a glove," Becca complimented, looking me over. I fastened the belt how I thought it should be done, trying to ignore the staring of my friends.

"*Perfect!*" Jill gasped, pulling out a pair of red, strappy wedge heels I had to match my red formal dress.

"Taylor, are you on makeup?" Becca asked.

"Yep!" She grabbed her makeup kit and bounded over, kneeling in front of me as I sat in my desk chair.

"I'm on hair!" Jill declared, walking to her bag and extracting her curling iron.

I was wringing my hands in my lap the entire time my three friends fussed over me, touching my face and pulling my hair, almost burning my ear twice and messing up the mascara when I flinched away.

Thirty minutes later, five minutes before we had to leave for Archangel, my friends backed away, triumphant.

"You look *amazing*," Becca said strongly.

"Put your shoes on and go look," Jill urged.

I leaned down and strapped myself into my shoes with shaking hands, thick curls of brown hair falling past my shoulders. I nervously approached my full-length mirror, not knowing what I was about to see.

I blinked in disbelief.

I did not look bad—in fact, I almost did not recognize myself. My makeup had been done to look mostly natural, apart from my deep red lipstick and the red tones around my eyes to match my shoes. My hair had been curled and parted on one side to frame my face in a surprisingly flattering manner.

"See what I mean?" Becca asked, breaking me out of my stunned trance. I turned to look at the slits in the pants, sucking in my belly as I studied my reflection.

"You guys deserve a medal. You performed a miracle."

"No," Jill disagreed. "There was a sex goddess inside you the entire time. It's time for her to come out."

"*Now,* you're ready for Archangel," Taylor said with a wink.

"We're really going to have to keep an eye on you tonight," Becca said. "Otherwise, every guy in town will be hitting on you."

Chapter Seven

My friends continuously slapped my hands away from adjusting myself, scolding me for messing with their hard work. I did not feel comfortable in the clothing or makeup, particularly with how often the other three commented on my transformation. Even my mother had complimented my appearance with wide eyes and a broad smile as I left. The praise only served to make me more uncomfortable, hoping I would not attract the same attention from others at the club.

Jill's father dropped us in front of the club, which I studied warily. For what felt like several minutes, I could only stare at the blue and white neon sign, listening to pulsing bass that escaped the confines of the building to flood the sidewalk as students walked through the darkened doorway into the flashing lights. The sign was intricate and alluring, summoning everyone inside and leaving a blue glow over the front of the building. My legs turned to jelly. I wanted nothing more than to get back in the car and leave.

Just when the urge became overwhelming, Becca's hand clasped my shoulder.

"No running away," she chided. "Don't worry. I told you, we'll be right here with you."

Once inside Club Archangel, the sound of the music was deafening and the flashing lights became disorienting. Becca led me to the small window in the wall where we were asked to present our school IDs. The cards were scanned and our purses were checked before we were allowed inside.

I had never seen anything like Club Archangel. It was mostly dark, making it difficult to gauge its exact size. There were circular platforms raised from the floor throughout the room where groups of friends were dancing above the others as the pulsing music rattled my chest. The lights flashed different colors as the strobe light kicked on and off in time with the beat. To one side there was a bar—likely only serving non-alcoholic drinks—and over the bar was a metal grate balcony where other students were chatting and bobbing their heads to the music, not as active as those on the dance floor. Across from the bar and balcony was a stage. The curtains were pulled shut and a large banner hung across the space, reading "Welcome Back!" covered with streamers and balloons.

"C'mon, Lily!" Taylor laughed, yanking me from my position by the door. I had been so entranced by the loud, disorienting club that I had not noticed my group of friends moving away. I followed Taylor's guide toward the bar, where we sat at a tall table near one of the two metal staircases leading to the balcony.

"What'd'ya think?!" Taylor asked over the pulsing music.

I took a deep breath. "I don't know."

"It'll be overwhelming at first, but you'll get used to it," Jill assured. "The most important thing is to have fun, and only dance with guys we have told you are okay."

"Oh, and don't *ever* go on the balcony," Taylor added, pointing at the grate metal above our heads. Confused, I asked why.

"That's for the Commish Kids," Jill explained. "You can't go up there unless you're part of the Commission of the People."

"Why?"

"It's an unwritten rule," Taylor said. "They can come down here and dance, but if anyone not in the Commission goes up there, they get real quiet and stare at you until you leave."

"They're their own little society, then?"

"*Oh*, yeah."

"Hello, *ladies*," a voice cooed as a boy our age leaned against our table.

"Hey, Todd," Becca greeted brightly.

Two other boys stood behind Todd, though it was difficult to discern their features in the constantly-flashing lights, so I just assumed the three boys were the other friends Becca had mentioned.

"Hey, baby!" Taylor squealed, kissing Todd. Todd kissed back briefly before standing straight, placing his arm around his girlfriend and looking around the table. When his eyes settled on me, my blood ran cold. I hated being pegged as the new girl, particularly when it came to boys.

"Who's the hottie?"

"I am!" Taylor pouted playfully.

"I know," Todd laughed, kissing her temple. "Who's *this* hottie?" He pointed at me.

"This is Lily Sandover," Becca introduced. "Lily, this is Todd Douglas."

"Nice to meet you."

"Lily's new here," Jill explained, pointing at him accusingly. "So be nice to her."

"I'm *always* nice!" Todd defended, playing along. "Well, Lily, I guess I better introduce you to these weirdos over here." He turned to the two boys behind him. "This is Devon," he introduced the taller one, "and that's Clark," he jerked his thumb to the shorter boy.

43

Devon was surprisingly handsome, his well-defined features making him look older than seventeen and his perfect smile stunning me. Clark, by contrast, was small and feeble-looking with dark hair and eyes. He wore thick glasses and looked as nervous as I felt. He did not make eye contact with me, though I could feel his eyes studying me whenever I turned away.

"C'mon, Clark!" Todd laughed, grabbing the smaller boy's shoulder and pulling him closer. "Be social! Say hello to the ladies."

"Hello," he mumbled.

"How are you doing, Clark?" Becca asked gently, smiling at the nervous teen.

"I-I'm alright. Thank you, Becca. How are you?"

"I'm alright. Do you wanna dance?" she asked, starting to stand.

"N-no, thank you," he said quickly. "I actually…I need to go."

"Aw, c'mon, one dance!" Becca insisted, grabbing his hand and dragging him to the floor as another song started. I watched them leave before turning to the rest of the group.

"Is he okay?"

"Clark? Oh, yeah, he's fine," Todd answered before resuming kissing his girlfriend.

"Clark is a Commish Kid," Devon explained, his voice strong and very fitting to his disposition. I, admittedly, found myself a little flustered by him, which was a new feeling for me. "Most Commish Kids are like that around us common folk," he joked.

"You're friends with a Commish Kid?" I asked as he sat in Becca's recently-vacated seat.

"Yeah, he's a good guy," Devon said. "We've had honors classes together for years, so we ended up becoming friends. He was always alone in the back of the class. I just wanted to make sure he had at least one friend."

"If he's a Commish Kid, why is he down here? Shouldn't he be up there?" I motioned to the balcony above.

"It's a system they have worked out," Jill explained. "The Commish Kids have rounds. A few will come down at a time and will circle the room to pick up gossip."

"That's creepy."

"Yeah, but that's what they're expected to do."

"Do you girls want anything?" Devon asked, standing. "I'll get us some drinks."

"I'd love an iced tea," Jill chimed. Devon reached across the table, smacking Todd in the shoulder.

"Hey, will you stop eating her face for a second?" he groaned. "Do you two want anything to drink?"

"No, thanks," they both said before resuming their previous task.

"What about you, Lily?"

"I didn't bring any money."

"That's okay," he said. "It's free."

"Just water, please."

I watched Devon as he went to the bar, unable to tear my eyes away, even as he walked back, balancing three glasses.

"So, Lily, who do you have in Central?" he asked, setting my water in front of me.

"My dad," I answered. "He's the Regulator for the Western Region."

"Impressive, the biggest region." He smiled. "What are you interested in? Do you want to do what your dad does?"

"Not really," I admitted hesitantly.

"Yeah, I don't blame you. I'm the same way," he laughed. He turned to look at the dance floor and nodded to Becca and Clark. "That's why I feel bad for Clark. He doesn't have a choice even though he's said often that he doesn't want to be in the government."

"What do you mean he doesn't have a choice?"

"Well, once you're in the Commission, that's it," Jill elaborated. "You don't get out. Clark has it really tough. He was born a Commish Kid and is mom is head advisor to Dana Christenson himself."

"No way," I hissed, my eyes shooting wide.

"Oh, yeah," Taylor interjected, having broken away from her heated makeout with Todd. "Mr. Christenson already has his sights set on Clark to take over as advisor one day. At least, that's what Clark's mom says."

"I thought they weren't allowed to talk about what happens in the Commission," I said.

"Not what goes on *inside* the Commission," Todd agreed. "But they have to release information about who is taking over. And when you have someone like Dana Christenson saying that your kid has potential, wouldn't you brag?"

Becca reappeared at the table as the song ended, smiling at Devon.

"You are in my seat!" she declared, playfully pushing him.

"That's what happens when you leave it unattended."

"Fine!" She sat on his legs, wiggling her hips. "I hope my bony ass doesn't hurt too much." When he just shrugged, Becca picked up his drink, taking large gulps of iced tea with a smug glint in her eyes.

"Hey! Stop, I just got it!" he laughed, trying to snatch the drink back. "You're going to drink all of it!"

"That's the idea!" Becca smiled triumphantly when she pulled the almost-empty glass away from her mouth.

"Thanks, Becca," he groaned through his smile. "Would you like a refill?" he asked sarcastically.

"Yes, please!" she beamed. She got off of his lap as he grabbed the glass and returned to the bar. When he was gone, Becca resumed her seat victoriously.

My attention turned back to the club, my senses overwhelmed. I knew a few of the songs, though most I had never heard before. The noise reverberated in my chest and rattled my eardrums. The flashing lights made me dizzy, and while part of it was unpleasant, another part was thrilling and I found myself bobbing my head in time with the beat as if by instinct, feeding off the energy of the other club-goers.

Devon's return with more drinks brought my attention back to the table. He had brought another iced tea for Becca and one for himself, but when he saw that Becca had taken his seat, he pouted.

"Where am I supposed to sit?"

"You're not," Jill laughed. "Stand like a gentleman and let the ladies sit."

"How about," he turned to me, "I take *you* out to the dance floor, instead?"

"No." I shook my head quickly, my heart jumping into a terrified pace. "I don't know how."

"You don't have to know anything fancy," he chuckled. "C'mon, it'll be fun!"

He grabbed my hand and pulled me out of my chair. I somewhat-willingly followed. Becca winked, giving me a thumbs-up when I glanced pitifully back at her.

Devon led me through the mass of people to the middle of the crowd, where he turned to me and began moving with the beat of the music. I bounced by bending my knees, but I was so nervous about dancing that it was the only movement I could manage, my eyes scanning everyone around me, self-conscious.

"You need to *relax*," he laughed.

"I don't know how to do this," I said with a broken chuckle, embarrassed heat invading my cheeks.

"It's easy," he said. "Just relax and feel the music."

"I don't know *how*."

"No, you're just nervous," he corrected. "Just feel it and move however you want. There's no skill to it and no one is watching. Trust me."

I took a deep breath and tried to relax, which proved impossible. Firstly, I was *way* out of my element, and secondly, I did not want to screw up. The last thing I needed was to fall down and make a fool of myself my first night at Club Archangel. There were too many people around us and my clumsiness could end up with some people hurt—though most likely just me.

I bounced a little more, trying to rock my upper body as Devon moved with the crowd, naturally one with the ocean of dancing students.

"You are trying *way* too hard," he said. "Come here," he motioned me closer. Nervously, I stepped forward.

Devon took a hold of my shoulders.

"Take a deep breath."

I smiled awkwardly, but did so, feeling silly at having to be coached on how to relax in the middle of the dance floor.

"Good, now let it out."

I found myself laughing and shaking my head.

"I'm sorry, I'm really no good at all this."

The end of the song slowly meshed with the beginning of the next. The teens around me cheered and began dancing enthusiastically. A smile came to Devon's face.

"This is a good song. Turn around."

"What?"

"It's alright. Turn around."

When I was facing the other direction, Devon placed his hands on my arms, leaning to my ear.

"Close your eyes," he whispered. I tried to suppress the shiver that ran down my spine, but it was entirely involuntary. My eyes slid shut, my attention focused on three things—his hands on my arms, his voice in my ear, and the beat resonating through my chest.

"Do you feel it?" One of his hands rested on the skin just below my collarbone. I jumped, startled, but his hand did not move. "Just relax," he whispered. "Close your eyes again."

I obeyed.

"Do you feel the music here? Feel the beat rattle your chest?"

I nodded.

"Do you feel it here?" His hand move to my abdomen, resting against my exposed stomach. I nodded again with a giddy smile. Both of his hands rested just above my hipbones. "Keep your eyes closed and move with what you feel."

My body began to sway, my hips acting of their own accord. I felt Devon's hands on my skin, felt his presence behind me, and my grin widened. My movements became more confident, my eyes remaining closed.

"That's it."

I continued to dance, his hands never leaving my hips, his mouth always close to my ear. Before I knew it, I was moving fluidly, feeling less self-conscious and allowing the beat to move me.

But I was not dancing only to the feel of the music, I was dancing to Devon. He was moving behind me, keeping me in rhythm. I knew I likely looked ridiculous with my eyes closed and a huge grin on my face while I danced with him, but in those minutes, I did not care.

The song ended too soon. The next one started and the change prompted me to finally open my eyes to the dancing teenagers and flashing lights. I turned to face a smiling Devon.

"I told you you could do it."

"Thank you."

"You just need to loosen up more."

"Yeah, I'll work on that."

Before I could help myself, I hugged him, feeling his strong arms wrap around my waist.

"Thanks," I whispered sincerely.

We returned to our table. Taylor and Todd had slipped away sometime while I was dancing, leaving Becca and Jill. Becca was beaming like a proud parent at me. Jill, on the other hand, wore a very different smile that made her gaze dark, and it was a look that only girls could spot easily.

It was jealousy.

She liked Devon, and was clearly irritated by the attention he had given me.

I sat nervously, trying to void eye contact with Devon. I knew if I expressed any interest in him. I would get into rocky territory with my new friends.

I did not dance again, though Devon continuously asked. I turned him down, saying that I had had enough for one night and 'maybe next time.' I suggested that Devon dance with Jill, which he did several times, taking Jill's attention away from me and hopefully showing her I was more interested in her friendship than in Devon.

A boy was not worth losing one of the friends who would help me survive my move to Central.

I remained at the table for the rest of the evening, bobbing my head to the music and admittedly enjoying watching the other students dance. Taylor and Todd eventually returned, noticeably having committed some intimate act elsewhere.

Announcements came over the speakers several times as the club began closing. As they listed the times each of the three busses would be leaving, the club began to empty and the dance floor cleared. Deciding we were ready to leave, our group caught the first bus. We found a collection of seats in the back and waited for the bus to fill as everyone talked excitedly, still riding the euphoric high of the party. Becca turned to me.

"What did you think?"

"Well…" I started slowly, "it was an experience."

"That's the spirit!" Todd laughed.

"Where's Clark?" I asked.

"He'll catch a later bus," Devon answered. "He always does."

"You looked like you had fun," Taylor noted.

"You did," Jill agreed. "You can keep that top, by the way," she assured with a wink.

"Oh, no," I said quickly. "I'll give it back on Monday."

"No, I won't wear it," she insisted. "It doesn't look as good on me. Seriously, keep it."

"And you can keep the pants, too," Becca added.

"I can't wear this every week."

"We'll go shopping next weekend," Taylor declared. "We can get you some makeup, some hair stuff, some clothes. Trust me, you'll be able to pull off just about everything."

"I don't know about *that*…"

The bus jolted into motion, taking the kids to the various stops that had been designated on the route back from Club Archangel. My stop was one of the last, so I had to say goodnight to my friends first. I agonized over how I would say goodbye to Devon, worried it would look like I was flirting with him in front of Jill. But I got lucky, as Jill's stop was closer than his, so she was gone before I told him goodnight.

"Thanks, again," I said as he stood.

"I'll dance with you whenever you want to relax a little," he assured with a gentle smile. He walked off the bus with several other students as Becca turned to me.

"You two looked pretty good on the dance floor," she leered, wiggling her eyebrows. I chose not to respond beyond a quiet laugh.

Becca got off the bus two stops before me, making my stop the last in my group of friends. I navigated my way home and used the secret key under the mailbox to open the front door, my exhaustion hitting me like a truck as I closed the door behind me.

"Lily, is that you?" my father's voice called.

"Yeah, it's me." I walked into the kitchen where my father sat at the table in the breakfast nook, surrounded by papers. He smiled when he saw me, though his eyes did go wide as he scanned what I was wearing.

"Well, you look…"

"I *know*," I groaned. "I was a science project for my friends."

My father laughed and motioned me closer. I leaned down, hugging him tightly, thrilled to be back in my quiet home.

"I was going to say that you look beautiful," he said. "Did you have fun?"

"Eh." I shrugged, breaking our hug. "I don't know…it was a bit overwhelming."

"Yeah, I remember being your age." He grinned. "It may have been long, *long* ago, but I remember getting out on the dance floor, too."

"*You*?"

"Your old man was pretty wild back in the day," he chuckled. His eyes softened. "I'm glad you had an alright time, at least."

"I did."

"Meet any boys?" he asked with an expectant eyebrow.

"No, Dad. No boys."

"Good, because boys are nothing but trouble."

"You used to be one."

"How do you think I know so well?" He patted me on the arm. "Go on, now. You must be tired."

"I am," I affirmed. "Where's Mom?"

"She went to bed," he said. "Oh, right, she told me to tell you to wash the makeup off your face, wash your hair, and soak your feet in warm water before you go to bed."

I laughed, rolling my eyes.

"Alright."

"I'm just relaying the message." He raised his hands peacefully. "I don't know anything about this girl stuff."

"You know as much as I do." I kissed him on the cheek before walking away. "Love you, Dad. Don't stay up too late."

"Love you, too, honey."

I left my father to his work, walking wearily to my room. When the door was closed behind me, I took off my shoes, surprised by the extent of my exhaustion. I carelessly threw them toward the corner before walking to my bathroom, tenderly running my fingers over Dex, who was sleeping at the foot of my bed.

Lazily leaving my clothes all over the bathroom floor, I stepped into the shower. I tried to wash myself as quickly as possible, knowing there was a good chance that the heat would cause me to fall asleep under the water's spray. I stepped out and wiped down the mirror only to see that the makeup around my eyes had smudged rather than come off. I washed my face vigorously, though it seemed impossible to remove all traces of black eyeliner.

My first task the following day would be to buy makeup remover—my old makeup remover wipes had dried up from lack of use.

Once I had given up on the black smudges around my eyes, I brushed my teeth, then my hair, finally pulling on my pajamas and crawling into bed with my eyes mostly-closed.

My intention had been to stay up after I got home to do some homework but I could not bring myself to stay awake. I was unsure what had made me so tired. Maybe it had been the loud music and flashing lights, or maybe it had been the large crowd of people, or just the overwhelming anxiety leading up to the party. Either way, my homework would have to wait until I recovered from my first party at Archangel.

Chapter Eight

I was in a daze for the entire weekend. My senses had been overloaded, leaving me exhausted from the experience at Archangel. Because of my fatigue, it took me an embarrassingly long time to read the assigned chapter of *An Angel Without Wings*.

I managed to complete my homework late Saturday and doodle Sunday away until my mother hurriedly reminded me of the politician coming over for dinner, demanding I get out of my sweatpants and put some effort into my appearance. With my fatigue turning my brain to mush, the dinner I had forgotten about with one of my father's new colleagues seemed like a harrowing task.

Our dinner guest was Benjamin Lloyd, the Chair of Regions in Leader Simon's administration, which meant he was extremely important and my father's most influential superior in the Chamber of Regions. The whole family needed to appear perfect and be on our best behavior.

My father often entertained others in the government back home, but never those as high as the administration of Leader Simon. Therefore, everyone was a little nervous about meeting with Mr. Lloyd, desperate to make a good impression. I was worried my foggy brain would make me seem like a moron, so I drank a cup of coffee while I dressed.

I dressed in a white blouse and black, knee-length skirt, pulling my hair back and trying to look modest but not old-for-my-age. I was used to society parties and high-standing officials in our home, but now I was in Central and the person we were entertaining was of much higher status. I felt like I was learning everything all over again, which caused me to fuss over my appearance far longer than necessary.

My father came home around seven and rushed to change suits and clean up, blurting a quick "I'm home! I'll be down in a minute!" as he ascended the stairs two at a time.

At seven-thirty the doorbell rang, signaling the arrival of our guest and causing my mother and me to share a nervous look.

I was not sure what I had been expecting of Mr. Lloyd, but I had not been expecting the small, thin man who appeared on our doorstep. He was balding and his eyes were surrounded by wrinkles, though the lines in his face were hidden by thick glasses. He did not immediately strike me as a man with enough ambition to become Chair of Regions— if anything, he seemed too weak and exhausted to be in Central's political arena.

"Hello, I am Benjamin Lloyd."

"Yes, it is a pleasure to meet you," I greeted, having been the one to answer the door. "I am Lily, Thomas' daughter. Won't you please come in?"

I stepped aside, immediately more relaxed once I saw the man we were entertaining was not of overwhelming stature—even his obviously-expensive and well-tailored suit did not make his shoulders look imposing.

"Thank you," he said. "I saw a picture of you on Thomas' desk. It doesn't do you justice."

"Thank you very much, sir," I said graciously. "Mom?" I called gently. "Mr. Lloyd is here."

"Oh, Mr. Lloyd," my mother greeted, walking into the foyer from the kitchen and extending her hand. "It's very nice to meet you. I am Karen."

"It is wonderful to finally meet you, Karen," Mr. Lloyd said, taking her hand and kissing the back of it. "I have heard so many wonderful things about you from Thomas. I was anxious to meet such an incredible woman."

"Oh, you are far too kind," my mother giggled demurely.

I always hated those kinds of dinner meetings. Everything was so flighty, consisting of denying compliments and skirting any real conversation for the first half of the evening. I especially hated how all of the forced smiling made my cheeks hurt, but I dared not scowl or roll my eyes at the obligatory pleasantries meant to cover the awkwardness of introductions.

"My husband will be down in just a moment. I apologize but dinner is not quite ready. It will still be about ten minutes."

"That is perfectly alright, Mrs. Sandover," Mr. Lloyd assured with a light chuckle. "It smells fantastic! What are you making?"

"Steak with steamed vegetables, mashed potatoes, salad, and an apple pie for dessert," my mom answered with a beaming grin.

"Absolutely wonderful!"

"I hope it is to your liking," she said, moving back into the kitchen. My father came down the stairs as my mother retreated to the kitchen, dressed in a new suit and tie and looking like a savior swooping in to rescue me from making small talk with Mr. Lloyd.

"Mr. Lloyd."

"Come, now, Thomas, we've discussed this," Mr. Lloyd chuckled, taking my father's extended hand. "None of his 'Mr. Lloyd' business. It's Ben."

"Ben, thank you for joining us for dinner."

"Absolutely. I always prefer to conduct meetings over food rather than in a stuffy office."

It took all my willpower to keep the disappointment off my face at having to sit through the whole dinner meeting when I did not care about politics and had no idea what my father was working on that would merit the meeting. I wished it had been a weeknight so I could have slipped away to 'do homework,' as was my typical excuse.

"I see you've met my daughter."

"I have," Mr. Lloyd affirmed. "She seems like a wonderful young lady, Thomas. You must be very proud."

We moved to the table where I asked Mr. Lloyd and my father what they would like to drink. While we waited for dinner to be ready, Mr. Lloyd and my father talked lightly, discussing their homes and how our family was adjusting to Central. They did not talk about politics or the purpose for the meeting, which I knew would become the conversation near the end of the evening.

I rarely joined the chatting as dinner commenced. My mother and father talked genially to Mr. Lloyd, asking him how long he had been in Central and if he had any children—all the normal questions one asked of a first-time guest. My mother asked about Leader Simon and inquired if he was a nice boss, which Mr. Lloyd replied by saying that he was a kind and gentle man.

I had never pictured the leader of a country as powerful as America to be "gentle."

I only joined the conversation when I was asked if I liked Central and was adjusting well to my new school. I answered politely but did not elaborate, desperate to stay out of the small talk.

When the time was appropriate, my father started the meeting part of dinner.

"So, Ben, what did you think of my proposal for the seventh route into the North-Midwest Region?" my father asked after we had wrapped up a story about traveling to the Northeast Region. Ben nodded, finishing the bite of steak he had in his mouth before turning to face my father fully.

"I thought it was brilliant," he said. "Did you work with Samantha on this?"

"I did," my father affirmed. "Mrs. Davis was the one who gave me the idea, actually." I blinked, recognizing the name of Becca's mother, who was the Official Regulator for the region they were discussing. "She told me that the northern most road was frozen for over six months of the year, and the transportation of goods becomes very difficult.

Reconstruction of the northern roads has been severely lacking since the revolution."

"It is a problem we have been facing for several years, ever since the closing of routes twelve and seventeen after the reformation. And that northern border is particularly dangerous with Canadian refugees desperate to get in." Mr. Lloyd mused with a pensive nod. I was completely lost and was trying to decide if I wanted to listen and learn what my father was suggesting or if I wanted to tune it out. "However, your thought of redirecting the seventh route is genius!"

"Do you really think so?" my father asked, his eyes alight with pride.

"Absolutely!" Mr. Lloyd said strongly. "In fact, one of the reasons I wanted to talk to you is because I want to submit this proposition to Leader Simon and the Commission of the People to see if we can get it approved as soon as possible."

At this, all of our eyes went wide. While I did not really understand the technicalities of their discussion, I understood the significance of the words and what they meant for my father's career. It took him several minutes to speak.

"You really think we should submit it already? There are still so many details to work out, like funding, and time—"

"The sooner we get this submitted, the more resources we'll have to figure out the details," Mr. Lloyd explained with a smile, seeing our stunned expressions. He leaned over and playfully hit my father on the shoulder. "It was about time you showed up in Central, Thomas. Time for us to crack the whip and get everyone back into shape."

The rest of dinner and dessert was spent discussing how the procedure would work and the revisions that my father would have to make before it was submitted to the eyes of Leader Simon and the Commission of the People. I was shocked that my father's first major proposal in Central would create such a stir, particularly as we had been in Central for only a short time.

Mr. Lloyd finally left late in the night when my eyes and limbs were growing heavy from exhaustion. We bid him goodbye at the door as he thanked us for hosting him. He complimented my mother's cooking and told my father, once again, that he should be very proud of his family. He told me to keep having as much fun as possible but not to let my grades slip. As he stepped over the threshold onto the front steps, he turned to my father one last time.

"I'll see you in my office on Monday, Thomas," he said. "And, just so you know, this kind of innovative thinking gets noticed quickly.

I wouldn't be surprised if you got your invitation into the Commission of the People for this."

My heart stopped and plummeted to the floor.

I knew what an immense honor it was to become a part of the Commission of the People—it was like being invited to the most exclusive club in the country. But the entire family was brought into the Commission. I had seen the way the "Commish Kids" were treated and how they acted around everyone else—how they struck fear in the other students. It was a group I was desperate to avoid. My anxieties were twisting around the food inside my belly, causing my body to lock up in confusion and terror. I knew my father wanted to do great things in Central, and being in the Commission was obviously something he aspired to, but it would be the final nail in the coffin of my future.

We bid Mr. Lloyd goodnight yet again and, when the door closed, my mother squealed, throwing her arms around my father's neck.

"I knew you would do great," she whispered.

Chapter Nine

Becca asked Monday morning if I had recovered from Archangel, and even though I said I had, my ears were still ringing. Jill became tense whenever anyone mentioned that Devon and I had looked good dancing together. I was not sure if the other girls noticed they were pushing her buttons or if they were purposely testing boundaries to see how long it would be before the issue was finally discussed.

I was relieved class gave me a reason to be away from Jill, but I knew it was only a matter of time before the issue of Devon would turn into a fight. I needed to tell her I had no interest in Devon—even though that was not entirely true. But I knew better than to approach her first and cause unnecessary drama. I had to wait for her to bring it up.

I purposely lingered outside my Lit class, waiting until the last possible moment to slip across the classroom and take my seat, making sure I would not have to discuss Archangel again.

"Hello, everyone, how was the party?" Mr. McDermott asked once the chime rang for class to start. The chorus of answers took several moments to quiet as Mr. McDermott smiled and nodded, telling us that he was glad the welcome back party was such a success. He did not allow the class long to talk about the party, holding up a book with an expectant eyebrow.

"Did everyone read the first chapter?"

"Yes," the class answered collectively.

"Great! Let's start with overall thoughts on the chapter." He looked around the room, waiting for someone to raise their hand and begin the discussion. After several long, silent seconds, Becca's hand went up.

"Becca."

"I thought it was interesting that the author told us that Thomas Ankell really didn't like *anything* about the America before the revolution. He didn't even want to save it. He didn't have any plans to start a revolution. He *hoped* America would fall. He had a lot of very negative and dark thoughts about the country."

"Excellent starting point," Mr. McDermott said. "This is a detail many have wondered about since this book was made public. Do you think that it's true that he hoped the United States would collapse? Or do you think that the author's making that up for the sake of good storytelling? A fighting-for-the-greater-good sort of narrative?"

A girl raised her hand.

"His feelings actually make sense, in a way."

"Why's that?"

"He was so unhappy with the state of the country that he didn't see any way to *save* it," the girl elaborated. "He ended up rebelling because he had to create a whole new system. The old one *had* to fall because it was beyond repair."

"That's a very good point, Jessica," Mr. McDermott agreed. He saw another hand in the back of the room. "Yes, Kevin?"

"I'm confused about something," he started. "The author says that there are some controversial things about Thomas Ankell's life. Is it just that he didn't like America, or…"

"No, no," Mr. McDermott laughed brokenly. "In the next few chapters, you will read some things that will make your eyebrows raise, that's for sure. Drug abuse, teen pregnancy, and intense violence." He sat on his desk. "Do you all agree with Jessica? That Thomas Ankell *wanted* to create a new system?"

Taylor raised her hand. "I didn't really get that impression," she disagreed. "I mean, there is a line—" she flipped through her book.

"Quoting!" Mr. McDermott grinned, also opening his own book. "Quoting is good."

"It's this line, where he says: 'I hate this country. I hope it destroys itself and burns to the ground. It deserves it.' To me, that doesn't sound like he wanted to rebuild anything. It said earlier in the chapter that he didn't *understand* the government, and that meant he didn't have any ideas for a better system when the revolution started."

"Excellent!" Mr. McDermott said. "And, actually, this is a perfect lead into what I wanted to talk about today. The author makes a point to start out this book by explaining that Thomas Ankell did not know *anything* about politics. Did anyone notice the way the author talks about the Ankell family?"

"They're repeatedly called ordinary and typical," one boy answered.

"Exactly. The author makes a point to stress that Ankell came from perfectly ordinary roots, even close to the point of poverty. This holds true to the American notion of the self-made man who makes his own way in the world due to his own determination. This sort of description of the family and the background of Ankell eludes to other great historical narrations of pre-Second Revolution American heroes, like Benjamin Franklin, which I think you all read a few years ago.

"So, why do you think this language was used in this first chapter to introduce Ankell's background?" Mr. McDermott asked. "If Ankell hated America and the Washington System, why would the narrative of his heroism be told in the same fashion as older American heroes who founded the very system he wanted to destroy?"

No one immediately answered.

One girl in the middle of the room raised her hand. I recalled that she was a Commish Kid, and a nasty one, at that, but I could not remember her name.

"Yes, Karmen?"

"It's true that he didn't like what the Washington System was doing, but when he was running the revolution, he was fighting for the 'true American Spirit,' and he rallied the people by talking about the Founding Fathers and how the American Spirit used to be one of the most powerful ideals in the world."

"Perfect," Mr. McDermott praised. "We must understand that Ankell became immortalized with the other American heroes because he fought mostly for the American Spirit and America as a whole. He looked at America as if the country was a person and, as we look further into the book, you will find one of his speeches where he talks about the 'Life of America' as if America was a human being, and not a philosophical idea of a country.

"Now, what do you think about the way the state of the world is described? Why do you think the author chose to include that section? Greg?" he motioned to a boy who had his hand raised in the back of the room.

"Well, this was written after Ankell died, so the state of the world had changed drastically between the time he was a boy and the time he died. The Second Revolution sent the entire world into a similar revolutionary state. The world we see today is nothing like it was back then."

"Very true. Yes, Karmen?"

"Going off what Greg said, it also seemed like the author was trying to say that Ankell's idea of revolution was brought to the world at the right time. All leading countries were ready for a change and, since America is a powerhouse with a lot of political influence, when Ankell organized the Second Revolution, it wasn't just a revolution of Americans, but it allowed the world to rally behind him, and to bring change to their own countries."

"You mean that everything was just about timing?" Mr. McDermott pressed.

"It just seemed that way from the way the author elaborated on the subject."

"That is an excellent point. It *was* all about timing. If Thomas Ankell had tried to launch that revolution at any other time, it would have never gotten off the ground. This is absolutely true."

Mr. McDermott went to the front of the room and turned on the projection screen to show a map of America divided into the six regions. "I hope you all know this map," he teased. "This is what America *used* to look like." He clicked a button on his computer and an older map appeared. The fifty states that used to compile America were outlined in relation to the current regions. "One of the greatest things Ankell did with the revolution was denouncing the idea of the United States. He claimed that America was no longer united and that the name was inappropriate. He stated that Americans needed to fight for America as a whole, not for their particular states with hopes that it would change the entire country.

"For the first several months of the revolution, this idea was considered preposterous, and many unified with their states, forming state divisions of the revolution. I know none of you are familiar with this map, so I will explain it. In the book, the horrible state of affairs started with Texas. This," he pointed, "is Texas." He pointed to the former state of California. "This is where Ankell is from, and this," he pointed to Washington D.C., "is where the former capital was." He motioned across the map. "Does it make sense why the revolution started in the western states?"

"Because the government was so far away…" I murmured before I could help myself. As teachers often did, Mr. McDermott heard my comment all the same.

"What was that?"

"The national government was too far away from the states on the west coast," I repeated louder.

"Absolutely right," Mr. McDermott said. "Ankell claimed that western representatives were too far away from their home states and they could not relate to their constituents at all, particularly with the sheer amount of corruption in Washington."

He explained the order of states that committed to the Second Revolution before class was finished and ended class by telling us that he would discuss the workings of the Washington System throughout the week in order to understand the roots of the Second Revolution.

I had never expected to learn that the bringer of the Second Revolution, the man Americans idolized as a hero, had been so angry toward his own country. I supposed the motives of some heroes had to remain secret to preserve the image presented to the public.

It was difficult not to ponder what life must have been like before the Washington System fell. I tried to imagine the deep-seated hatred in the American people and relate that anger to known facts of the bloody Second Revolutionary War. It was difficult to imagine just how angry the people had to be to wage war on their own government—one of the most powerful governments in the world that had no qualms killing its own people.

I found myself flipping back and forth between the pages in my personal sketchbook during art class, turning over dark thoughts of war and corruption. I added more shading to my recent sketch of an angel soaring above the clouds, waving his flag to rally the people. But, as I had been doing for weeks, I eventually flipped to what was quickly becoming my favorite sketch. It depicted the face of a man with eyes so full of emotions it was hard to believe all those feelings could be experienced at once. To me, the two pictures were connected to the Second Revolution. The man was America, full to the brim with anger, sadness, and general frustration about his own helplessness. The angel was flying high above all of it to rally people toward a better future.

I was not sure why the imagery was speaking so strongly to me. The war had already been won. America was at peace. But I felt as if all that anger and pain was still burning in my chest, and perhaps still within the American people.

* *** *

The week progressed quickly—*too* quickly. All too soon the subject of Archangel came up again.

My friends agreed to make me up once more. Our shopping trip was set for Saturday and, before I could complain about it, they made it clear that I had no choice but to participate.

Soon, the problems that Ankell faced before the Second Revolutionary War seemed insignificant compared to the problem I was facing Friday at Archangel. I was worried that Jill and I would be at odds over Devon, and I wanted to keep my friends more than I wanted a boyfriend. I was worried that Archangel would become the battleground of my first fight with my new friends.

I spent much of my time silently debating whether or not to pull Jill aside, but I could never find the right moment.

As I was mulling over the conundrum during lunch on Wednesday, tuning out the conversation around me, Taylor cut Becca off mid-sentence.

"Oh, no," she groaned, her eyes focused down the hall. "They're doing their rounds."

"Who?"

"Bitch Squad Alpha," Jill growled. Craning my head around Becca, I saw three girls walking toward us, one of whom I recognized as Karmen.

Becca turned to me, her expression pained.

"Brace yourself."

"Oh, Jill," Sarah Henderson, who was flanking Felicity Hanks, greeted. The girls seemed perfect, even while wearing the exact same uniform. Their hair and nails were impeccably kept and their makeup smoothed out all imperfections on their skin, creating an intimidatingly flawless image.

"Hi, Sarah," Jill greeted hesitantly.

"I haven't seen you since the summer trip."

"Don't act like you spent any time with her, Sarah," Felicity said, her tone lofty and cold. "She was too busy hanging out with Devon and Todd. Clark was with them for the first few days, remember?"

"Oh, right," Sarah agreed. "Jill, did you understand the chemistry homework?"

"Uh...yeah, kind of."

"Awesome. I need to copy it before class. Show up a few minutes early, okay?" Before Jill could protest, Sarah reached down and pat her on the head with a cold smile. "Thanks, you're such a pal."

"Who's this?" Felicity nodded to me, taking a few steps closer. She leaned down, inspecting me with ice in her gaze. "A new girl?"

"That's Lily Sandover. I told you about her," Karmen answered. "She's in my Lit class."

"*This* is her?" Felicity barked a laugh. "*You're* the Sandover kid? The Commission has been talking about whether or not to accept your family." She looked me over once more and pouted. "How disappointing. I thought with all the wonderful things everyone says about your father that you wouldn't be so plain."

The words stung more than I should have let them.

"Well, if you *do* get into the Commission, be careful," Felicity snorted. "There are a lot of perverted old men in there who really like the wide-eyed, naïve school-girl look."

"I wouldn't be concerned, Felicity," Becca said with a cold grin. "She won't take your father's attention away from you."

"Ah, Becca." Felicity turned to Becca as I blinked incredulously at my friend's bold words. "I thought the summer would soften you, but I guess even a debilitating illness can't cure you of being a cunt."

"Call me that again," Becca challenged, standing for the confrontation. We were all on our feet shortly after.

Taylor stood between them. "Don't start a fight in the hall."

"Keep your nose out of this, fat ass," Karmen snapped.

"What the hell is your problem?!" Jill bellowed as Taylor backed away, hurt.

"She just wishes she could eat whatever she wanted without having to stick her fingers down her throat afterward," Becca bit back. "Don't take it personally, Taylor. Remember, she has to have Luke do all her homework for her because even her boyfriend can't tutor her enough to pass her classes. Not only are you able to excel in all subjects, but you don't have to have Todd do the work for you."

"*Please.*" Karmen rolled her eyes. "I don't need my boyfriend to do anything for me."

"Not according to the Board of Education," Becca taunted.

"What's goin' on here?" a voice asked. The boy coming down the hallway appeared to be a fourth-year, his tall, lanky frame accented by the navy blazer, his thick curly hair falling to the side of his dark brown eyes.

"Just dealing with some trash," Felicity quipped.

"Why are you even bothering?" the boy sneered, putting his arm around Felicity's shoulders. "They're nobodies."

"Not all of them," Sarah corrected, motioning to me. "This is the Sandover girl."

"Oh..." After his eyes raked over me, inspecting every inch, he scoffed. "She's gonna get eaten alive."

The group of Commish Kids walked away, leaving a heavy, unsettled feeling in the air. Once they were out of sight, I let out a long breath, my heart thundering inside my ribcage.

"I *hate* those bitches," Becca growled around ground teeth.

"More importantly," Jill started, smacking my arm as I resumed my seat between her and Becca, "why the *hell* didn't you tell us that you're going into the Commission?!"

"Nothing's official!" I protested quickly. "I mean, it's a little early for my dad to get appointed to something like the Commission of the People, right? We just got here."

"You'd be surprised," Taylor said. "They're always on the lookout. It only takes one thing to catch the attention of Dana Christenson and you're in."

I hesitated.

"I guess I just don't want to believe that it will really happen…" I turned to them, forcing a wobbly smile. "I don't want to be a Commish Kid!" I whined.

Jill put her arm around me.

"It's okay. You can still be our friend."

"Of course," Taylor agreed. "It just means that we won't see you as much…"

"And that we have to be careful what we say around you…" Jill added.

"And that you have to be on the balcony of Archangel instead of with us…"

"You know, amazingly, this is not comforting," I groaned.

Chapter Ten

It was concerning how easily the taunting words of the Commish Kids had gotten under my skin. I mulled over the warnings about the Commission and how I would be "eaten alive," unable to keep the phrase from repeating in my head for days after the confrontation.

In many ways I was thankful to go to Archangel, as it provided the perfect, overly-loud distraction.

After donning a far-too-tight dress and being covered in makeup, we took a taxi to Club Archangel. The wide-eyed look from the taxi driver finally convinced me that the shopping trip the following day was a necessity—I could not let my friends dress me anymore if I was drawing so much attention.

Once inside Archangel, we found a table under the balcony again.

"Okay, tonight, you will participate in the activity that is called creeping," Taylor teased.

"I know what creeping is," I laughed.

"Now you get to practice," Becca said. "At one point, you'll get up and dance your way to the various sides of the club and listen to any gossip you can. If they're talking about anything interesting, stick around and listen in. Just dance close to whoever you're eavesdropping on."

"Don't you think that's too obvious?"

"Most people are surprisingly oblivious. Everyone knows that people do it, but if the conversation's interesting, they stop noticing things they should," Taylor told me with a shrug. "We'll all take turns tonight and then we'll meet up here and compare notes."

I did not know what would be considered interesting gossip, but I agreed to eavesdrop, though I was not sure how I was going to hear gossip when I could barely hear my friends over the thumping music.

I sipped the water Jill had brought from the bar and watched people dance in the flashing lights, feeling less out-of-place than before. My realization at how much more relaxed I felt made me believe that, *maybe*, I could handle the weekly trips to Club Archangel, as long as I had the protection and guidance of my friends.

When the boys arrived, they greeted me as though I had always been one of the group. Clark was looming around the back again and the sight of him made me realize I could ask him about my family joining the Commission of the People. He must have seen the realization in my expression because his eyes widened and he cleared his throat.

65

"I have to go," he said as he rapidly retreated.

"I'm going do my creeper rounds," I blurted, following him. I wove through the dancing students until I was able to grab Clark's arm as he tried to disappear into the crowd. He jumped and turned, his eyes wide with anxiety.

"Lily."

"Clark, hi," I started stupidly. "I know that we don't really know each other, but I was hoping to talk to you."

"I'm sorry, Lily, but I really have to go," he said, turning away.

"No, wait!" My hand closed around his elbow again. "Clark, I really want to talk to you."

"What about?"

"My family…and the Commission."

"I can't tell you anything about that," he said. "I can't reveal anything that happens in Commission meetings. Those are the rules."

"I know," I said, looking over his near-frantic expression. "Clark, are you *always* this nervous?"

"What?" I did not realize it was possible for his eyes to look more fearful until I asked the question.

"You look *terrified*," I noted, suspicious. "Why are you so nervous all the time? Is it because of the Commission?"

Clark's eyes moved upward and I followed his gaze to the balcony above. There was a small group of Commish Kids standing next to the railing, looking over the club like royalty surveying their subjects.

Only, they were not looking casually around the dance floor—they were looking directly at *us*.

I could only stare at the four Commish Kids in confusion before turning back to Clark. Once again, I was surprised. Clark's entire demeanor had changed. He was challenging them, staring at them as if telling them that they had no right to look down on him.

The group backed away from the railing, the final girl's eyes lingering on me one moment longer before she, too, turned her back to the rest of the club.

Clark let out a long breath, his shoulders slumping once we were no longer under scrutiny.

"You should not be talking to me," he warned.

"What the hell?" I gasped. "What was *that*?"

"You wouldn't understand."

"I might soon."

He closed his eyes, adjusting his glasses with a shaking hand.

"I know." His voice was full of regret. "I'm sorry, Lily. I understand you have no influence over this situation."

"Wait, Clark. Please, can you just tell me if it's true that the Commission has been talking about letting my family in?" My heart was thumping against my ribs as I watched his reaction. He closed his eyes again, his head dropping.

"Mr. Christenson has taken a great interest in your family," he admitted. "And I mean a *great* interest..."

My stomach turned.

"Does that mean..."

"I don't know," he said, his gaze locked on my feet, his voice almost too quiet to hear over the beat. "But, generally, if you have Mr. Christenson interested...you're in."

I had to focus on keeping myself from collapsing as nausea consumed me. If my family got involved in the Commission of the People, I would be locked in the world of politics for life—exactly where I did *not* want to be.

"Lily," Clark said, finally raising his eyes though he did not hold eye contact for longer than two seconds, "for your sake, I hope that Mr. Christenson's interest is only in the work your father does."

The heaviness of the words settled over my entire being.

"What do you mean?"

Clark's expression became pained.

"I wish I could tell you," he said. "But if Mr. Christenson's current fascination is anything to judge by...you and I are in the same boat."

He turned and disappeared into the crowd of dancing students before I could gain my bearings enough to ask more questions. I was so frightened, I simply stood in the middle of the dance floor, trying to wrap my mind around the probable new direction of my life, unaware of the sea of movement around me as the bass continued to pulse through Archangel.

I was not sure how many songs passed before I felt arms around my waist. I whirled around to see Devon's smiling face. I laughed nervously, forcing myself to relax.

"You looked lonely out here by yourself," he said, swaying us both. "I thought I would come and dance with you."

I laughed again, unable to help the nervous habit, and then I leaned forward and hugged him, my head against his shoulder as I took a deep breath. I needed someone to help me stand temporarily while I tried to yank myself out of the terrifying spiral of my thoughts. He continued to sway with me to the song's slow, heavy bass, his arms holding me upright.

"Hey, are you alright?"

"Yeah," I said, finally looking up at him. "I'm sorry."

He looked into my eyes before taking a deep breath and shaking his head.

"What?"

"You made me sad," he told me. "Someone as beautiful as you should never have such a sad look on her face."

I smiled genuinely but I had to look away, embarrassed by his words, heat singeing my face.

"You don't take compliments well," he noted with a teasing grin. "For making me that upset, you owe me a few dances."

"A few?"

"Yes." His bright expression managed to bring a smile to my face once more and chase way the heaviness on my shoulders. "We'll do our eavesdropping rounds together."

I could not bring myself to care about Jill's jealousy. I needed to be with someone who would take my mind off of the Commission. We moved to the edge of the room as we danced, his hands never leaving my waist, which helped keep me grounded in the moment.

When we approached another seating area in a distant portion of the club, we slowed our dancing to listen to the closest group.

"—that Jessica Bevins is going to get *another* younger sibling."

"Unbelievable," a boy groaned. "Her dad is making babies like no other."

"She's upset, since this will be her fourth half-sibling—"

We moved as Devon danced away from the group—apparently, that was not worthy gossip.

We passed by group after group, listening to bits of conversations. I did not hear anything of interest for me, particularly since I did not know who anyone was talking about. I just followed Devon's lead, eventually blocking out all conversations and dancing to turn off my troubled thoughts. Occasionally, I would glance at the balcony, paranoid that I was still being scrutinized. Every time I looked there were two different Commish Kids leaning against the railing, casually scanning the crowd—it was *creepy*.

The realization that I would likely be one of them made my heart plummet into the floor for the umpteenth time that evening. I turned to Devon and smiled weakly.

"Tired?" he asked.

"Yeah," I lied. "Did I pay back my debt?"

"Yes."

We returned to the table, though we had to hug the edge of the dance floor to make it back to our group of friends, as a popular song caused more students to surge into the crowd.

"Hey, you two," Becca greeted as we approached the table. "How was it?"

"Good."

"Hear anything interesting?"

"Nope," Devon answered for us. "Pretty dull tonight." He turned to me. "Water?"

"Yes, please."

As he slipped away, Becca smiled, leaning over to me.

"You really like him," she noted.

"I don't know," I mumbled. "I like him…but…"

"But what?"

"Jill likes him, too," I whispered, nodding to Jill, whose conversation with Taylor kept her distracted from me and Becca. Becca rapidly looked between Jill and me, blinking in surprise.

"Are you sure?"

"Yeah. Pretty damn sure."

"…huh."

I stared at her expectantly, my eyes wide.

"*Huh*? That's *it*?" I gawked. Becca's expression was confused and a little dazed, which was a reaction that made no sense to me. "Tell me what I should do!" I snapped. "You know her best."

"Um…I don't know." Becca shrugged. "This is news to me."

Her reaction was puzzling, but before I could press her again, Devon returned. Jill noticed him and smiled broadly, cutting off Taylor in the middle of her sentence.

"Hey, Devon, wanna dance with me?" she asked. I looked to Becca pointedly with my eyebrows raised.

"Sorry, Jill, I'm tired. Maybe in a little bit," Devon said. She pouted, half-playful.

"Fine," she whined. "I'll go by myself."

I busied myself gulping down water. I heaved a breath of relief when I had downed two-thirds of the glass and smiled at Devon once Jill was out of sight.

"Thank you for doing the rounds with me."

"No problem." He turned to Becca. "What about you, beautiful? Have you done your rounds, yet?"

"Nope." Her tone was clipped and short. As I watched her stare into her own glass, I noticed that somewhere in the time we had returned to the table and that moment her entire demeanor had changed. Devon made a confused face at me, seeing the change as well, but he shrugged it off while I turned back to Becca for two more seconds.

Drawing a deep breath, I gulped down the rest of my water, feeling things becoming uncomfortably turbulent.

* *** *

My friends met me in the downtown area the next morning to take me shopping. My mother gave me some spending money and then told me that I could use my card up to five hundred dollars. Her generosity surprised me—I assumed it was because she was thrilled that I was starting to act like a teenage girl instead of a hermit.

The first store was a large clothing store where I played dress-up for my friends. It got to the point where I was certain they were pulling anything they could off the racks just for fun, as their picks became more ridiculous and more revealing.

After the second store, I had spent nearly three hundred dollars on clubbing clothes. My friends then decided it was time to cart me to the makeup store, teaching me about the various products they had used to make me ready for Archangel the previous weeks.

Armed with everything I could possibly need, we returned to my house, laughing and joking as if we had been friends for years. All the awkwardness I felt within the group was gone and the naïve part of me wanted to believe that the tensions would just fade with time.

Once at my house the other girls showed me how to put on my makeup, explaining that I was expected to make myself look pretty every day to get into the habit of using makeup. I reluctantly agreed, too tired to defend my minimal morning routine.

We passed the afternoon in the way groups of girls did—talking and talking, not sure how we strayed from one topic to the next. The girls ended up staying for dinner, where my parents also had fun talking with them, though I could tell that my father was feeling outnumbered. My mother, conversely, was relishing in the girl-talk.

I hated to admit that I was enjoying it, too. I was starting to change, and I could not help but wonder how much more Central would change my life.

Chapter Eleven

The only thing that made school fun was Mr. McDermott. Even though we spent a full two weeks going over only two chapters, discussing the policies of teenage pregnancy—since Ankell had become a teen parent—his alcoholic behaviors, and his hatred of the United States, the class was fascinating enough to make the weeks fly by in the blink of an eye. Compared to Lit class, all other classes were too boring and standardized, combining in a monotonous blur.

But it only took two weeks to change my life completely.

I could feel the walls closing in around me. I was haunted by the inevitability of joining the Commission of the People. My life would no longer be my own. I was sure the Commish Kids were always watching me, judging if I was worthy enough to become a member of their elite circle. Horrible nightmares caused me to wake up panicked and sweaty, unable to discern nightmares from reality, and causing my groggy brain to mull over my anxieties during the day, unable to focus on anything else.

Clark scanned me at Archangel with a silent look of sympathy. I tried to talk to him again, but I was never able to stop him from disappearing into the dancing crowd once he saw me move toward him. He was too evasive. Even the gossip among the students had changed to rumors that I was going to become a Commish Kid even though my family was so new to Central.

Being the subject of such whispers made it impossible not to panic about the direction of my life. As far as I was concerned, the gossip was my proof that my family was already in the Commission of the People.

It was Wednesday when we received the invitation.

I was sitting at the kitchen table cutting apples for a pie with my mother when my father returned home earlier than usual.

"Karen? Lily?"

"We're in the kitchen, honey!" my mom called.

My father darted into the kitchen, tossing his briefcase to the side and running to my mother, scooping her up to spin her with a beaming grin.

"This is it!"

"What are you doing?" she giggled.

"We got in!"

"What are you talking about? Thomas, you're—"

"Read this," he gasped, shoving a folded letter into my mother's hands. The knot in my stomach tightened.

71

This was it.

We were in the Commission of the People.

I felt the urge to cry, or scream, or run away, but barely managed to stay in my seat. My mother unfolded the piece of paper and her eyes darted back and forth across the page.

"Oh my God, Thomas!" she gasped, throwing her arms around his neck and kissing him. "This is *incredible*!"

My father passed the letter to me.

"We've made it into the Commission of the People!"

I forced a weak smile and took the letter, my father wrapping his arms around my shoulders and planting a hard kiss on my cheek. My mother quickly began talking about who we were going to meet and the honor that came with being a part of the Commission of the People, my father joining the excited chatter.

I silently read the letter.

Mr. Thomas Gregory Sandover,

Due to your recent achievements on the NMW Region Seventh Route Expansion we wish to extend an invitation for you to join the Commission of the People, a branch of Central under the leadership of Mr. Dana Christenson.

Mr. Christenson personally invites you to attend a ceremony to be held during the next meeting of the Commission of the People on Saturday, September 7th, at 10:00 p.m. in honor of your appointment. During this ceremony, you and your family will be informed of rules and regulations within the Commission of the People, as well as receive a personal welcoming gift from Mr. Christenson.

We must remind you that the Commission of the People requires you to remain silent about your appointment to those outside your family until you have been inducted. Your names will then be announced on the new members list. This order of silence is in effect until the date of Sunday, September 8th.

The meetings for the Commission of the People start precisely at 10:00 p.m. every Saturday evening. For your first trip to the Commission of the People headquarters a driver will bring you and your family to the meeting on September 7th. After this meeting you are expected to bring yourself and your family on time to consecutive meetings.

Congratulations. We look forward to working with you.

> *Sincerely,*
> *Danielle Markus*
> *First Advisor of the Commission of the People*

"What do you think, Lily?" my dad gasped, leaning over my shoulder to look at the letter proudly. I could see the excitement in his eyes, so I smiled, trying to banish the suspicious fears in my gut.

"I'm so happy for you, Dad."

"Be happy for *all* of us!" He beamed, hugging me tightly again. "It's going to be great, Lily. I promise."

* *** *

"Little Lily..."

The voice was calling me again.

Fear bolted through my body as the words tickled down my spine. My eyes opened and I found myself in the grass of my backyard. I lifted my head, terrified and confused. Everything seemed darker. The shadows were thicker, and somewhere within the darkness, someone was watching me. I stood to scan my surroundings, hearing noises and quiet whispers from all angles.

"You're gonna get eaten alive..." a quiet voice hissed behind me.

"You're gonna get eaten alive..." another voice laughed to my left.

"You're gonna get eaten alive..."

"You're gonna get eaten alive..."

I tried to determine the sources but there was no one in the shadows. I backed away, turning to my house, which was devoid of light and just as cold as the surrounding darkness.

The voices got louder, laughing as they repeated their ominous message. My heart was pounding, panic swelling into a hot ball in my throat.

Even though my house was dark and obviously-not-safe, I ran to the glass door and tried to force it open. The sliding door would not budge.

I caught sight of my own wide-eyed, frightened reflection in the darkened glass. Behind me, a tall, menacing figure loomed, its features indiscernible.

I screamed, stumbling back, using the darkened windows as mirrors to track the menacing figure. In every window I saw it standing silently behind me. I could not escape no matter how fast I ran. He was always waiting for me in the next reflection.

I stopped running and turned, attempting another direction, but I tripped over my own feet and fell heavily to the ground, the dirt biting into my knees and hands.

The dark shadow approached. He glided closer and closer, his looming aura choking the air around me. I yelped again and turned to crawl away, but the shadow was instantly in front of me. I could only stare, breathing hard, terror coursing through my veins like icy needles.

The shadow leaned over, encompassing me in its arms as the voices started again.

"You're gonna get eaten alive..."

"You're gonna get eaten alive."

"You're gonna get eaten alive."

"You're gonna get eaten alive!"

I was trapped. I was never getting out.

"I am going to eat you alive," the dark voice whispered in my ear.

I screamed.

I sat up abruptly, panting, looking wildly around my bedroom. I had fallen out of bed, my knees and hands stinging from the sharp contact with the carpet. I swallowed hard, trying to moisten my throat and calm my breathing, but it did nothing to ease my panic.

Cringing at the pain in my knees, I moved clumsily to my bathroom.

I splashed my face with water, my heart still knocking against my ribs hard enough to almost break them, my hands shaking as I braced myself over the sink.

There was no way the dream had *not* been about my family joining the Commission of the People. The warnings I had received about the Commission haunted me to the point of giving me night terrors so realistic I still felt the shadowy figure's presence behind me.

I wet a washcloth to press to my knees.

I was angry. I wanted nothing to do with Central or the Commission. I did not want to think about how secretive I would become, or that I would be unable to hang out with my new friends at Archangel, and all just because my father had received a 'promotion.'

I was infuriated and overwhelmed.

After I had regained control of my breathing, I returned to my bedroom. When I turned off the bathroom light and was plunged into darkness, I scurried back to bed, clambering under the covers before scanning my room, just to be sure the shadowy figure was no longer looming over me.

* *** *

I knew I was acting out of the ordinary on Thursday because my group of friends continued to ask if I was alright. I lied. I had to. I was sworn to secrecy.

I managed to carefully avoid the worried questions, but I was concerned about my ability to keep up the act two days in a row.

When Friday came, I spent the day sick to my stomach. It was my last day before becoming part of the famous—*infamous*—Commission of the People.

Everything about the invitation into the Commission felt wrong. The fact that we had to stay silent and were meeting so late at night made me curious. I was constantly asking myself the obvious question—*why?*

Becca grabbed my attention during lunch while Taylor and Jill discussed something that had happened during Taylor's previous class.

"Hey," Becca said, nudging me, "are you feeling okay? You've been acting kinda strange."

"Yeah, yeah, I'm fine."

"You're not very good at lying, Lily," she teased. "C'mon, you can tell me if something's bugging you."

I wanted to spill my guts and tell her about my family's invitation into the Commission of the People. I wanted to tell her how much I hated the idea of being trapped in the government for the rest of my life. I wanted to tell her I was thinking about running away…that I felt as though I was drowning.

But I bit my tongue.

"I just have a lot of things on my mind," I said, forcing a pathetic smile to my lips. "I'm sorry."

"It's fine," she assured. "But if you ever need to talk, I'm here for you."

"Thanks, Becca," I said, fighting back tears, hoping she had not heard the cracking of my voice.

As had happened the previous week, I got ready for Archangel on my own and was picked up by Jill's father. I had made myself up slowly, constantly staring into the mirror absent-mindedly. I was losing myself deeper and deeper inside my dark thoughts. I was becoming the mask I had put on for the past two days. Numb.

At Club Archangel I tried to take in the noises and lights as if I was seeing the club for the first time. From Saturday on, I would be a Commish Kid. I would be on the balcony, overseeing the club like royalty, keeping my distance from the friends who had welcomed me so warmly into Central.

Our group moved to an empty table under the balcony and I sighed heavily, for the first time wishing I was old enough to drink alcohol legally, wanting anything to quiet my tumultuous thoughts.

The songs were heavy in bass and intoxicating, but even as I tried to lose my thoughts in the beat, I remembered that Clark would soon arrive. I began anxiously throwing glances at the door, desperate to talk to him before he tried to disappear again.

"What's with you?" Becca laughed. "The last time you were this nervous at Archangel you had never been here before."

"I'm not nervous."

"Then why do you keep looking at the door?" Taylor asked with a grin. "You waitin' for someone?"

"Devon?" Becca teased.

"Oh, um…well…" I looked at Jill and flinched from her cold stare. I glared discreetly at Becca, but she was already watching Jill's reaction. Her expression had changed again, almost appearing hurt over Jill's jealousy. Before I could question it, the boys startled me by appearing suddenly at the table. I jumped out of my seat when Todd leaned on the table next to me. Everyone stared at me, perplexed by the over-the-top reaction.

"Are you alright, Lily?" Todd asked, one eyebrow cocked.

"Yeah. You just scared me, that's all."

My eyes focused on Clark standing behind Devon. He was already watching me, his gaze apologetic.

"You look like you need to loosen up a little," Devon noted. "Dance with me?"

"Um…in-in a minute." I had not looked away from Clark, trying to silently communicate my need to speak with him. He took a deep breath, his eyes closing behind his glasses. When he opened them again, I saw the change in him. It was the same confident air he had adapted when we were being watched by the other Commish Kids.

"Actually, Devon, *I'd* like to dance with Lily," he said, his voice just barely shaking as he stepped to my side.

By the stunned expressions that befell my friends' faces, I could see they all came to the same conclusion at the same time.

My family's induction into the Commission of the People was no longer secret.

"You have got to be kidding me…" Taylor whispered.

"No way. You just *got* here!" Todd gasped.

"Why didn't you say anything?" Becca said, her hurt expression causing pain to radiate through my chest.

"I *can't* say anything. I'm sorry!" I burst quietly, feeling the tears coming too quickly for me to stop.

"Lily," Clark said, his voice lined with authority, "come with me." His hand locked around my arm, pulling me into the thick of the dancing crowd and away from my startled friends. The irrational fear that I would never see them again once I was engulfed by the swaying students became so strong I struggled against Clark, throwing constant looks back at the table.

"Clark, no, wait!" I choked, trying to pull away.

"You will see them again," he assured, somehow understanding my fear. "But I need to get you away before you say anything you're not supposed to."

I yanked my arm from his grasp.

"How *could* I know anything?!" I snapped. "I'm not even in, yet!"

"Will you keep your goddamn voice down?!" he snarled. We were in the middle of the dance floor, surrounded by dancing students as the beat pulsed through the club like a heartbeat. I was certain no one could hear me. Clark took a deep breath, the muscles in his jaw clenching. "Look, I know this is a shock, and I know that you don't want to be part of this. But, the fact is, you *are*…and there is nothing you can do about it. That means you have to abide by the rules, or you're going to find yourself somewhere you *really* don't want to be."

"Clark, I want out of this," I whimpered, surprised by the weakness of my voice. "Please, tell me how to get out of this."

"There's no way out," Clark choked, his own voice breaking. "If there was, I would have found it already." He looked at the balcony quickly and then turned to me. "*Don't* tell the others that I want out," he whispered so quietly I had to strain to hear him. "And don't let anyone know that you want out, either. Pretend to be honored."

I felt myself starting to cry no matter how much I tried to fight the tears. The authoritative look disappeared from Clark's eyes.

"I just…I want…"

"It's okay, Lily," he said. "I'm here to help you. I have been instructed to tell you about your protocol, as far as Club Archangel is concerned."

"My *protocol*?" I echoed in disbelief.

"If you want to travel with the other girls and spend some time with them at the beginning of the night, that's fine," he continued. "As long as you don't let anything slip about what has been going on in the Commission. After you have said hello and settled, you are to go up to the balcony. We take turns coming down and scanning the room for anything that would be of interest for the Commission."

"You mean...I can't spend more than the first few minutes with my friends?"

"No," he said reluctantly. "And, if you insist on staying down here, another child of the Commission must be with you."

"Why is this so secretive?" I asked. "What exactly is it about the Commission that no one is supposed to know?"

Clark glanced at the balcony again. I looked up to see one Commish Kid, but he was on the far side, looking over a different section of the club.

"I can't say anything here," Clark murmured. "Besides, tomorrow night, you will understand." He sighed heavily, his expression pained. "Listen, I know that Mr. Christenson has taken a very special interest in your family and that frightens me."

"What? Why does that frighten you?"

"Because anything that Mr. Christenson is this fascinated with...generally, the outcome is not good."

"What the hell are you saying? I mean—"

"Mr. Christenson has ordered me to be your protector at Archangel," Clark said, interrupting my panicked babble. "That's how I know he's interested."

"Ordered? My *protector*? What the hell are you *talking* about?!"

"He likes you...or your family, I don't really know which," Clark said. "Please, I need you to understand this, so listen carefully." I nodded, though I was so lightheaded and confused I was unsure I could pay close enough attention to his words. "The Commission is full of warped, cruel men and women who think that they are above the rest of humanity. This is a fucked up world you're about to step into, and you're going to need help adjusting. That's why I'm here. I'm going to help you."

"I thought...I thought the Commission was..."

"Everything you thought the Commission was is somewhat-true...but it is not clean, and it most certainly is not for the people of America to know," he explained vaguely. "This is why you need to stay *absolutely silent* about everything you hear and see in the Commission starting tomorrow."

"You're scaring me..."

"I wish I could help you more. I really do." He lowered his head and I saw that his eyes were also welling with tears. "...but I *can't*..."

He turned to the balcony yet again. This time, there were several Commish Kids at the railing—at least seven—and they were all watching us, whispering to one another with sneers painted on their faces.

"We need to get up there," Clark said hurriedly.

"No! Clark!" I cried. "Please…I just want one night with them. I *need* that. I'm not in yet, right? I can stay down here tonight."

Clark looked between me and the Commish Kids on the balcony, sharing a silent conversation over the crowded, deafening dance floor.

I saw one of the Commish Kids, an extremely pretty girl that I had never seen around school, shake her head and crook her finger for us to join them. My stomach somersaulted once more. I was legitimately concerned I would collapse then and there.

"Come on," Clark said, taking my elbow again. "I'll talk to them."

"Are you in charge, or something? I mean, with your mom being advisor to Dana Christenson?"

"Damn it, Lily, you *really* need to learn how to keep your voice down," he growled through his teeth. I bit my lip, feeling the tears burning my eyes. He weaved through the dancing sea of bodies to the stairs of the balcony. "I have a little more respect, but Mr. Christenson has three advisors and one of them has a seventeen-year-old and a sixteen-year-old daughter. If they want to meet you, I need to introduce you."

I tried to spot the girl who had motioned us to the balcony as we approached the stairs, but Clark was pulling me so insistently I had to look ahead to keep myself from falling or crashing into something, particularly since I was wearing shoes I could barely walk in under normal circumstances.

We reached the grated stairs and Clark ascended them, still holding my arm as I clumsily pulled myself up the stairs in my heels. Admittedly, I was curious to see the balcony. I thought it would be a simple balcony with some tables and chairs, but it looked more like a posh country club than a nightclub. There were couches and coffee tables spread around the balcony and a smaller bar in the corner. It was also warmer on the balcony due to the close proximity of the strobing lights.

As soon as we reached the top of the stairs I was the center of attention. Clark released me and approached the girl who had summoned us, leaving me on my own. The thumping of the music was almost drowned out by the thumping of my heart as the Commish Kids moved toward me, like a pride of hungry lions closing in on fresh meat.

"Hmm," one boy mused, looking me up and down. "She's pretty enough."

"Yeah, you clean up nice, Sandover," Felicity said, suddenly at my right.

"I don't know." Another boy shook his head, crinkling his nose. "I never did like the look of a virgin trying too hard to look sexy."

"Wonder how long she'll stay a virgin," a girl sneered.

"Back off, you vultures," a voice snapped. As they parted, I saw the girl who had beckoned us to the balcony. She looked me over, smiling thinly.

"I'm Melissa," she introduced.

"Lily."

"I know who you are." She looked me over again. "Clark, why did Mr. Christenson assign her to *you*?"

"I don't know," Clark snapped. "But it was his order, so you need to *back off*."

"Relax," Melissa groaned, rolling her eyes. "Mr. Christenson has been talking about your father a lot. He's excited to bring you in." She smiled in a superior manner that made me feel like melting between the grates and disappearing. "Figures."

"...what figures?"

"Oh, honey, don't make the mistake of thinking that Mr. Christenson only looked at your father's accomplishments," Melissa said, her smile dropping the temperature of the air around me. "He has seen pictures of you and your mother and he has researched both of you *very* thoroughly."

"W-why would he do that?"

"He has to be sure you're qualified for the Commission," Melissa said in a tone that suggested I was stupid for asking the question. "Now, listen here," she said. "You're the new one in the Commission, so you are on special watch until you become fully integrated. Do you understand?"

"N-no..."

"Oh, *God*, she's stupid." Felicity rolled her eyes, turning away.

"It just means that we're going to make sure you don't say anything you're not supposed to," Clark explained, his tone far gentler. I nodded, feeling unduly embarrassed, my eyes cast downward.

"Why are you being so nice to her, Clark?" a boy leered. "She's not gonna fuck you."

"No one will fuck you, either, until that strange little affliction of yours clears up," Clark snapped.

"What the hell are you talking about?"

"All medical bills are paid for by the Commission," Clark said, speaking to the other boy in a very condescending manner. "Didn't you know that?" His eyes softened as soon as he turned back to me. He took my hand. "Come with me."

I eagerly followed his lead off the balcony. My knees wobbled as we neared the bottom of the stairs. When we were back on the floor, I remained clutched to the railing, shaking uncontrollably.

"We're going to take a trip outside," Clark declared, his other hand steadying my shoulder. I followed his lead again around the side of the bar to a door leading to the alley behind Club Archangel. The cool night air hit my face and I gulped it in greedily, thankful that it helped me collect myself a little. I could still hear the heavy thumping of the music within even after Clark closed the door, making the club feel still-too-close.

"Just so you know," he started, "up on the balcony, you really have to hold your own or you will get eaten alive."

The words resonated far deeper than Clark realized.

"Take your time to collect yourself," he advised. "You're allowed to be on the floor tonight as long as I'm with you."

"I...I'm so..."

"It's difficult because you haven't seen everything, yet," he said, his hand finding my shoulder once more. As my swimming vision began to clear, I saw the color of Clark's eyes for the first time. They were a very bright hazel, gentle and sympathetic even behind his thick-rimmed glasses. "I'm here for you. I'll help you through this. We'll help each other."

"I thought you said you couldn't help me."

"I can't help you get *out*," he clarified. "But I can stand by you through it."

"Clark, I'm scared..." I breathed. "And I don't even know what I'm scared *of*."

"That will be cleared up tomorrow night," he said, his tone indiscernible. "Before we head back in, there are a few things I need to tell you."

"What?"

"For the first few weeks, when you show up at Archangel, you are to wait with the girls and I will take you up to the balcony when I get here," he explained. "Just...*please* remember that you *cannot* say anything to them. I really mean it."

"...I promise," I said meekly. "But why can't I just stay with them? They're my *friends*."

"Lily, I'm sorry to say this, but now that they know about your induction...they won't treat you the same way. They will be guarded around you. You are part of the secret police force of the government, and their parents are the politicians. It's a tough thing for them to ignore." Clark shook his head. "It's easier on everyone if you go up to the balcony."

"Clark..."

"Yes?"

"When you said that you and I were in the same boat...did that mean that Mr. Christenson took an interest in your family, too?" I breathed. "That you know what might happen to us?"

He hesitated.

"I won't tell you tonight. Next week, after you've seen everything," he promised. "Are you ready to go back in?"

I nodded, though all I wanted to do was run—run away from the Commission, from the balcony, the Commish Kids, the rules, the club, the capital...*everything*.

Chapter Twelve

Saturday was a nightmare.

After hardly sleeping, I then had to wait fourteen hours with my parents before the start of the Commission meeting—which meant waiting thirteen hours until the chauffer came for my family.

Time went too fast and yet too slow.

My stomach was in knots and my brain was a tangled mess of fear and incoherent fantasies about running away.

The final three hours of waiting were the worst.

My parents continuously barged into my room, detailing how they expected me to behave and how much better our lives were going to be as part of the Commission of the People. They told me what to wear, what to expect—though they had no clue what to expect, either—and then continuously came to check on me, likely to calm their own anxieties.

The hour finally came.

I paced anxiously around the kitchen. I was not the only one nervous. My parents were also moving around, fidgeting or picking at their clothes. They shared excited, yet apprehensive, glances with one another. The tension was palpable through the whole family.

The doorbell rang.

"This is it!" my mom squealed, leaping to her feet. She moved to the door, her heels clicking on the hardwood. On the front step stood three men, burly and emotionless, dressed in clean suits, looking like they were straight out of a movie.

"Thomas Sandover and family?" one asked in a clipped tone.

"Yes."

"Please, come with us. We are here to take you to the meeting."

Tunnel vision enclosed as dread consumed everything else in my mind. The three SUVs with tinted windows were lined menacingly along the curb, no doubt drawing the attention of the neighbors. The driver of the middle SUV opened the back door for us and we loaded into the convoy.

"Please pay very close attention to the route," the driver told us as he started the car. "This is the way to get to the meeting hall of the Commission of the People."

We glued our noses to the dark windows, memorizing the route as a means to distract us from our anxieties. He drove us through the quieting capital city, passing through the downtown lights. I enviously studied those enjoying their normal Saturday night on the town, blissfully unaware of the new members of the Commission of People passing by.

The expansive Leadership District housed the towering government buildings. Some of the more beautiful buildings were lit up from the outside to show off their impressive architecture. Others were darkened, making the area look eerily abandoned when the buildings had closed down for the night.

We entered a maze of dark office buildings and skyscrapers at the west side of the Leadership District, finally coming to a security gate. The three cars slowed and were cleared by the hard-faced guards. After two more turns we were at another gate. Clearing the second security checkpoint, we rounded the final corner and caught sight of the building.

The building of the Commission of the People was not at all what I had expected. It was a small, seven-story office building with dark letters over the illuminated lobby doors that read "Commission of the People." A few of the above offices were lit, but otherwise, the first floor was the only one casting light against the barely-visible foliage surrounding the building.

We pulled into the circular driveway and our driver hurried to open the door for us. I looked at the surprisingly-unimpressive structure, caught off-guard by the banality.

"Mr. Sandover," the driver called his attention, handing my father a key card. "This is your card to get through the security gates." He motioned back the way we came. "Keep this *on you* at all times. Don't leave it in the car."

"I will."

"That is also your card to enter the building," the driver continued. "The front desk will give you a secondary key for the meeting room."

The driver led us to the door, leaving the two other drivers behind.

He flashed his own key card in front of a magnetic pad and the doors slid quietly aside.

The lobby was so quiet the echoing of our shoes on the marble floor was deafening.

Four security guards and a woman stepped out from behind the only visible furniture in the room, an enormous reception desk. They matched the driver in the sense that looked like they had stepped out of a stereotypical espionage movie, dressed in dark suits with clear ear pieces in their left ears.

"Good evening, Thomas Sandover and family." The woman smiled, though her greeting was not at all warm. "My name is Madeline. I am in charge of admissions."

"It's a pleasure to meet you." My father shook her hand.

"Likewise," she said. "If you would please step over here," she motioned to the marble reception desk. "Thank you, David," she called to our driver, waving him away.

"Now, Mr. Sandover," Madeline started, "can you remember the route to get here?"

"Yes."

"Excellent." Madeline continued smiling in the same fake manner. "As your induction letter stated, meetings are held every Saturday at ten p.m. *exactly*. If you are late, you will not be admitted. If you are unable to make any meetings due to prearranged trips, illness, or emergency, you are to contact Mr. Christenson or anyone on his personal staff and let him know. We will download the contact numbers directly into your cell phones. All these numbers will be represented by a speed-dial number. Number one is Danielle Markus, number two is Vincent Greene, and number three is Sandra Hansell. These three are Mr. Christenson's personal advisors. Number four is Sean Jacobsen, Mr. Christenson's head of security. Number five is Mr. Christenson's private cell. Please use his number as a last resort if you cannot reach anyone else. Mr. Christenson is a very busy man." She repeated the information without falter, reciting a perfectly-memorized monologue. She extended a plastic tray. "Please place your cell phones here."

I nervously placed my phone with my parents' in the tray.

"Before each meeting, check your phones in with us at the front desk. You may retrieve them as you leave."

She moved the tray and picked up three substantial stacks of multicolored paper, putting one in front of each of us. I was sure my eyes were not the only ones that shot wide.

"Don't worry, it's not as bad as it looks," Madeline assured with a small laugh. "This is the contract for entering the Commission of the People. It's all very basic," she said, motioning her hand over the first page. "It really is just a glorified non-disclosure agreement stating that you will not discuss any events or topics of the Commission with those who are not members, and you will do your best not to discuss the Commission in a public place where things could be overheard, misinterpreted, etcetera."

Madeline set pens down for our use.

"Of course, we encourage you to read through it before you sign, but the meeting begins in twenty-three minutes. These are filled out with triplicate carbon copies. You are welcome to look over the contract at any time if you have any questions or so desire."

My mom and dad were already looking over the papers while I felt overwhelmed with the task before me.

"Um…"

"Feeling a little at sea?" Madeline asked, turning her attention to me.

"Yeah."

"You understand what we mean by a non-disclosure agreement, right?"

"Yes."

"Excellent. The rest of this outlines the situations in which you cannot speak about anything in the Commission, even if other members of the Commission are present." She motioned to that area in the contract. "Back here," she leafed through some papers, "is all on general conduct within the Commission meetings and outside respect for others. Basic rules, I don't think we really need to explain it to you. It's all common sense, but it's still a legal matter." She pointed to the blank spaces scattered within the text. "All the blanks at the bottom you sign and date. There are some blanks in the contract where you will need to print your name and date, so be sure you read what each blank is for."

I picked up the pen and started signing the contracts, feeling so nervous that my signature became warped by my shaking hand. I went through the papers, trying to press hard enough for the carbon copies. My eyes were focused only on finding the blanks, skipping over the fine print. I finished signing shortly after my parents and Madeline took the contracts and pens.

"Now, ladies, if you would please place your purses up here for the boys to check, and Mr. Sandover, if you could please remove your jacket and set it on the counter as well."

The amount of security around the Commission was both alarming and impressive.

The big guards opened our bags while a third felt through the pockets and seams of my father's jacket, all three men wearing gloves as they searched.

Our purses were returned and my father pulled on his suit jacket again before Madeline led us to the nearby elevators.

After pressing the button to call the elevator, Madeline reached into her coat pocket and produced a key, turning to us.

"This is the key to the meeting room," she explained. "When we are in the elevator, I will show you how to use it."

It was a short wait, but it was still long enough for me to slip deeper into the panic I had been swimming in all day. The elevator doors opened and I had to force my legs to stop shaking in order to command them to step inside.

Madeline pressed the button to close the doors and then pointed to the emergency keyhole once the doors had closed completely.

"Place the key in here," she did so, "and turn it to the *left*," she turned the key, "and then press floors two and one at the same time."

The elevator jolted before descending into the basement. We looked around, confused why the meeting room would be in the basement.

"Do not remove the key until the door opens again," Madeline instructed. "You will not need the key to come back to the lobby—just hit the Lobby button. We will have a car waiting to take you home tonight. Next week we will have the guards bring your car forward after the close of the meeting."

When we had been in the elevator for an abnormally long time, I became suspicious of just where we were going and why the meeting was being held so deeply underground—I was also unsure how a small building could have such an extensive basement.

I felt the elevator slow as soon as claustrophobia gripped my chest.

The doors opened and I had to take a deep breath before stepping out after my parents. We found ourselves in a narrow hallway with the other five elevator doors.

"Alright," Madeline concluded, handing my father the key for the elevator. "Go through that door and follow the hallway to the meeting room. Congratulations, again, for making it into the Commission of the People."

"Thank you," my father said. She stepped back into the elevator, forcing another smile as the doors closed.

I had not thought it was possible to be more nervous until the moment she left. There were two dim lights between each set of elevator doors, but it did little to illuminate the hallway of the abnormally deep basement. My dad smiled at me and my mother, placing a hand on our shoulders.

"Here we go," he whispered, nervousness barely audible in his voice.

My stomach was in such a tight knot I almost doubled over. We started toward the door Madeline had indicated and my father opened it for us. The next hallway was better lit, but still dark, the deep maroon of the walls swallowing the light and making the space feel cramped. The double doors at the end of the hall were propped open, allowing me to see into the room beyond. There were tables set up as if for a banquet dinner and, while the area of the tables was dimly lit, the front of the room brightly illuminated a slightly-raised stage with a podium.

My curiosity became equal to my anxiety.

Instead of place settings on the tables, there was a USB resting on top of laptop computers at each seat. No one was sitting yet but there were groups of people clustered around the room, talking as they enjoyed light drinks supplied by the bar in the back corner. The walls were a pale, unadorned white, interrupted by the dark brown doors throughout the room and the flags and curtains around the stage.

"Ah! There he is!" a booming voice called. Benjamin Lloyd approached us with a broad smile. "The man of the hour!"

"Hardly," my father laughed, shaking the offered hand.

"It's a good thing you made it here on time. Mr. Christenson is very strict about punctuality," Mr. Lloyd said. "Come, sit with us. We're generally near the back."

"There's no seating arrangement?" my mother asked, looking at the computers.

"No," Mr. Lloyd said. "All the USBs and computers are the same. It's just the agenda and any information we need for the meeting," the older man explained as we moved to a table. Mr. Lloyd nudged my father in the ribs. "We stay back here so it's less of a walk to the bar, of course."

"Ben, there was something that I've been meaning to ask you," my father started. "But, obviously, I couldn't say anything until now. The invitation says that Mr. Christenson has a gift for us. What should we be expecting? The invitation and induction alone is an honor."

Mr. Lloyd's face slowly broke into a smile with a devious edge.

"Mr. Christenson gives *everyone* a gift when they are brought into the Commission," he said. "And it's different for everyone, depending on what he feels the family would like and how much he thinks he's going to like the family."

"What did you get?" my mother asked curiously.

Mr. Lloyd chuckled, avoiding her gaze.

"Until you see your gift, it would be difficult to explain mine," he said. "There is always a very…*special* quality to Mr. Christenson's gifts. After you have had your gift for a little while, I will show you mine."

"That's making me very curious." I could hear the nervousness in my father's laugh.

"We all are," Mr. Lloyd said. "No one knows what your gift is, so we're excited to see what he has for you."

"Lily?" a familiar voice sounded behind me. I turned to Clark, who was wearing a button-up shirt and slacks and looked even skinnier than he normally did at Archangel. "Hi. I'm glad you made it on time."

"Ah, Thomas, let me introduce you to Clark Markus," Mr. Lloyd boomed, motioning to the other teenager. "He's quite the brilliant young man. His mother is advisor to Mr. Christenson."

"Is that so?" my father asked, turning to Clark. "Markus…oh, right, your mother was the one who sent the invitation letter."

"Yes, she is in charge of that," Clark said.

"You two go to school together, then. Do you have any classes together?" my mother asked.

"No," I answered. "We met at Archangel."

"Club Archangel is a great way for the kids to relax," Mr. Lloyd interjected with a strong nod. "I think that it's good for them to let go and actually be teens sometimes. Don't you agree?"

I wanted to tell him that it was nothing like that, particularly for kids in the Commission, but I kept my mouth shut.

"Lily, do you want something to drink?" Clark asked, moving away. I took the silent hint.

When we were far enough away from my parents, I leaned closer. "Everything okay?"

"I should be the one asking you that," he said with a weak grin. Clark ordered two iced teas for us before smiling at me apologetically. "I've seen your gift." My eyes widened and my jaw dropped.

"Are you allowed to do that?"

"Well, granted, I didn't get a very good look at it. I was walking by," he clarified. "But I saw enough of it to know that you and I…we *are* in the same boat."

"You mean…he's *very* interested in my family?" I asked, nodding thanks to the man at the bar as he handed me my glass.

"I'd say," Clark agreed. "Generally, the more beautiful the gift, the more interest he has in your family. I should also warn you…Mr. Christenson is in one of his moods tonight."

"…what does that mean?"

"Don't be surprised if he…well, if he seems a little…overly-playful."

"Overly-playful?" I repeated. "What does that mean?"

"It's difficult to explain," Clark said. "But he might seem a little…okay, actually, he'll probably scare the living hell out of you. Just be prepared for that, and know that you're not the only one he scares."

Clark turned away just as I was about to press further. His eyes focused on the clock above the door.

"We need to sit down. Where are you and your family?"

"Over there." I motioned to the table.

"I'm one table over. If you need anything, just lean across and ask me."

"Hey, Clark." I caught his elbow as he started to leave.

"Yes?"

"I just wanted to let you know, I really appreciate you looking out for me," I told him softly. He smiled shyly.

"You're welcome."

We moved to our separate tables as everyone began taking their seats. I sat next to my mother, who was between me and my father. My father was talking amiably with Mr. Lloyd, sitting mechanically as Mr. Lloyd lowered himself to his seat. I saw some other familiar faces of the Commish Kids sitting with their families, but much to my relief, no other Commish Kids sat at our table.

I watched the clock tick down to exactly ten. I noticed that there were only two minutes before the exact start of the meeting and no one was at the podium or trying to get organized.

"Where is Mr. Christenson?" my mother asked before I had the chance. "I thought you said he was all about punctuality."

Mr. Lloyd barked a laugh.

"When I mean punctual, I mean down to the second. He will be here as soon as the second hand is on the hour."

I rolled my eyes, knowing that was impossible.

I watched the seconds tick by. At thirty seconds to ten, a woman walked onto the stage. She was very pretty with short-cut brown hair and clear green eyes, wearing an expensive, well-tailored suit. She stepped up to the podium and switched on the microphone, but no one quieted, barely noticing her at the front of the room.

I looked back to the clock. Twenty seconds left…

The woman shuffled some papers and also glanced at the clock.

Ten seconds…

Conversation slowly died in the final ten seconds and, by one second before ten, the room was silent. When the second hand hit the ten, all open doors slammed shut to close off the room.

"Ladies and gentlemen of the Commission of the People," the woman at the front of the room started, "I am pleased to call this meeting on the night of September seventh in session. We have much to review tonight with concerns regarding the representation of regions and the security of our nation, as well as a general update and report on the status of our Enterprise experiments and the status of appointed officials currently facing charges," she listed. "However, before we start that, we have an induction ceremony." She looked around the room, smiling as a tremor of excitement radiated through everyone. "Where is Mr. Thomas Sandover and his family?"

"Here," my father called, raising his hand.

"Ah, there they are. The Commission of the People would like to welcome you and present you with a gift tonight. My name is Danielle Markus, and I am advisor to Mr. Christenson. If you are in need of anything, please feel free to ask me."

Speaking of this Mr. Christenson, where is he? I muttered to myself.

"Well, we can't very well do the ceremony or meeting without our leader, can we? Mr. Christenson," Mrs. Markus smiled, "the floor is yours."

Everyone around the room started clapping but there was no sign of the leader of the Commission. Then again, I had no idea what he looked like—no one outside of the Commission knew.

I waited for him to walk to the stage but he did not, and no one else thought of that as strange. They still clapped and smiled at one another, unfazed.

"You must be Little Lily Sandover," a voice whispered in my ear.

Naturally, I screamed.

Chapter Thirteen

More accurately, I screamed and leapt from my chair, tripping over my own feet as I spun around. My stumble caused a round of laughter from everyone other than my startled parents. But the moment my eyes locked on the owner of the voice, everything else in the room disappeared in a millisecond.

The man was tall, *very* tall, easily close to two meters, wearing an expensive, immaculate three-piece suit. He was younger than I expected. His jaw line was strong and his hair was a deep auburn, but what startled me the most were the sunglasses he was wearing. Inside. In such a dark room…

My first thought was that he was blind, but he leaned down and righted the chair I had turned over, placing it back at the table without missing a beat.

"Mr. Christenson!" Mr. Lloyd laughed. "You shouldn't sneak up on pretty young ladies like that."

"Indeed," Mr. Christenson agreed with a grin. He offered his hand, palm up, to me. "I do apologize, Little Lily."

The nickname moved down my spine like icy fingertips, simultaneously endearing and threatening. I nervously took his hand, my own shaking uncontrollably. He leaned down slowly, almost gracefully, and kissed my knuckles. The action was chivalrous and polite, but my body was screaming that I was in danger, like I was sticking my hand into the cage of a hungry lion.

He straightened and stared at me from behind his dark glasses. I could do nothing but stare back, frozen in place.

He released my hand, his lingering touch leaving pins and needles across my fingers.

"Mr. Sandover," he said, walking to my father and offering his hand, which my father shook firmly.

"Mr. Christenson, it is an honor to meet you," my father greeted, clearly not arrested by the same feeling of terror.

"The honor is mine," Mr. Christenson said. He turned to my mother. "Mrs. Sandover, correct?"

"Yes." My mother smiled, giving her hand to Mr. Christenson, who bent down, kissed her knuckles, then backed away with a flash of his perfectly-white smile.

"It is wonderful to have you here. The Commission is always looking for fresh blood," Mr. Christenson said as he walked away from our table. We resumed our seats as others in the room laughed at Mr.

Christenson's statement, understanding some hidden meaning. Mr. Christenson looked over his shoulder as he approached the stage.

"Mr. Sandover, you and your family will be a *very* welcome addition to the Commission of the People. We are all very pleased to have you here." His voice turned soft and gentle as he ascended the platform, standing to the side of the podium, ignoring the microphone completely—he did not need it as the room was commanded into silence by his very presence. "If the Sandover family would please stand, we will get the ceremony underway and get to the part everyone is waiting for."

The gift. That was what had everyone so eager.

Thankfully, Mr. Christenson still frightened and confused me enough from afar to keep the adrenaline pumping through my veins. I managed to pull myself to my feet alongside my mother and father, our eyes never leaving Mr. Christenson.

"Now, then," he started, clasping his hands in front of him, fiddling with something between his palms. "Do you swear full loyalty to the Commission of the People, its cause, and its belief in protecting the basic rights of the American people outlined by the standards set after the Second Revolution?"

His voice was clear, yet there was a rasp to his tone that sent a shiver over my body. I could not determine if it was a shiver of fear, or if I enjoyed the sound of his voice.

"I do swear," we recited.

"And do you understand that your words are bound under contract to remain within the confines of the Commission of the People, never to be extended beyond the members of this group?"

"I understand."

"Excellent," he praised. "Then, I welcome you, as my colleagues, into the Commission of the People."

We were surrounded by clapping and cheering. My father and mother beamed as they resumed their seats, filled with excitement at being welcomed into the exclusive group. I sat heavily, trying to sort through my fears. Clark had said that I had no idea the full extent of what I was getting into, but nothing had yet happened to justify my severe paranoia.

Well, aside from the secretive invitation, the secretive route that could only be taught through word of mouth, the non-disclosure agreement, the meeting room near the center of the earth, and the man wearing sunglasses acting as the ring-leader of a political circus.

"Now," Mr. Christenson continued, still fiddling with the object in his grasp. I saw a glint of gold as he dropped the object, the chain wound around his fingers to stop it from falling to the floor. The pocket watch hung just below his fist as he wiggled his fingers absent-mindedly, pacing to the other side of the stage. "Everyone is very curious about your present. I suppose it is time to end the suspense."

The double doors near the stage opened and a *very* large, cloth-covered box was rolled into the room. The four men wheeling the box in front of the stage strained as they pushed and pulled. There was an excited murmur around the room. No one seemed surprised by the size, which made me wonder about the nature of their own gifts. Even around the fear and anxiety pumping through my veins, I was undeniably curious.

With shallow bows of their heads, the four uniformed guards sporting their own sunglasses stepped to either side of the box, waiting for Mr. Christenson to speak.

"I know that everyone is very curious about this gift. I must admit, I am reluctant to part with this one," he said.

"That means that he thinks you're something special," Mr. Lloyd whispered to us with an enthusiastic thumbs-up.

"Because this is a very special gift, it will require some upkeep and maintenance," Mr. Christenson continued. "But I will be sure to provide said maintenance and pay the necessary expenses. However, if it becomes too much for you to handle, I will be willing to negotiate an exchange."

He gripped the pocket watch tight, sweeping his hand toward the box.

"But I think that you will *really* enjoy this," he said, his lips barely quirking upward. Even behind his sunglasses I could feel his gaze settle on me. I stiffened, somehow understanding that he was speaking directly to me—as if the gift was for me and me alone.

"Is the suspense killing you, yet?" Mr. Christenson asked the room with a mischievous grin. "Before I reveal it, a warning to the rest of you. I don't want to hear complaints about having never heard of this one before. It was a *one*-time test and we happened to be fortunate. It is not something we will be repeating. I will not listen to any whining."

Mr. Christenson nodded to the guards.

Two took one edge of the fabric and pulled.

I could not believe my eyes.

The box was not a box at all, but a large iron cage on wheels, intended for circus animals. But it was not a lion in the enclosure. It was a boy. He looked about my age with shimmering blonde hair that fell in wavy disarray over his eyes. But even through his hair and at our distance, the amazing color of his dark blue eyes captivated me. He was not wearing a shirt, revealing muscled shoulders, a broad chest, and toned arms—his abdomen was, admittedly, less-defined. A drape of white feathers cascaded down his back, nearly blending in with his white pants.

I was dumbstruck. The others in the room gasped and gawked, standing to get a better look, not at all horrified that Mr. Christenson's gift to my family was another human being. I finally managed to turn my gaze to my parents, but they were staring, just as petrified.

"This is a *very* generous gift," Mr. Lloyd hissed urgently, leaning close to my father. "*Thank* him!"

"This...is an incredible gift, Mr. Christenson," my father said, stumbling over the words, forcing his stunned brain to form the sentence.

"I know." Mr. Christenson smiled darkly, easily hopping off the platform to stand in front of the cage. "Go on. Show them," he urged the teenage boy.

The boy turned his head to Mr. Christenson, his eyes bright with anger.

The feather drape behind him shifted. I quickly realized—much to my morbid fascination—that the feathers adorned two extremely large, white wings.

My mother gasped but her expression had changed to one of wonder. My father's jaw dropped. I would have been lying if I said I was not also awed by the sight. He looked just like an angel, magnificent and powerful, his sharp eyes softened by his gentle face.

"I am sure you have questions about him and where he came from, but those can be answered after the meeting and in private." Mr. Christenson's voice startled me from my staring. "For now, he will be kept to the side of the room so that everyone can marvel at him. He is quite the specimen. He should be on display."

He nodded to his guards and they, once again, moved the cage, placing the angel against the side wall.

"We will discuss him after the meeting," Mr. Christenson said, pointing to us briefly. "Now," he nodded to Danielle Markus, "we can start the meeting."

Mrs. Markus, who had been standing quietly to the side of the stage, stepped back up to the podium.

"Alright, everyone, try to focus. I know that Mr. Christenson's gift will be distracting, but let's do our best to get through the meeting efficiently," she said. "If you will all open your computers and insert the USBs, we will begin."

I opened my computer absent-mindedly, the glare of the screen causing me to flinch. Very shortly after inserting the drive, a program launched itself, showing a quick opening sequence for the Commission of the People before settling on a pie graph littered with numbers and tiny words.

I blinked stupidly, not sure how I was supposed to understand the data being displayed. I wanted to ask my mother and father, but they were both studying the graph with some level of understanding. The most I could discern was that it had something to do with the population distribution in the regions and how the American people were represented in Central.

"Clark!" a voice snapped. Many, including me, jumped in surprise. Clark's head whirled to look at Mr. Christenson. "Come here," Mr. Christenson ordered, sounding angry despite his quiet voice. Most turned their attention back to their computers, ignoring the teenage boy approaching the leader of the Commission. I noted the nervous wringing of Clark's hands as he stood in front of Mr. Christenson, his head bowed.

Mr. Christenson spoke quietly, his shaded eyes turned down to Clark. The younger man nodded quickly. Mr. Christenson took Clark's chin, forcing his head up, though Clark's eyes remained averted.

When he nodded again, Mr. Christenson released him.

When Clark was nearly at his table again, I looked at Mr. Christenson. He was staring right at me.

My blood halted in my veins. I felt the power of his eyes even from behind the dark glasses. He held my gaze, hypnotizing me, making it impossible to turn away.

There was nothing else.

It was only him.

My instincts were screaming at me to run. There was something else behind the already-frightening façade of the Commission of the People. The unquestioning acceptance of another human being given away like an object and the knowing laughter in everyone's eyes made my stomach twist, tangling so tightly I could barely breathe.

As I stared at Mr. Christenson, a cold, impish grin split over his face, growing until it was almost unnaturally wide, filled with dark glee.

The sudden appearance of Clark at my side broke me out of the staring contest. I jumped and turned to him when he started speaking. "Relax," Clark said with a wobbly smile. "I've been sent over here to be sure you understand what we're talking about."

"Oh, t-thanks."

Mrs. Markus continued talking from the podium, her enhanced voice still not loud enough to break through my clouded thoughts or the ringing in my ears.

Even though Clark had broken me out of my trance, I could still feel Mr. Christenson's eyes raking over me. My skin crawled. I could almost feel his fingers tracing up my neck, ready to take my chin, preparing to lift my eyes so I would be entranced once again.

"Just focus on the screen." Clark advised under his breath, spotting my trembling. "Don't look at him. Keep your eyes down."

I heeded the advice, trying to focus on Mrs. Markus' words or Clark's whispered explanations. But I could still feel Mr. Christenson's gaze. I had to close my eyes and take several deep breaths to keep from screaming for a reason I could not comprehend, panic overpowering all sense.

Mrs. Markus kept on talking, Mr. Christenson kept on staring, and I kept myself from screaming.

When two, grueling hours had passed, the meeting was called to a close. I managed to breathe a little easier as the sounds of shutting laptops and people standing filled the air.

I forced an exhausted smile in Clark's direction when he removed the USB and handed it to me.

"Thanks…" I managed to whisper, my clumsy fingers closing around the drive.

"You're welcome." He looked at Mr. Christenson, who was still watching me—I dared not look to confirm but I could *feel* his gaze.

"Be careful, Lily," Clark whispered. "*Please* be careful." He grabbed his chair and returned to his table, his head low.

My father stood, followed by my mother, so I pulled myself onto quivering legs. When they had shaken Mr. Lloyd's hand and received the proper encouragement, my parents turned to me.

"Come on, Lily," they whispered urgently. The way my hopes of leaving the basement were dashed when I saw they were walking *toward* Mr. Christenson almost made me cry.

Mr. Christenson had joined the rest of the Commission around the cage, answering questions as we approached. I reluctantly trailed behind my parents as we reached the cluster of Commission members. My head remained bowed as the others parted for us. I tried not to notice the looks of envy shot my way.

I only lifted my head when we were standing in front of the cage and I could study the teenage boy trapped within.

At such close proximity, I could finally see the shackles that limited the range of motion on his pristine wings, the silver metal standing in sharp contrast to the white feathers, prongs facing his bare back, waiting to puncture him if he moved too much.

He was beautiful. His vibrant blue eyes scanned us warily, moving over my father and mother first, understanding evident in his expression. When his gaze turned to me, my breath hitched and heat invaded my face. I was starting to doubt that the boy was human at all. He was too beautiful to be anything but an angel. Our eyes remained locked, allowing me to become lost in the blue depths until my knees grew weak.

"He is quite the specimen, isn't he?" a cold voice said beside me. I whirled around to face the tall form of Mr. Christenson. His presence was far too intense to handle up close and it made me feel sick, my body shaking. I stared into the dark glasses, seeing my wide-eyed expression in the reflection. "Do you like him?"

"...we will enjoy him immensely," my father said slowly, unsure of his words. "Forgive us, Mr. Christenson. We just have so many questions."

"I know," he said. "I will explain the rules about him and how he is to be treated. Then, I will answer your questions surrounding his origins."

Mr. Christenson stepped even closer to the cage, reaching a hand through the bars.

"Stand up, Mykail," he commanded in his hypnotic voice. Mykail hesitantly took the offered hand and got to his feet. He pulled his wings upright, folding them to his sides as the feathers shuddered, the longest feathers still dragging by his feet.

"I don't understand, Mr. Christenson," one woman said in disbelief. "He is a perfect specimen. Why are you not repeating this experiment?"

"It was an expensive experiment I did on a kick of inspiration," Mr. Christenson explained, waving a hand abstractly. My blood turned cold. His answer was so casual.

Mr. Christenson turned to my parents, motioning a hand over the now-standing Mykail.

"This is Mykail," Mr. Christenson introduced. "He's pretty quiet so he shouldn't annoy you too much. Sometimes he has tantrums about the shackles, but otherwise, he's a perfect angel." Veteran members of the Commission laughed, but I could not bring myself to even crack a smile. "However, I cannot stress the importance that the shackles *stay on*. His wings are very strong and he *can* fly. We don't want him to escape. Imagine the PR disaster that would cause."

Mykail made no effort to hide the hatred in his eyes. Mr. Christenson merely grinned when he saw the glare. "He does tend to stare, though. If that bothers you, just blindfold him. Don't be afraid to discipline him, either, should he do anything unwanted."

My father was about to ask a question but Mr. Christenson held up his hand.

"We will transport him to your home and be sure you have the proper facility to contain him. I will pay for the modification costs. The most important rule," Mr. Christenson's tone turned serious, "is that he is *never* to leave the confines of your home. He cannot go outside. Not to the backyard, not on the roof, *nowhere* outside." Mr. Christenson's head turned slowly, his covered eyes scanning us. "Tell me you understand."

"We understand," we whispered.

Satisfied by the tremor of our voices, Mr. Christenson turned his attention to the still-gawking Commission members. He threw his hands in the air.

"Alright, alright," he conceded with a laugh. "You can admire him a while longer. I will take the Sandovers into the back and you can study him to your heart's content." Mykail backed to the wall, sitting again and resting his wings on the floor of the cage.

"I shouldn't have to say this but I know someone will try it. Don't stick your hands in this cage. He is not yours. Respect the Sandover's property." Mr. Christenson turned back to us. "Let's go to my office."

He brushed his fingers down my arm as he passed me, causing my entire body to shudder. It felt like torture to force my legs to follow him rather than run the opposite direction.

Clark and Mrs. Markus approached us.

"Are you in further need of me?" Mrs. Markus asked.

"I'm always in need of you," Mr. Christenson said in a sultry tone. Mrs. Markus blushed and smiled demurely, sheepishly turning her gaze to her feet. Clark also looked down, a noticeable shiver running through his body. I wanted to study their reactions but Mr. Christenson had started walking again, leading us to the double doors at the back of the room. The stationed guard bowed his head to Mr. Christenson.

"Leave him there for five more minutes and then tell everyone to leave," Mr. Christenson ordered. "Have Mykail taken back to his cell."

"Yes, sir."

"Has Sean returned?"

"He just called in. He is on his way."

We followed Mr. Christenson down a hallway and around a corner. There were several ornately-designed wooden doors down the long, dimly-lit hall, only a handful sporting a nameplate. We reached the end of the hallway, passing through a door to our left, startling the guard stationed there.

"Good evening, sir," he said with a hurried bow of his head.

Mr. Christenson did not acknowledge him. The new hallway was bare with only one door at the far end and an opening to the right. Mr. Christenson turned the corner into another hall, where he led us to the final door, holding it open for us.

I was already lost.

Mr. Christenson's office was dark and full of heavy-looking wooden furniture. His immense desk had papers scattered across its surface and the bookshelves around the room were lined with thick books on law and history. A table on one side of the room had six chairs and was piled high with even more disorganized paperwork.

"Over here..." Mr. Christenson said to himself, swerving to the table as if he had forgotten the layout of his own office. Sifting through the clutter, he grabbed a bulky file as we crowded around the table.

He flipped through the file silently, occasionally lingering long enough on a page for me to catch glimpses of photos and notes scribbled on typed reports. He finally found a folded piece of paper and pulled it free.

Once he smoothed it over the table's surface I saw the detailed blueprint of our new house. My heart began pounding against my ribs as I scanned the handwritten notes: *Master Bedroom: Thomas & Karen. Guest room 1: Empty. Guest room 2: Mykail? Guest Suite: Lily.*

When I lifted my wide eyes, Mr. Christenson was smiling at me.

"Is this correct?"

"How do you know what room I'm in?" I whispered.

"I don't," he said, though his tone suggested otherwise. "I merely assumed that a young woman would prefer a larger room with a private bathroom."

"This is correct," my mother confirmed.

"Is this where you want us to put him?" my father asked, motioning to Mykail's supposed room.

"This one will suffice," Mr. Christenson said. "According to the measurements, he will have just enough space. I wouldn't want to make a greater imposition. We will install barred grates over the windows and in the doorways. You will be able to close the door outside of the bars, that way you can hide him if you have company. My men will be there on Wednesday. They should finish construction by Saturday, so I can bring him to you on Sunday."

"This is all very generous, Mr. Christenson—"

"Please, call me Dana. There is no need for formalities."

"Oh, um, thank you, Dana, for this wonderful gift. It is very generous," my father completed.

"You're welcome," Dana said. "Now," he would not let my father speak further, "there are a few other things we need to discuss about Mykail that are a little more sensitive. I will review it with you when I bring him next Sunday to be sure you understand the kind of care he will need."

"Before that, Dana," my mother started bravely, "does he really need to be *caged?*"

"When you are not with him, absolutely," Dana said. "And the bars must be specially engineered to withstand the strength of his wings."

"I thought the shackles kept him from flapping his wings," I interjected, making the mistake of looking directly at Dana.

"That's correct," he affirmed. "But he does not need full range of motion to cause damage. Do not make the mistake of thinking that Mykail is human. He can hurt you if given the opportunity. He is *very* dangerous."

Dana placed the blueprint back in the folder before opening a smaller file. "This is all the information you will ever need on Mykail," he said, handing my father a USB drive from inside. "This is your copy."

My father hesitated in taking the flash drive.

Dana leafed through the papers swiftly. I could not help but wonder how he could see anything while wearing dark glasses in such a dimly-lit room.

He extracted a sheet of paper with three pictures of Mykail—one straight on, one from the back, and a profile picture, all with his wings spread.

"He has six tracers in his body, the same type used to track dogs and cats but a little bigger. This way, we'll be able to pinpoint his exact location at all times. Keep this in mind should something happen. There is one in each ankle, each wrist, and one in the major joint of each wing," he pointed to the places in the pictures as he spoke. "Up here," he pointed to the joint at the top of the wings, "he has his disciplinary chips. If *ever* he misbehaves, you will use these to punish him."

"*Punish* him?" we echoed, almost choking on the words.

"It's no different from owning any other pet," Dana explained. "You wouldn't let a dog who has made a mess in the living room go unpunished, would you?"

We could only stare, stunned into silence, unable to comprehend treating Mykail the same as an animal.

"When I bring him to you, I will give you clickers to activate the discipline mechanism," Dana continued, ignoring our obvious mortification.

"What will it do to him?" my mother asked. "Will it hurt him?"

"Oh, yes." Dana nodded enthusiastically. "It will be excruciating. It causes an electric pulse to temporarily paralyze his wings and trigger muscle spasms in his back. Puts him on the ground very quickly."

"That's *cruel*," I said.

"How else do you think he will learn?" Dana challenged. "Pain is the best way to teach an animal the rules." He rustled through some more papers. "I will reimburse your home for his food," he continued. "He eats the same as any other human but does prefer red meat over poultry for obvious reasons."

He and Mrs. Markus were the only ones who laughed at the joke.

"In any case, he does not have any special dietary needs or restrictions," Dana said. "Just be sure he always has access to water and feed him at least twice a day."

The way he spoke about Mykail made me feel sick. I felt like we were buying an illegal animal off the black market...only it was *far* worse.

"You will need to bathe him at least twice a week," Dana continued. "As I'm sure you can imagine, his wings are exceptionally heavy and he cannot maneuver himself to wash everything. You must be especially mindful of the skin by his wing joint," he pointed to the area on Mykail's pictures where the feathers touched his shoulder blades. "If he moves too much, the skin can rip when dry. After you bathe him, you will need to put a special lotion on this area for the following two days to avoid a bloody mess and possible infection."

"Every day, then?" my father deduced.

"Basically," Dana confirmed. "I will show you where and how to apply the lotion when I bring him to you."

He shifted through his papers once more.

"I believe that is all," he said. "Now, if he is in pain from his wings or complains of back pain, call my personal line. It will be number five in your phone. Also, if you have any other questions or concerns with him, you can call my line at any time, day or night."

"We wouldn't want to impose," my mother said. "I'm sure you are a very busy man."

"No imposition. If you are unable to reach me directly, call my head of security, Sean. He will relay the message to me. He's generally nearby. Mykail is very dear to me. I want to keep a close watch on him." Dana chuckled lightly. "After all, I spent *a lot* of money creating him."

My mother, father, and I looked at one another, wondering who was going to ask the questions of how and why Dana created Mykail.

"What is it?" Dana asked, seeing the glance. "Do you have a question?"

None of us found the courage to speak. In response to my pleading expression, Clark cleared his throat.

"I-I think, Mr. Christenson, that they are curious *how* you created Mykail."

"Oh, of course!" Dana snapped his fingers. "Forgot about that. Right this way."

He turned on his heel and left his office. I saw my parents exchange a concerned glance before following obediently. They felt the same way I did—trapped, dumbfounded, and frightened.

But we knew better than to raise a fuss in the heart of the Commission of the People.

Clark stepped to my side.

"How are you holding up?" he whispered.

"I don't know. Ask me tomorrow."

It was a very short walk to a door at the end of the hallway. Dana extracted a keycard from his breast pocket and tapped it against his other hand, turning around to face us.

I could not stop my gasp, halting as I felt the energy around him shift. His face looked darker, his shoulders broader, looming in front of the closed door with a cold air of warning emanating from his entire being.

"I should not need to remind you of the NDA you signed when you entered," he said. "Nothing you are about to see is to be discussed outside of the Commission. This is the same for Mykail. If you let anything slip, we will take care of you very quickly and discreetly." Dana let the comment resonate in our skulls. "Do we all understand each other?"

"Y-yes."

He grinned. "Excellent."

Dana pressed the keycard to the electronic pad and opened the door as we braced ourselves for the unknown horror waiting on the other side.

Chapter Fourteen

The air was colder beyond the door but the room was brighter, almost blindingly so.

We passed through an automatic sliding glass door and traversed a short, stark-white hallway to another set of automatic doors. My father cleared his throat as we entered a room lined with security monitors behind a reception desk manned by six burly guards.

"If I may, Dana," my father started, "why is the Commission running experiments? What are they for?"

"That's a bit complicated to answer," Dana said. He nodded to the guards that rapidly stood to attention at his arrival. One rushed to lead us through the next door, three more guards following. Dana continued the tour, ignoring the guards surrounding him in their practiced formation. "In simple terms, with the Commission's ties to the American military, we've been contracted to create a new breed of soldier."

"You're...altering humans to make *weapons*?" I choked in disbelief.

"Yes," Dana said without hesitation. "Some work, like Mykail. Others...well, they're not as fortunate." Dana motioned to the wall next to him. My heart plummeted at the sight that greeted me. The wall was a large, glass panel that gave us full view of the creature inside the unadorned white cell. There were no words to describe the hideous, blotchy skin seeping with thick, yellow fluid. The large eyes looked reptilian and the mouth had become horribly twisted. The fingers were webbed, the thin skin between the digits secured by black sutures. The back arched unnaturally, distorting the rest of the body and forcing the ribs to protrude sharply.

My mother yelped and I barely managed to swallow back my scream.

"*That* was once human?" my mother gasped.

"At one point, I think so." Dana tilted his head to the side, as if contemplating the question. "Not much to look at now, I'm afraid."

"How do you even *do* this?" my father breathed. "This is out of science fiction."

"Trial and error, really," Dana said with a shrug. "We decide to try a concept, lay them on a table, and change everything we can until we have something, well, like this." He motioned to the creature again. "We've created all sorts of fascinating things over the years. Learned quite a bit as well. Helped medical science more than military pursuits, if I'm honest."

"You...you said you were creating weapons," I said, tearing my eyes away from the experiment. "W-what kind of weapon were you making with him?"

"See the disgusting yellow ooze? It's highly acidic and extremely corrosive. It could melt just about anything, and anyone, it comes in contact with." He sighed dejectedly. "Unfortunately, it did cause problems with his hair follicles and skin pigmentation. Then it started eating through his nerve endings and into his brain. We're running some final tests before we put him down."

"Wait, you just...*test* on humans and then kill them when they don't work out?"

"Oh, it's all very humane," Dana said easily. "Come, I'll show you more. We keep all the ugly ones up front. Keeps people on their toes, which is good because the successful ones are far more dangerous."

Dana continued walking, almost *bouncing*, down the hallway, his four guards surrounding him. I turned to my parents, who were too shocked to move. Mrs. Markus smiled when she saw our expressions.

"There is no need to be frightened," she said, motioning us to follow. "Dana is trying to psych you out. All of the experiments are properly contained."

But who contains Dana? I growled to myself. I forced my legs to move down the bright, sterile hallway, following the adults. My curiosity demanded I look in each large cell we passed. Some experiments were hideous, looking like alien creatures with little resemblance to anything human. They shuffled about their cells, backing away when they saw us like terrified animals.

"Dana?" my father called.

"Yes?" Dana said over his shoulder, not stopping as we walked through two sets of doors, entering a section with a large "3" painted on the double door.

"All of your experiments were human?"

"Or some variation thereof."

"What the hell does that mean?" I grumbled under my breath. Of course, Dana heard me and stopped. His guards also halted. The head of the Commission of the People chuckled, turning around to face me.

"You obviously have not had enough experience in the world to understand that no one is truly human anymore, Little Lily."

"Where do you get your test subjects?" my father asked, trying to divert Dana's attention.

"Oh, all over the place," he answered. "They're people the Commission rounds up. You know, illegal immigrants, homosexuals, ethnic and religious minorities, those people."

We could only stare at Dana, stunned at how easily he had disclosed the information. Dana barked a laugh at our paling expressions.

"Why the looks of surprise?" he asked coldly. "What did you *think* happened to the undesirables collected by the Commission?"

I had never given much thought to the Commission cleansing the population of America. Since I had been born into a time where the population was considered purely American, it was not something I often had reason to ponder. Nausea overwhelmed me, sickened that I had never thought deeper into the Commission before.

The entire population ignored the basic question of what the Commission of the People did with its criminals.

"I've startled you," Dana noted. "But the detention and elimination of the undesirables is the reason the Commission of the People was created. This should not surprise you." He sighed heavily, pointing to his face. "Do the glasses bother you?"

"P-pardon?" my mother whispered.

"My glasses. You see," he said, pinching the frames, "I would rather not wear them at all. After all, an enormous component of nonverbal human conversation is done through the eyes."

My pulse thudded harder in my veins. I was overwhelmed by the horrific evening, but was undeniably curious to know the gaze that had been staring me down all night.

Dana pulled the glasses from his face.

The guards stepped in front of Dana and turned him around in the following instant.

"Our apologies, sir."

"What?" Dana whined. I could barely see his head over the guards as Dana turned to look at them. I craned my neck to see Dana's face but the guards were moving too much, attempting to get Dana to face the other way once again.

"Sean has asked that you are not to remove your glasses in front of new members of the Commission," one guard said.

"Sean is not here. And he does not create the rules, *I* do." Dana's tone changed, dropping the temperature in the entire hallway. "Move out of the way."

"We're sorry, sir."

"We're following Sean's orders."

There was a thick silence that hung in the air for three agonizingly-long seconds. Then, one guard cried out as his arm was twisted behind his back. Dana stepped close, looming over the cringing and collapsing guard.

"Who commands you?" he snarled.

"Y-You, sir!"

"If you want to lose your arm, defy me again."

"I'm sorry, sir! It won't happen again, sir!"

"Good boy," Dana cooed. "Now, are you going to bow at my feet and kiss my shoes like a good pet?"

"S-sir?" the guard gasped. Dana released his arm, placing his hand on the man's head and pushing him to the ground. The guard hardly dared to peer up at Dana once he was on his knees, trembling in terror.

"You heard me."

"Sir, this isn't fair. He was only—"

Dana swiveled, jamming his fist into the speaking man's diaphragm. He, too, fell to his knees, clutching at his stomach, gasping like a fish out of water.

"I will not tolerate such blatant disobedience," Dana snapped. "Do I make myself clear?"

"Yes, sir..." they chorused.

"Now, you heard me," he snarled, staring at the two guards on their knees.

I watched in fascination and horror as the two men leaned down to Dana's feet and kissed the tops of his shined, black shoes.

"That's better, you pathetic puppies."

Dana finally lifted his gaze.

His eyes were incredible. The intensity of the warm, honey color caused my legs to go weak as I fell willingly into their depths. I felt the pull from every section of my body. My knees quivered. My heart pounded. My mouth dropped open and a fire awoke in my belly that refused to be ignored. I shivered, lost in the color that seemed to sway and morph around the pupil, dancing hypnotically. Heat rose to my cheeks, but it was not from embarrassment.

Dana's gaze shifted to my mother and father. Even my father seemed flustered, seduced by the incredible power of Dana's gaze, rooted to the spot, unable to even blink.

"Sorry you had to see that display," Dana cooed. I could have sworn he was hypnotizing us with his eyes and his now-calm voice that dripped with heat. "Some pets must be reminded of their master's authority."

I barely heard the words. Every part of me was alight with fire and intense curiosity, lined with a palpable dose of fear. He was a beautiful predator and I was the defenseless prey, captured in his authority and splendor, willing to be his victim, desperate to get closer…to surrender to him…

"Are you frightened, Little Lily?" Dana asked, his deep, raspy voice tickling my spine, magnifying the flames along my nerves his eyes had ignited. I swallowed hard and shook my head. "You're not afraid of me?"

I nodded, my head attached to a string entirely under his control.

"That's a smart girl…"

The power of Dana's eyes was broken when a hand pushed his head sideways, turning him around. I blinked rapidly, trying to regain my bearings for the arrival of the newcomer. The man was even taller than Dana with tanned skin, dark brown eyes and hair, and the build of a wrestler clad in a simple black suit. Despite his impressive frame, his presence was comforting, soothing the intense heat that had filled the sterile hall.

"Dana, please," the stranger said with a tone of patience that I had to marvel. He sounded like a caring older brother who had caught his unwell sibling doing something mildly unacceptable. The man plucked Dana's glasses from his breast pocket and tenderly placed them back on his face. "I asked you to keep these on as often as possible, particularly around new members."

"You're no fun, Sean." Dana pouted.

Next to me Clark had visibly relaxed, as though he had just seen a dangerous dog leashed.

"Sir, I try not interfere with your affairs," Sean said. "This is the *only* thing I ask of you."

"Your rules for these idiotic things are bizarre," Dana growled, adjusting the glasses. "When can I take them off in front of the Sandovers, then?"

"I would prefer never."

"Nope."

"Then at least not on their first day," Sean groaned. "I'm sure they're overwhelmed enough. They don't need you staring them down. You are very aware of what your stare can do to people." He turned to the guards. "Parker, Jake, return to your post."

"Yes, sir," the two at Dana's feet blurted, scurrying away.

"Now that Sean is here, the fun stuff will have to wait," Dana said dejectedly, turning back to us and jerking his thumb over his shoulder. "This is Sean Jacobsen, my head of security."

I realized then that it was not Dana's security Sean was charge with, but the security of everyone who came in contact with the leader of the Commission. Though I was thrilled Sean seemed to have some control over Dana, it made me wonder why Dana was willing to obey when he had not tolerated the orders from the other guards. I entertained the thought that Sean *was* Dana's older brother—explaining the calm patience in his voice—but they did not look at all related.

"It is a pleasure to meet you, Sandover family," Sean greeted. His eyes rested on me for only a moment before rapidly flicking to Clark, filled with a silent question. I tried to ignore the churning of my stomach at their silent exchange, my overstimulated brain unable to even begin discerning the hidden meaning. Clark nodded next to me and Sean's gaze began studying me with interest.

"I was about to take them to Lab Two and show them the recent progress we have made with the Enterprise project," Dana told his head of security.

"Have you explained the project to them?"

"I was about to." Dana started walking again, Sean falling into step behind him as he began explaining the experiment over his shoulder.

"The ultimate goal of all this is to create a creature that is human in most respects and has no spontaneous mutations, which is the current hurdle." Dana walked us out of section three of the experiment cells and through the door across a narrow hallway marked with a large six. We moved through another hallway of glass cells filled with cowering experiments and into yet another hall where we immediately turned right, walking to a single door with a small window in the middle.

"This is Lab Two," Dana explained, extracting his key card again, sliding it over the electronic lock before opening the door.

We were immediately greeted by a bone-rattling scream. The sheer agony in the cry made my entire body go cold, petrified. Dana was the only one undisturbed by the noise.

"Oh," he said, "I guess they have someone on the table."

Everything inside me screamed not to peek around Dana, but I could not resist. Craning my neck, I saw the lab was filled with chairs like those in a dentist office, but bigger and flatter with metal restraints over the ankles, knees, hips, chest, wrists, upper arms, and neck. Sheets hung limply from tracks in the ceiling, several stained with splatters of old blood.

At the very far side of the lab, a group of people in white coats loomed over one table more brightly illuminated than the rest.

"Kyle!" Dana called. One man turned, lowering his surgical mask.

"Oh, good evening, sir," the man named Kyle greeted easily.

"Who do you have on the table?" Dana asked, stepping into the lab, not at all disturbed by the blood staining the front of the Kyle's lab coat or the pained whimpering of the subject on the table. Mrs. Markus also entered the room and Clark nodded, telling me to follow. I stepped into the lab after my parents, Sean trailing at the back of our group.

"Eina, sir," Kyle answered.

"I wasn't aware he was scheduled for testing today," Dana said, his pace hastening, his voice interested, as though he had walked in half-way through a movie he had been wanted to see.

"No testing, sir. Just a blood draw and vitals check."

"Sandovers, come meet my pride and joy." Dana smiled, stepping to one side of the table as the men and women in lab coats parted for us. I warily eyed the needles and other sharp instruments in nearby trays as I moved to the opposite side of the table with my parents, while Clark and Mrs. Markus stood at the foot of the modified chair.

A young man was secured in the restraints, his eyes rolling in their sockets as he breathed heavily, sedated and disoriented, whines emanating from his throat on each exhale. His pale skin was dotted with bandages and bruises, and his messy, sandy hair was oily from grime.

"Meet Eina," Dana said tenderly, placing a hand on the young man's head. "He might be the first success of the little project I was telling you about. I was just going to show you his file but, as luck would have it, you get to see him in the flesh. Not many have."

"...s-success how?" my father asked. Terror had seized my mother's tongue.

Dana lifted a hand to remove his glasses.

"Dana—" Sean started.

"Be quiet, Sean," Dana growled, his tone dangerous as he placed the glasses in his pocket. Sean obeyed.

"Eina is part of the program to create what we're calling the Machine of Neutralization," Dana explained. He leaned on his hands on the table, scanning us, his eyes still hypnotizing though there was no seduction in the gaze—there was only power and radiance that had me hanging off of every noise that dropped from his lips. "The Machine of Neutralization is the main goal of Dana Enterprises, a sub-branch of the Commission," he continued. "You see, wars are starting to get more complicated. Killing other humans in the traditional manner no longer seems to amuse or persuade nations the way it used to. War, as it was, is now unacceptable. We are trying to create a creature that is stronger than any human with the qualities of an animal that can be the ultimate weapon for the new kind of warfare."

"How can you do that?" I asked.

"The first step was deciding which animal DNA to use that wouldn't turn the subjects rabid, or put them into shock where their body shut down and they turned into living vegetables," Dana said with a shrug. "So far, we have had the best luck with the DNA for a *lion*, oddly enough. Even the monkey DNA didn't take. *Very* counterintuitive."

"Just...splicing DNA?" my father asked.

"God, no, it's *far* more complicated than that. There's work to coincide with the immune system, nerve endings, then altering the brain function to open up different pathways for command of the new DNA. Believe me, it's been a nightmare. We lost at least forty before we got the neural pathway alteration down to keep subjects from turning into vegetables after the first week," the head of the Commission elaborated. "We got some interesting results from *that*..."

"So...Mykail is not one of these...Machines of..."

"Neutralization. No," Dana finished my sentence. "Mykail was just for fun. He came out far too human for this particular project." Dana looked back to Eina. "Eina is the first one who has not been lost after the third part of the procedure. He seems to have retained basic motor skills as the DNA has been linked to his. The only side effect we had is that all of his body hair has fallen off, except for this, his eyebrows, and some downy, blonde hair..." Dana ran his hand over the young man's head. "We're checking him multiple times a day to see how he differs from the others who were unable to move past this stage. With this success we want to be certain he survives to reach the next stage." He turned to the scientists. "Is everything looking good so far?"

"Yes, sir," Kyle confirmed. "We're also giving him some supplements for his immune system, which seems to be slightly weakened, but not drastically so."

"Beautiful," Dana complimented.

"Does Leader Simon know about all this?" I asked, feeling surprisingly brave despite my mortification. "Do you tell him about this project?"

"Weekly."

"Do you tell him the *truth*?"

Dana smirked. "That's a smart girl you've got there," he said, glancing briefly at my parents. "As a matter of fact, Little Lily, Leader Simon is a regular visitor to this area of the Commission to watch the process himself." He looked at the others of my family. "Do you have any other questions for me?"

My mother found her tongue again.

"No," she said rapidly. "No, no."

"Oh, there is no need to be nervous," Dana assured, looking at Eina. "He's harmless right now."

"Oh…yes, I'm sure…" my mother agreed, her voice shaking. "Forgive me, Mr. Christe—Dana. I am feeling quite tired."

"My apologies," Dana said. "It is rather late. I shall walk you back to the main room. You can make it back to the lobby from there, correct?"

My mother turned, eager to escape. I followed everyone out of the lab, being the furthest from the door. I felt Dana approach, and despite my hastening step, his hand gently brushed through my hair, causing me to freeze just as I reached the door.

"I wanted to see if it was as soft as it looks," he whispered. He leaned down to my ear. "You are far more beautiful than my pictures show," he said. "It will be a *pleasure* getting better acquainted with you, Little Lily."

It was not just the tone of his voice that made everything in my body go on alert. There was a promise in the words that told me he would get to know me better by any means necessary.

Chapter Fifteen

The car ride home was silent. No one could speak, too overwhelmed to form any coherent thought, let alone maintain conversation.

I got into bed without thinking, not even noticing my actions until I was under the covers with the lights off, staring at the ceiling numbly. My brain, overloaded with terrifying images and upsetting realizations, had shut down, unable to take in more information.

It was unclear if I slept at all but when the numbers on my clock read ten in the morning, I decided to get out of bed and read the assigned chapters of J.A.N.E. I read slower than normal, needing to move my eyes over each sentence at least three times before I actually *read* it— even then, I was sure I had not retained any of the information.

When I made my way to the kitchen to silence my belly, heated arguing floated to me from downstairs. In a strange way, the sounds eased me. It was comforting to hear my parents sharing my disgust at the events of the previous night.

I descended the stairs slowly, listening.

"What do you want me to do, Karen?" my father snapped. "We signed the damn contract. Leader Simon knows what the Commission does. We have no one we can report this to!"

"Damn it, Thomas, they are taking *humans* and turning them into...who knows what!" My mother's voice broke, tears choking her.

"The people the Commission collects are *criminals*," my father said. "The Commission was created to get rid of these people. That's why it exists!"

"Then no one should care where they're taking these people and what they're *doing* to them? The people would start a new war if they heard about last night."

"*Exactly*," my father said. "If keeping quiet and accepting our role is going to keep the peace, so be it."

I trudged across the living room carpet as a weighty silence took over the argument.

"What?" my father finally growled.

"You're going to go along with this?" my mother asked incredulously.

"We don't have a *choice*, Karen!"

"Dana *gave* us a boy with goddamn wings as a gift!" my mom cried. "You're going to act as though that is *normal*?"

"Apparently it *is* normal for the Commission!" my father burst. "We are *bound* by contract. We can't get out. We're *stuck*. We need to accept that there is no other alternative. Who knows what they would do to *us* if we went public with the information."

My parents finally caught sight of me as I stopped in the archway into the kitchen.

"Come here, hun," my father coaxed. I rushed into his open arms. I desperately needed the hug. I closed my eyes and tightened my grip around him, refusing to let go, both of us shaking. "How are you holding up?" he asked, rubbing my back.

"...okay..." I said, though it was still too soon to tell exactly how I was faring.

"I'm going to make some lunch, Lily. Are you hungry?" my mother asked mechanically.

"Yes."

I helped make the simple sandwiches and we ate at the small table in the kitchen. At first, the meal was silent, but half-way through his sandwich—we were all eating slower than usual—my father sighed heavily.

"I know we're shaken up," he started, "but we need to gather ourselves and accept that we are now a part of the Commission...and everything it does."

"That's going to be tough, Dad."

"I know. I know..."

There was nothing more to say. We shared the same tension, all of us desperately tried to think of a way out of the Commission even knowing that we were trapped for life. My father stood, tears gathering in his guilt-filled eyes.

"I'm so sorry for all this..." he whispered in a choked voice.

Seeing my normally-strong father on the verge of crying brought the tears to my own eyes.

* *** *

I returned to school in a daze. As Clark had predicted, my friends treated me differently, but none treated me more bizarrely than Becca. When I walked to Jill's locker, as I had done every morning since the second day of school, Becca stiffened upon seeing me.

"What?" Jill asked, seeing the reaction.

"I just remembered...I need to talk to Mr. Peters," Becca said hurriedly, gathering her backpack. "I'll see you in class!" she called over her shoulder as she half-ran down the crowded hallway.

114

Jill and I looked at one another, confused. Figuring she actually *did* need to speak with Mr. Peters, I shook off my concern. But Becca avoided talking to me during class, avoided sitting next to me at lunch, and made it clear that she did not want to be anywhere near *me*. After seeing how easily she accepted Clark, another Commish Kid, even going out of her way to be inclusive toward him, I could not understand her avoidance of me.

Though I was hurt by her change in attitude, I also found myself indignant. I had seen things that they could never begin to comprehend, and learned national secrets that would make them run screaming. I was entitled to a period of numbness while I processed.

What made the day far worse was my inability to stop thinking about *him*. Dana's eyes haunted me, looming beyond my eyelids whenever I blinked. That cold, powerful gaze was always watching me, making me very distracted and jumpy, even occasionally igniting a dull fire in my abdomen.

That first week after my family's induction, *everything* reminded me of the horrors in the bowels of the Commission. Pictures of the massacre during the Second Revolution reminded me of the creatures in the pristine white cells. The loud, sudden laughter of students in the hall reminded me of the echoing scream from the lab…

I was trapped in constant, horrific flashbacks of that night.

That was why, on Wednesday, when I came home and there were strangers in the bedroom next to mine, I screamed. The construction workers creating Mykail's cage stared at me quizzically and then went back to work, trying not to send me skeptical looks. I forced a wobbly, apologetic smile and retreated to my room, slamming the door and crying on my bed, feeling as though I had just walked through a battlefield.

I was drowning in my own mind. All I thought about day and night was what I had seen at the meeting, and Dana's incredibly powerful eyes. I was plagued by the Commission. The calm, playful, deep voice of its leader was always looming behind me. Even the comforts of home provided no escape.

I existed in a constant state of fear.

Even my drawings had changed. I obsessively redrew the picture of an angel soaring over the clouds in battered armor, holding his flag high. I needed to see that beautiful creature I had encountered that horrible night out of his cage. It gave me hope that, someday, I could get out of my own cage—the Commission of the People.

The workers left the house just before dinner, giving me a few minutes before I was called downstairs to wander into the room and see what they had accomplished. They had created holes above the doorways and around the window frame, where I assumed the bars would go. I left the empty room when my mother called, disturbed by the thought of bars encasing the room—just another cage.

For the next few days, I tried not to feel time passing, which only made me hypersensitive to how rapidly the week progressed. It still felt unreal that we would soon have another member in the household— one that was an experimental weapon from the Commission of the People. What worried me most was not the fact that we were getting a human as a sickening gift, but that Dana Christenson would be coming to our house to deliver him in person.

The last thing I wanted was Dana in our home.

I was hesitant to go to Archangel that Friday, since my friends had been avoiding me and I had passed the week in an adrenaline-muddled haze. I was sure the noises of the club would be too much to handle.

Taylor turned to me Friday at lunch and forced a smile.

"So, same time to pick you up?" she asked. I blinked, surprised that she brought up the subject at all.

"Um…yeah, that would be great," I said before I could think of a better answer.

"Are you going to hang out with us at all?" Jill asked, trying to sound nonchalant.

"O-only until Clark shows up," I told them honestly. "Then we need to go up to the balcony, I think."

"Can I ask you something?" Taylor started, her eyes dropping to the floor for a moment as she gathered her courage. "This funk you've been in this week, does it have to do with the Commission?"

I did not know how to answer. I stared at the three sets of inquisitive eyes, frozen like a deer in the headlights.

"Well, you know I didn't want this to happen. I just…I'm just depressed, that's all."

"Is it as horrible as all the rumors say?" Jill teased, though her voice trembled.

I had to take a deep breath and turn away, pushing down the images of horror, terrified at how quickly the memories overwhelmed me yet again. When my friends saw my expression, their own eyes filled with worry—except for Becca. She looked frightened. I was too shaken to put much thought to her reaction, but I did take note of it.

The three girls did not speak to me for the rest of lunch, probably because I could not hold conversation, unable to shake the memories of the previous Saturday and the dread at the next meeting. Instead, the day at school became monotonous, moving around me, speeding toward the looming night at Archangel.

When I got home, my mother was there to greet me.

"Mom?" I said, surprised. "I thought you were working with Dad today."

"No, he's working with Mrs. Davis. They're pitching their idea in front of Leader today." She turned to me and sighed, her eyes betraying her own exhaustion. "How are you?"

"...it's been a rough week."

"I can imagine." She leaned against the kitchen counter. "I spoke with some of the others in the Commission about Mykail and their own gifts. They all seem very at ease. They say that the awkwardness passes after a few days."

"That's not much of a comfort."

"Maybe your father's right..." my mother whispered, her gaze falling to the floor. "It's our only option to accept everything that the Commission does...maybe it really *will* become normal for us. Why shouldn't it? It seems almost everyone felt the same way at first."

"But this is *wrong*, Mom."

"We need to adapt, Lily," she said. "I've been thinking about everything that happened Saturday...and I think that we might have to make an effort at first, but the Commission is not to be defied. Going against it would be suicidal."

"...I know."

"We'll see how it is living with Mykail and then we can discuss this further," she said with a decisive nod. "Are you going to Archangel tonight?"

"Yeah..."

"Let me know if you need any help getting ready," she told me, though her tone was distant, her thoughts clearly elsewhere.

I retreated upstairs, anger toward my mother bubbling inside me. She wanted to *adapt* to the Commission. The thought of pretending to be alright with the torture that the Commission put their subjects through made me sick.

It was routine to get ready for Archangel and climb into the car with my friends, but we did not exchange many words during the drive. Everyone in the car, including me, felt awkward.

I tried not to think about how dramatically my life had changed. Just as I had been getting into the routine of Central, the metaphorical rug was pulled from under me again. I found myself wiping away stray tears on my cheeks as we reached Archangel.

The loud music and bright flashing lights of the club disoriented me as I feared. I found myself eager for Clark to arrive so that I could go to the less-crowded balcony—I was too frightened to go up there alone.

When he arrived, he said quick hellos as I stood to walk to his side.

"I'll, uh, see you later..." I told the others clumsily.

"Okay," they chorused back. Becca said nothing, only offering a tight nod in response. I made a mental note to talk to her when I had my bearings again.

Clark and I ascended the steps to the balcony and, immediately, the Commish Kids descended upon us.

"Well, well, well," said one of the boys—his name was Frank, I think. "If it isn't the new favorite."

"W-What?"

"Don't act all innocent," a girl I did not know sneered, stepping to Frank's side. "Everyone knows that Mr. Christenson favors your family."

"Because of the gift?"

"Just ignore them," Clark said, his eyes hardening as he rounded on the girl. "After all, what was it that your family got, Gabrielle? Some kind of pretty boy your father immediately became far too attached to?"

"Shut up, Clark."

"Oh, you're here," a voice said behind me. Whirling around, I came face-to-face with Melissa. I recalled seeing her briefly at the meeting, but I had been so focused on Dana watching me that I had not paid much attention to her or any of the other Commish Kids the previous Saturday.

"Melissa," Clark greeted curtly.

"You all need to back off of her," Melissa said to the growing group around us.

"Why? Because she's a favorite?" another boy challenged.

"No," Melissa contradicted. "Because she's *more* than a favorite."

I turned to Melissa, confused, waiting to see if she would explain. She did not. In the silence, my gaze passed over the rest of the Commish Kids. They were staring at me with wide eyes and nervous glances, hesitantly slinking to the various shadows around the balcony. I looked at Clark, whose eyes were on his feet, as though ashamed that I had found out that I was "more than a favorite," whatever that meant.

"Clark?" My voice was choked.

"We'll talk over here," he said, motioning to one of the secluded corners at the back of the balcony. My feet shakily brought me to the appointed area, Clark guiding me to the small couch. "Do you want anything to drink?" he asked out of courtesy.

"No."

"How are you holding up after Saturday?" he asked, sitting next to me.

"Horribly."

"Yeah, you had one hell of an induction. Most people don't get that far into the back on their first day," he said sympathetically. "And I think you are the first to see Eina outside of Dana and his advisors."

"Clark, please," I said, my voice cracking. "You said you would tell to me more once I had seen what goes on in the Commission. Now, I wish I could unsee everything." I leaned forward. "What did Melissa mean by *more* than a favorite?"

"It means that you're like me." I had to strain to hear him over the thrumming of the music.

"How am I like you?"

"You're of interest to Dana," Clark elaborated, clearing his throat to strengthen his voice. "And now everyone understands why you've been assigned to me."

"Who else is more than a favorite?" I asked, turning over my shoulder to scan the other teenagers on the balcony. Whenever a Commish Kid arrived that night, one of the others would lean in and whisper something before pointing in our direction. I could only assume they were spreading the news that I was "more than a favorite."

"No one," Clark answered. "Until now, it's just been me…"

"Are you…upset about that?" I asked, hearing the strain in his voice.

"Yes and no," he said. "But not for the reasons you probably think. I am happy not to be alone in this position any more, but I wish that you didn't have to be subjected to him like I am."

"What…what do you mean?"

Clark clasped his hands together and shifted to sit on one of his legs, facing me, his eyes full of torment.

"As I'm sure you noticed, Dana is not…*all there.*"

"Oh, believe me, I noticed."

"He has no regard for any rules other than total obedience to him," Clark continued. "And his tastes are…questionable."

"I saw."

"What do you mean you *saw*?" Clark asked, his eyes going wide. Realizing that we were talking about two very different things, I narrowed my eyes suspiciously.

"…what are *you* talking about?"

Clark groaned and ran a hand through his hair in frustration, avoiding eye contact.

"...I'll give you an example." He looked around before leaning even closer, though his eyes were locked on the space between us, never meeting my gaze. "You remember that thing he did with his eyes when he took his glasses off?"

That I remembered all too well.

I nodded.

"One day, in a private meeting with Dana and his advisors..." He paused, lifting his eyes long enough to wildly scan the balcony to be sure no one was eavesdropping. "I was sitting near him and he got bored. So, he..." Clark swallowed hard and closed his eyes, his voice choked. "He took off his glasses and looked around, but everyone was watching my mother on the other side of the room."

I leaned closer, his voice getting quieter and weaker with each passing word.

"He, um...he looked at me...and he did that thing with his eyes...and...I-I felt..." He turned away, biting his lip. Seeing how difficult it was for him to talk, I placed my hand on his and nodded.

"I understand. You don't have to say it."

"And that night when I was going to his office to find my mother..." He trailed off, a shudder running through his body that had me jumping to all sorts of horrifying conclusions. "...I found them, alright."

My eyes widened. "They...they weren't..."

"Right there on his desk," Clark confirmed, his eyes finally turning to mine, cold. "And what was worse was that he *knew* I was there. He was showing off. He *knew* that I had seen them. He had *wanted* me to find them."

"How do you know that?"

"Because he *looked* right at me and smiled while he was...*screwing my mother!*" he hissed. I could tell by the pain and tension in his voice that he had been keeping the story to himself for a very long time.

"...does your mom know that you know?"

"No."

"Maybe...I don't know, it was a one-time thing?" I tried to comfort him stupidly.

"Yeah," Clark scoffed, rolling his eyes, "one time a week."

"*What?*"

120

"I'm telling you, Dana does not care," Clark said strongly. "He has had sex with all of the women in the Commission—with the exception of your mother—and even a good portion of the male members."

"You can't be serious," I whispered. "That's *illegal.*"

"That's why I said his tastes are questionable. Another thing I'm sure you noticed is that Dana doesn't care too much about the law, despite his position to uphold it."

I pursed my lips.

"So..." I started awkwardly, "since I'm...*more* than a favorite, does that mean he'll try to...I mean, has he ever..." I raised my eyebrows, motioning to Clark, hoping he understood what I was trying to ask.

Clark shook his head.

"No," he whispered, "we haven't." Relief engulfed me. "But..."

I tensed again.

"*But?*"

"He's shown explicit interest in me."

"You've said that before."

He sighed heavily, tears welling in his eyes despite how he tried to blink them away.

"He..." Clark stopped. My heart was racing and breaking at the same time. Clark had obviously been enduring far too much on his own for far too long. "He likes to..."

I took Clark's hand, but stayed silent, waiting.

"He gets playful," he said. "It started out as some kind of sick game. At first, he would send someone to get me—I stay at the Commission every day after school—and when I would go to his office, I would catch him with someone else, or sometimes with my mother." He took a moment to collect himself. "He wanted me to see him with all these people. But...one night..."

"Are you alright? You don't have to talk about this," I said after he trailed off yet again.

"No, I'm alright," he assured weakly, his voice tight. "It's just...it's really hard to talk about. I've never told anyone before." He cleared his throat. "One night...my mom was working late and I was doing homework in her office...but I got tired, a-and I fell asleep on the couch..."

The pain in Clark's voice was so powerful I could only listen, feeling the trembling of his hand and trying to keep my heart from shattering.

"And when I woke up…he had me p-pinned on the couch…and he just…kept touching…and k-kissing…I couldn't move…I-I *couldn't…*"

Clark hid his face in his hands, shivering, shying away from me when I tried to take his hand again. I did not know how to comfort him. I waited, fighting the urge to hug him, worried what the others on the balcony would think, sure that they would bully or tease either one of us about the display.

Clark ran his hands through his hair and took a deep breath, trying to discreetly rub away the stubborn tears behind his glasses.

"I'm sorry…"

"Don't be sorry," I whispered.

Clark dabbed away the escaped tears on his sleeve, turning to look distantly at the wall, taking several deep breaths. "He hasn't gone any further than that…but…every time it happens…I just keep wondering if that's when…"

He did not need to finish.

"You haven't told anyone else? Your mother? Your father? Does your father even know what's going on between your mother and Dana?"

Clark chuckled darkly.

"Oh, Lily, the world you are getting into is so fucked up you'll never believe it," he said. "Yes, my father knows about them. He even participates on occasion, if he feels like it."

"You're not serious…"

"Dana has that power over people. I don't know if they know about what Dana does to me, but I'm sure they must have some idea. They know how Dana can be."

"And they don't care?"

"Within Dana's inner circle, no one questions anything." Clark shook his head. "Dana does what he wants and no one stops him. No one *can.*"

"What about Sean?"

"If you can stick around him, you're more likely to be safe from Dana," Clark agreed. "He's the only one Dana listens to."

"Why?"

"Hell if I know," he said. "There have been rumors about family connections, or even a love affair, but no one really understands their relationship. I doubt even Sean understands it."

"Is there anything you can do to stop Dana when he…"

"No. To be completely honest, sometimes I don't think he's even human," he said. "He has ridiculous strength. I have never seen him sleep, or eat." The teenage boy's eyes became lost, filled with memories of the leader of the Commission of the People. "He's not just crazy, he's crazy with insane power, both physically and politically."

"Why does everyone put up with it? There have to be a lot of Commission members that think what the Commission does is wrong, or that Dana should be stopped."

"Many do, or *did*. Once you fall under Dana's spell, it's all over," he said. "He'll have you convinced that the testing is the right thing to do, and he'll turn any argument you make to be in favor of what he does. He just has that kind of power."

"So, for me..."

"I don't know what he has planned for you," Clark admitted. "But I saw him mulling over your pictures, so I know—"

"Whoa, *what*?" I had been hoping Dana had only said he had pictures of me to scare me.

"He has thoroughly researched you," he elaborated. "Don't ever think he's *not* watching you, Lily," he warned. "He is everywhere. He lives in the basement of the Commission, but at least once a day, he comes to the surface and he does something different every day. You never know when you'll run into him." Clark looked around the room. "And he has cameras everywhere and connections with the National Security Council. You're always under his eye."

I felt my skin crawl.

"That's how you know I'm *more* than a favorite?" I pressed. "The pictures?"

"Yes." His eyes turned apologetic. "I'm so sorry."

"No, don't be," I said reflexively. "I'm sorry that you've been carrying this weight alone for so long."

"I will admit," Clark started, smiling weakly, "it is really nice to be able to tell someone. I didn't mean to dump all my emotional baggage on you."

"It's fine," I said. "I'm sure we'll be sharing a lot of emotional baggage, considering our position."

The night wore on as I mulled over what Clark had divulged. It sickened me that he had had to bear up to such abuse for so long, and it worried me that I would also become the object of Dana's inappropriate affections with no one around willing to stop Dana's advances. Clark told me that Dana was more into mental torture than physical domination, and he explained that the molestations were a mind game, not an act of pleasure, but that frightened me even more, particularly if the rest of the Commission was already under Dana's spell.

Clark was clearly feeling uncomfortable having told me the secret he had kept for so long, so we sat in awkward silence amid the thrumming of the bass. The silence gave me too much time to think, to put myself in Clark's position, to grow the panic of being subjected to Dana Christenson's mental torment, unable to turn to my parents for help because it was only a matter of time before they, too, accepted Dana's whims as the norm.

As the announcement came over the club speakers that the buses were taking everyone home, I watched the Commish Kids continue their casual conversation, making no moves to gather their belongings.

"Are we catching the last bus?" I asked.

"No," Clark said. "We're having our own meeting here and then we'll catch the Commission bus."

"The Commission bus?" I repeated incredulously. "Seriously?"

"Yeah..." Clark groaned, understanding my exasperation. "Melissa," he called, "are you doing the report today?"

"Yes," she answered.

"Report? What report?"

"Don't worry about it. It's just for the advisors' children," he said. "After everyone leaves, we'll talk about what we heard around the floor and what, if anything, should be presented to the Commission at the meeting. One of us has to write a report about who said what and who they heard it from so more investigations can be done if warranted. Dana is training a new generation of Commission advisors."

"Wow," I breathed. "That is slightly terrifying."

"Only slightly?" he grumbled.

After the second announcement, the Commish Kids moved around the balcony, pulling chairs into a haphazard circle for the meeting. Some returned from the dance floor, talking quietly with those next to them as they assumed a seat. Each had an air about them that was stuck-up and cold, as though knowing the horrors of the Commission entitled them to be unfeeling about others. It was unnerving to hear the sharp comments and relayed gossip about possible Commission criminals who could be captured and imprisoned in the labs of the Commission of the People.

Melissa looked over the railing of the balcony for several minutes once the main lights turned on, white light flooding the building. It was the first time that I noticed the real color of the walls—a dark grey that was so plain, it was in complete contrast with what the club looked like in full swing.

"Everyone is out," Melissa announced, turning away from the railing to join the circle. "Who's not here?" When no one spoke up and her eyes had scanned each face, she nodded. "Great. It's my turn to do the report this week so, Clark, do you have anything you want to put in it before we start?"

"No."

Melissa extracted her phone from her purse and started a voice recording. "September thirteenth, Club Archangel Report. Who would like to start?"

A boy raised his hand.

"Brian Dunning," Melissa said for the record.

"I heard Susana Reynolds explaining to her friends that her father is interested in pitching an idea to Leader about the war in the far east," Brian said. "Apparently, he spoke to some of the locals when he was there a month and a half ago."

The others whispered to one another, shocked by the news. I looked at Clark, who also seemed interested. I tapped his arm to let him know I did not understand.

"Don't worry too much about knowing all this information," he whispered. "The most important thing is to listen. You'll pick up names and get to know people as long as you pay attention."

For a half-hour, the Commish Kids discussed the gossip they had heard in the club. Some of the teens were very accusatory. Others stated constantly that they were unsure if they had heard the information correctly or if it had been out-of-context. None of the gossip jumped out at me but, apparently, it merited something from those who had been in the Commission longer.

After the half-hour meeting, Melissa stopped recording.

"Now that that is out of the way…you all were at the meeting last week but because it was her first meeting, we didn't get much of a chance to talk to her. So, I would like to introduce Lily Sandover." She motioned to me, causing sweat break out on my palms from the sudden spotlight. "She is of particular interest to Mr. Christenson, something all of you need to keep in mind."

"Sure," the boy named Brian sneered, looking me over hungrily. "I guess it's no mystery *why*."

"*Please*." One girl rolled her eyes. "Mr. Christenson doesn't like virgins."

"And how would *you* know?" Felicity scoffed.

"Because he's always hanging all over your mother," the girl retaliated.

"If he doesn't go after virgins, that doesn't explain why *Clark* and *Lily* are his favorites," a boy I knew as Lance said, looking us over with contempt. "After all, we all know that no girl in her right mind would want to sleep with a faggot like Clark."

Clark got to his feet, his eyes alight with anger as he stormed toward the snickering Lance. I was unsure if I needed to leap up with Clark or if that would provoke further bullying. I could hardly think amid the tension suddenly swirling around the balcony. I felt like I was watching a terrifying competition where everyone *wanted* to be the target of Dana's attention.

"Say that again," Clark growled. "Call me a faggot one more time."

"Clark, enough," Melissa warned, her tone exasperated. Lance chuckled and leaned back in his seat, triumphantly crossing his arms.

"You're awfully defensive…"

"Oh, if you only knew the things I've seen your uncle do with Dana," Clark said with a dark smile.

Lance's features twisted in fury as he stood to match Clark.

"And what, did you *participate*?" Lance snapped. "Or did you just jerk off while you watched?"

"It's against the law to engage in any activities of a homosexual nature," Clark said. "Be sure to remind your uncle of that."

"No wonder you want to be so close to Mr. Christenson, then," Lance chuckled coldly. "Keeps you nice and safe as long as you *please* him, doesn't it?"

"Mr. Christenson won't take him to the lab until he gets tired of him," a girl taunted. "Little faggot that he is. He won't last another two years, probably."

"For the last goddamn time!" Clark barked, glaring at the other teens. "I'm not a fucking faggot, so back the *fuck* off!"

"Then why are you getting so defensive?" Brian challenged, trying to make his condescending tone sound innocent. "You've never fucked a girl, so they're no way to prove you're *not* a fag."

I realized that I was the only one who would step in on Clark's behalf. The cruelty of the Commish Kids was mounting as they reveled in tearing Clark apart, feeding on one another as he floundered. The only way to derail the bullying was to play the game on their level.

I walked to Clark, putting as much movement into my hips as I could muster. I wrapped my arms around his shoulders, leaning close to his ear.

"It's alright," I said. "Just ignore them. They don't know what they're talking about."

He turned to me, startled by my sudden close proximity. I could only hope that my wobbly smile was convincing to our audience.

"What are you—"

"The way he talks tells me he's never been with a girl, himself," I said, my arms remaining around Clark as I channeled my inner bitch at Brian. "And if he has, he probably had to beg for it. Or maybe even pay."

"What the fuck does *that* mean?" Brian snapped.

"Just what it sounds like," I said with a cold smile. Surprisingly, it was very easy to mimic their level of cruelty. I turned to Clark, leaning my head against his. "But I do know that he could never please a girl the way you did for me after the meeting…"

Clark turned to me, his eyes widening behind his glasses. But when he heard the questioning snickering around us, his body language changed. His shoulders straightened and his chin raised, a cold aura surrounding him as he committed to the charade. As he wrapped an arm around my waist and turned his gaze back to Brian, I could have sworn he exuded the same powerful, chilling demeanor as Dana.

"I feel sorry for any poor girl forced to deal with your ineptitude, Brian," Clark said. "Unlike you, I don't need to prove anything."

Clark turned us both, his arm still around my waist as I kept a hand on his shoulder, throwing a smirk back at Brian, who was trying to formulate a response. As Clark took my hand to guide me to my seat, he leaned close.

"What the hell was *that*?"

"I plead temporary insanity."

I scoot my chair closer to Clark so that we could appear like a couple once we resumed our seats. Since my bitchy demeanor had gotten everyone to shut up, I tried to keep up the same confidence. I sat proudly, throwing coy smiles at Clark occasionally, but I was internally smacking myself, wondering what the hell had possessed me to put myself in the bullying crosshairs of the Commish Kids.

"Is there anything else we need to argue about tonight?" Melissa groaned.

No one spoke up.

"Great," Melissa said. "As I was saying before you all decided to have a pissing contest, Lily Sandover is a particular favorite of Mr. Christenson. Her family will be a wonderful addition to the Commission and I'm sure we'll get along well." There was no sincerity in her words.

It took some self-control, but I managed to keep myself from snapping at her for not stepping in sooner, and for lying about how well I would interact with the other Commish Kids.

With the meeting wrapped up, we made our way to the bus idling in front of the club. I lingered with Clark at the back of the group.

"The others will talk," Clark whispered to me.

"They talk anyway." I tried to sound nonchalant. "We need to stick together and help one another. I hope you don't mind that I did that."

"No." His eyes went to his feet. "But…"

"What?"

"I am concerned about what will happen when Dana finds out what you said." My blood ran cold. He did not say *if* Dana found out. It was *when*.

"You don't think he'll take it seriously, do you?"

Clark chuckled brokenly. "You still have a lot to learn about Dana."

We descended the balcony stairs last. But since we were last coming out of the club, we were the last on the bus and had to sit in the back. As we were walking, Clark in front of me in the narrow aisle, a hand groped me. Lance and Brian laughed at my back. I flushed red and quickly moved to the back of the bus as some of the others who had seen the molestation snickered, amused. One more hand reached out and tried to touch me before I planted myself in the seat next to Clark, trying to keep my humiliated tears at bay.

Chapter Sixteen

I was nearly hyperventilating en route to our second Commission meeting. My parents were reluctant to go to the gathering, mirroring my hesitation for the first meeting. We had dressed for the formal affair slowly, dragging our feet to the car and driving at just the speed limit to remain outside the Commission of the People as long as possible.

Silence pervaded the vehicle. While I knew my parents were unnerved by all we had seen at the Commission, I was worried that they were trying to accept the dealings of the Commission, feeling trapped and that the only thing to do was submit. My mother had already suggested we adapt, which told me she was already succumbing to the fear-fueled influence of the Commission of the People.

I did not want to adapt—I wanted to fight. I had spent most of the day creating fantastical scenarios where the American people were shown the truth of the Commission and rallied to bring an end to the cruel institution. I had no idea if such a change was possible, but it brought me small comfort in the hours before the meeting.

We reached the Commission building and went through the same security procedure as the previous week. Our phones were checked in and our purses and jackets were searched before we were led to the elevators.

We were fifteen minutes early so we had no choice but to interact with other members before the meeting started. I stuck close to my father, but it was not long before other Commish Kids honed in on my location.

Brian came to my side even as I tried to hide behind my parents.

"Good evening, Lily," he greeted. My anger flared, remembering the previous night in the club. I tried to force my bitchy attitude to the surface, though I was hesitant with my parents within earshot.

"Hello, Brian."

"Why don't we get something to drink?"

"No, thank you."

"Go on, Lily," my mother urged. I rounded on her, trying to convey with my eyes that I did not like the boy in the slightest. But she was oblivious to my silent cues, thinking I was just being antisocial, not trying to avoid a bully. Not wanting to raise a fuss in the meeting room, I begrudgingly followed Brian to the bar.

"What would you like?"

"Nothing," I snapped. "What do you want, Brian?"

He scoffed. "Seriously? *Clark*?"

"It's none of your business."

"Come on. He's a faggot," Brian jibed. "Everyone knows it."

"That's not what *I* know." I was digging myself into a deep hole, but I could not compel myself to stop. I needed to protect Clark. We had to help each other survive inside the Commission.

Brian's eyes roved over me, trying to catch my lie. His gaze gradually changed, turning from inquisitive to hungry.

"Is that so?" He cocked a sick smile. "Why don't you get with a *real* man, then, if you're that desperate?"

"I don't see any nearby."

"You've got some fight in you," Brian noted. "I like that."

"Ugh," I rolled my eyes, "that is so cliché. I'm not some project or conquest and I'm sure as hell not stupid enough to fall for your bullshit, so leave me the fuck alone."

Brian laughed. "They all say that."

"*They*?" I scoffed. "In your dreams…"

"But deep down inside," he said, placing a hand on my hip, which I smacked away, "you know you want it."

"Stop."

"C'mon," he said. "You were obviously desperate enough to fuck *Clark*, of all people."

"I told you, that's *none* of your business." I smacked his wandering hand away again.

"What the hell is your problem?" Brian growled, finally fed up with my attitude. "What? Just because you're Mr. Christenson's favorite, you're *better* than everyone?"

"Yes," a voice answered behind me. My blood halted as the voice ran down my spine like icy fingers. His sudden presence was cold and all-encompassing. I turned as though his voice commanded me to face him, confirming that the leader of the Commission had appeared behind me, Clark next to him. Dana was wearing another immaculate three-piece suit, fiddling with his pocket watch as his dark glasses shielded his powerful eyes.

His arm snaked around me, his large hand holding my waist as he fixed the startled Brian with a dark, veiled stare.

"She *is* better," he said. "I don't give special attention to just anyone."

His hand was warm, sharply contrasting with his cool appearance and frightening demeanor. My heart began thundering, though it was not only from fear. A part of me was excited to have him near me, to have such a powerful man *touching* me, protecting me. As Clark had said, Dana had "that kind of power."

"Mr. Christenson," Brian greeted with a half-bow of his head, unsure how to behave after Dana had caught him being so aggressive. "I apologize, I didn't see you come in."

"I tend to sneak up on people." Dana smiled coldly. "And you were just heading back to your table."

Brian dared not disobey the order. "Yes, sir, I was. Excuse me."

As he scurried away, I kept my eyes down, waiting for Dana to move his hand.

He did not.

"Young boys," Dana said with a disapproving click of his tongue. "They don't know the art of seducing a woman."

Dana moved in front of me, his hand skimming up my arm to my face, his fingers gently caressing the skin of my cheek.

"Good evening, Little Lily."

"G-good evening," I stammered, backing away and turning from his touch. "Uh…thank-thanks."

"I don't like sharing, Little Lily," he told me bluntly. The movement of his head told me he looked to Clark as he spoke again. "You would *both* do well to remember that."

Dana turned away. With each step he took to the other side of the room, my body relaxed a little more, no longer feeling the acute power of his presence. When I felt I was able I turned to Clark, who instantly dropped his eyes to the floor.

"What was all that about sharing?"

"Nothing," Clark mumbled. "Don't worry about it."

His tone told me it was something I *should* worry about. I wanted to question further but my mother suddenly placing her hand on my shoulder caused me to jump and whirl around.

"It's alright," she said with a concerned once-over following my reaction. "It's just me. Come sit down. The meeting is about to start."

Once again, at exactly ten the doors locked us in the meeting room. Dana walked around the room as the meeting commenced, prowling through the tables like a teacher looking for cheaters during an exam. Clark moved next to my seat to help me understand the material again but as had been the case the previous week, I found it impossible to concentrate. I was too focused on Dana's movements, watching the predator slink about, trying to decide his next prey among the complacent herd.

My attention was only diverted from Dana when Mrs. Markus mentioned the Enterprise project and my mind was flooded with memories of Eina. The information Mrs. Markus shared was promising, but vague, leaving me to wonder how much those in the Commission knew about the experiment and how much Dana kept secret even from the Commission of the People.

The meeting finished around midnight and Dana made a beeline for our table as members of the Commission departed.

"So, Sandovers," he started, claiming the chair next to my father, practically pushing Mr. Lloyd from his seat, "how have you been?"

"Fine, thank you, Mr. Christenson," my mother responded stiffly.

"Oh, what's this Mr. Christenson stuff?" he asked lightly. "I told you, call me Dana."

"Yes, sorry, Dana," my mother corrected herself, her voice shaking, her eyes averting from his dark glasses.

"Are you ready for Mykail to join you?" Dana asked, beaming with excitement. "Are the workers almost finished?"

"Yes," my father affirmed. "They finished earlier today."

"Excellent. What time should I bring him by? Eleven?"

"Um, sure, eleven works," my mother agreed.

"Wonderful." Dana's bright smile turned to me. "And you, Little Lily? Excited for your new pet?"

As much as I tried, I could not stop my scoff of indignation.

"I don't think of him as a *pet*, Mr. Christenson," I growled. My parents' heads snapped in my direction as the eyes of all nearby turned to me. Clark leaned to my ear.

"Lily, *don't* pick a fight with him."

"Why wouldn't you see him as a pet?" Dana asked, leaning forward, interested.

"Because he's a human being."

"Not anymore."

"He was at one point."

"So were corpses," Dana said with a shrug. "And yet, we can't think to treat them the same as anything other than a corpse, can we?" He cocked his head. "Think of it this way. Our experiments are like a death and a rebirth combined. The human part dies, we spend a few days observing it, and then we put the human part in the ground and get a new puppy."

"No, it's not that simple," I said sharply.

"Why not?"

"Because it's *not*."

"Because you see him as human?" Dana prompted. "Then how about this? Humans are creatures of attachment. They need interaction, other life forms—human or animal. Humans cannot be alone. That's the reason societies exist at all. So what happens when a human is ostracized by society? What can a human do if they cannot find a group to understand and accept them? All they do is hurt because there is no attachment, no interaction. Whatever human part you see residing in Mykail surely craves interaction. That is why I am giving him to you. He can become a part of your family, your loyal pet who loves you unconditionally because anything is better than being alone."

"He must have had a family before," I snapped. "Why did you take him in the first place?"

At this, I heard everyone around us gasp. Apparently asking about the crimes from which the Commission acquired its subjects was taboo.

"*I* didn't," Dana answered. "*You* did."

"What does that mean?"

"You, as part of American society, decided what was acceptable and what wasn't," Dana continued, his voice almost playful, clearly enjoying the argument. "People, like you, cannot handle those who are different. You ostracize them, hurt them, murder them…so, to protect yourself, you, as a society, decided who needed to be removed. I am simply following your wishes, making sure you can sleep peacefully at night."

"That was not a personal decision."

"Then, if I told you that Mykail used to allow other men to fuck him, you would be able to accept that without judgment?" Dana asked, his voice turning cold. "If I told you that he peddled his ass and helped his older half-brother smuggle illegal drugs over the border, you wouldn't let that information determine the way you treat him?"

"Well…I…" I was losing ground rapidly. "Even with all that, he shouldn't be punished in *this* manner."

"*Punished?*" Dana raised an eyebrow. "This is not punishment. It's rebirth. After everything that he did, every law that he broke, he has been given a gift. Just look at him. He's become an angel."

"Against his will."

"Nothing is a willful choice anymore," Dana said with a gentle laugh. "If it was, you wouldn't be here, would you?"

I could feel Dana's eyes working through my soul behind his glasses.

"No," I said with as much strength as I could muster.

"At least you're honest," Dana said with a crooked smile.

"Dana, I am so sorry about my daughter," my father interjected. "We didn't raise her to be so rude."

"No, of course not," Dana said. "It's been a while since anyone has had the backbone to give me this kind of shit. It's actually quite refreshing."

I dared to glare at him, which only served to widen his grin.

"Little Lily, I am going to enjoy you very much."

"Don't count on it."

"Lily!" my mother gasped.

"Your spirit is very familiar," Dana noted. He turned to my father. "I knew a man when I was about her age that possessed this kind of defiance." He stood, striding easily around my chair to lean over my shoulder and whisper in my ear. "It took a lot of time on the table but he eventually broke." He leaned closer, pressing his jaw against the side of my head. "In time, you will, too."

He straightened, turning his attention to the group of spectators around us.

"What?" he asked, waving them away. "Go on, go home."

They dispersed slowly, looking at me with appalled expressions, not believing that I had said such things to Dana Christenson, of all people. Picking a fight with the leader of the Commission of the People was not just stupid, it was suicidal.

"We're so sorry, Dana," my mother repeated. "I can't believe she—"

"It is of no concern," Dana assured, his voice turning soft and sultry. "I am not upset."

"Oh…" my mother whispered, clearly tasting the honey in his voice. "Th-thank you for your understanding."

"It is no trouble," he said. "After all, you are her mother. I know she was raised very well."

"Oh…Dana…you are far too kind." My mother smiled, her cheeks flushing brightly as I marveled at how easily Dana had flustered her.

Clark's hand was suddenly on my shoulder.

"Are you out of your *mind*?!" he whispered, pulling my attention from Dana's flirting.

"I'm sorry," I said meekly.

"Don't be, I'm really impressed. But are you out of your mind?!"

"I don't know, I guess so," I said. "I don't even know why I said all that."

"I will see you tomorrow morning," Dana said to my parents. "If you could open your garage door for us, we'll bring him in that way so none of the neighbors see him."

"Thank you, Dana," my father repeated, shaking his hand. "We look forward to tomorrow."

"As do I." Dana grinned mysteriously, throwing a final glance at me from behind his glasses.

I could feel it. I was in far over my head.

As Dana left the room, my father grabbed my arm.

"What was that?"

"I'm sorry," I mumbled. I could not stop the pain I felt at my father being upset about my argument with Dana. I had thought that my father was also against the dealings within the Commission, but his anger made me wonder if he had already started adapting to the norms of the Commission of the People, and wanted me to bow to Dana's will like everyone else.

"You do realize that you were arguing with Dana Christenson, right? This is *not* a man you want to upset!" my father snarled. "He practically runs the country under Leader Simon."

"Dad, do you really think that Leader Simon can control a man like Dana Christenson?"

"No, why do you think I'm so worried about what you just did?!" he snapped. "You might have put yourself in danger!"

A wave of relief flooded me. He was worried for my safety. The realization relieved my fears on many different levels which, oddly, brought a smile to my face.

"This is not a laughing matter!" my father growled. "Come on. Let's go home."

Chapter Seventeen

Dana was coming to our home. The dangerous predator leading the Commission of the People was going to be walking through our house. After the previous night's debate, my parents were insistent that I do anything and everything to please him while he was our guest to atone for my behavior—though even the *thought* of playing nice sent my stomach lurching.

I fretfully watched the minutes tick by, dreading the impending visit. Amazingly, I was not as worried by the idea of an experiment of the Commission living with us as I had been when the workers first started preparing Mykail's room. All apprehensions about Mykail living with us were overshadowed by Dana Christenson's imminent arrival.

Far too soon, it was ten-thirty and my mother called me down to sit with her as we waited for the leader of the Commission of the People.

"I want you on your best behavior," my mother reminded sternly. "We don't want a repeat of last night."

"Mom, can you lay off that, already?" I groaned. "Dana wasn't upset, why are you?"

"You don't know that he wasn't upset. He was probably just being polite."

"Something tells me that, if he *was* upset, he would have no problem telling us," I grumbled.

We sat in silence, watching the hands on the clock move closer to the hour. I spent the quiet minutes wondering if Mykail was going to easily fold into our family, or if he was just supposed to stay in his room like a piece of furniture. It was unclear what we were supposed to *do* with him.

My father opened the garage door ten minutes before the hour so we would be able to hear the car's arrival. Two minutes to eleven, we still had not heard a vehicle idle in our garage.

"You don't think he's scarily punctual *outside* of Commission meetings, do you?" I asked.

"I don't know," my father muttered, apprehension clear in his voice as he stared pointedly at the door to the garage.

Our ears were trained on the garage, our breathing shallow so we could ear even the smallest of noises.

One minute to eleven and still no sound of Dana Christenson.

Thirty seconds...

Ten seconds...

When the second hand hit the hour and our clock began chiming its tired song, there was a knock on the door to the garage. I barely suppressed my startled yelp as I jumped out of my seat. My father stood, throwing us an exasperated, yet impressed, look as he went to answer.

"Dana," he greeted.

"Good morning, Tommy," Dana greeted happily. I cringed—my father *hated* being called Tommy.

"Oh, um…" My father took Dana's offered hand, taken aback. "Actually, sorry, but I really detest the name Tommy." He tried to laugh off his unease.

"Really?" Dana asked, surprised. "How interesting." Dana turned away from my father to greet us, not at all deterred. "Karen, Little Lily."

It took all of my self-restraint not to snap at him that I hated the name Little Lily.

"Welcome, Dana," my mother said, extending her hand. Dana turned her hand over and kissed the back, his lips lingering on her skin, his eyes meeting hers over the top of his dark glasses. When he turned to me, I shakily extended my hand and he pressed his warm lips to my knuckles, turning his eyes up to me, making my blood grow hot—though I struggled to say it was only from anger.

"Ah, Sean," my father said, inviting the Commission's head of security inside. My body relaxed upon hearing that Sean was also there. Dana smiled, amused by my obvious relief.

"Before we bring Mykail in, I should double-check the arrangements," Dana declared. He walked up the back stairs before anyone had a chance to show him the way. I shivered at how comfortable he was in our home.

He turned right at the top of the stairs and opened the door to the guest room. Looking over the barred door, Dana grabbed and shook it—the door did not even rattle.

With an approving nod, Dana reached into his suit pocket and pulled out a paper bag, extracting a key. He placed it in the lock and turned it twice, the bolt clanking loudly to the side. "Excellent. That sound will let you know if anyone is letting him out," he explained. "You should be able to hear it from just about anywhere in the house."

As Dana stepped into the room to check the bars over the window, Sean placed himself in the doorway, watching Dana closely as Dana walked around the new queen-sized bed which made the room appear even smaller.

"Sean," my mother tried to strike up conversation as we stood awkwardly by him, "how long have you been head of Commission Security?"

"About four years," he answered. "But I worked security in the Commission for two years before the promotion."

"Do you enjoy your job?"

"I do, thank you for asking, Mrs. Sandover."

"He's lying through his teeth," Dana called from the bathroom. "He hates it. He's lying because I'm here."

"Dana…" Sean groaned.

"What?" The head of the Commission shrugged as he returned into view. "It's true."

I looked between them, not sure whether to believe Dana or Sean. Sean looked far too kind-hearted to *enjoy* working for a man as cruel as Dana, and he did not protest Dana's statement, but it made me question why he put up with working for the Commission at all if he hated it so strongly.

"Everything appears in order," Dana mused. He retrieved the paper bag from his pocket again, pulling out four keys. "One for each of you," he distributed them, "and a spare."

"Then, we *can* let him out," I deduced.

"You can let him out into the rest of the house," he affirmed. "But no further. He *cannot* go outside. If he does, I *will* know," he said dangerously. "Do I have your word that you will not let him out of the house?"

"Yes," we chorused.

"I will hold you to it." Dana turned to Sean. "Let's go get him."

Dana pulled off his glasses, placing them inside his breast pocket as he descended the stairs. My father held the door open so we could watch. Sean closed the main garage door as Dana moved to the daunting black SUV that barely fit inside the space.

In the back seat, Mykail was bent forward, his wings folded, cramped at an awkward angle that I knew had to hurt as he tried to fit in the car. The sight was made more painful by the black bag over the experiment's head, making him look like he was heading to execution.

"Why do you have his head covered?" my father asked as Dana reached into the car.

"So he doesn't know how to get back home," Dana said mysteriously. "Mykail." The angel reached out with both hands, turning his upper body in search of guidance. His wrists were chained together, hindering his movement. Dana gently took one of the angel's hands. "Wing's down," he instructed. The angel folded his wings even closer to his body, maneuvering around the seats of the SUV, bumping them as he tried to disembark.

Dana placed his hand on the top of Mykail's head and then touched his wings, guiding him more tenderly than I expected.

"Very good," he praised. Mykail's wrists were chained to his ankles, making him shuffle awkwardly away from the vehicle as he tried to find his balance again while being unable to see.

"You have to have him *chained* as well?" my mother said worriedly.

"Well," Dana chuckled, "*I* do."

The leader of the Commission of the People removed the bag from Mykail's head. The boy looked around, his eyes wide with surprise and fear as he adjusted to the sudden light.

"Sean, let him stretch his wings. That was an uncomfortable car ride for all of us."

Dana's head of security pulled a ring of keys from his pocket, searching through them before unlocking the cuffs on Mykail's wings. We watched in fascination as Mykail lifted his wings and spread them wide, the muscles in his shoulders flexing with the movement. Once his wings reached the expanse of the car, he sighed in relief and settled into a normal position, rotating his neck as the feathers ruffled on his wings.

The movement was hypnotizing, graceful, and natural, as though he had been born with the extra appendages.

My heart fell as I watched Sean fasten the cruel cuffs once again.

"Why do you need him chained?" I asked.

"He can get playful," Dana answered vaguely, taking the keys from Sean. Dana unlocked the cuffs on Mykail's ankles, handing the restraints to Sean before starting on the cuffs on the angel's wrists. "But that's only with me. I'm sure he'll be a perfect angel for you."

As soon as Dana removed the second cuff, Mykail snarled and lunged forward, taking advantage of the sudden freedom.

"And here we go," Dana groaned, ducking and grabbing Mykail's wrist, twisting him. Mykail fell to his side on the cold garage floor, his heavy wings throwing him off-balance. He let out a quiet shout of pain, but surged forward on the ground to latch onto Dana's ankle.

"Will you knock it off?" Dana droned, kicking Mykail away, annoyed more than threatened. "See? Sometimes, he needs a little discipline."

Reaching into his pocket, Dana pulled out something that looked like a car remote. He pressed the only button and Mykail let out a pained wail, backing away from Dana on the floor, his back arching and his wings trembling as the muscles quivered.

"Stop it!" I cried as Mykail's pained features began to turn red

"After he attacked me?" Dana asked darkly. "No." The leader of Commission looked back at Mykail, his gaze cold. "We generally have this conversation once a week, as it is. He should know better by now."

"And you wonder why he hates you?" I snapped.

"Ah, he doesn't hate me." Dana crouched next to the cringing experiment and placed a gentle hand on his pained face. "He just likes to test my limits. We have a healthy relationship, I think."

The tension gradually left Mykail's body as he lowered his head to the cold cement floor, panting through clenched teeth as his pain ebbed.

"Mykail, can we make it up the stairs and to your room without repeating this?" Dana asked condescendingly. Mykail turned his head, but did not respond. The leader of the Commission of the People nodded once.

"Good boy."

He offered his hand, helping Mykail to his feet. The experiment's wings trembling as he was forced to lift them with the rest of his body. Dana walked to us, leading the experiment. I retreated out of instinct. Mykail's eyes lifted to mine as he passed and I felt my entire being gravitate to the magnetic stare—so different from Dana's while being surprisingly similar. The gaze was powerful and alluring, but failed to spark the same primal fear as Dana's molten irises.

"To the left, Mykail," Dana instructed, keeping his hand on the angel's shoulder. Mykail ducked his wings through the doorway and turned up the stairs. He walked into the guest bedroom and looked around briefly before sitting on the bed, eyes downcast and shoulders slumped, his wings relaxing at his sides to rest on the mattress.

"Sean, get the box out of the car," Dana ordered. As Sean went back downstairs, Dana motioned us closer, though we still kept a fair distance from the experiment, uncomfortable. "Mykail, these are your new masters," Dana introduced. "This is Thomas Sandover, his wife Karen, and their daughter, Little Lily."

Mykail kept his eyes focused on the grain in the hardwood floor at his feet.

"He's not much of a talker," Dana lamented. He turned to my father, pulling out two identical clickers to the one he had used to discipline Mykail in the garage, each clicker attached to one key. "Here is the key for the cuffs on his wings. You can remove them *only* when you bathe him and apply the lotion. Then, they have to go right back on. Sean is getting the lotion and other things now. I'll supply it for you."

Dana snapped his fingers.

"Something I forgot to tell you last week," he said quickly. "Every other month, I will be coming over to give him his shots."

"Shots?" we echoed.

"They're for his wings. It's medicine," Dana explained. "It'll take me ten minutes, at most. Unless I decide to stay for dinner, of course." He grinned, obviously not joking.

"Ah, I see," my mother said, trying to laugh at his banter.

"So, the clicker." Dana nodded to the two remotes in my father's palm. "Whenever you have him out of this room, keep that in your pocket. If he gets out of hand that is how you can subdue him quickly. The other one is a spare, you'll keep it with the spare key to his cuffs and the spare to his room. Always be sure you know where the keys are so he doesn't try to take them. Not that he can reach the cuffs himself to unlock them, but it's best not to tempt him to try. He might harm himself."

Sean returned with a small, cardboard box and set it on the far bedside table. Dana opened it, pulling out an unmarked yellow bottle.

"Alright, everyone, over here. I'll show you what to do," Dana said, beckoning us with his finger.

I had been locked in a staring contest with Mykail's vibrant blue eyes once he raised his head at Sean's return. As cliché as it seemed, there was something otherworldly about his beauty and that beauty was too captivating to comprehend. I followed my parents toward Dana, constantly flicking my eyes to Mykail, more interested in him than Dana's instructions. His gaze followed me, like he was trying to communicate something silently.

"Take a fair amount of this on the palm of your hand," Dana explained. "You want to smear it all over his shoulder blade." He ran his hands over the area he was talking about on Mykail's back. No one missed the way the experiment flinched from the touch. "Be sure to get under the feathers around the main joint of the wing."

"Every day?"

"Yes," Dana affirmed. "Pick a time, make it a habit. It shouldn't take long. He'll sit still. If he doesn't, hit him a few times with the discipline chip to make him behave."

I cringed at the thought.

"You have a few choices for feeding him," he continued. "Be sure he gets at least two full meals a day. Three is nice, if you can swing it. But I know sometimes no one will be home to feed him. Just be sure he doesn't go hungry. I'll reimburse you for his food. If you feel comfortable with it, you can have him eat at the table with you. If not, just bring him a plate of food and keep him in here. I doubt he'll make a mess. He's pretty clean."

"Are you sure he's safe to let out of this room?" my mother asked, clearly thinking of the incident in the garage.

"He's very docile, really," he assured, placing the unlabeled bottle of lotion back in the box. "He and I just have a certain type of relationship."

I resumed staring at Mykail, unable to turn my eyes away, barely hearing Dana's words beside me.

"So…" Dana mused, looking at Mykail, Sean, and the box on the bedside table before clapping his hands together once. "Shall we have some lunch?"

Dana exited the room without waiting for an answer. My mom blinked at my father, who shrugged and led us out, Sean closing and locking the cage door behind everyone. I glanced back once more, catching a glimpse of Mykail staring at us through the bars as we went out of sight.

My mother and I made quick sandwiches, feeling desperate to get Dana out of the house and opting for an easy lunch.

"So, Tommy," Dana started, leaning against the counter as he watched us work. My father cringed at the nickname but chose to ignore it. "What made you go into politics?"

"You could say that it runs in the family. My father was a Regulator, as well."

"Your father," Dana repeated slowly. "Mister…Johnathan Sandover, correct?"

"Yes."

I listened over my shoulder, occasionally throwing glances at the three men. I could hear the tension in my father's voice. I never knew much about my paternal grandfather, since my father never discussed him other than his political dealings, so the conversation piqued my interest, particularly since he had died before I was born.

"I'm amazed he was able to continue his career in politics after the scandal with his wife," Dana said simply.

At this, both my mother and I turned, confused. My father's frantic eyes turned to us, trying to think of an explanation while Dana waited patiently, impervious to the awkward mood gripping the kitchen as my father stumbled.

"I'm surprised you know that," my father evaded with a nervous smile.

"His wife *did* kill herself, didn't she?" Dana continued.

"Uh…yes…she did…"

Dana nodded, backing off the subject. My mother turned back to preparing lunch, though I took longer to resume the task. I watched Dana settle against the counter, triumphant.

"Did you think you would get so far as to work directly in Central?"

After a few boring exchanges about my father's advancement in America's capital, my mother turned again.

"Shall we eat in the dining room?" she asked, bringing the platter of sandwiches to the bigger table. My father turned to Sean and Dana.

"Would either of you like a drink? A beer or something?"

"I'm fine," Dana said. "Sean?"

"A beer would be great," Sean murmured with an apologetic smile. "Thank you."

Dana moved into the dining room behind me, his cold smile causing me to shudder.

"That dress looks beautiful on you, Little Lily."

"…thank you…" I scurried away to sit at my normal place at the table—across from my mother and next to my father. Dana took the seat next to me.

"Dana?" My mother offered him the tray of sandwiches as Sean and my father walked in with their beers. Sean sat on Dana's other side and my father assumed his normal spot at the head of the table.

"No, thank you," Dana declined the food.

You were the one who suggested lunch… I growled internally, barely suppressing the urge to roll my eyes.

"Sean?" my mother said, offering him the tray.

"Thank you very much, Mrs. Sandover." Sean said, his tone even more apologetic than before as he grabbed one of the sandwiches. He scarfed down the food as though he had not eaten in days.

When the tray came my way, I picked the smallest sandwich, knowing I would be unable to eat with Dana seated right next to me, but not wanting to decline and seem rude after my defiance the previous night.

"Well, Dana," my father started, taking his own sandwich to keep his eyes averted, "how did you come to lead the Commission? You look too young to be in such a high position."

"Appearances can be deceiving." Dana smirked. "Actually, I worked under Bryant Morris and took over after he died."

We all stopped and stared, dumbstruck.

"Impossible," my father breathed. "The man who founded the Commission of the People? You worked under him?"

"We knew each other on a very intimate level, yes," Dana affirmed. "I was quite young, then. I didn't think I'd come to *lead* the Commission after his death, but here I am."

"Bryant Morris died forty years ago," my father said, skeptical and confused. "How could you have worked under him? You look to be in your forties. When were you born?"

"I wish I could answer that question for you," Dana said. "But, along with several other memories, my mind decided that such information was not important and promptly discarded it."

There was no way to respond other than stare at the head of the Commission of the People incredulously.

"…I wish I could forget my age," my father tried to joke, his voice straining. "If you knew Bryant Morris, then you could tell me if he started the Commission with the idea that…*this* would happen."

"*This*?" Dana repeated, confused. "You mean the testing? Oh yes, he's the one who started it." He nodded enthusiastically. "He ran over four thousand experiments when he was head of the Commission. Probably more, if we count the ones that were kept off-record."

I choked. Coughing, I reached for my water, hating that the table's attention was now focused on me. Dana's hand rested on my shoulder and I recoiled, frightened by the touch.

"Are you alright?" he asked, unfazed. I nodded quickly and tried to get my throat to dislodge the food.

"Over four thousand?" my mother repeated when I stopped making such a commotion.

"Yes. We still have some of them lurking around the cells today."

"Why did he start doing the experimentation? The same reason you continue it?"

"…you know, I don't remember," Dana said with a smile, looking thoughtful for a moment before shrugging. "I actually believe it was a request from one of the early Leaders who wanted military advancement. They used to be quite worried that the American people would stage another coup so soon after the revolution."

"Then…you're doing this because you're worried about the domestic safety of America," my mother concluded hopefully.

"No," Dana corrected. "Not at all. That was the original plan, when there were still illegal immigrants, homosexuals, and other filth wandering the streets. No, everything is much calmer now."

"Then why continue the testing?"

Dana smiled wickedly, winking. "I'm a stickler for tradition."

I took a deep breath, my appetite leaving as my nausea grew stronger. I looked at my mother.

"I have to finish my homework. May I be excused?" I asked as politely as I could around the tightness in my jaw.

"Of course, honey," my mother said reflexively. I gathered my plate and took it to the kitchen before darting upstairs, not caring how much noise I made. I spared a glance at the room at the other end of the hall. Mykail was on his side on the bed, his eyes dark and gloomy as he stared into space, lost in troubled thoughts.

I ducked into my room.

I collapsed onto my bed and tried to catch my breath, but panic and disgust were already deeply seated in my chest. Dana was too much to handle in concentrated doses. I could not help but wonder if he had always been so intense, or if working for Bryant Morris, running gruesome experiments at such a young age, had molded him into the terrifying man running the Commission of the People.

I put my head in my hands, my entire body in panic no matter how I tried to calm myself.

Everything Clark had told me could not prepare me for the reality of Dana. A part of me knew I was in greater danger than I was willing to admit to myself, particularly with Dana's obvious interest in me. He had something planned. Somewhere inside the twisted workings of his mind, he was devising a way to break me—I could feel it in the marrow of my bones.

"That wasn't a very subtle exit."

I scrambled to my feet, biting back my scream. Dana was leaning against my doorframe, smirking. He stepped into my room, closing the door behind him. The clicking of the latch made my heart pound angrily and my muscles tense. My hair stood on end and everything in my body screamed at me to run.

"What are you doing up here?" I choked, trying to sound angry.

"Coming to see you."

"W-What do you *want* with me?"

"Oh, no, Little Lily," he said disapprovingly, as if I had made a mistake about which line to say next. "No, it's too soon to tell." He tilted his head to the side in a terrifying manner that made me shudder, my laboring heart threatening to break my ribs. "I must confess, I am quite impressed that you were willing to stand up to the other kids in the Commission and tell them that you were sleeping with Clark, but I am not at all happy about the lie."

He took another measured step forward. My legs hit the bed and I sat heavily, unable to retreat further. He placed a hand on my face, closing the space between us. I felt immobilized in his presence.

"But you are new, and you do not yet know the rules, so I will let it slide this time."

"…y-you don't like to share…" I recounted. "Does that mean that you're going to start molesting me? Like with Clark? That's how you learned about our lie, isn't it? You tortured it out of him?" I hated that my voice was trembling even as I hurled such heavy accusations.

Dana smiled dangerously.

"He'll tell me anything I want to know," he said, leaning closer. I backed away, falling to my elbows as he placed his hands on either side of my hips on the bed, his face hovering over mine. I was trapped under his energy, hypnotized, every muscle in my body rigid. "I just have to know," his hand ran up my side until his fingers lightly traced over my neck, "which buttons to push."

The touch sent a different kind of spark through my body. My mouth fell open, my breath shaking as I exhaled.

The seductive power was in his eyes again, pulling me toward him as my barriers crumbled. His eyes slowly closed before opening again, the blink cat-like and carefully choreographed to hypnotize me.

"Lie back."

The voice ran up my spine and I collapsed, losing all strength in my arms from the command. He leaned over me, his hand cupping the back of my neck tenderly, no other part of his body touching mine.

"You are *mine*, Little Lily," he said. "And you always will be."

"No…"

"Yes," he contradicted. He brought his face even closer. I felt his breath on my lips. My eyelids fluttered shut at the sensation. "That's it…" he cooed. "I can tell that you've barely been touched." I could hear the smile in his voice. "You've never even been kissed before, have you?"

I could not respond.

His voice turned sultry, dripping with heat and sex.

"Let's fix that."

His lips were upon mine, warm and surprisingly gentle. He overpowered all of my senses. My body went hot, fire ravaging my veins as his presence made desire radiate along every nerve. I gasped against his lips and, while my mouth was open, his tongue slipped inside. It was wet and foreign, but I did not move away. Overwhelmed, I was filled with a pleasure I never knew existed. He was barely touching me, but there was no doubt he set off a primal chain reaction within my body.

Dana broke away, standing straight.

The rush of air cooled my body and, when my head stopped spinning, I came back to reality. Fear crashed over me. In the resulting panic, I curled up on the bed, hiding my face in my hands, my brain turning to static as I tried to understand my reaction to the forced kiss.

"I guess I should be more careful," Dana whispered, his hand tracing my exposed calf. I flinched from the touch. "I'll have to take my time training you."

Tears pricked at my eyes, but I refused to let them flow while he stood beside me. I did, however, curl tighter into the fetal position.

"I'm going to ask for a tour of the house," Dana told me, his fingers leaving my skin as he walked to my door. "I'm warning you now, I will ask you to join, so don't break down the moment I leave."

He swept from my room. Once he was out of sight, chills spread through my body, causing goose bumps to rise over my arms and legs.

I swallowed back the swell of adrenaline at his departure, barely holding myself together. The bastard knew I was on the verge of a meltdown and had patronized me about it, telling me so easily not to break down because I would have to show a strong face to my parents so they would not know what had occurred.

I refused to let him have the satisfaction of turning me into a blubbering, frightened mess.

I counted my breathing, listening closely as voices moved into the small living room at the bottom of the stairs outside my room.

"Lily's room is just up there," my mother's voice said.

"Could she join us?" Dana asked innocently. The task of walking without my legs shaking seemed impossible, but I knew I had to be stronger than Dana's influence. I had to show him that he would not be able to break me, no matter how much he frightened me.

"Lily!" my mother called. I took a deep breath, counted to five, and stood, my legs miraculously managing to hold my weight.

"Yes?"

"I'm giving Dana and Sean a tour of the house. Come join us."

"What the hell does he need a tour for? He owns the house blueprints..." I sneered under my breath.

I joined the group on quivering legs, avoiding Dana's eyes as we moved through the kitchen, living room, into the backyard, and then up the main stairs to the master bedroom and the other guest room.

"Well, you certainly have turned the house into a home," Dana complimented, stopping at the top of the stairs outside my parents' bedroom. He turned to where the family photo wall had been established, looking over the pictures with a hint of dark glee in his eyes. Every smirk, smile, and blink had me teetering on the edge of fleeing my house entirely to escape him. But I managed to stay, trying to determine what he was plotting based on his expressions.

"Look at all these pictures…" he mumbled, his voice distant. His eyes stopped when he saw one of the pictures and his face fell. He leaned closer to study it. It was the photo of my father and grandfather with the fish—my dad's favorite picture.

"I'll be damned…" Dana said in what sounded like disbelief.

"What is it?" my mother asked.

"This picture of little Tommy and his father."

"Oh," my father grinned, "it's one of my favorites."

Dana looked it over and then straightened, looking thoughtful as his eyes remained locked on the picture.

"Wasn't there someone else in this picture, too?" He motioned to one side of the photo. "Right here? They've been cut out…"

We all blinked, confused.

"No," my mother said with a gracious smile. "It was just squeezed into a smaller frame."

"No," Dana contradicted, "there was another person in the picture." He looked at it a while longer and then his eyes widened as he snapped his fingers. "Your brother! He was next to you in this picture!"

"No," my mother repeated. "Thomas is an only child."

I turned to my father and my blood ran cold. My father was staring at Dana with wide, terrified eyes while the leader of the Commission smiled knowingly back.

"…how…how could you possibly…" my father stammered.

"I researched your family *very* thoroughly."

"Thomas, what is he talking about?" my mother asked, her eyes roving over my father's stunned expression.

"William Sandover," Dana answered for my father, his attention diverting to the picture again. "He was…ten years older than you, correct?"

"Thomas, that's not true…" my mom said slowly, glancing between my father and Dana, trying to convince herself that she knew her husband better than Dana.

"It's true, Karen," the leader of the Commission told her. "Tell them, Tommy. Tell them why you never spoke of William."

"…well…I-I…" My father was too flustered to form his response rapidly. "I haven't seen him since I was eight."

"Why not?" Dana prompted.

"He was disowned."

"Why?"

"…for…" my father looked at us, pained, "for aiding criminals of the Commission of the People in escaping the country."

"There we go," Dana praised my father. "And that was why your mother killed herself, wasn't it? She couldn't bear your father disowning his oldest son, particularly when said son disappeared." He stepped closer to my father, the air becoming colder between the two men. "Do you know what it means when people 'disappear' in this country, Tommy?"

My father closed his eyes, his expression creasing with pain as he hung his head.

"Say it," Dana commanded.

"It means that he was captured by the Commission of the People," my father whispered, his voice choked. "Which means…he was made into a test subject, wasn't he?"

"Yes," Dana said. "I handled his case personally many years ago. No wonder your name sounded so familiar."

My father closed his eyes, trying not to flinch at the words.

"You were very close to him, weren't you?" Dana asked, his eyes back on the picture.

My father nodded slowly.

"Huh…interesting that you never tried to figure out what happened to him after your father reported him to the Commission. Never crossed your mind again, did he?" Dana stared at my father for a few moments, before sighing heavily and turning to Sean.

"Sean," he started, "I think we should go. We have other work that demands our attention." Dana put his glasses back on and smiled at us with a short nod. "We'll see ourselves out."

Chapter Eighteen

"Thomas, how could you not tell me that you had an older brother?" my mother said disbelievingly. It had taken us several minutes to move from the top of the stairs to the kitchen after Dana and Sean left, and still several minutes of silence before my mother finally asked about my father's older brother.

"What was I supposed to say?" he asked. "I was eight when he disappeared."

"Dana said you two were close," I muttered.

"We were." My father put his head in his hands. "But you don't understand what it was like…"

My mother sighed heavily, pressing her fingers into her eyes.

"Better late than never, I guess."

"…I loved Liam. He was my idol. He was so loving and generous…he cared about everyone over himself." My father's arms went flat to the table, his eyes remaining downcast. "With a father who never thought of anything other than his political career and the power he could gain, Liam practically raised me."

He hesitated.

"But they fought almost every day, Liam and our father. Liam was so brilliant that my father liked to show him off. Liam *hated* it. They would get into screaming matches every night, and my father would…well…he'd beat Liam with his fists if he had to. He didn't tolerate disobedience."

I knew my grandfather had not been a loving man, but had never known he was abusive.

"…and he…" my voice trembled at the words, "he helped people escape the country?"

My father drew in a deep breath.

"When the Commission began taking people more forcefully, Liam was at all the rallies against the Cleanse. He even started smuggling people over the borders if they were marked by the Commission," he explained. "When my father learned of his sympathies, the fighting got far worse."

He closed his eyes.

"I didn't really understand what was going on. I was too young. I just remember…I remember my father kicking Liam out in the middle of the night after one of their fights…and then my mother and father started fighting…and I never heard from Liam again.

"I only found out that Liam had been called into the Commission the night before…" My father stopped, cringing at the painful memory. "My mother was screaming about what my father had done…that he had called Liam in. The next morning…I found her hanging in the laundry room."

"Why didn't you tell me any of this?" my mother gasped. "Don't you think this is something your *wife* deserves to know?"

"I put it out of mind!" he snapped. "My father used to beat me whenever I asked about Liam. I learned not to think about him."

"And now we're *in* the Commission of the People!" my mother snarled. "What if someone were to find out what your brother did? Smuggling criminals out of the country? What would people think?"

"Now you want to be *accepted* by those in the Commission?" my father asked. "What happened to last week, when all you could talk about was finding a way to get out?"

"*You're* the one who said there's no way out!" my mother barked. "We have to adapt, and if the others were to hear our own brother was a criminal—"

"The only danger I see in others knowing is that Dana would find out. But, lo and behold, he already knows! He's the one who brought it up!" my father interrupted. "And he *still* wanted us in the Commission. We're one of his favorites. Everyone has said so. My father stayed true to the Commission and reported a man who was dangerous to America. Dana respects that, and the others will, too."

My mother shook her head, abruptly standing from the table.

"Where are you going?"

"I'm going to pick up some things for dinner," she said, snatching her purse from the counter.

"What do you want me to say, Karen?!" my father called, turning in his seat as she left the kitchen. "You wanted me to adapt to the Commission? I'm adapting."

"I'm glad it's so easy for you."

"You've accepted the experiment!" my father retorted, standing to follow her as she went to the garage. "You've agreed to accept *that* as the norm! But when *I* accept my brother was a criminal, I'm suddenly in the wrong?!"

My mother sharply shut the garage door behind her and my father's shoulders slumped.

I remained silent and still. Even after he left, Dana was still tearing my family apart. I had every intention of telling my father what Dana had done to me, secretly hoping it would anger him into finding a means for our family to escape the Commission of the People. But as I left the kitchen table and walked to my father's side in the living room, he leaned over the back of the couch, one hand pressed over his eyes as the tears fell down his cheeks.

I could not upset him further that day.

Instead, I wrapped my arms around him and hugged him tightly.

* *** *

The entire week was filled with tension.

My parents were fighting every day about the Commission of the People. They did their best not to fight in front of me, but I caught bits and pieces of their arguments, which was often worse because I did not know what had started the confrontation. In my mind, though, the root of their arguments was always the same—Dana and the Commission of the People.

School offered no relief to the stress. Becca was still acting strangely, and overshadowing my concern about her behavior was my annoyance. I was dealing with too much at home and with the Commission of the People to devote energy into figuring out why she was avoiding me. The only one I felt I could talk to was Clark, but no one knew where he ate lunch and I was not brave enough to search the school alone for him.

The final source of anxiety was Mykail. Dana had been right that he was quiet, but that also meant he stared—*a lot.*

Every time I saw him, he was staring at me. For the first two days, everyone in the family was far too nervous to be around Mykail alone, or without the discipline clicker in-hand. After the second night of all being present for the application of the lotion and the delivery of his dinner, we realized that Mykail *was* docile. He never fought against us, never spoke…he only stared.

Wednesday night my mother was brave enough to invite Mykail downstairs for dinner, unlocking the barred door, constantly looking over her shoulder as she led him downstairs. He entered the dining room hesitantly, his expression betraying his worry as he sat with us. It was a tense, silent meal. Everyone only ate half of what we were served, including Mykail, unable to muster more appetite amid the tension.

But after that night, it was much easier to have him eat with us. We felt it was kinder than isolating him during meals. My mother was the one who bathed Mykail and took care of most of his needs. He soon became the family pet, and the questions about his care became commonplace—"Did you feed Mykail?" "Did you buy bottled water for Mykail?" "I'll bathe him tonight."

152

His care became part of our routine in little less than a week.

By Friday I was ready to get away from it all.

I went to Archangel with a lot on my mind and every intention of venting to Clark. But when the other boys in our group of friends appeared, Clark was not with them.

"Where's Clark?"

"Oh, he's not coming tonight," Devon answered. "He's sick or something."

Realizing I would be alone that night at Archangel, I formed a plan to go to the balcony, get a drink, and sit in one of the chairs to pass the night as inconspicuously as possible. I said goodbye to my now-estranged group of friends and joined the other Commish Kids.

No one bothered me, which was a relief. I was not in the mood to defend myself against their cruelty. Once or twice some Commish Kids approached, but I kept my head down and ignored them until they walked away. I never bothered to look up and determine who had approached.

I remained in the back corner of the Archangel balcony, trying not to dwell on the new reality of my life. It was already difficult to breathe in the heat of the balcony, but occasionally, unwanted memories of what I had seen at the Commission, or the eyes of the silent Mykail watching me, would cause a sharp spike in panic that had me closing my eyes and counting my breathing, my body growing clammy with fear. Everything I thought of as normal had been turned upside-down in as little as two months. I was existing in a state of turmoil, leaving me with constant, insidious exhaustion and desperation.

I wanted nothing more than to escape.

I stood, leaving my drink behind, and descended the metal stairs to the dance floor, weaving through students. I needed to move, which was difficult in the tight blue dress, but I still found myself moving with the music as Devon had taught me my first night at Archangel, shifting my hips and shoulders with the beat, letting my body act on its own, ignoring my racing thoughts.

The song faded for only a second as another took over the speakers, the lights flashing in sync with the opening as the students cheered around me. The bass was heavy and the thrumming of the song was intoxicating, though I could not discern the lyrics. Even though I didn't understand the words or recognize the song, it was easy to move to, my hips swaying as the pulse of the song raced down my spine.

I danced until my mind had blocked out everything else and I felt as though I was alone, the beat of the song my only companion.

I *felt* him approach. That strong, searing power was at my back before I could react, large arms encircling me, hands flat against my belly pulling me tight to him. I gasped, my head falling back against him as his mouth went to my ear, his breath ghosting over my skin.

"Keep moving, Little Lily."

I obeyed.

His voice and hands sparked something deep in my belly. My mouth fell open as my hips moved against his. The flex of his fingers caused the fire to swell inside me, consuming every nerve. His hands moved from my abdomen to my hips, anchoring them against his as we moved together. I lifted my arms, my fingers linking together behind his neck.

His hands were powerful on my body, one hand resting over my lower abdomen while the other snaked up my side before lightly grazing over my chest as the hand crossed my shoulders, tracing my collarbone with a delicate touch. I danced with the music, feeling his mouth against my neck and his hips pushing against mine in rhythm.

I moaned, surrendering. I was sweating in the heat of the club, dizzy. My hands tightened at the back of his neck, helping me to remain upright. My body trembled. Some hazy part of me knew what was really causing the tremors.

I was a puppet in his hands, responding to his every move. His thigh slid against my behind and I moaned openly, grinding and feeling nothing other than the heat of the room and the sparks his touch left on my skin. His fingers moved from my shoulder back down my body, over my breast again, which he squeezed before moving his hand to my abdomen, over my hip, and to the skin of my thigh.

I spun around to look at him, ignoring everyone else in the club. He was smirking, his glasses nowhere to be seen. The unnatural color of his irises in combination with the predatory look made my knees give out from under me. He was not in his normal three-piece suit. He was wearing a black shirt with the V-collar exposing the dip of his collarbone. He was clad head-to-toe in black—perfect camouflage for the dark club. He smiled when I looked him over appreciatively, mimicking my scrutiny. I could feel the trail of his gaze as he scanned me before his hands on my hips and my lack of coherent thought caused me to keep writhing to the heavy, powerful bass of the song, losing sense of myself entirely.

His arms encircled my waist, his fingers pressed into my backside as his other hand, once again, skimmed up my side to palm my breast. I moaned and swiveled my hips against his, hungry for sensation.

"Perfect, Little Lily," he whispered, his mouth close to mine. My eyelids felt heavy. I was drunk off his presence and the heat of the club—it was becoming too much to bear. "This is the way I want to see you...in need...begging..."

"P-please..."

I stretched against him, feeling the need in my belly elongate to encompass my entire body. I pressed my chest to his, bringing my mouth closer, but he pulled away, smiling with the familiar dangerous expression. He chuckled coldly, dancing with the music against my body, working my nerves until I was incapable of control. I felt like a rag doll.

He lifted my leg over his hip, canting his hips intimately. I choked back a moan, my eyelids fluttering wildly. The hand that had been on my breast moved to tangle in my hair. I gasped as he yanked my head back, exposing my vulnerable neck so he could kiss the underside of my jaw, smiling against the sweat-slicked skin. I didn't think about everyone else in the club, or how the others could be watching the very intimate dance between me and the one-and-only Dana Christenson. The students on the dance floor wouldn't recognize him, but the Commish Kids in the balcony would know him immediately and would see us only layers of fabric away from having sex.

I didn't care. His intoxicating power had turned me to putty in his hands.

"You are mine," he growled against my throat. He yanked my head further back, towering over me with a devilish smile. "Do you feel this?" he whispered, pushing me against his hips again. The spark that ran through my body was as sharp and bright as lightning. "That is from *me*. You cannot run from this."

I shook my head. It was too hot. I couldn't breathe...

Dana's hand was over my mouth.

"Shh...shh, Little Lily," he cooed. I started to panic even as my body continued to grind against his. His other hand continued to grope my thigh, keeping it hooked over his hip. The touch had turned cold. "Submit everything to me. You cannot escape."

I couldn't breathe. My eyelids fluttered shut again as I tried to move my mouth away from his hand. It was too hot. The music was too loud. I couldn't *move*...

I opened my eyes, my vision blurry. I was no longer in the club. I was against the side of a building, hearing the thumping of the music in Club Archangel nearby. I tried desperately to regain my senses. I was sweating and light-headed, finding it difficult to keep my eyes open, dizzy and disoriented. My leg was hooked over someone's hip and a hand had slipped under my dress to press fingers into my panties while the other hand remained firm over my mouth.

I forced my exhausted eyes to focus on the boys around me. One had pinned me to the wall as he pressed his body against mine, grinding roughly. All four boys I recognized from the Commission of the People.

"Aw, shit, is she coming to?" Freddie groaned to my right. "Her eyes are open." My heart began racing, knowing, even in my drugged state, that I was going to be raped if I didn't fight back immediately.

"Get the fuck off of me!" I snapped, trying to push Brian away with my weak, useless limbs.

"Ha! She's still pretty feisty!" Lance cackled. "Better tame her quick, Brian."

Panicked, I regained enough strength and coordination to reach for the front of his pants. I felt sick touching him, but I grabbed, twisting my wrist as fast and as far as I could.

Brian cried out in pain and crumbled, falling away, his hands releasing me. I also fell to the ground, my legs the consistency of jelly.

"Holy fuck, dude! Y'alright?!" Justin gasped.

"Fuckin' *bitch*!" Freddie barked, backhanding me. The pain was sharp and tears sprung immediately to my eyes. Before I could see around the pain, another set of hands clasped my ankles, yanking me flat to the concrete in the alley.

"No!!" I screamed, kicking at them and flailing my fists.

"*Fuck*! Hold her still!"

"Excuse me." A calm, cold voice filled the alleyway. My eyes shot open and my breath hitched in my throat. I craned my head to see a tall figure, his eyes bright even in the dim alley lights. Beside him were four men—one I recognized as Sean.

"Mr. Christenson?!" the boys cried, their faces paling as they backed away from me.

"Get them," Dana ordered shortly, his voice disinterested.

The guards descended upon the boys in an instant, Sean included. Lance and Justin jumped up and started running, but that just caused the guards to, quite literally, tackle them to the ground. There were sounds of struggling and pained shouts as Sean and the other men angrily pinned Freddie and Brian to the asphalt.

Dana crouched next to me. His eyes were not compassionate for the situation in which he had found me. I shivered, remembering my strange—hopefully drug-induced—fantasy about dancing with him. I prayed that he had no way to read my mind to see the fantasy for himself.

He tenderly tucked my hair behind my ear, ignoring the way I flinched from his touch.

"Aren't you a fortunate little one?"

He offered me his hand. I stared at it, and then at him. He looked into me with those eyes that could see everything and, before I knew it, my hand was in his and he was scooping me into his arms. I was carried, half-naked, to the limousine parked at the entrance of the alleyway. He placed me in the vehicle before climbing in himself. I hastened to straighten my dress but my fingers were clumsy and I was on the verge of tears as fear of moving from one assault to another consumed me.

"Allow me," Dana said, pinching the hem of my dress and pulling it back down over my hips at an agonizingly slow pace. My breath was stuck in my throat as I watched his hands, anticipating having to fight him off next.

When the dress was straightened, his gaze moved to my face, a dangerous light playing in the golden color. I felt as though I was trapped in a cage with a hungry, wild animal.

"A-Aren't you…going t-to ask me i-i-if I'm okay?"

"No," he said. "I know you're fine."

"Like hell I am!" I snapped, shoving him angrily, though he hardly moved.

"They didn't do anything to you. Not yet, anyway."

"The fuck they didn't!"

"Oh my, what language," he chided playfully.

"Wh-what the hell are you doing here, anyway?! Are you fucking *following* me?!"

"Yes."

I blinked, not expecting a blunt confession. He cocked his head to one side, waiting for my reply, a smirk tugging at his lips.

"What do you *want* from me?" I whimpered.

Dana's face moved closer, stopping mere centimeters from mine. *"Everything."*

My body was frozen, and the longer I remained under the assault of his eyes, the weaker I felt.

"Please…" I whimpered, sobbing. "I want to go h-home…"

"I am going to take you home," he assured. "As soon as Sean gets back."

I could not take comfort in the words—there was no telling how long it would take Sean to get in the car or what Dana would do to me in that time.

"It was probably a date-rape drug," Dana noted, backing away from me to grab a bottle of water from a cabinet in the limo.

"What?" I choked, pushing my tears away with the heels of my hands clumsily.

"The drug they gave you."

"How do you know?"

"That you were drugged?" Dana clarified, breaking the seal on the bottle. "I've seen the signs before."

"On girls *you've* drugged?" I said angrily, though I knew there was very little malice around my blubbering.

"Let me assure you, Little Lily, when I want a woman in my bed, I don't need to use any drug," he purred, his eyes shining with a very intimate light.

He moved the bottle toward me and I reached out. He pulled it away and shook his head, clicking his tongue.

"Oh, no, no, no, Little Lily," he said. "You have no coordination. You would drop this and spill water all over the limo."

Tunnel vision was encroaching as my heart threatened to break my ribs. The only thing keeping me from passing out was Dana's presence and the instinct to never be vulnerable around him.

His eyes locked on mine again, hungry and cruel. He lifted the bottle.

"Tilt your head back and open your mouth."

Every joint and muscle in my body was locked. The car was getting smaller and smaller. There was no escape. The doors were locked and his gaze was powerful enough to paralyze me.

"Come now, Little Lily." He showed me the bottle. "Aren't you thirsty?"

I was very thirsty, but more than anything I was frightened, both to obey and to disobey. Slowly, I tilted my head back and opened my mouth, trembling uncontrollably.

"Open your mouth wider," he said, his voice laced with something that made my shivering worse. My lips parted wider and he moved the top of the bottle to the side of my mouth. I tried not to choke as he poured the water, but as he pulled the bottle away and I dropped my head, droplets ran down my chin and neck, soaking into the front of my dress. His eyes darkened and lit with fire at the same time. He ducked his head to my neck, kissing the trail of water.

I whimpered, unable to move away.

Tears tumbled down my cheeks again as the frightened sobs rose in my throat. "Please don't..."

I closed my eyes, cringing at his lips on my throat. His lips closed over my pulse before planting a long kiss to the underside of my jaw.

I continued to cry, backed against the limo door, trying to put as much distance between us as physically possible in the cramped space.

"Ah," he breathed, "there are those tears again." He moved to my cheek and I tried to turn my head. He kissed the moistened skin. "I want to make more of these."

I nearly leapt out of my skin when the driver's door opened.

"Sir?" Sean said as he climbed into the driver's seat.

"Yes, Sean?" Dana said, backing away. I went limp against the door, lifting my hands to my face, my whole body heaving with silent sobs.

"The boys' names have been taken and we will be sure to contact their parents. The police have also been called. The others are waiting here until the police arrive."

"Excellent." Dana nodded approvingly. He turned to me and I tensed, my eyes wide behind my fingers, fear rocketing through me that he would continue the molestation even with Sean in the car. "We are taking Little Lily home."

"Yes, sir."

Dana did not touch me nor speak to me for the entirety of the drive. Instead, he stared, watching me cry and sob, refusing to let me look away from his gaze. There wasn't a smile on his face, but there was a frightening fire in his gaze that caused my anxiety to triple. I wished my heart would give out right then—it seemed to be the only way to escape him.

He appeared to be fascinated by my crying. He was enthralled, and the more interested he seemed, the more I tried to compose myself. I had pushed my tears away completely and sat straight, holding myself together with every ounce of strength I had within me by the time we had reached the suburban sprawl around Central.

I sat as far away from him as possible, our eyes locked in battle. I wanted to watch the scenery pass, to see how much longer I would be trapped in the limo, but I could not look away.

When we entered my neighborhood, Dana sighed and reached for the cabinet in the limo again, releasing me from the prison of his gaze.

"Here," he said, handing me a mirror and a box of tissues. "Clean yourself up."

I looked at my reflection, not really caring about my appearance after everything I had endured that night. Still, I looked like hell. I removed the runny mascara from my cheeks and did my best to look normal again. His gaze remained observant, as though fascinated. When I was finished, I handed him the mirror and the box of tissues.

"…thank you…" I choked on reflex.

He took the box of tissues first, carelessly placing them back on the top of the cabinet. He then took the mirror, his fingers lingering on mine and sending the cold pangs of fear into my belly again.

We finally pulled up in front of my house.

"Thank you again," I said hurriedly, hoping the forced nicety would prompt him to unlock the doors so I could escape.

"You best be on your guard, Little Lily," Dana whispered. "You are far more delectable than you realize." His hand went to my knee before moving slowly up my leg. I shivered, unable to recoil when his mouth once again went to my neck, kissing my racing pulse.

"But always remember," he breathed. "You are *mine*."

He kissed my pulse again.

"One day, Little Lily, I *will* take you. And you will never be able to escape."

"Sir," Sean said from the front, "curfew is in a half-hour. The bus will be here soon. Her parents will begin to worry."

"You are right," Dana agreed. He backed away, his fingers lingering as his hand left my skin. "Good night, Little Lily."

The doors unlocked and I clambered out of the car. My legs wobbled, threatening to give out from under me on our front lawn. I stumbled my way to the front door and opened it clumsily, falling inside and nearly slamming it shut behind me. When my overwhelmed brain registered that I was home, I stood completely still, listening to the silence, worried that my parents were still awake and would see me in such a disheveled state. I made my way toward the stairs, keeping a careful ear out for any noise. They were so sure I was coming home by curfew that they rarely waited up for me anymore. Hearing the silence of the house was a relief—I could not handle explaining to them what had happened. I needed time to collect myself.

I moved through the living room and ascended the back staircase, turning off the lights as I moved through each room. As I was climbing the stairs, I spotted the light from Mykail's bedroom and turned to his large, barred door. He was sitting on his bed, staring directly at me as I rounded the corner.

I sniffed my tears back and cleared my throat, trying to ignore the way his blue eyes stared at me.

"It's time to sleep now, Mykail," I told him. He continued to stare, unblinking. "Turn off your light and go to sleep," I said, trying to adopt a stern tone. "I mean it, Mykail."

He did not move, his eyes still on me.

I lost my temper.

"What the hell is *wrong* with you?!" I barked. "You just sit there and stare *all day*! Why don't you *say* something?! Why are you being such a *dick*?!" I slammed my hand against the bars and turned away, mostly to hide my cringe from the pain that radiated through my hand.

"I didn't mean to be a dick," he said when my back was turned. I whirled back around, my heart stopping.

"You...you can talk?" I stammered.

"Yes."

"W-why haven't you said anything before?!"

"No one was speaking to me," he answered.

I wrapped my hands around the bars and fell to my knees, at my limit for surprises in one night.

Chapter Nineteen

"This can't be happening…" I whimpered.

Mykail walked to the bars, crouching in front of me.

"I apologize for startling you," he murmured. "But you looked extremely upset. Are you alright?"

I raised my gaze, feeling my cheeks flush. Being so close I was under the full power of his brilliant blue eyes. My heart skipped a beat at the compassionate gaze.

"W-what?"

"I'm sorry I frightened you," he repeated. "I just wanted to…" He trailed off, becoming awkward as well. "I was worried."

The tears overcame me. I tried to hold them back, but the evening had been so horrible that I could not keep my emotions in check.

"It's…fucking *Dana*," I growled, hiding my face in my hands, grinding my teeth against the scream building in my chest.

"Say no more," Mykail said knowingly. "I understand."

"I'm sorry," I sniffed, raising my gaze. "I have no right to talk after what you've been through."

Mykail looked at the ground, his wings ruffling in response. When he looked back at me, he motioned his head into the room.

"Do you want to come in and talk?"

It took me an embarrassingly long time to understand the invitation. My first reaction was to say no, but I didn't want to be alone with my brain constantly replaying the events of that night.

I looked down at myself, mortified to see I was still clad in my alley-dirtied club dress.

"Um…I'm going to change…"

"Okay. I'll be here," he said with an easy shrug.

I smiled, as did he, and pulled myself to my feet, my legs still shaking. I decided against a shower—I might fall and crack my head open. Once in my room, I slipped out of my dress, going into the bathroom and looking in the mirror.

I was embarrassed at the horrible state of my face. I scrubbed hard at my skin, ridding it of the stains of makeup and tears, though it only reddened my blotchy expression.

"What the hell are you *doing*, Lily?" I whispered, staring at my reflection.

I did not know how I rationalized that going into the cage with the "angel" Dana Christenson had given my family was a good idea. In fact, the more I thought about it, the worse the idea seemed. I considered not going back to his door at all…

I concluded that sitting outside the bars of his room and talking would be safer, and would give me time to calm down and process everything that had occurred in the previous hours.

I pulled on my sweatpants and a tank top, checking myself over once more before nervously rejoining Mykail. The shakiness of my legs had ebbed to an exhausted weakness, though I still held a nervous knot in my stomach, embarrassed and worried about discussing the events of the night with someone I hardly knew.

"Lily?" Mykail called as I lingered just beyond his sight. "I can hear you."

I took one more deep breath and stepped closer. He was still sitting by the bars, his heavy wings resting on the floor.

"You look more comfortable," he complimented.

A hot blush rose to my cheeks. His eyes were so warm they made me feel safe, the tender gaze pushing away my anxiety. I lowered to my knees, smiling like an idiot but unable to stop the moronic expression.

"Why haven't you said anything before?" I asked. "What do you mean no one was talking to you?"

"Well, maybe I should say no one was calling me a dick," he teased.

"I'm sorry," I groaned with a cringe. "It's…been a rough fucking night."

"What happened?"

Hesitation flooded through me again. Even knowing he had undergone horrible experimentation at Dana's hand, I was afraid how he would respond to me recounting the events of that night.

When I did not speak for a long time, he nodded back into the room.

"Are you going to come in?"

"Um…I…I don't think that's a good idea," I said, a small part of me worried he was trying to get me in the room to hurt me. Despite his warm demeanor and captivating eyes, I knew I could not trust him—I hardly knew him.

"That's fine. Whatever you feel comfortable with. But I am worried. What happened tonight?"

"A-are you sure you want to know?"

"If that asshole Dana did *anything*, I swear…" he growled, his lip curling in disgust. "Did he hurt you?"

I looked down at my lap, wringing my hands nervously.

"Um…he…well…you know, it's not that big of a deal." I shrugged it off, my nerves getting the best of me. I could feel Mykail's eyes on me, reading every muscle movement and flick of my gaze avoiding his.

"I'm sure that some things are a little embarrassing to talk about, particularly with someone you don't know, but believe me when I say that I will understand. I spent eight months with Dana. I know how he can be."

"What do you mean you spent eight months with him?" I asked. "Is that how long…" I trailed off, my attention focusing on the wings.

"No, the testing only took two months. The other six months were just when he was fascinated by what he had made me into and decided to test the rest of my family the same way."

"Wait, the rest of your family? The same way? He said that you were the only one…like this," I explained awkwardly. "The rest of your family is still in there?"

His gaze turned to the floor.

"I…I'm sorry," I blurted, realizing I was being insensitive.

"No, it's not you," he said. "My older brother is still in the Commission. But my younger brother and sister…they died about two months ago."

"What happened?"

"My young brother died during his testing," he explained. "My sister went into a coma during testing and that *bastard* continued to test on her, even in the coma. And, just like my brothers, when she came to with her wings, she had lost her mind…so they killed her. They wanted to take her apart to see what had gone wrong."

I stared at him, agonized by the immense pain in his eyes and the tremor in his voice. Before I could stop myself, I was reaching forward, my hand resting on his around the bars.

"I'm the only one who was a success…" he completed quietly, his eyes not even lifting when I touched his hand.

"And your other brother?"

"He's still being tested on. He did not fare as well as I did. Last time I saw him, he was almost incoherent…"

"I am so sorry," I whispered, squeezing his hand.

"You have no reason to be sorry," he said. "Out of curiosity, what did Dana tell you about me before he brought me here to live?"

I opened my mouth, unable to find the words at first. I spent several silent moments trying to decide if I should tell him the truth.

I swallowed hard, shaking my head.

"I want to know what he told you," he insisted. "He must have told you why I was taken into the Commission. Please, tell me what he said."

"But, it's Dana. He was probably lying," I evaded.

"That's exactly why I want to know."

"Why? No matter what he said, it doesn't really matter," I avoided gently. "And it will only make you angrier."

"Being angry will help," Mykail said. The bright fire in his eyes was enough to make me back away from the bars. For a brief moment, I was reminded of Dana's eyes in the limo. "I plan to kill Dana."

Everything went very still, an eternity hanging on those few small words.

He smiled darkly, but I was no longer frightened by the expression. I was intrigued.

"I am going to kill that evil son of a bitch. Anything you tell me about what he's done will just fuel me." His grin was terrifying, but I was excited by it, a smile threatening to break across my own face. "Tell me what he told you about me, and then tell me what he did to you tonight."

Even though there was a rational part of my brain screaming at me not to anger Mykail, I wanted to stoke that fire. I, too, wanted to kill Dana, since that seemed to be the only way I would ever be free of his influence.

"He...he told me that you were a homosexual...and that you smuggled drugs across the border."

He blinked at me in shock and then rolled his eyes with a groan.

"He must have been wanting to prove a point," he noted. "What a *bastard*..."

"Is it true?"

"The part about me smuggling drugs is true, yes. But I am not gay."

For some reason, even though I knew he had to be a criminal for the Commission of the People to capture him, Mykail's confession still surprised me.

"You...smuggled drugs?"

"Hard not to when that's the family business," he sneered, his eyes focused elsewhere. I backed away a little, startled by the tone. His eyes softened immediately at my reaction. "I'm sorry, I didn't mean to snap at you."

"No, i-it's fine..." I turned my eyes to the carpet, starting to feel uneasy and awkward.

"What did Dana do to you tonight?"

My heart raced and the fear returned in an instant, but I could not lift my eyes to look at Mykail. The thought of recounting the events aloud was more terrifying than I expected. I felt as if I could make the entire night disappear if I didn't tell anyone, if I never spoke of it again and told myself it was all just a bad dream.

Mykail placed his other hand on mine.

"I understand it's painful, but if you keep it inside and push it away, it will come back to haunt you in some other way," he said. My gaze finally lifted to meet his stunning blue eyes, which were warm and caring—so different from how he had looked only moments earlier. "I'm here to listen."

"I was at the club…" I started, my eyes averting, though I was able to keep my head up. I began to spill the story, finding myself close to tears and hyperventilating when I explained my time in the limo with Dana. Mykail's hand kept me anchored to the present moment. I was unable to finish the story, stifling my sobs in my hand, feeling the same powerless dread wash through me.

His hand reached through the bars and he carefully wiped the tears away from my face. I blinked, my sobbing ceasing in an instant when his warm fingers came in contact with my skin.

"I'm sorry…" I hiccupped. "After everything you've been through…this…this is nothing." I shook my head, mentally slapping myself for thinking that my problems outweighed the torture Mykail had suffered at Dana's hand.

"No, what he did to you is *unforgivable*," he snarled. "No one has a right to treat anyone like that. I don't care if they're a homeless man or Dana fucking Christenson, no one has the right to do that to another person."

"But he *is* Dana fucking Christenson," I groaned. "He can do whatever the hell he wants. Who is going to stop him?"

"Someone will eventually," Mykail said. "Don't you dare give in to him," he said strongly, his eyes locking with mine in a determined stare. "Don't stop fighting him. Because I'm going to kill him one day. But if you give in, he will take you down with him."

I smiled and took his hand in mine.

"You're very together considering everything you've been through," I noted, sniffing back more tears.

"The only thing that keeps me going is the thought of one day killing that son of a bitch."

"Can I help?" I asked, only partially joking.

"After what he did to you, of course you can."

"Mykail…" I started, "he's not going to stop, you know."

Mykail sighed, turning his hand to clasp mine, moving his thumb against my skin. Despite the tenderness of the action, I was startled by how easily his touch soothed my nerves.

"I know," he whispered. "Try to bear up to it. Keep fighting. Don't let him overtake you."

I bit my lip, thinking about the fantasy of dancing with Dana. It was already so easy for Dana to enthrall me and make me a puppet in his hands. I had no idea how I could stay strong against him when all it took was a single glance to set my body on fire.

"What is it?" Mykail asked, studying my conflicted expression.

"Nothing," I said, shaking my head. "I'm sorry, I'm tired."

"Of course," he agreed. "You should get some sleep."

I stood, as did he, but I hesitated outside his barred door.

"Mykail?"

"Yes?"

"Could I ask a favor?"

"What is it?"

"Do you think…I could have a hug?" I chuckled, feeling embarrassed for asking the silly question. He smiled and nodded, stepping back to allow me to open the door.

I reached into my pocket and pulled out the key, slowly turning the bolt so it was as quiet as possible. I was aware of the discipline clicker in my pocket, but was confident I wouldn't need it.

Once I had worked the loud door open enough for me to slip in, I extended my arms. He wrapped his arms around me, securing me in his warm embrace.

It was the best hug I had ever received.

My arms circled his neck, my fingers brushing the feathers of his wings. They were soft and I had to resist a very strong urge to bury my fingers in them.

"Thank you for listening to me tonight," I whispered. "I really needed someone to talk to."

"If you *ever* need to talk, I'll be here."

"Ooh, better be careful about saying that," I laughed lightly, pulling away. "I can complain a lot if I want to."

"I'll listen, but I don't mean just when you have something you want to get off your chest. I mean, even if you just want to talk to someone about anything. I like talking with you. I've been wanting to talk to you for quite some time, but…I wasn't sure how you would react."

I smiled, the hot blush rising yet again to my cheeks. I wanted to stay up and talk to him the rest of the night. But I *was* very tired, and I was starting to feel an interest in him that I needed to ignore. The last thing I needed was to become infatuated with the "gift" Dana Christenson had given my family. I told myself that I was feeling attached to him because I was able to turn to him so quickly after such a traumatizing night.

However, when Mykail leaned forward and kissed my forehead, my heart leapt for joy and I smiled, giddy.

"Please, get some sleep, Lily," he said, my name on his lips sounding like honey. I melted again and turned away so he could not see my blush deepen. I fumbled with the key to lock the door again, accidentally making it louder than I wanted. I threw one last look at him before I went to my room, smiling, my heart thumping against my ribs.

* *** *

"Aren't you a fortunate little one?"

The words scurried up my spine like spiders. I turned to the side of my bed to see Dana, but I did not recognize the room beyond. I was in some foreign bed, nothing distinct about the white walls surrounding us to give indication of where the room was located.

"Wh…where am I?" I barely managed to breathe, unable to sit up no matter how hard I struggled to get out of the vulnerable position.

Dana crawled toward me. My heart thundered as the fire in his eyes revealed his dangerous intentions.

"Where do you want to be?" he asked suggestively, placing one knee on either side of my hips as his hands rested near my shoulders.

He swooped down, kissing me hard. I struggled, trying to get away yet finding no strength as I flailed pathetically on the bed under him.

He sat back on my hips, unbuttoning the jacket of his three-piece suit with slow, deliberate flicks of his fingers. My eyes widened and my panic turned to terror.

"No…"

"I'll sway you," he promised. His hands drifted down his body to rest on his thighs as he looked me over, smiling when he watched my eyes follow the path of his hands. "I told you, Little Lily, you're mine."

"G-get off me." I pushed against his weight, but he just smiled triumphantly, placing one finger against my lips.

"Now, be good," he cooed. "I told you I don't like to share, and since you fucked that angel, I have no choice but to punish you."

"What?" I snapped, my eyes flying wide. "We *didn't*! I swear!"

168

"That's not what he said," Dana sang. "Then again, I guess he would say anything if I inflicted enough pain." He winked. "Why don't we check anyway?"

"No!" I screamed. I started kicking. I felt his large hands on my ribcage, tearing my top away. I screamed louder, my arms and legs flailing, weak and heavy.

Dana started laughing as his hands went to the waistband of my sweatpants.

"No! *No!*" I screeched. "This isn't happening!" I cried. "This can't be happening! You're not here!"

"Feel me, Little Lily," his voice said in my ear as I covered my face, trying to rid my eyes of the scene. "Do you feel this? That is from *me*. You cannot run from this."

"No! No!!"

"Lily?!"

"*No!*"

"Lily! Wake up!"

I snapped awake, sweating and breathless, my eyes moving wildly around the familiar walls of my bedroom to finally rest on my mother, who was sitting on my bed, her hands holding my shoulders as her concerned gaze searched my expression. Dex was at the window, watching curiously.

"Honey, what happened?" my mother asked, pressing her hand to my forehead. "Are you alright?"

It took several deep breaths to get my heart out of my throat. I almost spilled the entire story of the previous night—I *barely* refrained. My parents had been fighting all week about the Commission, Mykail, and the situation we had fallen into. There was no need for me to make the situation even more complicated. Also, I did not want to accidentally let it slip that Mykail could talk and had plans to kill Dana Christenson in case my parents told anyone else.

I shook my head and swallowed hard.

"I'm fine," I lied. "Just…a nightmare…"

"Oh, honey." My mother ran her hand over my hair, her expression softening. "I know that things have been very stressful lately, but, you know, maybe this will work out. We just have to keep thinking positively, right?"

"Right," I responded mechanically, knowing she had no idea how bad things were becoming.

"I was thinking we would all go out for lunch today," my mother said with a wary smile. "Your father found a restaurant he would like to take us to."

"Sure," I agreed, not really processing the suggestion.

"Are you sure you're alright?"

"Yeah, I'm fine," I said too quickly.

She left my room and I let out a long, shaky breath, running my hands through my hair.

I was dreaming about Dana. *Fantastic*.

I got dressed, trying not to think about the nightmare, the night before, or that there was a Commission meeting in twelve short hours. I could feel myself spiraling into a dark place inside my mind that I had never visited before.

Then, I thought of Mykail. He was probably downstairs eating breakfast with the rest of the family as he had the previous few mornings. Thinking of the silent boy downstairs and the conversation we had shared the previous night made a goofy grin creep over my face. I wrapped my arms around myself, remembering the hug…him wiping away my tears…the gentle kiss on my forehead…

That had not been a dream.

What I had felt with Mykail was not an overpowering physical impulse as it was with Dana. What I felt with him was a deeper connection, one that felt sincere and strong. And yet, despite that strength, it was overshadowed by the terrifying power Dana held over both of us.

I took a deep breath, running my hands through my still-tangled hair again. I had to remain calm. I had to find a way out, or I would lose my mind. I could not give in to Dana. I could not let him win.

I glanced at the sketchpad on my desk, covered by my binder and copy of *An Angel Without Wings*. My brain clicked in a profoundly frightening way.

I grabbed my sketchpad and flipped to the drawing of the angel flying above the clouds, holding his banner high.

The position of defiance, of rallying others while dressed in battered armor, suddenly took on an entirely new, powerful meaning.

I glanced at my copy of *An Angel Without Wings* and then back at the picture.

I removed the page from my sketchbook and took a piece of paper from my binder, writing a quick message before sneaking into Mykail's open and vacant room to slip the sketch and message under his pillow, where my mother and father could not see it. I was worried what my parents would think if they saw the message: "Maybe you can lead the next revolution. I'll stand with you."

But I knew Mykail would understand.

Chapter Twenty

Even though my father took us out to lunch and we enjoyed the unseasonably warm weather and good food, it was obvious none of us could get our minds off the impending dread about the meeting that night. My thoughts were a tumultuous mess of fear and confusion. There was so much adrenaline coursing through my veins, I was worried at any moment I would just scream, not caring that we were in the middle of a restaurant.

But every time my mind replayed the events at Archangel, I would remember Mykail's understanding gaze and gentle voice.

Remembering my conversation with Mykail helped me remain composed. I even found a warm blush creeping over my cheeks as I thought about his arms enveloping me in the hug.

"Lily?" my mom called my attention.

"Huh?" I looked up, blinking back to reality.

"Are you sure you're alright?"

"Yeah," I said. "Yeah, sorry, just spacing out. What did you say?"

"Your father might need to go abroad for a meeting with the Prime Minister of the Greater United Kingdom," she said, clearly not convinced that I was alright but not bothering to push the subject. "If we end up having to go abroad, would you be alright in the house alone for a week or longer?"

"Sure." It was not uncommon for my parents to go on long trips and leave me at home. When I was much younger they would take me with them, but when I turned fifteen, they let me stay home alone, knowing I was bored on the political tours and I was capable of taking care of myself.

"That means you would be in charge of Mykail," my father added. "Can you handle taking care of him?"

"I'm sure I can," I said. "Um...has he said anything to either of you?"

"Said anything?" my father repeated.

"No, honey. He doesn't talk," my mother said lightly.

I tried not to question if my conversation with Mykail had only been a dream.

After lunch my mind focused on the rapidly-passing hours before the Commission meeting. My mother asked me to help sort some of my father's papers in an attempt to distract us both, but I spent my time monotonously sorting paperwork trying to convince myself I had *not* imagined my conversation with Mykail the previous night.

Becoming more anxious by the minute, I used the age-old excuse children used to get out of tasks assigned by their parents.

"I'm going to go do my homework."

I stopped at the top of the back stairs, glancing behind me to be sure my parents were not within earshot.

"Karen?" my father called from somewhere in the large house.

"Yes?"

"Where is my tie from Thursday?"

"It should be in your tie drawer!"

I heard her heels move over the hardwood floor to the main stairs.

I hurried to Mykail's door and found him sitting on his bed, staring at the wall, his expression blank with boredom. When he saw me, he stood.

"Mykail," I whispered, "*please* tell me that I did not imagine our conversation last night."

"Of course you didn't imagine it," he said, also keeping his voice low as he approached the bars. I heaved a sigh of relief, leaning my head against the cool metal.

"Lily," he started cautiously, "did you mean it?"

"Mean what?"

"The note." He spoke so quietly that I strained to hear him. Mesmerized by the clear blue eyes, I felt my head nod shakily. He moved his hand through the bars and I placed my hand in his. He squeezed my fingers tenderly, a gentle smile spreading across his face.

"Thank you." Moving slowly so as not to spook me, he pulled my hand through the bars and dropped his head to kiss it.

When his lips left my hand I yearned for them to return. I was desperate to feel something other than fear when someone was close to me, and even the simple kiss had chased away my anxieties in the brief moment his mouth made contact.

"Go," he said. "We'll talk tonight when your parents are asleep."

"Why don't you want to talk to them?"

"I don't really trust them yet," he said with a sheepish shake of his head. "We'll talk tonight."

* *** *

The elevator descended into the basement far too quickly. My stomach was doing so many somersaults I was sure that it would soon knot itself enough to kill me.

There was no avoiding facing Dana again.

The doors slid open and we stepped into the dim hallway, moving into the meeting room already abuzz with conversations.

As we entered, I kept a careful eye out for Brian and the others who had attacked me. It was not until I was searching for them that I wondered what had happened to them once Sean and the others had interfered. Uninvited, the sickening realization that Dana had the power to have those boys thrown into the cells in the back of the Commission rocketed through my mind. I found myself desperately hoping Brian and the others were alright—they may have assaulted me, but no one deserved that cruel fate.

I absentmindedly trailed my parents to our spot, continuing to search for the boys as they struck up conversation with another member of the Commission.

Just as I was getting frantic at not spotting them, Freddie entered the room with his parents and younger sister.

Even though I quickly ducked from his line of sight, I was relieved to see him.

Spotting Clark's mother near the front of the room talking to Sean, I ventured away from my parents, drawing off of every ounce of bravery I had to cross the expanse of the room toward the two adults.

My pace slowed as I approached, waiting to be seen before trying to speak.

"I understand," Mrs. Markus said.

"Dana said to ask if you needed any help," Sean said before turning his gaze to me. "Good evening, Miss Sandover."

"Good evening, Sean."

"Hello, Lily," Mrs. Markus greeted with a warm smile. I could not stop the confusing storm within me, remembering the kind woman was having an affair with the man abusing her son. It was uncomfortable knowing such intimate information about the Markus family. "How are you tonight?"

"I'm doing well, Mrs. Markus, thank you," I lied. "Is Clark alright? I didn't see him last night at Archangel." I tried desperately to keep the tremble out of my voice.

"He's fine," Mrs. Markus assured with a light laugh. "He was very busy with a school project and ended up falling asleep around six. He hasn't slept very much in the last few days, poor thing. I didn't have the heart to wake him for Archangel."

"Is he here tonight?"

"Yes, I saw him with Dana a little earlier," Mrs. Markus answered. "He's around here somewhere."

"Thank you." I started to turn away.

"Lily," Mrs. Markus called. "Thank you for being so good to my son," she said with a sincere smile that brought a twinge of pain in my belly as the hurricane of complicated feelings swelled. "I know he can be a little awkward, but he is a good kid. I can't tell you how relieved I am that he has a friend like you."

The truth about Clark and Dana was on the tip of my tongue, the words threatening to erupt, but I bit them back, understanding that telling her would only complicate things for everyone.

"Thank you," I said awkwardly, turning away to rejoin my parents across the room.

I watched the door and the clock, waiting for Clark—I was desperate to tell him about what happened and my subsequent conversations with Mykail. I hoped Clark would be as thrilled at the idea of an escape from the psychotic man who ran the Commission of the People as I was.

But the doors closed before Clark entered the room.

Mrs. Markus called the meeting to order as my anxiety turned into dread.

"Our leader, Mr. Dana Christenson, has an announcement to start the meeting."

Everyone started clapping and, just like that, Dana appeared from somewhere behind me, his fingers lightly brushing my hair as he stepped through the tables to the front of the room.

Mrs. Markus stepped out of the way as Dana ascended the platform and took his spot at the podium.

"I now give license to start the meeting," he said. "I would like to start with a very important reminder for all of you." He turned to one of the men sitting at the side of the room. "Kenneth, this is *in* the meeting. This *will* go on record."

"Yes, sir."

"Now," Dana started, his voice cold, "I will not mention names or explain what prompted this announcement, but this is something *everyone* in this commission needs to understand. It is our job to keep the population of America content and safe. We achieve this by apprehending criminals and the corrupt." Dana's shaded eyes rested on me. "That does *not* mean that we are exempt from those laws. Recently, there was an attack on one of our younger members by other young members of this commission. These individuals know who they are and the youngsters are going to take responsibility for their actions, but the blame rests with all of you, *especially* the parents.

"You *cannot* allow the children of this commission to become the criminals that we detain. You were all inducted because of your knowledge, experience, and appreciation for the intricacies of our young government. *Do not* make the mistake of thinking that this will keep your children safe from the Commission's laws. If I discover *one* more instance of such behavior, the offending children will be taken into the back and that will be the last we hear of them. Do I make myself clear?"

The room was gripped by a heavy silence.

"Understand that this is not only about the future of the Commission of the People. This is about the future of America. These children are members of one of the most powerful institutions in the world, but that does not mean they can forget what this commission does, and the task it must accomplish.

"Therefore, parents, I order this of you. When you are home with your children, raise them to be upstanding, but *obedient* and *Dana-fearing* children, because I will have no qualms taking your children and turning them into whatever the fuck I want. When they are within these walls they are not your children, they are your colleagues. If they are committing crimes, you are bound by law to report them, just as we are obligated to take them."

The weight of the responding silence grew.

"For example," Dana smiled, his hands holding the sides of the podium as his attention turned to our table, "take a page out of Tommy Sandover's book." The sound of weight shifting on chairs as everyone turned to look at us bombarded my ears. "His older brother harbored criminals over the border for years as part of the group called The Coalition, which some of you may have heard of. Even though they were related, Tommy's family reported him to the Commission, and another threat to our now-stable society was removed."

He began clapping, as if applauding my father for the act when it had been my grandfather who had betrayed his oldest son so cruelly.

More clapping sliced through the silence. Some members of the Commission were genuinely applauding my father, while others were hesitant in the praise, their bodies still tense from Dana's words. My father's shoulders had slumped and his gaze had turned to his lap, trying to hide his discomfort.

"We want the children of the Commission to become future leaders and that means we must weed out those who are not worthy," Dana concluded. "Be sure you all keep that in mind."

Dana stepped off the platform, abruptly ending his speech. Mrs. Markus shook off her stupor and returned to the microphone, her parental concern clear in her features.

"Uh…thank you, Mr. Christenson," she said awkwardly. "Very well, we will get started with the first item…"

I ignored her, as I always did, turning my attention to Clark's empty seat behind me.

Two large hands fell on my shoulders, my terrified gasp catching in my throat.

"If you don't mind, Little Lily," Dana breathed in my ear, "I have something I would like to show you."

Every part of my body screamed not to follow him but his hands guided me out of my seat before claiming my wrist.

"There is something I would like to show Little Lily," Dana explained to my confused parents. "I will bring her right back."

The words eased my mind a little bit—at least he had told someone that I was *supposed* to come back.

Dana brought me through the door at the back left corner of the meeting room that I had never been through before. The hallway on the other side was dark, the sparse lighting barely illuminating Clark as he fidgeted and paced, his eyes cast to his wringing hands.

"Clark!"

I was so relieved to see him that I could not stop myself from rushing forward to hug him. His arms hesitantly went around my back, patting my shoulder stiffly.

I pulled away and opened my mouth, but Dana's voice interrupted me.

"Clark has something to say to you."

Clark drew in a shaky breath, his gaze falling to the ground.

"Lily, I owe you an apology," he whispered. His entire body trembling, he went to his knees, his head bowed. "I…I was selfish, and I left you at Archangel alone last night. Because of that…you were assaulted and nearly raped. I accept full responsibility and understand the pain that you endured because of my carelessness."

He lowered his forehead to the ground, prostrating himself as mortification gripped my bones.

"Stop…"

"I have been thoroughly educated on what you experienced, but if you think…I need more punishment…I understand and accept the punishment."

"What the hell are you talking about?" I asked weakly. "Please, get up."

He did not.

"Clark! *Please!*" I begged. Still, he did not move.

Dana wrapped his strong fingers around my shoulders as I took a step toward Clark, halting my advance.

"I took the liberty of punishing him for you," he breathed against my ear. "But there is no harm in reinforcing the lesson…"

"What the hell did you do to him?"

"Nothing more, nor less, than what happened to you last night," he said. He leaned his head against mine—I could feel that he had taken off his glasses. "Oh, Little Lily, I told you already. You belong to me. I ordered him to protect you and he failed. I could not let that behavior go uncorrected."

"I do not *belong* to you," I said as strongly as I could manage through my trembling lips.

Dana chuckled, the sound causing my skin to crawl.

"Do you feel the power, Little Lily?" he murmured. My body became weak, partially from fear and partially from the exhilaration that tingled along my nerves from his voice. "It's intoxicating, isn't it? Having so much power over someone…" His mouth teased the shell of my ear. "One might even say it's," his hand slid down my arm to my hip, pulling me against him, "*arousing.*"

"Stop," I said, trying to wriggle from his grasp, though my thoughts remained stubbornly consumed with my drug-induced fantasy the previous night.

"*Look* at him," he ordered. "He is humbled at your feet…completely at your mercy. Don't you have the urge to abuse him? Just a little bit?"

"N-no…" I had no urge to hurt Clark. He could not have stopped what happened at Archangel even if he had been there. I was not about to punish Clark for *my* inattention and the other boys' malicious intents, even with the urgings of Dana Christenson running down my spine.

"Really?" Dana challenged. "You don't want to use this power? You know he can't do anything to fight back. You are in complete control."

I tried to turn away from Clark, who still had not moved, but Dana's hand was firm on my chin. I closed my eyes against the frightened and frustrated tears, determined not to let Dana see me cry. He had seen too many of my tears already. I refused to give him the satisfaction yet again.

"Open your eyes," Dana snapped. Reluctantly, I obeyed when his strong fingers dug into my jaw. "That's it. See the power you have, Little Lily? You could kick him right now and he wouldn't fight back. Don't you want to see how far you can push him until he begs for mercy?"

"No."

"I know, you want to see how it feels to dominate someone."

"No…"

"You want to feel someone's life," his other arm wrapped around me, "in your hands. You want to hear their cries…see their tears…"

"No…I-I *don't*."

My head was spinning. I wanted to turn back time. I tried to remember how I felt my first day in Central, when I met Becca and how happy I was to have a new friend. I wanted my new school to be my biggest concern. But unlike my classmates, I was fighting to keep my sense of autonomy, trying not be swept up in Dana's frightening storm of torment and power. I could not allow myself to fall under the spell to which so many in the Commission had already succumbed.

"You want to feel that power rushing along your nerves. I know you do," Dana cooed, holding me tighter. "You must have *some* idea what to do with him."

"Please…*p-please*…let me go…" I whimpered.

"Don't be afraid of it, Little Lily…Succumb to it."

"Please…don't make me do this." I needed to run. I needed to get out of the basement. I needed fresh air…I felt sick…

"Lily," Clark's voice pierced through some of the fog in my brain, "…I understand that what I did was unforgivable."

"Clark, stop!"

"I will accept my punishment."

"Stop it! Please! Don't say things like that!"

"Listen to him, Little Lily. He's willing…"

"I won't do it!" I nearly screamed, hoping the adults in the meeting room would hear.

"You will," Dana breathed before kissing my temple, his lips grazing my skin as he said, "I know you will."

"I…I am n-not your…goddamn toy." There was no bite in the statement. My throat was constricted, making it almost impossible to breathe. "I won't…I won't let you do this to me."

"Do what to you?"

"I…I am not like the others…i-in the Commission…"

Dana chuckled.

"Of course you're not, Little Lily. Why do you think I like you so much?"

"I-I won't…let you manipulate me," I near-sobbed, trying to will him to release me as all my physical strength drained away.

"But I told you," he said, "you are in control. Go ahead…take control. Make him pay."

"Lily, you can punish me…"

"Stop it!"

I melted from Dana's grip, crumbling to the floor in a shivering heap as I tried to keep the hallway from closing in on me. My sobs choked me, my body jerking, but I refused to let my tears flow, acutely aware of Dana's lingering eyes.

Desperate for any relief, I dragged myself to the nearest wall, sitting against it in the hopes it would provide some stability.

My eyes fell on Clark, who was still on all fours, though he had looked up when I had fallen, his gaze apologetic. I stared at him, unable to catch my breath no matter how I gulped in air. The tears started blurring my vision but I angrily blinked them away.

I refused to cry.

Clark started to crawl toward me, but Dana's foot lifted in front of the younger man's face, effectively stopping his advance.

Dana stared down at me with his unnaturally-colored eyes, making it even harder to draw in a full breath around my fear.

He lowered his foot and took a step before crouching and placing a hand against my face. I flinched from the touch as if it burned.

"I didn't get any tears from you tonight." Dana held my eyes in his cold stare. "Good. We're making progress."

He stood, plucking his glasses from his lapel pocket as he turned on his heel and left me and Clark alone in the hall.

Even after the door had closed behind him, we remained still, the anxiety and fear lingering. The dam finally broke as I let out a sob and curled around my knees, trying to keep myself from splintering apart.

Clark's hand on my shoulder forced me to uncurl as his arms secured around me. I threw my arms around him.

"I'm sorry!" I gasped. "I'm so sorry!"

"It's okay…don't be sorry…" I could hear the tears in his trembling voice. I held him tighter. "*I'm* sorry. I know I pushed you. I was just trying to get him to stop."

"What does he *want*?" I hiccupped.

Clark's arms tightened around me, but he did not answer.

* *** *

Clark and I were only present for the final five minutes of the meeting, which meant we received a lot of strange looks upon our return. Some of the Commish Kids were making no effort to hide their suggestive expressions, which only made me feel worse.

I sat at my table, forcing myself to smile at my parents as though nothing was wrong. I avoided turning my eyes toward Dana, who was positioned to the side of the room, watching the meeting with his usual hawk-like intensity.

"To wrap up the meeting, we would like to report that Gregory Altereye and his men, who, you will remember, have now been in space for two and a half years, have sent us tentative reports of finding other planets that could possibly sustain human life."

Everyone in the Commission of the People gasped in awe and excitement. I would have been excited as well if my brain had not numbed from over-stimulation.

"As we get more detailed information, we will let you know what we find," Mrs. Markus concluded. "And, with that, I believe we're finished for the evening."

She closed the meeting and everyone gathered their belongings to leave. However, as happened after all Commission meetings, friends gathered and socialized, talking about work or something that they were planning to do over the course of the following week. I turned to Clark, who motioned me closer.

"Are you alright?" he whispered. I nodded, even though we both knew otherwise.

"What is he doing right now?" I asked, not daring to look in Dana's direction.

Clark's eyes flicked over my shoulder.

"He's in the same group as your parents," he answered. He placed a hand on my shoulder again and asked me once more if I was alright.

"I guess so," I said. "I am so sorry about what happened."

"Don't be," he said. "I pushed you, I just..." He looked away, embarrassed. "I just didn't want him to keep tormenting you like that. I wasn't sure when it was going to stop." He dropped his voice even further. "You know, if you had just done something, it would have ended sooner."

"I don't care," I said strongly. "I could never live with myself if I hurt someone just because I was pressured into it."

Clark gave my shoulder a squeeze.

"You're a much stronger person than I am, Lily."

"You would have done the same for me, right?"

"I hope I would have your same strength," he said honestly. "Of course, I would never *want* to harm you, but...I don't know how much of Dana's pressure I could withstand."

I nodded, satisfied with the answer.

"Is he still talking with my parents?" I asked, casting a wary glance around us. He looked up discreetly and nodded. "We don't *have* to put up with this, you know. We can find a way to stop it."

"That's dangerous talk. *Treasonous* talk."

"I know, so let's not discuss it here. How do I get in contact with you?"

Clark glanced up yet again at Dana and his gaze hardened. My heart leapt at the subtle change. The look told me everything I needed to know. Mykail and I would need help, and Clark, with the inside knowledge gained from his years in the Commission, would know invaluable information about Dana that could help us fight against him—maybe even kill him.

"I know where you live," Clark said. "I will come over tomorrow."

"Okay."

"Are you *sure* you're alright?" he said once final time.

"I'll see how I feel tomorrow. It's a little hard to think right now."

"Clark?" a voice called from across the room. We both saw his mother motioning for him.

"Tomorrow," he promised. I took a deep breath, trying to steady myself as he walked away, and then turned toward my parents, who were still in discussion with Dana.

"Then would you recommend her for the Commission?" Dana inquired. I stood as far away from Dana as I could, feeling my heartbeat race when I got too close. Despite what I had already endured that night, I felt proud that I was able to even stand that close to the leader of the Commission. My mask was strong enough that my parents didn't even notice my gaze refusing to lift to Dana. I supposed Clark had also perfected hiding his fear to keep his family from seeing how much anxiety he endured in Dana's presence. Either that, or our parents had to ignore the warning signs of our abuse because they were just as trapped as we were, and had to hold on to what they could of their sanity within the Commission of the People by pretending all was well.

"She is a very intelligent woman, and she has been a great help to me," my father said nervously. I was thrilled to see that he was hesitant in recommending another person to be inducted into the Commission of the People. He had not been put under Dana's spell yet, and still found the practices in the Commission horrific.

"Karen, I was just telling Samantha here about your wonderful imagination for charity events," a woman said excitedly, approaching my mother and diverting her attention. The woman turned to Dana. "Oh, please forgive me, Mr. Christenson. I did not mean to interrupt."

"No trouble." He nodded, giving silent permission for my mother to leave the conversation. I watched her be pulled away, worried that someone was going to distract other members of the group and leave me alone with Dana once again.

"We already know all that," Dana laughed, as if scolding my father for saying something foolish. "I was wondering what you thought about her ability to be a part of this commission in the broader sense. She knows much about border control, being from so far north, and we have been having difficulties with illegals along that northern border trying to flee civil war in Canada."

"I am not sure," my father said. "Mrs. Davis might not be able to handle certain aspects of the Commission…"

I blinked, surprised to hear Becca's mother brought up as a potential candidate.

Dana looked at his hands, fiddling with his pocket watch pensively.

"I see…" he said. "Well, that is a shame…poor woman. Her husband is such a well-known philanderer that she must be desperate for *some* sense of belonging and purpose."

My father started a bit, as did I. I was, once again, unsure if Dana was telling the truth or if he was trying to get under our skins—then again, Dana had *truths* that got under my skin.

"I was not aware…"

"Oh, yes, the poor thing," Dana confirmed, though the words passed like acid on his lips. "She really should have someone to take care of her. She works so hard at what she does, and she is quite brilliant, it seems wrong to have her do all the work in her private life, as well, with such little reward."

There was something about the sentence that made a disgusting shiver run through my body.

"Dana," Sean said, walking to Dana's side and leaning in to whisper something.

"Very well," Dana said with a nod. He turned to us. "If you will excuse me."

Without another glance, he swept out of the room by the door near the platform, Sean in tow. I relaxed, not realizing the tension that had claimed my muscles for such a prolonged period of time. My father offered me a wobbly smile, which I forced myself to return.

"Are you alright?" he asked. "You look a little pale."

"I'm fine," I said before I could stop myself. "Just tired."

"I agree. It's late. Let's go home."

I told my parents Clark was coming over to help me with a project for school once we got home, but they were so exhausted they just said "fine" and wished me good night.

I walked to the back stairs, hoping to hear them go upstairs, too.

To my misfortune, they stayed in the kitchen. I heard my mother rustling around in the cabinets as I ascended each stair slowly. When I reached the top, I sat, listening. For a few minutes, I heard nothing other than my mother walking across the kitchen and pulling out a chair at the table.

"What are we going to do, Thomas?" she said, her tone defeated.

"I don't think there is anything we can do," my father muttered. "We're in for life."

"This is insane," my mother breathed. "You heard Dana tonight. The kids are starting to commit crimes against one another and he wants us to turn in *children* so that he can experiment on them. There has to be something we can do to get out of this. Maybe...maybe we can call the media—"

"Are you out of your *mind*?" my father snapped. "That's treason. Do you have any idea how quickly Dana would stop that from getting out before hauling *our* asses in as experiments? It's too risky. We have to remember that Dana is the most powerful man in America apart from Leader Simon. We have no idea how extensive his network is, or the extent of his power."

"So, the only thing to do is accept it..." my mother whispered. She was silent for a long moment. "Why do you think he has such an interest in our family?"

"...I don't know..." my father admitted. "My biggest concern is Lily. We don't want her to become the victim of the other children in the Commission."

I stood and peered around the corner into Mykail's room only to come face-to-face with him, startling me so much I had to clamp a hand over my mouth to keep from screaming. He held up his hands peacefully.

"Sorry," he whispered. "It seems all I do is startle you."

I took a few deep breaths before lowering my hand and shaking my head strongly.

"What do we need to do to take that son of a bitch down?" I hissed. "Because I am not putting up with Dana's shit any longer."

Chapter Twenty-One

Mykail insisted that we talk after my parents went to bed, telling me to set an alarm for two-thirty in the morning. Desperate to pass the time, I took a long shower, thoroughly washing my face and brushing my teeth, going through my bedtime routine methodically. But even when the routine was finished, I remained in the bathroom for another half-hour, staring in the mirror, scrutinizing the imperfections on my face. I hardly realized what I was doing until I became irritated at being unable to change my appearance in the short hours before going to Mykail's door.

I could deny it all I wanted, but I knew I had a small crush developing for Mykail. I had never bothered to worry about my appearance for a boy before, and the realization that I wanted to look beautiful for Mykail was enough to make my blood run cold. I stared at my hands on the bathroom vanity, trying to slow the swell of feelings within me. My situation was dangerous enough—the last thing I needed was to develop feelings for someone with whom I was plotting treasonous acts.

Even though I tried to sleep, my alarm meticulously set, every time I closed my eyes I could feel Dana's icy gaze on me. A few times I even leapt out of bed for fear that he was looming over me. His influence was working deep under my skin, making sure I would never feel safe again, even in my own bedroom.

I ended up tossing and turning until my alarm sounded, convinced that Dana was going to emerge from the shadows at any moment. I could still feel his breath on my ear, his strong fingers around my shoulders, his words of domination and power…

The shrill call of the alarm made me launch across my bed to silence it. I could make out a faint glow under my door coming from Mykail's bedroom. I kept my hand on the doorknob, drawing in a few calming breaths before cautiously stepping into the carpeted hallway and to the other side of Mykail's barred door. He was waiting patiently, seated on the floor, his heavy wings causing his shoulders to droop as they rested on the floor behind him.

He smiled as I sat in front of him and I could not help but grin goofily back.

"What brought on this sudden revolutionary spirit?" he asked.

"I cannot put up with Dana anymore."

"Did he attack you again?"

"It's not just me he's attacking. He's also attacking Clark."

"Who's Clark?"

"Another kid in the Commission, like me. And also like me, Dana likes to…" I trailed off with a dismissive wave of my hand.

"Likes to what?"

"Uh…" I tried to think of a delicate way to elaborate. "T-test our limits?"

"You mean molest and abuse you?" Mykail corrected. I nodded, looking at my lap, unable to quell the embarrassment at the severe words. "I see…seems Dana is grooming the younger members so they'll be completely obedient from a young age."

I cleared my throat. "Clark…actually wants to help us."

"You *told* him?"

"He knows more about Dana than I do. Probably even more than you do," I defended. "He can help form a plan."

"It's good that he has inside knowledge," Mykail admitted, "but I bet even he doesn't know what we need to pull this off."

"Then…what do you plan to do?"

"I'm trying to figure out the best course of action," he said. "Even if we manage to kill Dana, it wouldn't mean the Commission of the People would stop doing what it's doing. His death could be seen as an act of terrorism, not revolution, and the Commission could become more solidified in its ways if this is done poorly."

"So we would have to expose the Commission of the People so they don't *let* it solidify," I deduced. He nodded. "How the *hell* do we do that?"

"We would have to do it in one shot. That is all we will have," he said. "We would have to make a big spectacle to bring a lot of attention and make sure the Commission can't explain it away. We would have to flood the media with the truth about what the Commission does with those they capture. We are going to need a lot more people and many more experiments to show the true horrors of the Commission."

"Like the experiments Dana gives to members of the Commission?"

"No, not the gifts," Mykail said quickly. "The gifts are given because they are easily controlled by Dana, and they don't have any ideas about bringing down the Commission. They're obedient. Otherwise, Dana wouldn't let them out of the Commission lab."

"Wait…" Something stabbed the side of my mind. "What about *you*? You're not obedient to Dana."

"But I'm quiet," he said with a shrug. "And Dana knows I hate him, but…" He looked away, his eyes troubled as he looked back at his wings. "He knows that I can't do anything on my own."

"If it means getting rid of Dana and stopping the Commission, I'll help you. And Clark will help, too."

"You *must* be careful about talking to others about this," Mykail warned. "If you start spreading the word, those loyal to Dana might pretend to help only to expose our plans to him. Same with the experiments."

"But how would we even expose the experiments to the people?"

"We break them out."

I blinked at him stupidly, my mind needing several extra seconds to process the words.

"*How?!*"

"I...haven't gotten that far, yet," Mykail said with a sheepish smile. "I really only know a few in the Commission. I don't know who in the experiments could be trusted and I don't know which of the more powerful ones would be able to help us break others out."

"Do you know any of them?"

"Not really. There are a few I know the names of through rumor...like Eina."

"Eina?!" I gasped, placing the name with the memory of the young man strapped to the experimentation table during our tour of the Commission labs.

"Do you know of Eina?"

"Yes." I nodded quickly. "We saw him our first night at the Commission. Dana was talking about that ultimate weapon project..."

"The Machine of Neutralization?" he asked. "You certainly know a lot about the inner workings of the Commission lab already."

"That first tour was very in-depth," I grumbled.

"Eina is definitely the first one they've had this much success on, and who knows how much further they will go with that project. I don't know much about the project other than how often they yank Eina into the lab."

"Think he would want to expose the Commission?"

"I don't know," he said. "Don't get me wrong. It's well known through the Commission that Eina hates Dana more than anyone else on the planet. But all the security around him would make breaking him out more difficult. He is Dana's pride and joy, so he is protected extensively." Mykail's eyes were cast to the floor, pensive. "I don't know that it's worth the risk. It might be better to start with the experiments in Ward Seven and Ward Eight."

"Wards?"

"The Commission experiments are divided up into ten wards depending on the success of their testing and how dangerous they are.

Wards One and Two are the ones that did not have great success, and are going through final tests before the Commission kills them. Wards Three, Four, and Five are where the gifts come from. They were successful tests, but they are docile and some look at Dana like he's some kind of god that gave them superpowers."

"Some of the experiments actually *like* Dana?"

"Some of them worship the ground he walks on," he said with an exasperated roll of his eyes. "That is why I'm hesitant to ask any of the gift experiments."

"Which ward were you in?" I asked meekly, trying not to picture Mykail's face behind the glass of one of those stark, white cells.

"I was in Ward Five," he answered. "I am a little stronger than the experiments in the gift wards. Originally, I was in Ward Seven but I was eventually moved to Ward Five."

"Why *did* Dana move you to a gift ward?" I asked nervously. "He said he was reluctant to…give you away…" The words stumbled out of me as disgust seeped into my bones.

"I'm not sure," he said. "I guess he wanted to give you a gift that would show his favor toward your family." Mykail wrapped one hand around a bar of his door, his smile touching his eyes and making my heart leap. "But I'm glad that he did. It's been a while since I have felt so comfortable with anyone." He offered his hand to me through the bars. "I can't tell you what it means to me, Lily…having someone to talk to after so long alone in those cells."

My heart knocked against my ribs, flustered. My hand was in his before I could realize what I'd done. We were silent as we held the other's hand, the bars between us, a furious blush setting my face alight.

"You're a good person, Lily," he said. "I feel very comfortable with you. And I really like talking to you."

I had to drop my head as my smile grew and my heart picked up pace.

"Even though…" I started, my voice quivering. "Even though I hate what the Commission has done to you, and I want nothing more than to be able to give you your normal life back…I am glad to have met you, and that you were strong enough to keep your sense of self even after everything you've been through."

Mykail looked surprised. I could feel my panic rising that I had said something wrong when he leaned forward, stretching his hand through the bars again to rest his fingers against my cheek. My flush grew hotter as I stared dumbly at him, not sure how to react.

"Thank you for saying that."

Finally unable to handle the embarrassed thundering of my heart and flustered by the giddiness within my chest, I leaned back, mourning the loss of his touch when his fingers retreated.

His face fell as he drew his hand back to his side of the bars.

"Lily," he said hesitantly, "are you sure you want to do this? Do you really want to go against Dana?"

"Of course I do. Don't you?"

"Of course. But it's going to be extremely dangerous. Once we start planning…"

"I know," I said. "But if we get others to help, I think we'll find more and more allies. And if we can break out experiments, we can expose the Commission easier. Although I guess we'll have to find a way to hide them until we can expose them to the media. And in planning that, we'll have to be sure anyone who helps us won't expose the plan to Dana. And then—"

"Slow down," Mykail laughed. "If Clark is as close to Dana as you say, he'll probably have ideas that can help us form a plan. Has he been with the Commission long?"

"I think so. He's the son of one of Dana's personal advisors."

"Wow, he *is* close to Dana." Mykail's face pinched in confusion. "I don't recall ever hearing about Clark around the Commission…But he probably knows a lot about the other Commission families and who would be willing to entertain these treasonous plans. Getting support from within will probably be crucial."

He looked me over, his eyes brightening with an idea, but the light dimmed and his shoulders slumped.

"What?" I asked.

"Never mind, it's too dangerous."

"What is?"

"I was just trying to think of ways to get more information on experiments in the Commission."

"Tell me." I was willing to take any measures needed to take Dana down, and if that meant I had to do something dangerous, then I would—after all, we were already talking about treason.

He hesitated again.

"I was going to say that you could work your way into Dana's inner circle and then you might have access to the labs. Once there, you can look for a means to get the experiments out and maybe decide what experiments would be best for exposing the Commission's cruelty."

"I might be able to do that."

"Dana is too unpredictable. It would be dangerous to try and get closer to him. Especially if he's already so abusive to you."

I tried to think of how Dana would react if I showed more interest in the experiments. If I asked for a tour, he would likely get suspicious—or he would become even more enthusiastic. It was impossible to predict his reaction.

"I'll do it," I said with a definitive nod.

"No, it's too risky. It will just give him more opportunities to attack you."

"I'll take the chance as long as we can get some information out of it," I insisted. "I'll just keep in mind that we're doing this for a reason. It's a means to an end."

"There is no need to put yourself in that kind of danger. We'll think of something else."

"All of this is already dangerous. If this doesn't work out and we get caught, we're dead. Either way, the risk is huge. So we're going to have to gamble a bit if we want to make this work."

Mykail smiled, shaking his head.

"You are very strong…Alright, but if there is *any* sign that things are getting worse, you stop immediately."

"Deal."

"If you want to get close to Dana, you'll have to take it slow," he advised. "Dana will know you've got ulterior motives if you're too forward."

"I know," I said. "I figure maybe if I just show enough interest and ask the right questions, he'll offer information on his own."

"Perfect. And once we can break experiments out, we'll need a place to hide them. Do you know of any abandoned areas in the city? Like an abandoned building we could use as some kind of base?"

"No. I haven't been here long enough. But we can ask Clark. He's coming over tomorrow."

"Tomorrow?" Mykail repeated. "Did you tell him I was willing to help take down the Commission?"

"Um…no," I said sheepishly. "We were in the Commission room and couldn't really talk about it too much. I didn't know if anyone was eavesdropping."

"You shouldn't have talked about it in the open!" Mykail gasped, his eyes wide. "That's like entering a tank full of sharks with an open wound."

"I know," I defended strongly. "I don't need to be lectured. We were careful."

His eyes softened.

"I'm sorry," he said. "I didn't mean to lecture…I just…if you were caught, you would be taken to the labs and tested on. I couldn't bear the thought of that."

"…I know, but I'm being careful," I said, deflating. I shifted uncomfortably, clearing my throat to diffuse the tension. "So…you think we need to expose the Commission through the media?"

"I think we need to walk the experiments on the streets and have live broadcasts so we can show people exactly what the Commission does to its prisoners," Mykail elaborated. "The problem will be organizing all that in a way that will still take Dana by surprise. The Commission will scrub any report unless it's live."

"We could organize something around a big event that would already have a lot of media exposure. Like one of the parades."

"That's what I was thinking," he said. "We could also have to have some of our own secretly filming to post on the internet to reach as many people as possible. Even if the videos get taken down, the more that people see the experiments, the better chance we stand at dismantling the Commission."

Stifling a yawn in my hand, I nodded. "We can ask Clark for more ideas about upcoming parades."

"You should get some sleep," Mykail said with a tender smile. "We can talk more tomorrow."

"I'm alright." Despite my exhaustion, I was certain the hallucinations of Dana standing at my bedside would make it impossible to rest. "I haven't been able to really sleep lately, anyway…"

He stared at me for a moment and then cleared his throat, averting his eyes.

"If…if you want, I can stay by your side until you fall asleep," he offered. "I know what it's like…you know…to always be afraid. Sometimes having someone else close helps."

Yet another confusing wave of emotions reared in my chest. A part of me still wasn't sure I could trust Mykail, despite our treasonous discussions. But even through the glimmer of doubt, it was comforting to think of someone else being in the room, someone able to confirm that the undulating shadows were *not* Dana Christenson.

Still feeling the heat of embarrassment in my face, I stood from my kneeling position and slipped into my room, grabbing the key to Mykail's door off my desk. When he saw me reappear with the key, he stood, obviously startled that I had returned.

I moved the lock slowly, hoping to minimize the sound and hide my nervous trembling.

"I'm trusting you, Mykail."

"Thank you," he said. "I promise, I would never do anything to hurt you."

My heart thundering and a nervous smile threatening to split over my face, I opened the door. Even though Mykail had been allowed to roam the house, as the door swung open his presence felt different. I felt self-conscious as I led him the short distance to my room, hyperaware of how close he walked. I set the key back on my desk and turned to him, an endearing feeling overtaking the others when I saw he had stopped in my doorway, waiting for further invitation.

"You can come in."

His step was hesitant, glancing around my room, unaware of my racing pulse as he drew closer. Dex lifted his head and hissed, something he had done every time he saw Mykail.

"Just ignore him," I said, waving absentmindedly at the cat as Mykail eyed him warily. My legs were trembling as I passed Mykail to close my bedroom door. I felt Mykail's eyes follow me as I did so and I tried to gather even more courage as I turned to face him when the door was closed.

We stared at one another, awkward and nervous.

"Can I..." I took a shaky step in his direction, faltering when I saw him tense. "Sorry, I just...would it be okay if I touched your wings?"

Though his hesitation was evident, he nodded, turning so I could see the profile of his wings. Stepping closer, I rested my hand on the feathers, flinching when they lifted in response to my touch. The feathers were impossibly soft.

"Are they heavy?"

"Very," he answered. "Took me a long time to learn how to balance, especially when they're moving."

"You can really fly?"

"I love flying," he said, his eyes brightening. "It didn't matter how hard it was to learn the coordination, once I was in the air..." He shook his head, unable to find the words.

My fingers continued to brush over the feathers, tracing the edge of the wing until they were wrapped around the long flight feathers, marveling at the softness. As my hand drifted lower, releasing the feathers, Mykail's hand reached back, gently taking mine as he turned to face me. I watched his fingers tighten around mine as he lifted our hands between us.

I turned to his bright blue eyes.

"You're not afraid?"

My head was shaking before I could sort out the feelings within me.

With a relieved smile, he brought our hands higher, tenderly squeezing my fingers as his thumb passed back and forth over my skin. His eyes held mine, mesmerizing me, holding me captive as I began to wonder if he would lean forward and kiss me.

He did not. His fingers squeezed my hand again as he guided me to the bed, lifting the covers. Blushing and smiling like an idiot, I followed his guide, trying to quell the fluttering in my chest at the thought of him lying in bed with me. I cursed my hormones for making my blood run hot at the idea.

I slid under the covers as he pulled them over me, sitting next to me and taking my hand again.

"Sleep well, Lily."

"You'll stay until I fall asleep?"

"Yes." His thumb began stroking my hand again as one of his wings lowered over me, the weight comforting. "I'll stay until you fall asleep."

Chapter Twenty-Two

I woke with a start from a dreamless sleep, my eyes darting around the room as I tried to orient myself. A swirl of relief and embarrassment grew within me as I saw the numbers on my bedside clock read eight-thirty. I had slept through the night but had only fallen into a deep sleep with Mykail standing guard. I ran a hand through my hair, my fingers catching on the tangles as I fought the smile trying to take over my lips.

I extracted myself from the blankets and crept to Mykail's door, trying to peer around the corner to spot him before he could see me. Mykail was fast asleep on his bed, his peaceful face and draped wings contrasting with the severity of the bars on his door.

I was tempted to open the door, seeing it was still unlocked, so I could thank him—and possibly get a closer look at his sleeping features—but I could already hear the sounds of my mother cooking breakfast. I could not risk her catching me sneaking into Mykail's room.

Giving him a long, appreciative look, wanting to throw my arms around him and thank him profusely, I reluctantly returned to my room to dress. Remembering that Clark was coming over and that I could not spend all day in my pajamas, I pulled on jeans and a blouse, running a brush through my hair as my eyes flicked to the makeup on my vanity.

I shook my head of the thought, roughly pulling my hair into a ponytail as I wondered why I was suddenly so concerned with my physical appearance. It was uncomfortable thinking about wanting to make myself up just so Mykail might think I was beautiful. It was jarring to think that my first real crush could change me so drastically.

I joined my parents downstairs, where my father was reading something on his phone at the breakfast table while my mother was cooking.

"Good morning, Lily," my mother greeted when she caught sight of me. "Have any plans for today?"

I sat in my seat at the table, trying to act nonchalant. "Clark is coming over to help me with that project."

"Oh, right, you mentioned that," she said distractedly.

"What project?" my father prompted. I attempted to hide my fumbled answer behind a tired sigh.

"It's for J.A.N.E.," I said. "A presentation-type thing."

"Are you enjoying that book?"

"It's interesting so far. But we're still not very far into it."

"What time will Clark be over?" my mother asked. "I was going to go grocery shopping. But if you're busy, I'll just take your father."

He hung his head. "You know I *hate* grocery shopping."

"Oh, surely a strong, strapping man like you can handle carrying grocery bags for your loving wife," my mother teased, kissing him on the head as she placed a mug of steaming coffee in front of him.

"Well, when you put it like that…" He turned his playful grin to me and winked.

Had we still been in the Western Region, their behavior would have been our comfortable normalcy. But the behavior following the defeated discussion the previous night was unnerving. It felt as though they were blatantly ignoring the terrors of the Commission looming over us—as though they had accepted it just like everyone else.

"I'm not sure when Clark will be here," I said. "Maybe around ten?"

"Sounds like you're coming with me, Tom," my mother jeered, plating the scrambled eggs. "Breakfast is almost ready. Lily, will you go and wake Mykail?"

I tried not to hurry to the stairs in fear of raising suspicion, and even when I reached his door I hesitated, just to be sure that my parents didn't think I was *too* eager to go to Mykail's room.

Mykail stirred when I opened the door, lifting his head before his sleepy eyes slid shut again and he let out a groggy sigh. With an endearing smile, I stepped to his bedside and placed a hand on his shoulder.

"Mykail?"

His eyelids fluttered and he groaned, pushing his face further into the pillow in childlike defiance.

"Come on, breakfast is almost ready."

With a huff, he pulled his face away from the pillow and blinked, a tender smile gracing his lips.

"Good morning. Did you manage to get some sleep?" he asked, his voice rough. I tried to will away the blush staining my cheeks.

"I did," I said. "All thanks to you."

"I'm just glad you were able to rest." He inhaled deeply, his wings stretching as he reached under his pillow. "Your key." He extracted the small key and placed it in my palm.

I tried not to shudder at the warmth of his fingers as they touched my palm. Despite my giddiness, I was also quickly becoming irritated with the teenage hormones ruling every moment with Mykail.

"Breakfast is almost ready," I told him again, pocketing the key. Heaving himself upright, Mykail stretched, his wings nearly spanning the length of the room. I held the door open for him, watching him pass, my heart dropping when I saw the cuffs on his wings and the cuts that his stretching had lanced open.

I followed Mykail as he stepped into the kitchen, greeted easily by my parents. He bowed his head in silent answer, and I found myself hesitating when I remembered Mykail saying he did not trust my parents enough to talk to them—perhaps he was feeling the same apprehension about their apparent acceptance of the Commission of the People.

We ate our mostly-silent breakfast in the dining room. I could feel that my parents wanted to say something to break the silence, but the only topics they could think of had to do with the Commission. Every time they opened their mouths to speak, I tensed and they would deflate.

Around nine-thirty, as I was helping my mother clear the table, the doorbell rang. Being close to the door, my mother answered.

"Clark," she greeted, inviting him inside with a wave of her hand. I shot Mykail a discreet smile.

"I am sorry for coming over unannounced, Mrs. Sandover," Clark greeted. "I hope I'm not disturbing you."

"No, not at all," my mother said. "Lily told us you were coming over."

Clark looked at me, and I could see hesitation in his eyes. I gave him a smile to reassure him.

"Looks like I caught you at the end of breakfast," Clark said apologetically, turning back to my mother. "I'm so sorry. Is there anything I can do to help?"

"You're such a sweetheart." My mother grinned broadly. "No, that's alright. You and Lily go do what you need to do."

I looked at Mykail and then at my mother.

"Do you want me to put Mykail back?" I asked, trying to think of a way to get him back upstairs to include him in the conversation.

"Oh, no, Lily. Let him stay out here for a while longer. He has been cooped up in the room too long. I'll put him back when we leave, alright?"

Trying not to look as though I was silently communicating with both Mykail and Clark, I motioned for Clark to follow me to my room. I closed the bedroom door as Clark rounded on me.

"What did you tell them I was coming over for?"

"I just told them you were coming over here to work on a school project for J.A.N.E.," I defended.

His shoulders slumped, turning my desk chair as I motioned for him to sit. He took the seat heavily as I plopped down on my bed facing him.

"I'm sorry," he muttered, rubbing his face roughly with a groan. "I'm just…nervous about this whole thing."

"But you agree that we need to do *something*."

"Of course I do," he said. "But…you're talking about something that is nearly impossible. Dana is the most powerful man in the world, and taking him down wouldn't stop the Commission. This entire problem is very deeply rooted."

"I know. I was talking to Mykail about it, and—"

"Wait, wait," he interrupted, lunging forward in his seat. "The experiment?" When I nodded, his eyes bulged from his skull. "Are you *crazy*?!" he snapped. I leaned back, startled and slightly-offended by his tone. "Lily, just talking about this with *me* is a reckless venture. You cannot just talk to anyone about it, particularly those who have been close to Dana. You don't know where their loyalties lie."

"What about you then?" I challenged. "I'd say you're pretty damn close to Dana. Yet, you're here. Should I be worried about *you*?"

Clark's sighed.

"Lily, look," he started, "I have seen the damage Dana can do, and I have seen how blindly loyal others are to him. Dana is *dangerous*. We have to be careful in any and every way possible. Otherwise, you and I will be strapped to those tables in the back of the Commission, being turned into who knows what."

"I know that," I said strongly. "But Mykail is the one who told me that he was planning on killing Dana. He has actually been through the testing. He knows how horrible it is. Don't you think that he hates Dana for it?"

"Maybe," Clark said. "I don't know. I've seen some experiments worship Dana, despite the testing. We can never be sure. And there are plenty of people who are desperate for Dana's favor, and would turn us over in an instant to save their own skin."

I huffed, exasperated. "Are you going to help me with this or not?"

Clark opened his mouth, but hesitated.

"As much as I know it's suicidal, I want nothing more than to be free of that psycho," he grumbled. "So of course I'll help."

"Good," I said with a sigh of relief. "Because we could really use your expertise."

"What do you want to know?"

"I think first thing we need to figure out is how to organize. We are going to need people inside the Commission first, since they already know what the Commission does. Can you think of anyone who may have had thoughts of taking down Dana and the Commission before?"

"Maybe a few people, but not many," he murmured, his eyes going distant. "And they are around our age. I don't think we can approach the adults about this. Most of them are under Dana's spell, or are too terrified to even think about trying to defy him."

"I agree. Mykail was talking about how some of the experiments are against Dana as well. And, if we could get them out—"

"Get them out?" he interrupted with an incredulous laugh. "Now I know you're insane. Do you have any idea the amount of security that's inside the Commission?"

"No, not yet," I said. "But I've been thinking about trying to get closer to Dana so I can learn more. Maybe I can find a way to explore the back of the Commission and come up with a plan–"

"It's too dangerous, Lily." Clark shook his head. "You might as well run right into the middle of a tornado. If you show the slightest interest in Dana, he will sweep you up and tear you apart."

"He hasn't for you."

"No, but I didn't go looking to get closer to him," he said. "Dana is too unpredictable to try and play. And even though he's insane, he's not a moron. You'd never know if he was toying with you."

"I am willing to risk it if it gives us a chance against him."

"You don't know what you're saying…"

"It's dangerous to go against this, but it's even more dangerous to just sit back. We have to take risks if we want to fight against him. Dana is kidnapping, torturing, and killing people with impunity, and we can't let him get away with it."

"I just don't know that *we* have what it takes to change that," Clark mumbled.

"Isn't that what Thomas Ankell thought about going against the Washington System?" I said. "But he did it."

"That was different. A majority of the country was already against Washington when he started the Second Revolution."

"I'm starting to wonder if you really want to do this," I grumbled, slumping back.

"Of course I want to, but you're talking about doing something that is *exceptionally* dangerous," he said. "You're going to try and get closer to Dana, hoping that he will take you on a tour of the Commission so you can figure out weaknesses in the security and break out experiments?"

"Yeah, pretty much."

"And you want me to try and figure out who would be willing to help us with this insanity?" Clark raised his eyebrows. "Then what?"

"We need to find a place to keep the experiments until we are ready to reveal them." I relayed to Clark what I had already discussed with Mykail. He did not interrupt, listening intently, his eyebrows sometimes rising or a sigh leaving him as he thought over the information. When I was done, he was silent, his eyes distant as he pondered everything I had said.

"So?" I pressed when he had been silent for an uncomfortable length of time.

"We are going to need a lot of luck and, more than anything, we are going to need to be careful and *slow*. If we rush this, we're likely to make a mistake and be killed."

I agreed, though I was a little irritated to admit that we could not eliminate the problem quickly. "Do you think you could convince others in the Commission to help us?"

"I honestly don't know," he admitted. "I can try, but I have to warn you, we might not get the type of response you want. Most are probably too afraid to risk it in the first place, even if they do want Dana gone."

"We'll just need to convince them otherwise, then, won't we?" I said. Clark's eyes were sharp, the nervous boy vanishing and startling me as he studied my expression. I had to turn away from the expression, scratching a fake itch on my face.

"You're really serious about this, aren't you?" he said slowly. "You really want to kill Dana and tear down the Commission?"

"Don't you?"

"...If you really mean it...I guess we better get started..."

I perked up. "Really? You think we can do it?"

"I have no idea," Clark groaned. "But...the way I see it, our lives already rest in Dana's hands, and we are already fucked just for being in the Commission of the People, so...we might as well go down swinging."

"I think if we can expose the Commission, we can get the American people behind us. Even Dana Christenson can't stop millions of people."

"We can hope we get that far," he said. "I can think of a few people I can approach about helping us. They are in my rotation at school. I'll start asking questions to see where they stand."

"What classes are you even in?" I asked, curious why I never saw him at school.

"I'm on a prep track for political science, and I also study genetics and advanced sciences."

I gawked. "I had no idea our school even offered those classes."

"Generally they're the pre-med classes," Clark said with a sad smile. "I've actually thought that, if I wasn't in the Commission, I would have liked to become a doctor."

"Even after seeing everything they do in the Commission?"

Clark fiddled with his hands in his lap, nervous. "To be truthful, from a scientific perspective, what the Commission does is fascinating."

I was unable to school my expression at the words.

"That doesn't mean I agree with it," Clark blurted, raising his hands. "But, admit it, Mykail is fascinating. Being able to give someone the ability to fly, to give a human being *wings*...the possibilities become endless."

"That's the problem." I said. "Dana is trying to create an ultimate weapon out of *people*...What happens when he achieves it?"

"I don't know..."

A knock at my door nearly made me jump out of my skin.

"Yes?"

My mother poked her head around the door.

"How are you doing in here?"

"Fine," we both answered.

"Great. Do you need anything before we leave?"

"No."

"We're going to the grocery. We'll be back in a little bit," she explained. "I put Mykail in his room, so he shouldn't bother you."

"Okay," I said, hoping she did not see how anxious I was for her and Dad to leave the house. She bid us goodbye once more and closed the door. Clark and I both listened as the garage door under my room opened. I walked to my window, peeking through the blinds to see my parents drive away.

As soon as I could no longer see the car, I left my bedroom and went to Mykail's door where he was already waiting for me. He trailed me to my room, but I could feel how nervous he was as I stepped into my room and waited for him to join us. His step was even slower when he met eyes with Clark.

"Oh, I remember you," Mykail said quietly.

"Hello, Mykail," Clark greeted. My eyes flicked rapidly between them, not sure what to make of the tension.

"Clark," Mykail started, "are you sure you want to take this risk? Going against Dana?"

"Of course I am," Clark answered. "Are *you*?"

"I am not like most of the others," Mykail assured. "I want Dana dead and the Commission taken down. You may know about the Commission, but you know nothing about what it is like to be strapped to the table and made into something no longer human."

I flinched at the words.

"If you're lying to us, then we all may become well acquainted with the feeling," Clark sneered, looking between Mykail and myself. "I am willing to do as much as I can, but we are playing with a very dangerous and brilliant predator. There is no way to be sure that he does not know what we are doing, even now."

"I understand how dangerous Dana can be," Mykail said. "I am willing to risk my safety for the possibility of bringing him down. But I don't want to force anyone to risk their lives unless they have the desire to see the Commission dismantled, preferably before there is a lot of progress with Eina."

"I do agree with that time problem," Clark muttered. Mykail turned to me, a silent question in his eyes.

"What choice do I have but to fight him?" I snapped. I could feel the anger and hatred swell inside me, bringing stinging tears to my eyes. "If I *don't* fight, I am submitting to being his amusement for the rest of my life. The only way to change that is to fight. We may not win, but we need to be sure that, if we do go down, at least the country knows what really happens inside the Commission of the People."

Chapter Twenty-Three

The plan started very simply. The first thing we needed to do was see how many allies we could gather within the Commission. Clark agreed to drop hints to other young members of the Commission, and I finally convinced both Clark and Mykail that I would attempt to get close enough to Dana to be shown around the labs again.

I went to school that Monday as though nothing was different, but my nerves were humming. That day it was not fear that plagued me, but excitement, an electric tremor that made me feel alive...*powerful*...

As I passed my classmates in the hall, I smiled to myself knowing they were oblivious to my plans to take down the most powerful man and most powerful institution in the world. I figured Thomas Ankell must have felt the same way when he started organizing the Children of America to take down Washington.

I was helping to start a new revolution, and no one knew, yet.

My quiet, brooding attitude as I mulled over my conversation with Clark and Mykail kept my friends from conversing with me through the beginning of the week. I hardly noticed, throwing on a quick smile whenever they asked if I was alright. I did not realize that I had withdrawn so much until Becca, who had not held a real conversation with me in several weeks, tapped me on the shoulder one day at lunch.

"Hey, I'm gonna get a soda...wanna come with?" she asked. I blinked back to the present, surprised by the invitation. My heart picked up pace when I realized she was asking to speak to me privately, and I scrambled to my feet.

As it was Wednesday, the hallways were even more deserted than usual, as most of the students were watching the unofficial soccer match that always took place on Wednesdays at lunch, which afforded us even more privacy as we stopped at the vending machines.

"Hey, Lily," Becca started, fishing in her pocket for her student card, "everything okay with you?"

"Yeah, why?"

"You've been acting weird since you became a part of the Commission. And, lately, you've been..." She hesitated, keeping her eyes strictly focused on swiping her student card and selecting her drink. "I dunno what I'm saying...I know you can't tell me what happens in the Commission, but I'm worried. You just seem...off."

"I could say the same about you..." I grumbled. "I feel like you've been avoiding me."

The clunk of the soda hitting the bottom of the vending machine did not prompt Becca to retrieve her purchase. She stared blankly at the drink selection, her drawn face giving me pause. She looked older, paler, as though she had hardly slept for weeks.

"You're part of the Commission now," she whispered. "You're dangerous."

"I'm not," I defended. "Becca, I swear, I would never do anything that would hurt you or any of my friends."

"You're part of the Commission," she repeated, turning her darkened eyes to me for the first time. "Even if you don't mean to, the circle you travel in is too dangerous to ignore." She turned away to retrieve the soda, shaking her head minutely. "I wish I could ignore that, but I can't."

"Becca—" I stopped myself. I desperately wanted to vent my hatred for the Commission, and tell her that she had no reason to worry about the Commission because I was going to do everything I could to take it down, but the words were stuck in my throat, knowing they were too dangerous to be set loose.

At my silence Becca turned to me, clearly seeing the turmoil on my face. With a huff, she began tapping her finger on the top of the soda.

"What the hell makes all of you Commish Kids so nervous around everyone else?" she grumbled. "It really doesn't ease the rest of us, you know."

I turned away from her that time, looking around the hallway, trying to make my scanning of our surroundings appear casual.

The hiss of the opening soda filled the space between us, but Becca did not take a sip, staring down at the beverage.

"What's he like?" she mumbled.

"Who?"

"Dana Christenson." She still refused to meet my gaze. "We never see him or hear about him, we just...sort of know who he is. What's he like?"

The image of terrifying amber eyes flooded my mind without my bidding. I could feel the explanations building in my chest, desperate to tell someone about the night terrors, the twisting anger and helplessness that filled me every time we went to a Commission meeting, about the torment and abuse occurring in that hellish basement—but I could almost feel Dana looming over my shoulder, waiting for the confessions, waiting for the slightest crack in my armor to exploit...

"Lily?" Becca asked, grabbing my attention and causing me to blink back to reality. "You're going pale. Are you okay?"

202

"...I just wish I could tell you everything," I choked on the words. "Becca, please...I know I'm part of the Commission, but you have to believe me that I would never do anything to hurt you or the others. I just really need some friends outside the Commission. I need to *not* be a Commish Kid at least somewhere."

"Oh, Lily, I'm sorry..." she whispered, stepping forward and hugging me. I did not realize how desperately I needed the hug until I was blinking back tears against her shoulder. "Of course you can just be yourself with us. I'm so sorry...I just..." She backed away from the hug. "The Commission's fucking scary, you know?"

"Believe me, I know," I agreed, rapidly pushing the tears away from my eyes.

"Lily?" a voice called behind me. Becca's eyes turned dark as I turned to see Felicity approaching. "I thought that was you. What are you girls doing?"

"Nothing."

"I don't think I need to remind you that we were recently told to be very careful of who we speak to," Felicity said, sending a sneering look in Becca's direction. "I would think you would heed that advice perfectly. You don't want to lose your spot as a favorite, do you?"

"What do you want, Felicity?" I asked, stopping whatever Becca was about to say in response.

"I was wondering if you had heard a rumor floating around that Miranda was smuggling drugs," she said.

"Miranda Jacobs?" Becca asked. "Yeah, right. She would never do something like that."

"Are you sure?" Felicity pressed. She turned to me. "What do you think, Lily?"

"I don't know her."

"She's in the Commission," she said. "Since last week's meeting, every rumor is being taken very seriously. I'm trying to find the source of this rumor about Miranda. If it gets too far, she could get into some real trouble." She looked between us once more before giving me a cold, half-smile. "If you do hear anything let me know. This is a very damaging rumor. So if you want to make yourself useful, use your favorable position to be sure Mr. Christenson doesn't hear about it."

Felicity spun on her heel, her coiffed hair bouncing as she strutted down the hallway, her head high.

"What the hell is happening?" Becca asked, watching Felicity grow smaller in the distance. "All the Commish Kids have gotten even nosier since you joined." Her eyes turned suspicious as she turned back to me. "And what did she mean by favorable position?"

My stomach twisted around itself and I shifted uncomfortably under her gaze. "I can't tell you…at least, not here."

She nodded contemplatively. "Do you want to come over this weekend?" she asked, taking the hint. I nodded so quickly I almost made myself dizzy.

* *** *

No matter how I wracked my brain that week, I could not think of any way to get close to Dana without showing interest in his predatory advances. I had been unable to meet with Clark during the week to discuss things with him, and I also had no way of knowing if he was successful at finding others to help our cause. During the nights, once I had finished my homework and my parents had gone to bed, I would stay up and plot with Mykail.

The discussion of our plot and the discussions we would have over the hand-drawn maps Mykail had made of the Commission, would always turn to talks about what Mykail remembered from his imprisonment. We tried to keep up the guise that we were discussing his time in the Commission labs as a part of our plotting, but I was more curious about what he had endured because I desperately wanted to get to know him better.

Once Thursday came around, I finally found the courage to ask some more burning questions.

"Can I ask you something?" I asked, staring at my hands as a wrung them nervously in my lap.

"Anything."

"How did the Commission find out about your family?"

He lowered his gaze to the bedspread between us, picking at imaginary lint to avoid meeting my eyes as he answered.

"We had been smuggling drugs over the border, so it's really no surprise we were eventually caught," he said. "I'm not sure who turned us in. Someone must have overheard someone and it was the break the Commission needed to find us and take us in."

"…what happened when they caught you?" I asked, my voice so quiet I was unsure if he heard me.

"It happened so fast…" he answered just as quietly. "We lived in an average house in an average neighborhood up north, so they waited until after curfew so be sure everyone was at home and there would be no one in the streets to stop them or hide us…" He gave a short snorting laugh. "It might not come as a surprise that we lived a very unstructured life, so my brother and sister and I were up very late. We were playing video games in the living room. And the door just," he motioned his hands in a bursting motion. "Once the door was broken down, everything was chaotic. There was a bunch of yelling and screaming, a few gunshots were fired. I was on the floor before I could even register what was happening."

He lifted his hand to rub his forehead. "There was so much screaming and yelling…" he continued. "And then a bag was put over my head and I was carried to a van. Before I knew it I was in the Commission…everything is kind of a blur…"

I reached out to place my hand over his.

"I'm so sorry for what you've been through…"

"You know while we've been planning this…" he motioned to the hand-drawn maps next to us on the bed, "I've been wracking my brain trying to remember what the holding cells look like…how I got from there to the lab…how I got *out* once I was loaded into the car to come here…and I can't remember." He groaned, hanging his head. "Once you're down there, it's like everything happens in a fog. You're just so focused on surviving the next minute you don't notice anything else."

My fingers tightened around his hand, feeling his fear as though it were transferring from his skin to mine.

"I don't want you to go through that," he murmured, lifting his head. "None of this is worth you being trapped down there at Dana's mercy. So if you *ever* feel that this is becoming too much, please just tell me and we'll stop."

I forced a smile, my other hand reaching forward to encase his. His other hand mirrored the action.

"Once this gets going…I don't think we'll be able to stop," I said. "The more people that get involved, the more momentum we're going to achieve. We just have to work carefully, and we'll take that son of a bitch down."

His smile was weak, clearly wanting to believe my words, but unable to trust that we could execute our coup.

"I just don't want you to get hurt," he said.

"The best way to ensure that is for us to dismantle the Commission," I insisted. "And we have to make some progress before Dana finishes Eina's testing, remember? If he figures out how to make his weaponized human, who knows how many more he'll make."

"I'd be more concerned about everyone getting caught and turned into the same thing," Mykail said. "Maybe…maybe we shouldn't…"

"Don't," I said quickly, squeezing his hand. When I felt him squeeze back, a smile pulled at my lips that I desperately tried to ignore. "Don't doubt that we can do this. This is the right thing to do. If we give up now, hundreds if not thousands of others will be captured, taken down into the Commission, turned into who knows what…this *has* to happen. If we don't stand up for them, we're no better than everyone else who has just sat back and let things get to this point."

His own smile grew and he lifted his eyes.

"I'm in awe of you, Lily Sandover," he said.

Before I could respond, he leaned forward, pecking a kiss on my cheek before retreating, turning his head away in embarrassment. I was too stunned to move, though I was certain my cheeks were stained a bright red as I could feel the heat radiating from my face. He was blinking rapidly, only throwing one quick glance to see my reaction before his gaze fell to the bedspread again. He cleared his throat to speak but, worried he would try to apologize for the kiss, I moved forward and kissed his cheek in turn.

His stunned expression turned back to me, eyes wide, one hand going to cover the area where my lips had made contact. My heart was thundering, my breathing becoming shallow as I desperately waited for him to say or do something in response.

It seemed like an eternity before his hand left his cheek and cradled mine, his thumb stroking over my skin. My breath shuddered out of me, my lips parting as every nerve in my body started to buzz with excitement. I saw he was coming closer, his head slanting as he drew near, but it was not until I could feel his breath fanning over my lips that my brain finally registered he was going to kiss me.

My eyes slid shut as his lips met mine and in that moment, everything around us melted away.

The kiss was tender and sweet, and in that blissful moment, I wished it could last forever. When he kissed me, we were not planning a dangerous coup, we were not putting our lives on the line, we were not trying to hide our feelings…we were just together and nothing else in the world mattered.

When he pulled away from the kiss, it was another eternity before I could properly breathe again. I opened my eyes slowly, trying to focus on the tingling his lips had left on mine. I knew I was wearing a stupid, goofy grin, but I didn't care, especially when I saw his tender smile in front of me.

I was so happy I was sure I would burst.

"I really like you, Lily," he said. "I just…I can't even explain it. There is just something about your very being that is so…incredible."

"You're just saying that," I mumbled, though my lips struggled to form the words around my smile. I dropped my head, too embarrassed to face him.

"No, I'm not," he insisted. "You look at me as though I'm a person, not some freak show or some pitiable creature. I feel like you're the first person who has seen me for years. I mean, really *seen* me. And I can't tell you what that means to me."

I lifted my gaze.

"I feel the same way," I said. "I mean…I've always just sorta shadowed my parents, trying to be the good daughter, trying not to raise a fuss. Even with all this going on in the Commission, I haven't told my parents a lot of what's going on because I know it will just cause them more anguish. But with you, I can actually say what I'm feeling, and tell you what's been going on, and you don't make me feel guilty for doing it."

He squeezed my hand again.

"You can tell me anything," he said.

"And you can tell me anything."

With another squeeze of his hand that made my heart pick up pace again, thinking he was going to lean in and kiss me again, he drew in a deep breath and then slumped, glancing at the clock on his bedside table.

"I should let you get some sleep," he said. "We've been up late every night this week and you have Archangel tomorrow."

Trying not to appear too crestfallen, I nodded, slowly releasing his hand, still smiling like an idiot no matter how I attempted to school my expression.

"I'll see you tomorrow then," I said, climbing off his bed as he remained seated, watching me go toward his door.

"Sleep well, Lily."

I carefully opened his door, trying to keep the sound to a minimum, before turning around to wish him good night. When I saw him, sitting on the bed, a small smile tugging at his lips and the lingering blush warming his cheeks, I bounded back to him, wrapping my arms around his neck and planting a kiss on his lips. He fumbled, having to brace on one arm to keep from falling off the bed at my enthusiasm, before smiling into the kiss and meeting my weight with his.

I was the one to break the kiss that time, and I wished him a mumbled good night before scurrying back to my room, embarrassed and giddy.

Chapter Twenty-Four

I could not stop thinking about the kisses. All through Friday I was grinning like an idiot, recalling at random times the sweet gestures as my heart bloomed with affection for Mykail. It was only when I got home from school that I remembered I was expected at Archangel that night and my face fell. I had hoped to spend time with Mykail when I got home, but breakfast had already been awkward, as we could not do more than share embarrassed blushing glances with my parents seated at the same table.

As I slowly ascended the stairs to my bedroom, I debated turning toward Mykail's door, but when my heart fluttered and embarrassment burned at my cheeks, I refrained, doing my best to press myself to the wall as I rounded into my room.

Preparing for Archangel proved challenging as I became distracted with how I wanted to look that night. It was the first time that I looked at some of the more risqué things I had purchased with my friends. I felt a mix of embarrassment and confidence as I put on the tight, short bandage dress. Heat swept through my entire body when I imagined what Mykail would think if I were to step out of my room in the outfit, but the fire was immediately cooled when I realized I would be seen by everyone in Archangel in the same outfit.

There was danger all around me now that I had already started thinking about how to take down Dana. I had to be very careful how much attention I attracted.

I settled on a simple black dress and boots. Having spent so much time picking an outfit, I had only ten minutes to do my hair and makeup before Becca and the others were expected at my door to pick me up.

Again, I became distracted trying to cover all the imperfections I kept finding in my face, wondering if Mykail had noticed my large pores or the pimple starting to form on my forehead when we kissed the previous night.

When my phone buzzed, I abandoned my futile effort with the concealer and stumbled to put on my shoes and meet my friends at the curb.

Scurrying back to grab my purse after I opened my bedroom door, I heard a voice at the top of the stairs.

"Lily?"

I hesitated, the blush rising to my cheeks against my will. After confirming my parents were not near the stairs, I went to his door. He was standing by the bars looking at me with his beautiful, yet concerned, eyes. "Are you going to Archangel?" I nodded. "Are you going to talk to Clark?"

"Hopefully he'll have some news," I said, very pointedly moving my eyes away from his lips when he licked them nervously.

"Just please be sure you don't talk about this around a bunch of people, even if there is loud music," he said. He reached through the bars, his hand resting against my cheek and forcing my breath to catch in my throat. "Please be careful."

My legs turned to jelly, but I somehow managed to stay standing. Drawing in a deep breath, I nodded quickly. My heart was thundering. I knew it was dangerous when my friends were waiting outside and my parents were just downstairs, but I leaned forward, following his hand's guide. The bars hitting my cheeks cooled them as our lips touched for half a second, not daring any more contact.

He smiled when I pulled away.

"I can't tell you how relieved I am," he murmured.

"Relieved?"

"I've been worrying for weeks that you wouldn't like me the way I like you. Not that I would have blamed you with..." The feathers on his wings ruffled as evidence.

"I don't care about those," I said. "And I do like you. A lot."

"It's just so dangerous for you," Mykail said, his bright blue eyes shining with concern that only deepened the affection taking root in my chest.

"I know," I said. "But I'm willing to take the risk. With everything else we're doing, what's one more?"

He smiled, reaching through the bars again to take my hand, squeezing it. "You should go. Your friends are waiting."

"Will you be awake when I get back?"

He nodded.

I practically skipped to the car idling at the end of the driveway, trying not to appear *too* happy so as not to raise suspicion.

The car ride to the club was full of meaningless chatter that girls often had when in a group with adults in earshot. I was grateful for the silly talk. While I had been trying to adapt to the terrifying changes in my life since entering the Commission, I had not had the will to participate in the chats with my friends. Feeling my heart thrumming excitedly in my chest, it was surprisingly easy to fall back into conversation with them.

When we arrived at the club, we were all surprised to see Clark already waiting for us. Devon and Todd were nowhere in sight, and when we approached our normal table, Clark stood immediately and half-ran to me.

"We need to talk," he said urgently, grabbing my hand.

Fear consumed me.

He pulled me away while my friends opened their mouths to ask what was wrong, confused.

Clark yanked me onto the dance floor, creating a path through students and stopping near the stage. He ducked behind one of the cylindrical platforms, finding a clear space for us to stand without being in the direct line of sight to the balcony.

"Have you said anything to anyone about what we talked about?" he demanded, rounding on me.

"Of course not!"

"Are you sure?!"

"Clark, what the hell? You're scaring me."

"Yeah, well, I'm pretty fucking scared, too," he snapped, his eyes wide and his breath shuddering out of him as his frame trembled. He cast a quick glance around us, causing me to do the same, before he extracted some folded pieces of paper.

"I've been asking around," he started. "Nothing direct, just feeling around with some people I know have had doubts before. Everyone is too nervous about the announcement Dana made last week to say anything. But at the same time, more people have been hesitant saying outright that they support what Dana is doing, so he scared them enough to make them question some things. It might be a while before we can ask anything directly."

"Okay..." I said. "Then what's got you so freaked out?"

"Yesterday when I was at the Commission, Dana came to see me while I was studying. He told me that he's thinking of recalling some of the gift experiments."

"Recalling? Taking them back?!"

He nodded. "He asked for my opinion. I told him it would upset a lot of people and that, with his announcement last week, recalling experiments was going to raise even more questions and doubts. He told me that he thought I would say that and just walked out." He leaned closed, running his fingers along the creases in the papers. "Have you broken any of the rules Dana gave you for Mykail?"

"No."

"Then why would he say that? Especially since he seemed to know what I would say."

"I don't know," I said. "Who's to say it has anything to do with us? Maybe something else happened."

"I asked my mom but she said there hasn't been any talk of rogue or unruly gift experiments." Clark tapped the papers against his palm. "Then, today after school, I found this with my bookmark for *An Angel Without Wings*." He lifted the papers between us.

It took me longer than it should have to unfold the pages, but my fingers were trembling too severely to perform fine motor functions. The first page had scrawled letters that were extremely difficult to read in the sloppy handwriting and the dim light of the club. I brought the pages close to my face, utilizing the occasional flashing spotlight to read the information.

Even when I was able to make out the letters and numbers, the eleven lines were clearly in code, each starting with the letter W, one number, then the letter R and another number, finally ending with a random grouping of six numbers. The last line was the only one that had an extremely long sequence of twenty-two numbers.

"Does this make sense to you?" I asked, glancing up at Clark.

"No. The only thing I can think of is that the W numbers are the different wards in the Enterprise Lab. Otherwise, I have no idea what this could mean. And there's more there." He nodded to the other pages.

The next page had more confusing scribbles of numbers and letters, accompanying symbols that were very basic and primitive, appearing like some ancient math problem more than a coded message.

"This is ridiculous. What the hell even is this?" I groaned, frustrated.

"I told you, I have no idea," Clark said, just as frustrated. "The other three pages are more of the same nonsense. But it's the same penmanship, same paper, just different numbers."

The more I stared at the code the more confused and worried I became. I worried it was some sort of warning, that someone had learned of our plan and was trying to tell us.

"Look at the last page," Clark said, his voice tight, likely in response to the way my hands started to shake too violently to read the numbers.

I flipped the final page frantically. It was the only page where a legible message had been scratched in the same fine-tip pen.

There are more who can help. Be careful.
Memorize this and burn it.

My heart stopped, my ribs feeling as though they were closing tighter around my lungs and making it almost impossible to breathe.

"*That's* why I'm nervous."

"I...I..." No words could be summoned forward. My brain was awash with fear and confusion. I could not even lift my gaze from the message to look at Clark when he spoke again.

"Are you *sure* you have not broken any of Dana's rules or told anyone about what we're doing?"

"Of course I haven't. If I had, don't you think *I* would have gotten these before you?"

Clark let out a heavy sigh, troubled. Swallowing down the lump in my throat, I finally found the will to raise my head, though I gripped the papers so tightly they were starting to bend and crease. I had hoped that hearing there were those who supported our idea about taking down the Commission of the People would invigorate me, but there was something terrifying about the new development. Not only did we not know who our new ally was, there was no cipher for us to decode the messages they had given us that could, potentially, be crucial in taking down Dana.

Of course, there was no way to know if we could trust the anonymous note.

"Do you recognize the handwriting?"

"No," Clark said, rubbing his face with one hand roughly. "Somehow someone who has access to my things put it in my book, which means someone knows what we're doing."

My heart was trying to climb into my throat, stubbornly refusing to let my words come out louder than a petrified squeak.

"You...don't think anyone would put these there just to lead us into some kind of trap, right?"

"Even if they were, it's not like we can *read* them," he groaned. "I'm more worried that *Dana* would be able to read them and if I was caught with the information, he would catch on to what was happening."

I shivered at the thought and looked around us quickly, the changing of the song reminding me that there were hundreds of teenagers around us who could have snuck up at any time to eavesdrop—as was the way of Archangel.

I refolded the papers and shoved them into my boot.

"What are—"

"Maybe Mykail can read them," I said. "Maybe it is some sort of code that only those in the lab can understand."

Clark hesitated, but nodded begrudgingly.

"As for the other Commish Kids," he said, "I think we need to wait a week or two. Maybe by the end of October we will have an idea about who we can safely approach."

I nodded, trusting his judgment of the people he knew better than I.

"Clark?"

"What?"

I drew in a deep breath. "What should I do? In order to get Dana's attention? To get closer to him?" I barely managed not to choke on the words. "Do I just fawn over him like everyone else?"

Clark stared at me, the desire to warn me against getting closer to Dana clear in his expression. His shoulders curled forward as he dropped his gaze.

"No," he mumbled. "You want to get his attention? Challenge him."

"Challenge him?"

"Don't take any bait he throws at you. Don't praise him. Ignore him, make him come to you, play his game. Every time he looks at you, glare at him or look away. When he calls you over, don't go. When he speaks to you, pretend not to listen. That's when he tries harder to bring you closer. He enjoys the chase."

I could feel the deep instinct in my body screaming at me to abandon the plan, that trying to play Dana by making him eager to chase me was more dangerous than the plot to take down the Commission of the People.

"I don't know if it helps to hear this," Clark continued, "but it's clear he's already interested. He's shown you a lot more attention than other Commish Kids already. You probably won't have to do much to get him to bring you close. And if you only show interest in the experiments, he'll probably lead you into the labs that much sooner and you can look around."

I opened my mouth to ask Clark more about how to resist Dana, but stopped myself, feeling shame lick my throat sickly. It was one thing to fight Dana, to pretend not to be interested, but I also knew that, when Dana was close, his intoxicating charisma and power was far more difficult to resist. And I knew that I did not know Dana well enough to gauge when I was getting *too* close and would be in true, physical danger.

But I was determined and I had to take the risk.

If I wanted to have any hope in breaking apart the Commission, I had to take risks early, before I was so wrapped up in it that I could not muster the will to fight back.

"We should go up," Clark declared, peeking out from behind the cylindrical stage. I nodded numbly, following him through the crowd of dancing students and toward the balcony stairs. As we cleared the dance floor, I barely caught sight of Jill at the bar, getting drinks for the others at the table.

"Clark," I called to him, "I'll be up in a few minutes. I just want a few minutes with them."

Clark followed my gaze toward Jill and nodded silently, making his way to the stairs while I approached Jill, who was having to wait longer than usual since there were only two working behind the bar that night as opposed to the normal five.

"Hey," I said.

"Hey!" she gasped, startled. "Everything okay? You and Clark just disappeared."

"Yeah," I groaned, rolling my eyes for effect. "Just some stupid drama for the Commission." I tried not to feel the scraping of the folded papers in my boot as I spoke.

"Well, if the other Commish Kids can spare you for a few minutes," Jill said, turning her attention to the bar attendant handing her several tall glasses of sodas, "you should come hang out with us. Devon was asking about you."

There was ice in her voice. I watched her reach for the sodas, trying to gather them all, and feeling more bold than usual, I reached forward and grabbed two from her hands to help.

"Look, Jill," I started, "about Devon, I'm not interested in him that way."

Jill looked at me, her lips parted to speak, though she shook her head and laughed instead.

"All I said is he was asking about you."

"I know you like him," I continued, leaning against the bar counter to show her I was not planning to help carry the sodas until she heard me out. "And I think you two look good together. Devon and I just danced those few times. I'm not interested in him."

She stared at me some more, scrutinizing my face, looking for any sign that I was lying so she would drop her guard.

"You really don't like him that way?" she asked. "Because I would totally understand if you did."

"I don't," I insisted, unable to stop myself from thinking about Mykail, knowing that the little flutters in my belly I had for Devon were nothing compared to the fire that Mykail sparked within me. "Really."

Jill's smile was no longer forced, growing into a full laugh.

"You like someone else!" she gasped. I tried to school my expression immediately. "Who is it? Someone we know?"

214

"No!" I said too quickly. When she gave me a startled, yet impressed, sideways glance, I could not stop myself from talking. "I mean I don't like anyone! I swear! I just meant—"

"Uh-huh, whatever you say," Jill leered, taking the three sodas between her hands and turning away from the bar. I groaned, grabbing the other two glasses and walking to the table behind her, knowing I had just become the topic of gossip that night.

As I reached the table with Jill, I was eagerly greeted by the others.

"Hey! There you are!" Becca said. "Everything okay with Clark?"

"Yeah, nothing major, just Commission nonsense," I said. "Sorry if we worried you."

"Are you able to stay down here and hang with the plebs tonight?" Devon asked, leaning forward to catch my attention.

"I'd love to, but I do need to go up pretty soon," I lamented. "I just wanted to come over and say hello. I really miss hanging out with you guys."

"We miss you, too!" Becca whined, hugging me with one arm.

I allowed myself a few minutes to sit and chat with my friends. They talked about some of the funny stories the boys had from their classes, though it did not go unnoticed when Todd pointedly stopped a part of the story and stared at me, unsure if it was safe to share in front of a Commish Kid. I had been enjoying not thinking about the Commission with the other stories, but when the tone of the conversation shifted, I was once again reminded that, even if they looked at me as a friend, there was a level of distrust they would always have.

I took the opportunity to excuse myself and trudge up to the balcony, reminded with each step of the folded papers in my boots they scraped my calf.

When I reached the top of the stairs, my way was blocked by Brian, Freddie, and Will, glaring daggers at me. Drawing in a deep breath to steady myself around the fear bolting in my belly, I dropped my eyes and tried to push past them. Brian grabbed hold of both handrails, planting himself directly in my path.

"What the hell did you tell Mr. Christenson?"

"I didn't tell him anything," I defended, trying to push his arm out of the way. Will flanked his friend, staring down his nose at me.

"Really?" he snapped.

"Because he sure as hell did a number on us because of you," Freddie added.

"I don't care," I sneered. "You brought it on yourself." I tried to push past once again.

"It wasn't just us that got the punishment," Brian said, locking his arm in place. "Our parents have been put on notice with Dana Christenson. They're worried that they're about to be kicked out because of that night."

"Which, I'm sure, you know what that means," Will said.

"*You* were the ones who attacked me," I reminded them. "And I didn't tell Dana anything. He was *there*."

"What the hell does he see in you?" Freddie asked, his gaze scraping over me. "You really must be something if he's willing to go to such lengths for you."

I scoffed at Freddie, rolling my eyes and trying to push past Brian once more. When he still did not move, I punched him—admittedly not very hard—in the stomach. He stepped back more out of reflex than pain, giving me enough room to muscle my way onto the balcony and away from them.

I immediately went to Clark.

"Are you alright?" he asked, straightening at my angry stomping as I approached.

"I really hate some of the kids here," I huffed, sitting opposite him and crossing my arms as I slumped back.

"Preaching to the choir…" he grumbled.

It seemed as though I had been in the club for days by the time the announcement came that the buses were leaving. I had hardly spoken the entire night. Even when I glanced at Clark, wondering if he was about to say something when he straightened, I would see him look among the other faces of the Commish Kids before shaking his head and leaning back, deciding against it. Each time he did so, I absentmindedly scratched at the papers against my calf.

When the club lights came on and everyone had left, the meeting for the Commish Kids began. Clark was conducting the meeting, and I zoned out through most of it, my mind too busy with other conundrums. I was eager to get home, change out of the dress that was digging into my armpits, and show Mykail the notes we had received.

But the atmosphere of the meeting changed when Clark asked if there was anything any of the Commish Kids wanted to bring up.

"I think we need to discuss what Mr. Christenson said last week about the kids in the Commission," Felicity said.

"What about it?" Clark prompted calmly, though his shoulders had tensed at the topic.

"Well, first of all, why the hell he made the announcement," she continued, seconded by a round of agreements. "Who the fuck was attacked?"

"What does it matter?" Melissa asked. "Mr. Christenson might have just said that to keep us on our toes. You know how he can be."

"I don't give a shit, it's still stupid," Lance snapped.

"Yeah, we're all being punished for something we didn't do," Gracie scoffed. "My parents have been on my ass ever since that stupid announcement. They hardly leave me alone."

"Someone *was* attacked," Clark said. "The situation's been dealt with and we should leave it at that."

"So someone fess up," Felicity said, glancing around the circle of Commish Kids.

"This isn't an interrogation or an investigation," Clark interjected. "The parties involved have been warned. Mr. Christenson just wanted to keep the rest of us in line. If he wanted us to know who did it, he would have called them out at the meeting."

"That's hardly the point," Anne said. "We were all *threatened* at the meeting. He said he would take us into the back and turn us into experiments. And we're supposed to just accept that? Fuck no!"

Clark looked among the faces of angry teens, watching them nod enthusiastically.

"Are you saying you're unhappy with the way Mr. Christenson is running the Commission?" he asked, his voice flat.

The nodding stopped. The whispered agreements silenced. Most eyes turned to the floor, knowing that any answer they gave had to be exactly right or they could be reported for treasonous discussions.

"I say if you have a complaint about what he said last week at the meeting, take it up directly with him," Clark said. "We can sit here and complain all we want, but it won't change anything. His word is law in the Commission. You all know that. Got a problem? Talk to Mr. Christenson."

Clark amazed me. For as nervous and awkward as he often seemed, when he needed to, he could don a mask of authority one would never expect from him.

"Apart from the announcement," Clark continued when no one else spoke, "are there any other issues to be discussed?"

"Actually, I have a question," Sarah said, raising her head. "There have been a lot of rumors going around about Miranda Jacobs."

Again, the Commish Kids became unsettled, whispering to one another.

Clark nodded slowly. "I've heard the rumors. And I'm sorry to say, but this has also been brought to the attention of the Commission. There is an investigation being run to test the validity of the rumors. We should know soon what they determine."

"None of the rumors are true," Felicity said strongly.

"If it's not true, then where is she?" Sarah demanded. "She's been gone for nearly a week. No one has seen her."

No one could provide an answer, and it left a heavy, uneasy feeling in the air.

* *** *

I rushed to change into my pajamas the moment I got home, throwing my dress and boots haphazardly into the corner once I had retrieved the notes. I then peered out my door, listening carefully to the noise downstairs. My mother had been awake when I got home, but she was dressed in her robe and slippers, waiting for me to return home before going upstairs.

I heard her slippers scuffing over the hardwood followed by the click of a few light switches. When the glow from the kitchen disappeared, I crept to Mykail's door, unlocking it as gently as I could. He helped me open it slowly to reduce the noise, a process with which we were becoming extremely skilled.

"How was Archangel?" he asked as we sat on his bed.

"Boring for the most part." I fiddled with the papers in my hand, tapping them against my palm. "But this was really interesting."

"What is it?" he asked, unfolding them slowly.

"Clark said he found them in his book today after school," I explained, watching his long, lithe fingers smooth over the top page. "We can't understand them and we don't know who gave them to Clark. I was hoping you would understand. It's just gibberish to us."

My hope in his comprehension of the code waned when his brow furrowed in confusion at the top page. But when he turned to the next page, his eyes shot wide before his gaze flew back to me.

"Where did Clark get these?" he demanded.

I leaned away from him, startled by the reaction.

"Lily, *where* did he get these?"

"I-I don't know," I stammered. "He said he found them in his book. I don't know who put them there."

His bright blue eyes bore into mine, searching for any indication that I was lying. When he finally turned his attention back to the papers, I could feel my muscles quaking, worried about his reaction and yet extremely excited that he could decipher the message. He scanned the complicated equations on the first page before turning to the next page, his eyes growing wider the more he read.

"I can't believe this…"

"What is it?"

"Very valuable and very dangerous information," he answered distractedly, looking at the next page. "This is information on twenty-seven experiments. It has *everything*. Ward number, cell number, their rotation, general testing schedule, checkups, security rounds…"

"How can you tell?"

"It's a code used by the scientists and security staff in the Commission," Mykail explained. He began spreading the notes out on the bed between us. "When we start our experimentation, the older experiments teach us how to read the notes so that we can know what day of the week it is, since we're underground and there's really no way to tell. Every experiment gets a few hours of socialization a week, to test how severely the testing has affected the mental capacity of the experiments. That's how I learned this code."

"So this gives you information on some of the experiments?"

"Yes, but I'm rusty at reading this…" he said, running his fingers along the lines. "It might take me a while, but this right here is the ward and cell number, this is the day of the week they generally have their physical checkups…" His finger continued to pass over the code. "This is incredible…the amount of time it would take to gather all this information…"

"Then it would have to be another experiment who gave us this?"

"Most likely, but it's definitely someone *inside* the commission," he mused, not lifting his head from the notes. "It could be one of the scientists…could be a member of the security staff…" He glanced at me. "Who is Clark's gift?"

"I don't know, he's never talked about it," I said with a one-shoulder shrug. "And he goes to the Commission every day after school, so he's down there *all* the time."

"Then it really could be anyone."

"Do you think it's real? Or do you think it could be a trap?"

"Normally, I would be suspicious of that," Mykail said, lifting the last page with the simple warning scrawled on it. "But this would be a very convoluted way to set a trap. You would not be able to read this without me or another experiment or member of the Commission staff. And this states to burn this information." He sighed, setting the note down and rubbing the back of his neck with a groan. "The problem is that this information will only be good for a few more months. The rotations change every two to three months, which means we have a limited amount of time to use this information."

"Would this information help us break these experiments out?" I asked, my heart leaping at the thought.

"It could. Or it could at least give us a timeframe where we could plan an escape," he said. "The problem is getting them *out*. We have to get into the back of the Commission and start looking for a way to sneak everyone out." He turned his worried gaze on me. "The meeting is tomorrow night?" I nodded. "Do you have any idea how you're going to handle Dana?"

"No," I admitted. "I don't know how I *could* prepare for him, he scares the hell out of me."

"He should," Mykail agreed. "He's incredibly dangerous." He reached forward, taking one of my hands, his thumb rubbing tenderly over my skin. "Are you sure you want to do it this way? There has to be a way that doesn't put you in his direct line."

"Do you think we could find another way before this information is outdated?" I asked, tapping the notes. Even though the fear was still sitting heavy in my gut, even thinking about more people being brought into those labs, where they were strapped to the table and tortured, turned into things that could no longer be recognized...it was too sickening to bear.

"...no," he murmured. "But I don't like this. Dana is too unpredictable."

"I know," I agreed. "You and Clark both have told me how much you don't like it, but it might be our only way to get the information we need to finally kill that bastard. He's already interested in toying with me. We might as well toy right back."

Mykail's eyes softened, the piercing blue color making my heart flutter as all fears of the danger ahead flitted away. I had to wonder if I would ever become accustomed to his gaze, or if it would always hold such power over me.

His other hand reached forward, his fingers gingerly tracing my jaw, though his touch sent an electric shock through me, my body shivering in response. My hair stood on end, my lungs releasing what little air they had been able to take in under his powerful gaze.

It seemed impossible to become so attached to Mykail in such a short amount of time. There were moments where I had been rendered unable to pay attention to what he said because the sound of his voice was hypnotic. Other times, I would find myself mesmerized merely by the way his eyelashes brushed his high cheekbones whenever he blinked. Every day I found something else about him that electrified me.

He leaned to me, our lips brushing together once again.

The world disappeared and I tentatively moved my lips over his, not entirely sure what I was doing. Our mouths worked awkwardly together, our teeth hitting—kissing was harder than it looked in the movies. I was blushing furiously at my inexperience, trying not to giggle awkwardly when he took my face in both hands to slow my pace and teach me.

The next thing I knew, my head was on a pillow and Mykail was reclined beside me, his fingers dancing over my cheek.

"What happened?" I asked, not remembering how I went from sitting to a horizontal position.

Mykail's amused smile took my breath away.

"I'm not entirely sure," he chuckled. "I'm not sure if I should be flattered or insulted. When I stopped kissing you, you had a cute smile on your face, but your eyes were still closed. Then you were unconscious." He smiled brilliantly. "I don't know if you were so tired and bored that you fell asleep, or if it was such a good kiss that you fainted."

My cheeks were burning so hotly I was certain my entire face would combust into flame. I buried my face into the pillow, appalled.

"Oh my God…" I groaned, so embarrassed I hoped the bed would swallow me whole so I would not have to face him again.

"It's alright," he laughed, his hand rubbing my shoulder.

"That is so *embarrassing*..." I whined. I turned my head, barely peeking up at him. "Can we just say it was the latter?"

"I would be flattered."

Taking my shoulder, he turned me back to face him before moving forward and capturing my lips in a long, warm kiss.

When he backed away, it was impossible to remember how to breathe.

"While you're awake," he said, "you should probably go back to your room. I was going to relocate you if you didn't wake up."

"How long have I been out?!"

"About three and a half hours," he answered, sitting upright and offering his hand to me. I took it, trying not to let my embarrassment turn me into a puddle of shame.

We tiptoed out of Mykail's room and went to mine. He held the covers up for me as I climbed under them, giddy and smiling like a moron. I laughed harder when he took his time pulling the covers up to my chin and securing them around my shoulders with a smile of his own.

He then leaned over and pecked a chaste kiss on my lips.

"Get some sleep."

"Mykail?" I called as he started to move away. He paused. "Stay with me until I fall asleep?"

The request sounded childish and right out of a cheesy romance film, but I wanted him close. I wanted to lay beside him. I wanted his protection from the terrifying nightmares of Dana Christenson that were waiting for me when I fell asleep.

With a tender smile that sent my heart dancing in my ribcage, he maneuvered himself to lie next to me, his wings resting over the edge of the bed and on the floor as he draped an arm over my abdomen, pinning me under the covers and making me feel safer than I thought I ever could in Central.

Chapter Twenty-Five

As a young child, Saturdays had been the days I looked forward to the most.

Now, they were my most dreaded days.

I woke up late that Saturday morning and, because of that, I was somehow conned into grocery shopping with my mother. She like to go marathon shopping, so on our way to the supermarket, she saw a clothing outlet she insisted we visit first.

"I think your father and I will be in Europe for about a month," she said, talking about the trip she and Dad were not even sure they were taking yet. "Would you be alright on your own for a month?"

"Of course," I assured yet again. "Is…uh, Mr. Christenson going, too?"

"No." She shook her head, the bulk of her attention focused on the blouses she was scanning on the rack. "Too dangerous for him to travel abroad."

"Does that mean…I would have to go to those meetings by myself?" I was suddenly much less comfortable being left alone.

She paused, thoughtful.

"I'm not sure," she mused. "We'll ask at the meeting tonight."

My stomach turned over for the millionth time that morning.

I turned to the clothes on the rack next to the one my mother was browsing, my trembling fingers struggling to slide the hangers as I pretended to shop. "Hey, Mom?"

"Hm?"

"What do you think of him?"

"Who?"

"Mr. Christenson," I clarified, glancing over at her. She hesitated for a split second before shrugging.

"I don't know," she answered nonchalantly. "Why do you ask?"

"Just curious…"

"What do you think of him?" she turned the question back to me.

"He scares me."

I saw her nodding as I turned my gaze back to the clothes.

"That's understandable," she said. "But some people who are extremely smart are very different, and that can be scary."

"Smart?"

"He has a different way of looking at the world," she continued, though I noticed she had made a point of not meeting my gaze. "If you really think about it, it's a very clear way to see things. His view makes sense."

"Wait, *what*?" I turned away from the clothes, gawking at her.

"Lily," she said patiently, placing her hands on the hangers and turning to me, "he's one of the most important men in the entire world. He is commander of the most powerful organization in our country. He must be able to make decisions quickly and efficiently. To us, his judgments may seem rash, but he knows this world better than we do. He's probably dealt with these things hundreds of times. He knows what he's doing."

"I can't believe I'm hearing this," I gawked. "You're *defending* him?"

"He doesn't need defending. He does what he has to for the good of the country."

"How can you say that?" I choked. "After seeing what he does to people? What he did to Mykail…to Dad's brother?!"

"They were dangerous."

"And that makes it okay?"

"Do you realize how fortunate you are that the Commission does what it does?" she demanded, her tone sharpening. "Have you ever heard the stories about how things were before the Commission? The Commission of the People keeps us safe."

"At what cost?" I growled. "People being tortured? Tested on? Made into weapons or killed?!"

"Will you keep your voice down!" my mother snapped, glancing around to be sure we had not been heard. "You're too young to understand. I was the same way, once. When I heard about the revolution, about all the people who were displaced, I was horrified. But…as you get older, you realize that sacrifices like that must be made for the greater good. Not everyone is equal."

I felt as though I was staring at a stranger. My mother had always been driven and stubborn, but she had also been loving and caring, not just to the family, but to everyone she ever met. Hearing her justify Dana Christenson and the Commission of the People, even knowing everything happening inside the institution, made me disgusted to even look at her.

"I'll be in the car," I whispered, my voice choked.

I ran out of the store and the tears overwhelmed me the moment I slammed the passenger door behind me. Anger and revulsion swam inside me as I bitterly watched the door through blurred vision, my teeth grinding. My arms were crossed to hold my chest together as I tried to tell myself that my mother was not already succumbing to Dana's influence. I would have never expected those words to leave her lips, and they continued to replay in my mind until she emerged a half-hour later.

My tears had stopped, but I could still feel the swelling in my face. I wasn't sure if I wanted her to comment on my appearance or not, but I was still disappointed when she acted as though she could not see the evidence of my crying at all.

After we had left the grocery store, she tried to lecture me about how I would understand things differently as I grew up, that my view of the world would change. I told her that I didn't want to talk about it—not that that stopped her. I was left to sit bitterly in my seat, shrunk down with my arms tight over my chest and my gaze firmly locked out the window as she continued on and on about how naïve I was and that my idealism would eventually change to realism.

My jaw was firmly clenched as we unloaded the groceries. Mykail was sitting in the smaller living room with my father, but the moment I met eyes with him, I had to pointedly keep my gaze averted, knowing I would break down crying again if I met eyes with the boy who had suffered so severely in the Commission of the People.

As soon as I was able to escape, I fled to my room, threw myself on the bed, and silently fumed.

Fury consumed me to the marrow of my bones. I was sure I had never felt that kind of anger before.

I could not even begin to wrap my mind around the idea that any humans was "less than" another. I did not understand why different meant dangerous, nor what gave a small group of people the right to decide who was given the right to live and who was to be subjected to torture and death at the hands of the Commission. I never wanted to accept that as part of my world, and I sure as hell didn't want to be party to the group tormenting others.

My mother's words echoed in my head again, running down my spine and reawakening my disgust. My mother had always taught me to respect and cherish others, but she had just stated outright that people were not equal—that she had come to believe that there were those who were not deserving of respect and trust. And yet, she clearly respected the most dangerous man of all, the one at the helm of the Commission of the People.

I was not sure how long I remained on my bed, staring at the wall, irate and grinding my teeth, but I was surprised to hear my father calling to me from the bottom of the stairs to tell me we were leaving for the meeting in a half-hour.

I crawled off my bed, disturbing an indignant Dexter, to get ready for the weekly Commission meeting.

Just as I had the previous night, I started panicking about what to wear. At first I wanted to wear a turtleneck and slacks to cover up as much of my body as I could, but then I wondered if a low-cut shirt would be better for attracting Dana's attention. Did I want to play hard to get? Or entice him?

Running out of time, I decided on slacks and a blouse, but I left the blouse open to show some cleavage and a large necklace to draw attention to the area.

Painting on some light makeup, I hurried to my calling parents.

"Lily!" Mykail's voice hissed. I backpedaled to his barred door, where he was looking at me pleadingly. "Please be careful."

My family hurried to the meeting despite not being at all pressed for time, which left us with far too much time to socialize before the meeting. While my parents mingled with the other adults, I quickly sought out Clark.

"Hey," I greeted.

"Hey, how're you?"

"Fine, you?"

"Fine," he echoed, trying to be discreet about looking around him before he lowered his voice. "So?"

"He understands," I said vaguely, hoping my eyes would convey my excitement.

"Who understands what?" a voice quipped behind me. Spinning, I came face to face with Brian, Freddie, Lance, and Will, closing in like jackals.

"Leave us alone," Clark groaned. "Can't you find someone new to torment? We have to be boring prey by now."

"Torment?" Freddie blinked, feigning shock.

"Who said anything about torment?" Brian seconded.

"We were just trying to join the conversation," Will said. "After all, you two are the topic of the gossip, now."

"That's a nice necklace, Lily," Lance leered, leaning closer as I backed away. He reached toward my neck. "Is it a family heirloom or something?"

Clark smacked Lance's hand away, taking a step to shield me.

"Back off," he snapped.

"Ooh...aren't you possessive?" Lance said, his fist clenching as he turned his full attention to Clark. "Is she really worth what's about to happen to you?"

Brian tapped Lance on the shoulder and shook his head, nodding to the other side of the room.

We all turned.

Dana was lurking half-behind the curtain that outlined the stage at the front of the room, looking at us from behind his dark glasses.

My blood halted and I barely stopped myself from retreating, unable to tear my gaze away from the man peeking out from behind the curtain with the innocence of a five-year-old and the malice of a ravenous wolf.

I shivered, unable to turn even as I heard the boys that had been harassing us back away.

"Monday, during lunch, come to the east court of the school and we'll talk there," Clark whispered, though I could see out of my periphery he had also not looked away from Dana.

"I-I'll be there." I could hardly hear the words leave my lips, shuddering as Dana stepped from behind the curtain and began crossing the room in his gliding, dangerous stride. It took all my willpower to stop my legs from folding under me in fear as he stopped in front of us.

"I am pleased to see that the two of you have become such close friends," Dana said. "And Clark, good job protecting Little Lily this time." Though I dared not raise my gaze to his glasses, I knew his bright eyes were boring into me. "Little Lily," he said with a disapproving tone, "you have to be more careful around these young men, or I will have to keep closer watch over you."

His hand raised to my blouse and while I wanted to retreat, petrified, my body was frozen. His fingers expertly buttoned another button on my blouse to cover my cleavage and the pendant.

"Or perhaps you would like me to make another announcement to remind them of their place?" His voice had turned to honey again, and while I felt my skin grow hot as his fingers dropped from my blouse, I drew on all the strength and confidence I could muster to raise a hand and unbutton my blouse again.

"No," I told him, boldly raising my gaze to look at my reflection in his glasses. "Because I'm not yours to keep watch over."

The corner of his mouth quirked before he turned to Clark.

"Clark, we're running a few more tests on Eina tonight, so tomorrow I would very much like you to look over the results," he said. "Your input has been very helpful."

"Wait, what?" I gasped, turning to Clark expectantly. I saw the quirk in Dana's mouth turn into a half-smirk. Clearly he had been expecting my reaction.

"Clark offered to be a fresh set of eyes on Eina's testing results," Dana continued as Clark shrank under my gaze. "He really is such a bright boy. I can hardly wait for him to finish university so I can fully utilize that amazing brain with legal employment."

When Clark refused to meet my gaze and Dana continued to loom next to us, I turned back to the leader of the Commission.

"I thought Eina was *your* prized experiment. Why are you asking for extra input?"

"Nothing wrong with a new perspective," Dana said. "And Eina has been behaving oddly lately, so I thought it was time to get fresh eyes on him."

"Oddly how?"

"He doesn't seem interested in moving anymore," Dana said, retrieving his pocket watch and passing it between his hands distractedly. "There's nothing wrong with him that we could find, but thanks to Clark's input, we're going to see if his pain receptors are over firing, which might have prompted his recent behaviors."

"Or maybe it's nothing physical," I said shortly. "Maybe it's mental."

"Possibly," Dana agreed with a half-hearted shrug. "But he refused to even attack me when I walk into his cell, and that troubles me."

"Do you always expect your experiments to attack you?" I barked a laugh. "One day one might overpower and kill you."

"Quite possibly," Dana said. "And that's fully how I expect to go. That's how Bryant Morris died, after all."

Even Clark turned his gaze to Dana in shock.

"He was killed by an experiment?" I asked in disbelief. "I thought it was a heart attack."

"Of course you did, that's what we told the press," Dana said. "But as brilliant as Mr. Morris was, when he was obsessed with a goal, he couldn't see anything beyond his ambition, even if death was standing right in front of him." Dana cocked his head to the side in that dangerous way that sent shivers over my body. "And in the end, he was killed by his most prized experiment."

I could tell Dana was no longer looking at me, his shielded eyes focused elsewhere, as though seeing through time to the day Bryant Morris, the founder of the Commission of the People, was killed.

"Of course, we've made improvements since then." Dana snapped back to the moment, his face turning down to us again and causing both Clark and me to jump in surprise. "To properly keep things in order, we had to change quite a bit after his death. We had to learn how to think

228

like the experiments. There is always a concern that some of them will get together and rise up. It's happened before..."

Dana trailed off again, shrugging after a few beats of uncomfortable silence.

"I guess that just proves that you can never trust that you know anyone," he said. "You never know which of those closest to you will stab you when your back is turned." He placed his hands behind his back, still holding the pocket watch, and leaned to my ear. "Remember that, Little Lily."

He brushed past me, and I finally felt I could breathe. I had to inhale deeply several times to get my lungs back in order as I tried to shake the instinctive fear from my muscles.

I was relieved to see Clark's startled jump mirrored my own when the meeting room doors shut and everyone started taking their seats. We shared a trembling grin with one another before sinking into our own chairs.

The meeting was exceptionally boring. A few topics caught my interest, such as the trip to Europe that the Commission was organizing. Apparently, foreign leaders wanted to discuss government structure with the Commission of the People, and Dana was forming a delegation to go abroad and speak with them—a delegation that possibly included my parents.

There were a few brief reports on the experiments and the number of people the Commission was taking into custody from all the regions. That month, apparently, they had taken in fifty-seven people in the entire country. Mrs. Markus said it was a vast improvement and that things were starting to look up—whatever that meant. There was also a short discussion on Gregory Altereye and his men, who had found planets that could potentially support human life, and they were considering falling into orbit around one of them to see if there was already life on the surface.

Other than those topics, I ignored the contents of the meeting.

After the meeting was adjourned, my mother motioned for me to follow her. Despite still being furious with her, I fell obediently into step, hesitating only momentarily when I saw we were approaching Dana, who was in deep conversation with Freddie's mother.

We stood by the conversation, waiting for a moment to step in while I stared at Freddie, who glared at me. I tried not to let it scare or anger me, but I was upset. I was indignant that he was acting like the victim.

"Thank you, Mr. Christenson," Freddie's mother said.

"You're welcome, Alyssa." They walked away as Dana turned his attention to us. "Karen and Little Lily Sandover," he greeted. "What can I do for you?"

"We're terribly sorry to bother you, Dana." My mother was flushing, as if embarrassed, but the shy smile on her face told me that she was flustered just by being near him. Annoyance caused my jaw to clench yet again. It was no wonder she was so quick to defend the Commission. She was becoming fascinated with its leader, just like everyone else. The anger reignited hotter than before, realizing I was rapidly losing my mother to the Commission of the People.

"No bother at all."

"I know that you haven't finalized who is going to Europe, yet, but for those who have children and are going to leave for a month, do the children still have to come to the Commission meetings?"

"Come, now, Karen," Dana said. "I have not officially announced who is in the delegation, but you know that both you and your husband are indispensable. Of course you are going." My mother smiled shyly and fiddled with her wedding ring.

To divert the worst of my anger, I took comfort in the idea that it would be much easier to plot our rebellion with my parents gone.

"That would leave Little Lily all alone, though, wouldn't it?" Dana said slowly.

There were no words to describe how rapidly my ease deflated. I had been so focused on being able to spend time with Mykail alone and plot our rebellion with my parents gone, that I had not considered that my parents would not be around to stop Dana from appearing at my house whenever he pleased.

"No, not entirely alone," Karen said. "She would take care of Mykail, of course."

Dana turned to me quickly and the action startled me. Behind the glasses, I could feel his intense eyes boring into mine.

"Yes, she will need to attend the meetings," he said, his voice dangerous. "I will be sure to have one of the other families or one of our drivers bring her."

Dana had clearly seen the possibility that Mykail and I would get closer, and it was the last thing he wanted. He had already told me that he didn't want to share me, as if I was some sort of possession, and he viewed Mykail as competition.

"In fact," Dana continued, turning to my mother, "I was thinking of asking Little Lily to stay here at the Commission after school during the week."

"I'm sorry?" my mother asked, confused. My body tensed.

"Considering the young people are getting more aggressive in the Commission, I would not want anything to happen to Little Lily, particularly when you're abroad. I already feel like she's family, and I know that several of the boys here would love to call her their girlfriend."

"Really?" My mother sounded interested and I could not stop the roll of my eyes.

"Yes, but if I may say so, none of the boys are really worth her time. In order to keep her safe, I would like to have her come to the Commission after school."

"Oh...well..." My mother turned to see my reaction. I tried to tell her with my eyes that I was vehemently opposed, hoping she would get the hint and say no. She turned back to Dana. "I don't know," she mused. "You are such a busy man, Dana. I would not want to impose. Besides, she would be all alone down here after school."

"No, not at all," Dana said with a gleaming smile. "Clark stays with me every day as well. There are plenty of ways for the young ones to amuse themselves down here."

"I think I should talk to Thomas about this."

"Oh, yes, of course," Dana agreed. "Discuss it with him and let me know. The invitation is there."

"Thank you." She turned to me and nodded. As we turned away, Dana smirked at me.

My pace halted at the expression. The smile was an invitation. He was waiting to see if I would turn away from him and run, or if I would stay and defy him in the same manner as earlier in the evening. Trying to hide my deep breath in my turn, I looked at my mother.

"Hey, Mom, I'll be over in a little bit," I told her. "I want to ask Mr. Christenson something."

"Alright," she said, walking away, somehow convinced despite my shaky voice. I turned back to face Dana, who was waiting patiently.

"Little Lily," he greeted as I approached again.

"What did you mean?"

"Mean by what?"

"About not knowing who close to you will stab you in the back," I clarified, my voice stronger than I expected. "What did you mean?"

"Just some words of warning."

"Shouldn't you be heeding those warnings more than me?" I challenged. "If Bryant Morris was killed by an experiment that he was obsessed with, doesn't that mean that Eina is probably going to kill you one day?"

"Astute of you," Dana agreed. "Thankfully I am not *quite* as obsessed with Eina yet. Mr. Morris would spend many sleepless nights mulling over his prized experiment's charts, trying to memorize every detail. To be fair, experiment four-eleven forty-one was an anomaly from the beginning, so everyone was quite fascinated by him. He was rebellious and powerful, and never one to quietly submit to anything anyone told him to do. I found him puzzling, but Mr. Morris found him enthralling. He even started bringing the experiment into his quarters, just to spend more time with it. And that was all it took. One instance of him letting his guard down and four-eleven forty-one killed him." He cocked his head to the side. "I'm not quite ready to let Eina *that* close."

"What happened to the experiment?"

"Oh, he was dealt with accordingly." Dana smiled darkly and my hair stood on end at the hidden meaning in the words. "I can't say I blame Mr. Morris. It's quite easy to become obsessed with these experiments." He paused, lifting his gaze around the room before turning to the side and motioning to the door near the stage of the meeting room. "I think we should have this discussion in my office."

"Why?" I asked a little too quickly.

He chuckled. "I won't harm you, Little Lily. Where would the fun be in that?"

Before I could protest, he dropped his arm and walked past me to approach my parents. I forced my feet to follow. Even though I wanted to entice Dana and get close enough to him so that I could see more of the lab, I was starting to realize that meant *actually* spending time with Dana...just the two of us. Everything in my soul screamed at me to never be alone with such a dangerous predator.

"Tommy!" Dana called. My father cringed, but turned and forced a smile.

"Dana," he greeted, shooting me a curious glance when he saw me following the leader of the Commission.

"I am going to take Little Lily back to my office. She wanted to ask me a few questions," Dana stated matter-of-factly.

"Oh...o-okay," my father said, caught off-guard and wary of agreeing. "How long will you be?"

"I—"

"Actually," Dana interrupted me, "Clark and his mother are staying late tonight. They can drive her home. There is no reason for you to stay. It is already quite late."

"We can wait," my father said quickly. "We wouldn't want to impose on Danielle."

"Nonsense." Dana waved his concern away. "They have a driver. He can take Little Lily home if Danielle wants to stay later." He smiled and placed an arm around my shoulders. "I promise I will return her to you safely."

My father was torn but my mother seemed to have no problem with the idea. She smiled and turned to my father.

"It's alright, Thomas," she said. "She's perfectly safe."

"Yes, of course," my father said, though his hesitation showed he did not believe the statement. "Okay, then…we'll see you at home, honey."

I barely managed a nod, stuck in the storm between wanting to get closer to Dana for my own gain and wanting my parents to rip me away from the leader of the Commission and take me home. Dana's hand on my shoulder was warm, insistent, turning me away from my mother and father and guiding me through the door I had not been through since our first night at the Commission. I tried to remember the turns in the hallways that would lead me to Dana's office, but the memory of that night was fuzzy, disjointed, as though I had been in a dream when I last traversed those halls.

Dana steered me into his office, holding the door open and motioning me inside before closing the door with a click behind us. The office was dimly lit, papers still scattered over the large table and ornate desk. The room was messy and disorganized, file folders and open books even littering the floor amid folded and overturned papers, a few marked with a shoeprint.

"Now then, Little Lily," he started, walking past me to lean against the front of his desk, crossing his arms and tapping the toe of one shoe against the floor, looking me over as I stood helplessly in the middle of the office, "why are you suddenly so interested in my warnings about backstabbing? And when it comes to the experiments, at that? The last time we spoke about the experiments, you basically told me to go fuck myself."

"…not in so many words," I said coldly.

He smirked. "This is exactly why I wanted to have this discussion here," he mused. "I like you when you're away from everyone else, when you're not playing the role everyone wants you to play."

"What makes you think I'm not just playing the role you want me to play?" I challenged. "You said it was refreshing to have someone challenge you."

His continued scrutiny caused my heart to pick up a terrified pace, though I refused to back away from him or turn my eyes from his face. I had to play his game. I could not show my fear.

With an agonizingly graceful motion, he dropped his head and slowly removed his glasses.

"May I ask you a personal question, Little Lily?"

Figuring he would ask regardless of my answer, I waited in silence.

"Do you hate me?" he asked coolly, his amber eyes grabbing my gaze. "Or do you just fear me?"

I stared into the molten color, watching the hues shift and billow like smoke, trying with all my might not to fall into the depths of his eyes.

"...I hate you."

"And do you hate me merely because you're afraid of me?" he pressed. "People are afraid of what they do not understand, and that fear can very easily turn to hate. How else do you think the Commission was able to cleanse this country of the undesirables?"

"What the Commission does is beyond responding to hatred," I said. "It's creating even more hatred. What you do is *evil*."

"Hatred, evil, cruelty...that's all fear under different names, nothing more," Dana corrected. He stood straight, closing the space between us slowly. It took all my self-control to keep my feet from retreating, though I could not stop my body tensing.

His step halted midstride, a smile growing over his face.

"See? You are afraid of me."

"...everyone is afraid of you."

"To an extent," Dana agreed. "Until they learn to embrace the fear, to fall into it, to let me control their fear so it no longer controls them." He took two additional steps toward me and I barely managed to keep myself from running. "Doesn't that sound enticing?"

"No."

"You can be honest with yourself," Dana said, drawing uncomfortably close. I could feel my breathing coming heavier and faster, my eyes unblinking as I watched his golden gaze come more and more into focus. "No need to put on a front for me, Little Lily."

He stopped with only one stride between us, his towering height forcing my head back as I maintained eye contact, his expensive suit making his frame seem even more imposing.

He was beautiful, there was no doubt about it. A predator wrapped in a human disguise, his appearance luring unexpected prey into his clutches. Even as my heart raced in terror, my body began to grow warm, his all-seeing eyes reaching deep into my soul, lighting a fire there that I could not name nor contain.

I stared, captivated by the creature looming over me, flinching when he lifted a hand and brushed his fingers over my cheek.

"Do you feel that?" he whispered.

I could not respond, but I could also sense that he did not expect me to speak. His fingertips were warm, soft, brushing over my face and leaving sparks in their wake. Despite the gentle touch, my heart was beating so hard my ribs were aching from the abuse. My hands tingled, fear consuming my extremities.

I was under his spell. His eyes seemed brighter, filled with fire. The precise motion of his fingers as they trailed down my jaw and neck felt as smooth and threatening as a knife edge. There was a faint scent lingering on his suit, and the gentle rumble of his quiet laugh as it radiated from his chest tickled my ears and sent my hair standing on end.

"That adrenaline coursing through you is heightening every sense…" he murmured. "Every sensation is sharper, more vibrant, setting your body and mind alight." His fingers traced over my collarbone, finally resting in the indent at the base of my neck. "This is more alive than you have ever felt, because everything in your life has been the product of fear, starting from your conception all the way to this exact moment. It has consumed and controlled your life in ways you have never understood."

"T-That's not true," I stuttered, hypnotized by his voice, his eyes, and the gentle pressure between my collarbones.

"It is," he cooed. "Fear is what rules humans, and it's the way humans train one another. Evolutionary fear of not spreading genes leads to conception. Learning how to walk and stay balanced is induced by the fear of falling. Eating when hungry is out of fear of starvation…any sort of pain or discomfort will lead a human to do anything, and to build a cohesive society, everything must be imbued with fear to keep the masses in line."

"You're insane…" I whispered.

"Am I?" he challenged, the rippling color of his eyes hardening and causing a shudder to rush down my nerves. "And how am I insane? Because the fact that I don't follow the rules of our society causes you to feel uncomfortable? Frightened?" His head tilted again. "Why are you so willing to conform to societal expectations when you claim that our society is evil?"

"Not society, the Commission of the People," I said, stepping back so his fingers would finally leave my skin.

"That society gave birth to the Commission of the People. One would argue that the apple rarely falls far from the tree."

235

"But the American people would *never* accept the way you experiment on people!" I snapped. "That's not acceptable by *any* society."

"You are very young indeed," Dana mused, taking another step. That time I retreated, backpedaling until I felt the papers slipping under my feet and my back hit one of the chairs at the large, disheveled table. "One of the greatest fears humans have is the fear of their own frailty. That's how medicine evolved to the point where our experiments can happen, and if you think it got to this point without a mountain of bodies behind it, you are truly naïve."

"Of course you would justify your cruelty," I grumbled, trying to back away even more as his hands came to rest on the table behind me, effectively pinning me against the back of the chair, his face coming close to mine.

"Society might not like their delicate sensibilities being prodded with the knowledge of what we do down here, but there is something to be said for the morbid curiosity that comes with being human." He smirked at me. "Don't tell me you've never thought about it. I'm sure even when you looked at Mykail with that terror in your eyes, a part of you wondered what it would be like to fly like he can. What it would feel like to be physically changed to do whatever you want. Infinite strength, ability to fly, see in the dark…those are the abilities that make superheroes."

"Or supervillians," I tried to bite back, irritated when the response caused his smile to grow. "And what about all the downsides those superhero stories talk about?"

"What about them?" he asked. "It's just like the downsides of being human, but since they're not the common human experience, they're fascinating to ponder. Wondering what *you* would do if you were faced with those dilemmas. That's no different than these experiments, pushing things to the very edge just to see how far we can go as a society, or even a species."

"Until those experiments kill you when your back is turned," I said. "Even that doesn't worry you?"

"Not at all," Dana said easily, his face drawing so close I could no longer bring his face into focus, his breath hot against my cheek. I tried not to shiver, tried to pull my thoughts together, realizing I had been compliant in Dana pinning me to the chair and had not even tried to push him away. It was so difficult to think in his dark office. My mind was swimming in a fog, thoughts elusive, my body only responding to whatever Dana Christenson did.

"I bet you will be afraid." The words had no strength, but I still managed to say them clearly. "I bet when you see Eina coming after you to kill you, you'll be afraid then."

"I'm not afraid of death."

"Everyone is afraid of death."

"Except those who have already known it," he whispered, leaning even closer, his lips barely brushing the skin of my cheek. "Would you like to know it, Little Lily?"

The words were gentle, inviting, whispered with loving care, but my body reacted as though they had splashed ice cold water over my head. My hands raised to his chest, shoving him with as much strength as my trembling muscles could muster. He backed away but his smile only grew. The force of the shove pushed me back against the chair harder, so I stumbled to regain sense of my legs, turning my head toward his office door, intent on running out when a knock sounded and the door opened without waiting for an answer.

Mrs. Markus walked into the room.

"Sorry to disturb—oh, Lily, hello. I didn't know you were in here."

"Hello, Mrs. Markus," I said weakly, wanting to feel relieved at the sight of her though the feeling did not come.

"I didn't mean to intrude," Mrs. Markus said, turning to Dana. "I can come back later."

"No intrusion," Dana said, motioning her inside.

"While we were in the meeting, I missed a call from Leader Simon's Finance office. Edgar wants to meet with you about the funding of the Europe delegation. I looked at your calendar. I figured we could meet with him Thursday when Leader Simon visits."

Despite the fog of fear and confusion in my mind, the words resounded through the haze and brought me into sharp focus. Dana had already stated that Leader Simon was made aware of the experiments happening in the Commission, but I did not think that he would make the journey to the Commission himself. Thinking about how Dana had already told my parents that he was interested in having me come to the Commission after school, I had to wonder if it would ever be possible to meet Leader Simon—maybe even ask him how he truly felt about the goings-on in the Commission of the People.

"Thursday is fine," Dana said. "Danielle, how late were you planning on staying tonight?"

"Not much later," she said. "Why? Is there something you need?"

"Not exactly." Dana nodded to me. "Tommy left his little girl here to talk to me and I was hoping you could take her home when you leave."

"Oh, of course," Mrs. Markus said with a bright grin. "Clark is in the first conference room. She can wait with him until we leave."

"Thank you, Danielle. I'll take her to Clark when we're done and then I'll be in the back for the rest of the night, so feel free to head home whenever you're ready," he told her. The sentence was spoken with gentleness, but there was authority behind the words that bespoke a few hidden orders that I did not understand, but could still feel.

"Very well. Good night, Dana," she said, backing out of the office and closing the door behind her.

As Dana's attention returned to me, I glanced at the desk clock next to his powered-down computer, seeing it was already nearing one in the morning.

"Don't you let your people sleep?" I grumbled.

"Of course."

"Then why are you going into the back with the experiments at this time of night?" I asked. "Unless you're more obsessed with Eina than you're willing to admit."

The cold smirk returned to his lips. "The experimentations are constant, Little Lily. We're never closed down here."

I didn't expect to have such a visible reaction to the statement. I jumped a little, my eyes going wide as a cold stab of fear hit my gut, wondering how we were supposed to sneak anyone out of the labs of the Commission if it was a twenty-four-hour operation.

"You seem surprised," he noted, quirking an eyebrow.

"You just said you let your people sleep, and now you're saying you're never closed," I said, hoping I could explain my startled response. "And what about you? Surely you sleep at some point."

"I gave up the habit."

Trying not to roll my eyes at the statement, I crossed my arms as a barrier against him and cleared my throat to strengthen my voice. "And you're such a control freak you have to oversee all the experiments yourself?"

"Of course not," he said. "I'm a busy man, I don't have time for that. But Eina will be on the table tonight and I wouldn't miss his testing for anything." He tilted his head. "Care to join me?"

I faltered and I knew he saw it. I hoped he would think that I was actually considering going to see Eina's testing rather than debating with myself how much interest I could show in the Commission before Dana figured out I was trying to infiltrate so I could break experiments free.

"I don't revel in cruelty like you," I responded.

"But you are fascinated by it," he said. "You're fascinated by what we do down here, by all the test subjects we have in those cells."

"*Humans*," I snapped. "They're *human*."

"And what is your definition of human, Little Lily?"

I faltered again. There was no way I could explain why I felt that every human confined in the Commission was undeserving of the torment they were enduring. It seemed so obvious, like common sense, that one was not to cause harm to another human.

He nodded knowingly. "That is what will limit you, Little Lily," he said, raising a finger like a patient teacher. I wanted to punch him at seeing the gesture. "You're taking on the fears and pain of everyone else. Don't you think you have enough problems in your own life without worrying about them?" He motioned behind him to signify his prisoners.

I felt like we were playing tug of war. Even though we were no longer physically close, I could feel the tension between us, pulling me closer as I tried to yank him to my side of the room.

"I'm part of the Commission now," I said. "Which means what happens to those people back there is part of my life, and therefore part of my problems."

"Oh, so you're willing to admit you're part of the Commission now?" he said mockingly.

"I didn't have a choice in becoming part of the Commission," I continued. "But you dragged me in here, and I am disgusted by you and everything you do." His expression remained mocking, his eyebrows going high. "You shouldn't decide who is *acceptable*. Who should live and die. You have *no* right to do that."

"And you have a right to tell me that I don't have that authority?" he retorted. "Interesting argument, considering the people of America as a collective were the ones who decided who was acceptable and who wasn't. *I* didn't decide the criteria for the undesirables. The American people did."

"Like hell!" I snapped. "If the people knew what happened to those people, they would never—"

"Don't continue to disappoint me, Little Lily," he tutted, shaking his head. "Of course the American people decided who was an acceptable member of society, and they continue to defend that choice every time a neighbor calls in someone who doesn't meet the criteria. Sure, they may not know the specifics, but don't for one moment think that their neighbor disappearing in the middle of the night was a gentle act. Often even if we have to tackle fleeing undesirables in the middle of the street, the neighborhood will shut their blinds and turn the other way."

"This wasn't why the Revolution was fought," I tried to say, though I could not put any conviction behind the words I knew were untrue. "Thomas Ankell didn't tear down a corrupt government so the government he built could become even worse."

"He most certainly did," Dana corrected. "Ankell and Morris killed hundreds of thousands in one form or another. Even I am nowhere near the body count achieved by either one of them. But they were marketed as heroes, as warriors for a better cause, and they both agreed on the duties of the Commission of the People."

"That was during a time of war. The country is peaceful now. There's no reason to keep acting like barbarians and killing our own countrymen, or-or turning them into experiments."

"Then as long as it is in the name of peace and prosperity, the violence is justified?" He clicked his tongue and shook his head. "You sound more like Ankell and Morris than you know."

"No, that's not—"

"You think that everyone is equal, but if everyone was equal do you think we would need to exploit and rule each other? Do you realize how many people line up for slaughter at a single word from someone who holds title over them alone? Because fear is the currency of a stable society, and peace is the commodity being sold. Fear of what you could tell the Commission is the reason your friends are so reluctant to spend time with you, because they know you're more powerful, which makes you one to fear. You don't even have to do anything. All you have to do is tell them you're part of the Commission and that shadow looming behind you will force others to scurry out of your way so you can keep gaining power and instilling fear, which will keep those around you from misbehaving, and that in turn, perpetuates the peace in America.

"That is exactly how the government operates, as well. The laws and legislations passed are meant merely to dissuade those who might consider pushing their luck. And you can wipe that disgusted look off your face," he chided. "This is nothing new. Humans have lived this way for thousands of years, long before the Commission of the People came into being. It is merely the way humans were built to coexist. And if you think that humans will let their compassion and empathy overrule their fear, you still have much to learn about the world.

"Humans cannot live without fear," he concluded, "Fear of what's different, fear of pain…it's the only way to keep people from tearing themselves to pieces. So if I have to take all those people into the back to keep the peace, I will do it because, overall, it is better for everyone in the country."

"...I pity you," I said before I could understand why those were the words that came to mind. "I can only imagine how young you were when you were surrounded by all this, to the point where you think this cruelty is the default for humanity."

Dana smirked—there was a challenging edge to the expression that sent a shockwave of excitement through me.

"And do you think you're the one to prove me wrong?"

"Maybe. But I don't know that there's enough human left in you to save." I wanted the words to be sharp and biting, but they sounded defeated.

"There's not," he stated simply, raising an arm to look at his expensive watch. "But it should be most entertaining to watch you try." Plucking the pocket watch from his suit jacket, he twisted the chain around his fingers and jerked his head toward the office door. "I'll take you to Clark now."

* *** *

Clark was so startled to see me when I walked into the conference room that he clambered out of his chair, hissing when he banged his hand on the corner of the table.

"Lily?"

"Clark, you and your mother will be taking Little Lily home tonight," Dana ordered, his hand finally leaving my lower back as he leaned against the doorframe.

I had never seen a conference room in the Commission before, but the half-wall of windows showing the hallway and a long table with a shining, mirrored surface surrounded by plush rolling chairs were the only details I could notice in my goofy state. Clark's small laptop was opened next to a stack of textbooks, meriting some notice as I drew closer to my classmate.

Dana said nothing more, though I could feel his eyes land on my back before he retreated from the conference room, closing the door behind him.

I fumbled for one of the chairs, pulling it away from the table and slumping into it heavily as Clark watched Dana through the windows until he was out of sight. He then diverted all his attention to me, placing a hand on my shoulder as he resumed his seat and wheeled it closer to me.

"Talk to me, what happened?"

"Nothing," I whispered. "I just...I can't...I can't think when I'm around him."

"He has that effect," Clark agreed.

I lifted my eyes from the smooth, black table top and looked at his eyes hidden behind his thick-rimmed glasses. I could see the fear in his eyes, the acute worry, and the way his gaze passed over me as if scanning for injuries. Normally, seeing anyone so worried would force me to pull myself together, not wanting to appear weak or frighten anyone. But there was a knowing edge to his scrutiny. He knew exactly how I was feeling. He had clearly felt it several times before. I could almost see the gears in his mind taking account of how I clenched my fists in the fabric of my slacks, the cadence of my voice, the rate at which the tears gathered in my eyes...able to determine the severity of my encounter with the leader of the Commission of the People based on those reactions.

The tears could not be stopped.

I bent forward, hiccupping in the final few attempts to keep the sobs at bay. Clark pulled my chair to him, pulling me into a hug and allowing my hands to grip in his shirt as I cried.

"I'm here," he said.

"I...I couldn't argue against him," I managed to choke out around my sobbing. "I wanted...he has to understand...he can't do that to people. He has to..."

Clark's hands were steady on my shoulders, holding me tight.

"You don't have to explain," he whispered. "I know."

"But...what if he's right?" I asked, my fingers slowly loosening as I managed to draw back and search his expression for more reassurance. "That the Commission is necessary because humans are too cruel to be trusted to govern themselves without this type of control."

Clark's thumbs moved over my shoulders, holding me steady as I sniffed and tried to dispel the steady stream of tears falling down my cheeks.

"Everyone knows that humans can be exceptionally cruel, but the way I look at it, if what the Commission did really was the best thing for the country, we wouldn't feel this strongly about fighting against it. If Dana wasn't such a severe threat, our instincts wouldn't scream at us to run every time we saw him. And I'd much rather listen to my human instinct than whatever Dana fucking Christenson says."

I drew as much air into my lungs as I could stand, holding my breath, hoping it would clear my head. But as always happened in the basement of the Commission, my mind was fogged with a confusing storm of thoughts I was unsure I could weather.

When I exhaled, Clark squeezed my shoulders before releasing me with a nod.

"You're too strong to let Dana break you down," he said. "I know you have no choice but to listen to what he says and think about it, but don't let it get under your skin. At least, as much as you can." The last sentence was said in an exasperated laugh.

"...do people really still call in their neighbors? Like they did during the population cleanse?" I asked meekly, barely managing to remember I was wearing mascara in time to be more careful about how I dabbed the tears from my eyes.

"Not as often," Clark said. "Most of those in the back now are found by electronic traces or criminal histories. It's not as rampant as it was when the population was all mixed together."

I nodded slowly, sniffing, peering down into the reflective surface of the table to assess the evidence of my tears on my face.

"I guess it's harder to spot undesirables when there aren't distinctive physical features," I mumbled. "Although I guess those differences are what led the people to thinking they were less than human and turning the other way when the Commission rounded them up." I turned back to Clark. "Are there are lot of people of other ethnicities back there?"

"Unfortunately," Clark said with a somber nod. "Even knowing the danger, people still try to sneak into the country on their way to Canada or Mexico and get caught within our borders."

"I don't think I've ever seen one in person," I mused.

"The Commission is, unfortunately, frighteningly efficient."

I slumped back in my chair, running my hands through my hair with another heavy sigh.

"...what the hell are we doing, Clark?" I whispered. "What if we can't pull this off?"

"We can't think about that," he said, flicking his eyes to the windows by the conference room door and the security camera in the corners. "Sometimes, we have to act just because we see hope and change on the horizon."

"...how the hell did this become our lives?"

"Our parents?" Clark suggested lightly.

I laughed. "Come on, do we really blame our parents for everything?"

"I don't mind doing it," he said, cracking a weak smile.

Smiling with him, I shrugged one shoulder. "Dana wants me to start coming here after school," I told him. "I don't know that my parents will go for it, but you might have some company down here."

"Certainly will be a welcome change from how boring it can get being stuck down here until Dana tells my mother she can leave," Clark huffed.

"He really runs this place with an iron fist, doesn't he?"

"You have no idea…"

Clark glanced at the clock on his laptop before groaning, muttering under his breath about how many hours he had already spent in the basement that day and that he wanted to go home as he packed his books into his backpack and shut down the laptop. I watched him numbly, feeling the heat in my face slowly subside as my tears gave way to bone-rattling emotional exhaustion.

Being around Dana was draining. I would need to slowly increase my exposure to him to build up a tolerance if I had any hope of playing our game at his level.

My eyelids were drooping when the conference room door opened and Mrs. Markus stepped into the room. A man followed, about the same height as Clark's mother, wearing a simple black suit and sunglasses, his black hair slicked way from his face. I assumed he was the Markus' driver and could feel the relief that washed through me wake me enough to stand, eager to get out of the Commission of the People.

"Are you two ready to go?" Mrs. Markus asked sweetly. She turned to me as the driver stepped into the room and took Clark's backpack from him without prompting. "Oh, Lily, are you alright? You look as though you've been crying."

"Oh, no, sorry." I wiped at my eyes again, that time forgetting about the mascara. "When I get really tired my eyes start watering. Contacts," I lied.

"…are you sure you're okay?" she asked again. The tone was meant to be comforting, but a crushing sadness fell over me. I could hear the tenderness in her tone, her genuine worry about my well-being, and I could not understand how she could work for Dana and be so loyal to him when she clearly felt such empathy.

"Really, I'm alright," I said quietly.

The driver held the door open for us before following Mrs. Markus loyally to the elevators so we could grab my phone from the reception desk. A sleek black car was idling outside the front doors, waiting for us when we finally stepped into the chilly night air. The driver opened the door for us before assuming his seat, silent and stoic, never removing his dark glasses.

"Clark, did you finish your homework?" Mrs. Markus asked. I leaned against the door of the car, watching the dark scenery pass as Clark, seated between me and his mother, nodded, clearly just as tired.

I did not ask how the driver knew where I lived despite my never telling him. I was too thankful to see the house still glowing with light when the car bumped into the driveway. I mumbled a thank you to the driver and mustered a more enthusiastic sentence for Mrs. Markus as I opened the door and climbed out of the car.

"Lily," Clark called, catching me just before I closed the door, "don't forget about Monday. I'll see you in the courtyard with the notes."

"Right," I said quickly, glad he had reminded me as I had forgotten in my haze. "Thank you again for your help. I'll see you Monday."

I closed the car door and half-jogged to my front door, finding it unlocked as I was sure my parents were waiting for me. With one foot over the threshold, I waved to the car that was waiting for me to get into the house before leaving. As the car slowly backed away, I closed the front door and was immediately ambushed by my father.

"Lily?" Before I could notice he had not even changed out of his suit yet, he had enveloped me in his arms. "There you are," he murmured.

I folded my arms to my chest, letting his hug encase me completely, squeezing me tightly as I felt the relief at being home mix with the relief of my father's relaxing muscles.

That hug was all the proof I needed.

Dana was wrong. Cruelty was not the core element of a human. The love I felt in my father's arms, the safety and warmth that chased away the lingering needles of freezing fear Dana's words had left under my skin...those feelings were unmistakable.

And if something as simple as my father's hug could dispel the fear Dana had brought into my body, then I could find a way to remove Dana's fear-fueled influence and bring down the Commission of the People.

Chapter Twenty-Six

It took a while for my father to leave me alone. He was acting as though he had not seen me in months, offering to make me some herbal tea and sit with me a bit. My mother, who had been in the shower when I returned, came downstairs and playfully scolded my father, saying he was being silly for thinking I was in some kind of danger.

The words hurt more than she could have known.

But I was finally able to sneak away, going to my room to quickly wash up and change into my pajamas, trying not to be horrified at the state of my makeup—nor angry at my mother for not wondering if the mascara on my cheeks was the result of tears.

Pushing down the anger and the residual fear, I peered out of my room, confirming the downstairs lights were off before going to Mykail's door. With practiced precision, we unlocked and opened the door, sitting on his bed, keeping only the one bedside lamp on so as not to alert my parents if they were to see a bright glow coming from his room.

"How was it tonight?"

"Dana wants me to go to the Commission after school," I said.

Mykail's beautiful expression became conflicted, his eyes falling to the bedspread between us.

"What's with that expression?" I asked. "You're not getting cold feet are you?"

"Not exactly," he mumbled. "I'm just...not fond of the idea of Dana having such easy and constant access to you. He's too dangerous."

"I know," I agreed. "I actually managed to spend some time with him alone in his office tonight."

His head snapped up, his eyes wide.

"Did he hurt you?"

"No, no," I said, waving my hand awkwardly, hoping the action detracted from the embarrassed blush that rose to my cheeks. "I mean, he scared the hell out of me, and I kinda got shaky..." I drew in a deep breath, puffing out my cheek as I exhaled. "I think if I can slowly increase my exposure to him and his...whatever the hell it is he does, his presence won't be so overwhelming."

"...maybe..."

"And the more often I can roam the Commission, the more snooping I can do."

"Speaking of which," Mykail started, reaching into his pillowcase and extracting the notes Clark had given me and the crude, hand-drawn map of the Commission Mykail had drawn. "I looked over the notes and deciphered them as best I could."

"As best you could?"

"Well, whoever wrote this has really sloppy handwriting," he said, leafing through the papers with a huff. "But there is a lot of great information in here, assuming we can trust it."

"Like what?"

"What took the most time to figure out was the first page, but it's the security access codes for each of the wards," he explained, pointing to the double-us followed by a string of numbers. "These are the door codes that would allow you to get into each ward without one of those electronic cards."

"But that wouldn't be the code for the cells in those wards?"

"No," he said with a shake of his head. "And these security codes change every few months. Although considering the rest of the information was written in the code used by experiments, I'm worried about how accurate the information is. This is very likely another experiment, and they might not have the most up-to-date codes."

"But it's a start," I said, desperate to feel that we were making some sort of progress. "What about the other pages? Do they have the codes for the cells?"

"No access codes for the cells, but," he raised a finger as though sensing the exasperated sigh that was about to escape me, "it does detail the cell numbers and schedules of twenty-seven experiments throughout the different wards."

"Twenty-seven?"

"Unfortunately, no names were given and I never bothered to learn other experiments by their numbers, so I'm not entirely sure who they all are. I think I have an idea of the one experiment in Ward Ten just based on the location of the cell, but I can't be completely certain."

"You mentioned that experiments would interact with one another to test how severely the testing affected social interaction," I recalled. "I'm assuming that does not mean they just let the experiments wander through the halls…"

"No," he agreed with a grin. "That's what these schedules are for." He motioned to a scribbled table he had scratched on the back of one of the papers, the days of the week spelled incorrectly and tiny letters and numbers detailing which experiments were to socialize on which days of the week. I desperately tried to find patterns or similar days when the twenty-seven experiments were interacting on the same date, but I could not stop myself from looking up at Mykail at the severity of spelling errors in the days of the week.

He cleared his throat nervously. "Sorry about all the misspellings, I know they're all wrong."

"No, sorry, it's not a big deal," I said quickly. "It just startled me, that's all."

"Safe to say I didn't get far in school," he mumbled, his eyes very pointedly avoiding my gaze. "But I was actually the most literate member of my family, if you can believe it."

"I...I never really thought about it," I said. "I shouldn't have just assumed. I didn't mean to make you uncomfortable."

"Let's just say criminal families don't really care if their kids can spell the days of the week," he said, his voice sharper than I anticipated, but before I could think of a way to tactfully ask him more about his childhood, he promptly dropped the subject.

"Anyway, these are the days and approximate times that these experiments are in the Dome."

"Dome?"

Mykail nodded slowly, drawing in a deep breath. "The closest we get to going outside once we're taken into the Commission," he said. "It's an artificial environment. It basically looks like a giant, domed greenhouse. There are plants, even a stream with running water, and giant light panels that are supposed to give off UV light. This schedule is the time of day these experiments go to the Dome."

I took my time studying the overlaps and gaps in the schedule.

"There are a few that seem to coincide with one another," I mused. "But I don't think we're going to be able to take these experiments a few at a time and break them out. Once one or two go missing, I'm sure the Commission will crack down on security quickly. We would have to try and get them all in one go."

"Again, assuming we can trust these experiments," Mykail said. "Even though it took me a long time to figure all this out, once I realized how varied and classified this information was, I have to admit I got a little suspicious."

"Maybe it's all of these experiments working together to gather the information," I suggested, trying not to show how unnerved I was at the idea that we were being baited. "Surely there were experiments who talked about rising up and trying to take over the Commission."

"That hasn't been done in many years," Mykail said. "Of course everyone whispers about it, but it's really just a way to keep ourselves sane in there. And even if some experiments were trying to organize a breakout of some kind, they would never leave a paper trail." He tapped the pages between us. "They would plot using the sign language so the guards wouldn't catch on."

"There's a sign language between the experiments?"

"Best way to communicate with the cameras everywhere. Everything is disguised as normal movements, like scratching your arm or tucking hair behind your ear. It's one of the first things experiments are taught by the older ones when they start going to Dome." He drummed his long fingers over the papers, shaking his head "I wish we could get blueprints of some kind. There have to be secret passages, or emergency staircases out of the Commission that could be used to break these experiments out. And even if you do manage to get closer to Dana, I don't know that you'll be able to do too much searching in the far corners where only security personnel or scientists are allowed."

"Maybe if I get down in the Commission more, I can get into Dana's office," I suggested. "Surely he's got blueprints."

"It's a good place to start," he agreed. "As long as you are very careful."

"Our other big obstacle is gathering people to support what we're planning," I said. "Everyone is probably too afraid of the Commission to even listen if we tried to say anything against it."

"Then just wait for Dana to do something particularly ugly to anyone you want to approach," Mykail said. "It's always better to approach people when they're in a high emotional state if you want to convince them."

"I'm sure it won't be too long before Dana does something," I huffed. "But it seems like so many people are willing to just accept what he does."

"In the Commission, a lot of people think falling at his feet is the best way to gain his favor, and Dana's favor means survival. But Dana also strikes a lot of fear, and fear can be manipulated in a lot of ways."

For a brief second, Dana's bright, molten eyes and crooked smile flashed through my mind, as if to say "Sound familiar?"

The shudder passed unpermitted down my spine, and I had to draw in a deep breath and rub my eyes roughly to hide the action from Mykail.

"Getting cold feet?" he asked with a subtle smirk.

"No," I said, straightening and pushing the thought of the Commission leader's face far from my mind.

"I know it's daunting but if you're serious about this, we'll find a way. I'm sure there's more than a few Commission members unhappy with the state of things even if they don't want to admit it," he said, gathering the papers and smoothing them into a neat stack. "And obviously there are experiments ready to stage a coup." He turned and placed the papers back into his pillowcase. "And once we have the support we need to pull off the breakout of the Commission, we can anger the people into the revolution we'll need to take down the Commission of the People."

"Oh, only all that," I laughed sarcastically.

"The revolution wasn't that long ago," Mykail said, smiling at me, trying to raise my spirits. "There are still plenty of those raised with the spirit of fighting the corruption of the government. I doubt it will take much to reignite that spark."

I pursed my lips and nodded, blaming my exhaustion for the flutters I felt in my belly.

I could feel Mykail's eyes on me, picking apart each feature to read my mood. I swallowed down the knot in my throat and shook my head.

"Sorry, I think I'm more tired than I realized."

He reached toward me, placing his hand against my face and tenderly rubbing his thumb over my brow. My eyes fluttered closed.

"Then enough plotting for tonight."

He leaned to me, one of his wings pressing into the bed to stabilize him as both his hands took my face, tiling my head to capture my lips in a tender kiss. Startled by his boldness in that moment, my exhaustion melted away and my heart picked up pace, my blood going hot at the contact. When I felt his tongue tentatively press against my lips, asking for entrance, I felt my face grow hot under his touch, both from the rush of hormones and embarrassment.

I had heard plenty of stories from my friends that had taught me a lot, but I had never made out with a boy before Mykail, and felt clumsy and awkward, unsure what I should do to show him that I was very interested in continuing the activity. My body quivered, the touch of his fingers and lips electric on my skin. The feeling of his tongue left me weak. I leaned into him for support, unable to move my hands beyond placing them between us on the bed as I leaned into the kiss.

I did not falter for long. Mykail's strong hands took my waist, lifting me enough to turn me on the bed so I was on my back, allowing him to settle over me as my hands closed around his face. His wings pressed into the mattress on each side, giving him the ability to drag his fingers up my waist, to my shoulders and down my arms as his lips found mine yet again.

We were encased in the protection of white feathers, the furniture of the room and the glaring of the lights above blocked by the wings. My hands went to his neck, holding onto Mykail as I longed to draw him closer, weaving my fingers into the thin, soft hair at the back of his head. The heat in my veins was hot enough to burn away my fears, even if temporarily. The conversation with Dana earlier in the night, the tears Clark's worried gaze pulled out of me, the growing anticipation of planning a revolution did not exist in those moments. There was only Mykail. Only his lips, only his hands, only the cocoon of his wings.

Though I felt clumsy and awkward as my lips tried to react to Mykail's more practiced movements, our tongues tangling together, I eagerly participated, my body growing hotter and hotter under his gentle caresses. I could not open my eyes. All I could do was hold him to me, feel the way each tender ministration sent fireworks along my nerves, and try to catch a short breath every time our lips parted for the briefest second.

It was messy. No finesse. But it was incredible.

My focus was drawn sharply to the heat in my body when Mykail shifted above me and pressed his hips down on my thighs. A wildfire sparked in my abdomen, drawing a strangled groan from my throat that should have embarrassed me, had the flames devouring my nerves not charred all rational thought. His hips pushed forward, a gentle undulation, but it felt so intimate, so intense, that I gasped and our mouths broke apart. Mykail drew back as though I had bitten him, breathing hard, sitting back on my legs as his hands promptly left me.

"Sorry," he whispered, turning his head to the side as he tried to catch his breath. "We should take this a little slower."

I could hardly hear his words, the pang of disappointment causing a dull ringing in my ears. The light seemed too bright now that I was staring directly at it, and my body was eagerly craving the heat that had been snatched away when Mykail retreated.

I reached for him, my fingers lazily drifting over his knee.

"Do you hear me complaining?"

"We need to be careful," he said, taking my hand and encasing my fingers in his to keep them from teasing his knee. "Sorry, but I think we should stop this for now."

"No, don't say that," I pleaded. "We can slow things down if you want, but don't just pull away like that…"

"I have to be careful, Lily," he said, squeezing my fingers. "I can't lose my head like that. I could have hurt you."

"I know you won't," I insisted.

"…I don't," he whispered, his fingers squeezing even tighter, almost to the point of pain. He climbed off me, sitting next to me as his wings unfolded around me and went to rest on the bed behind him. I stared at the ceiling, trying not to let the disappointment crush me, needing a few moments of deep breathing before I sat upright.

"I'm not trying to be difficult, Lily," he said quietly, his eyes downcast. "What Dana did to me...I'm still learning who I am now that..." His feathers bristled to complete the thought.

"I can understand that," I said slowly, kicking myself for being so wrapped up in physical desire that I was disappointed when he pulled away from our heated kisses. "I just don't want you to think I'm afraid of you. Because I'm not."

His smile was sad when he lifted his gaze to meet mine.

"I can't tell you what it means to me to hear you say that," he said. "You just answered my prayers."

"You pray?" I asked, unable to stop the smile spreading over my lips.

"The irony is not lost on me," he said. "And I don't so much pray to God as I pray to have the strength to stay alive long enough to see things get better in my life. That I would find someone who could see beyond what the Commission did to me. Who could accept it?"

"I don't think accepting is the right word," I said quietly. "I can never accept the pain Dana put you through. But I can accept who you are, no matter what, even if I am filled with pain and anger at the thought of what happened to you to get you here." I scoot forward on the bed, taking both his hands in mine. "And if you ever want to talk about what happened, I'm here to listen."

I saw the way the muscles in his neck tensed, so I squeezed his hands tighter.

"To be honest, I don't remember most of it," he mumbled. "It's all a little foggy...like everything that happens down in the Commission."

It was a small relief to hear that I was not the only one who struggled to keep my head on straight once in that basement.

"Really the only memories that are distinct are the later tests...when the wings were stitched together."

Again, his feathers ruffled. I turned my attention to them, to the way they dipped the mattress where they sat, the way his shoulders drooped with their weight...

"How did they even manage..." I did not need to finish the question.

"They have technologies that the world doesn't even know exist yet," he said. "With such a large sample of test subjects that can be tested on and killed without repercussions, the scientists have made leaps and bounds in science and medicine. Originally, I was part of the

Machine of Neutralization project, but…" He stopped his eyes going distant. "After what happened to my brother…"

"Your brother was part of the Machine of Neutralization program?"

"…he didn't last long," Mykail whispered. "None of my siblings did. And when it was my turn, they decided my genetic makeup was not compatible with what they were attempting to do, so they decided to see if they could attach wings so that, when they did manage to do whatever the hell they're trying to do with those experiments, they would know if it was possible to attach wings to a human."

"…I can't even imagine," I choked, my hands tightening around his even further, shaking.

"I'm actually lucky," he said, lifting his gaze. "My testing is over. Dana isn't interested in changing anything more with my case. Others like Eina are not so lucky."

"You've met Eina?"

"Briefly," Mykail said. "He was almost always kept separate from the other experiments, if not by the scientists, then by the other experiments."

"What do you mean?"

"There is something…wrong with Eina," Mykail said, not dropping his head, though his gaze went distant, drawn back to his interactions with the Machine of Neutralization. "You can feel it when you're around him. He's more dangerous than anything the Commission has made before. I'd go so far as to say he's even more dangerous than Dana."

I could not stop the skepticism from taking over my features.

"I know it sounds crazy," he said, "but I'm telling you…there is something completely unnatural about him. Sometimes when I looked into his eyes…it was like I was watching an asteroid approaching earth, or the detonation of a nuke. It was just…devastation and destruction in his gaze. And he's so strong, and so fast, and it's like he can see into your mind."

"Do you think, if we break these experiments out, we should also break out Eina?"

"No."

It was said so strongly and sharply I recoiled from the word.

"But he could help," I insisted. "I'm sure if we let him out, he could at least kill Dana for us."

"Maybe, but it's not worth the risk," Mykail said, his gaze capturing mine again, though there was no warmth or compassion in his expression. "Eina is too dangerous to be kept alive. It's best to stop

Dana and dismantle the Commission of the People before Eina's testing is finished, and then kill Eina. Let that data and technology die with him. It was not meant to exist to begin with."

His expression was so cold my hands pulled away from him unconsciously, unable to stop myself from flinching in response to the lack of compassion toward another experiment.

"I'm sorry," he said, his shoulders dropping further as he sighed. "I know it sounds harsh, but you haven't seen what I've seen. Eina is dangerous. Best to leave him out of our plans entirely and focus on being sure the Machine of Neutralization is never completed."

* *** *

I barely remembered that I had agreed to go to Becca's the following day, and had to scramble to get dressed and head out the door so I could get to Becca's once she texted me, asking if I was on my way over.

Becca's mother answered the door. I had not yet met her, and was startled at how similar she and Becca looked—clearly Becca had inherited more from her than her father. Mrs. Davis had a very natural beauty to her that made her both inviting and a little intimidating, though her broad smile that nearly caused her eyes to close had me smiling right back when she greeted me.

"You must be Lily." She motioned me into the house to escape the growing chill in the air. "I've heard so much about you from your father."

"From my father?" I repeated. Having stayed up nearly the entire night with Mykail, I had only obtained an hour and a half of sleep, so I was very slow in remembering that she worked with my father. "Oh, right!"

"You look exhausted," she noted, looking me over as she closed the door. "Do you want some tea? I know those Commission meetings run pretty late."

"You do?" I asked suspiciously.

"We may not know what the Commission of the People talks about, but we do know that Mr. Christenson is a very busy man and only has time to have the meetings late in the day and night. It's common knowledge for all who work in Central."

"Oh," was the only response I could manage. I could not stop my suspicious thoughts from turning over possibilities of what the people in the city knew—or believed they knew—about the Commission of the People.

"Can I get you some tea?" she offered again.

"No, thank you."

"Lily?" Becca called, descending the stairs. I smiled at seeing her grinning at me. I hoped that the awkwardness between us was finally gone, and that she had returned to acting like my first friend in Central. Though I had hoped to figure out what had caused her strange behavior, I was so relieved to see her bright expression that I temporarily forgotten we had a falling-out.

"Hey."

"Hey!" she said brightly. She grabbed my hand, turning to her mother. "We'll just be up in my room."

"I know, I know," her mother said teasingly. "Gossiping away."

"I would never!" Becca said with fake indignation.

Becca was far more energetic than me, and even mustering the strength to follow her fast pace up the stairs to her room was draining. She stopped at the top of the stairs and waited for me, her expression beset with suspicious concern as she led me to her room. She sat on her bed next to me with a small smile.

"How have you been?" Her tone told me she already knew full well I was struggling.

"I've been better."

"You've been worrying us for a while," she said gently. "I guess not just you. All the Commish Kids have been acting strange lately."

"Yeah..."

"I'm assuming you can't tell me what that's all about."

I drew in a deep breath. "Believe me I wish I could. It would be nice to talk to someone about it." I pursed my lips in a forced smile. "But don't worry. It's only those in the Commission, nothing that involves the rest of Central or the country."

"That's a relief."

It was not the response I had been expecting, particularly with how severely Becca's frame slumped, as though the words had taken an enormous weight from her back.

"What do you mean?"

"Just...with all the rumors going around about Sweeps, I thought—"

"*Sweeps?*" I gasped, straightening. "As in the post-revolution Sweeps? Like during the Cleanse?"

"Haven't you heard those rumors?" Becca asked. "Everyone's been talking about it since Miranda Jacobs went missing. A few other kids have been talking about Commission vans staking out neighborhoods. It's getting scary."

"I haven't heard anything about that," I said. "That hasn't come up in any of the meetings." Seeing the darkness that had taken over Becca's being again, I realized her distance was not because of me being a Commish Kid as much as it was her fear that the Commish Kids were scouting for possible Sweeps—one of the most notorious periods in American history.

"Don't worry, you have nothing to worry about," I said strongly, forcing a broader smile in an attempt to ease her concern. "If anything was going on with your family, I would have heard about it. And I don't care what the Commission rules are, I will tell you."

Becca let out a sound that was somewhere between a sigh and a laugh.

"You would?" Her voice was trembling and my heart plummeted into my stomach.

"Is that why you've been so nervous around me?"

She closed her eyes, shaking her head in disappointment. "I'm sorry, Lily. I know you would never do anything to any of us…but people change once they're in the Commission. I mean, Felicity actually used to be one of Jill's best friends when they were still in First Tier. Felicity even used to be kind of a tomboy, and then within a few months of joining the Commission, she became a completely different person."

"…and you're waiting for me to change, too."

"You already have," she said slowly. I felt my eyes widen at the statement before I could stop them. She pointed at me. "Right there. That's what I mean. You're constantly afraid. We can all see it, and since we don't know what it is that's scaring you, we're coming up with all kinds of worst-case answers."

"…I…" Words had evaporated from my tongue.

"You were kinda shy when you first showed up, but you also had a quiet confidence that I could see. Now…that's gone. It's like you're constantly waiting for someone to leap out and attack you. Just like Clark."

"…sometimes it feels like that's what's going to happen," I admitted. "I guess I'm just trying to adjust to the Commission and it's been…*very* difficult."

"Well, if you're wanting to adjust to the Commission, I don't think Clark is the one to help you. He never seemed comfortable with the Commission the entire time I've known him." I saw the smile threatening to pull at her lips. "Although, it's nice to see how well you two have hit it off. You've been spending a lot of time together…"

I smiled. "It's not what you think." I wanted to explain to her that Clark was helping me navigate garnering such attention from the leader of the Commission of the People, and that the reason neither of us felt comfortable with the Commission was because of the constant threat of Dana Christenson looming over us. But I bit my tongue against the urge to confide in her—literally.

Becca's eyes narrowed.

"Look, Lily, if you're in some kind of danger, tell me. Maybe I can help. And how are they going to know if you told anyone?"

"I don't want to test that," I said with a quick shake of my head. "And really...I don't want to scare you."

"The Commission already scares me," Becca said. "It scares the whole country. That's its job. But I won't tell anyone, and it's not like there's anyone listening in right now."

"...we don't know that..." I mumbled, though my thoughts were not directed to any cameras or microphones in the room, but to the sharp, golden eyes I could feel piercing the back of my neck.

Becca looked around the room, nervous.

"What are you talking about? You're scaring me."

"...can we walk outside?" I asked, straightening and rubbing the hair standing on the back of my neck. Becca jumped, rapidly looking around the room again.

"Outside? Are we...is my house bugged?" she whispered.

"I doubt it," I said quickly. "I just...would feel more comfortable talking about this outside. I don't want to take any chances."

"But we could be followed or seen by other Commish Kids," she said, standing when I did, her frame tense, her eyes wild about the room, falling on each corner as though expecting to see the glint of a camera lens.

"If we just go walk in the park or something, it won't be suspicious. And we'll be able to see when someone approaches."

I was too tired to put too much thought to my paranoia about Becca's house being bugged, but I was puzzled by the reaction as Becca grabbed a coat and scarf to fight the approaching winter weather. I had never considered that my own house was bugged, which horrified me considering the conversations I was having with Mykail nightly. But it felt more likely that the Commission—or more likely Dana himself—had put surveillance on my friends' homes to catch me reaching out to others outside the Commission for help.

Even if I was plotting against Dana and could use all the help I could get, I refused to risk Becca's safety.

There was a park not far from Becca's home, but we walked slowly, huddled in our coats, fighting off the growing strength of the wind as we traversed the clean sidewalks of her neighborhood.

"Mind if we talk about something else for a little bit?" I asked with a weak smile, my hands deep in my pockets and my shoulders drawn as closed to my ears as I could bring them. Thankfully my posture to fight the cold made it easier to ignore the growing ball of anxiety in my belly.

"What do you want to talk about?"

"Anything," I said. I shivered, turning to her. "How about what happened after I left on Friday? Jill seemed pretty happy I told her I was not interested in Devon."

Becca laughed and nodded into her scarf, her eyes watching her feet on the sidewalk, mimicking my own hunched pose. "Yeah, she really likes him. But she also was thrilled that you were interested in someone else. That's why I asked about Clark."

"Oh," I said, feeling the anxiety in my gut grow and the heat rising to my cheeks battle back the acute cold in the air. "No, no, not Clark…"

"Wait." She stopped, turning to face me, her eyes wide. "You *do* like someone! I see it all over your face! Is it someone we know?"

"No, you don't know him," I said, unable to stop myself from smiling like an idiot at the sidewalk at the thought of Mykail being my official boyfriend.

"Now I'm really curious," she said with a broad smile.

"Well…maybe one day you'll meet him."

"That's just mean," she pouted. "Let me guess, he's at university, right? An older guy?"

The words were threatening to burst out of me. I could feel myself start to gather all the ways I wanted to describe Mykail and the way he made me feel, but I forced the urge down, smiling broadly and digging my hands deeper into my pockets, turning away and continuing down the sidewalk toward the park I could see only a block away.

"Unless…" Becca caught up to me, her bright eyes darkening, "you're afraid to tell me because it would get you in trouble with the Commission."

"…it might," I whispered, unsure if she heard the answer, though judging from the way she fell silent as we crossed the street and started on one of the winding paths through the park, she had certainly heard and did not know how to respond.

I was startled when she was the one who initiated the conversation as we walked through the falling leaves littering the park.

"Do you feel comfortable telling me what's going on now?"

I drew in deep breath, debating if I truly wanted to tell her more about the Commission, even knowing the danger I was putting us both in. Also, there was no way to predict her reaction. And based on her reactions earlier in the day, I was worried that telling her about the Commission and then telling her that I was trying to think of a way to dismantle it, would make her believe that I was trying to trick her into traitorous acts. I had not heard the rumor about the Commission starting Sweeps again, but if it was widespread among the school, it would be even harder to convince others to join our cause—the fear would outweigh the anger.

"It's just been really difficult lately," I mused to my feet, my step slowing. I looked up when I heard the sound of children on the jungle-gym and swing sets we were slowly approaching, oblivious to how dangerous their country could be if they did not fall in line with the ideal of an American citizen. They were too happy to be playing with their friends on the weekend to even notice the chill in the air, let alone our dark expressions as we passed by them. "Everyone thinks they know what it's like in there. A lot of people even want to join. But it's…not what anyone really expects."

"How do you mean?"

"Well, don't you think the institution is a little obsolete now that the population is cleansed?" I mused, drawing closer to Becca and dropping my voice as a mother stood from her bench and called for her daughter. Becca waited until we had passed the woodchips surrounding the jungle-gym before answering.

"Maybe a little, but there are still undesirables in the country," she said. "And the Commission doesn't just keep the people in line. It's the reason the American people can put such trust in the Central government. They handle dirty politicians."

"What if they *are* the dirty politicians?"

I looked around us rapidly, being sure no one was in earshot. Becca did the same, before dropping her gaze to the pathway, her step slow and rhythmic.

"Those are heavy accusations," she murmured. "But…sadly, it wouldn't surprise me."

"And I'm angry that it surprised *me*," I said, huffing. "I mean, I knew that politicians always walked in the gray area of morality, but I wasn't expecting it to be so cruel."

"If it's really as bad as all that, you should bring it up to someone in the Chamber of Regions, or maybe you go a step further and go right to Leader Simon's cabinet."

"There are dozens of Regulators and cabinet members in the Commission who are doing nothing to change it," I said. "I think it's like we read in *An Angel Without Wings*. Just like the Washington System, everything is so corrupt that there's no power within the government to correct it. At that point…it's up to the people, right?"

"Lily." She held out her hand to stop me, her brow creasing as she shook her head slowly. "Do you realize what you're saying? Or what I *think* you're trying to say?"

"I'm just talking, it's not like I'm plotting anything," I said, trying to sound casual, though I was now starting to question if I really *could* talk to Becca about my plans to take down the Commission. "It's just…people don't really think about what happens to everyone the Commission apprehends…and they really should."

As soon as the words left my mouth, fear overwhelmed me. It was alright to pose questions and talk abstractly about how past events could have influenced our current day, but there was very little chance she would mistake those words.

Her face noticeably paled.

"You're scaring me…"

"I know, I'm sorry," I blurted, lifting a hand to my face to brush away imaginary hairs, allowing me to look away from her. "Don't-don't read too much into that. I'm tired. I haven't been sleeping well lately."

"Lily," Becca said strongly, raising her hand to stop me as I tried walking again. "I'm worried about you. Are you in danger? You can tell me, I want to help."

My mouth opened, but again, the words lodged into my throat with icy claws.

"…I can't," I said.

"I won't tell anyone, I promise," she said. "I just want to help you. I can see how scared you are."

"I just don't want to put you in any danger," I said. "Everything is so fucked up right now and I-I-I just don't know what to *do*."

"Okay, okay," she said, her hand leaving her pocket again to rest on my shoulder. "Right now, you don't have to do anything. Just know that I'm here to listen and if there is anything I can do to help you, I will. I just want you to be okay."

I stared at her, seeing that she was petrified at what I had hinted at about the goings-on in the Commission of the People, but I could also see the sincerity in her gaze.

"Thank you," I whispered. "But you might regret those words." I tried to laugh, turning my eyes away from her so she could not read too much into my expression. "Things get much worse down there, I might just have to start another revolution."

I let the words sit between us, trying not to let them become *too* heavy and give away my plans so early.

"Well, if you think there's a reason to fight one, then I believe you," Becca said with a smile and a nod. "But if we're not doing it today, I would love to go back to the house because it is *freezing* out here!"

I could not tell if she was trying to lighten the mood, or if she was trying to end the conversation, but I was also eager to get out of the cold, so I laughed and we turned back to return to her house, fully intending to talk about *anything* other than the Commission of the People.

Chapter Twenty-Seven

On Monday, I anxiously waited for my lunchtime meeting with Clark. I had stayed up with Mykail transcribing the information from the anonymous notes so I could share with Clark, though I was worried that my exhaustion had caused me to write down the wrong information. Even when I was sitting in class, pretending to listen to the teachers, I could feel the pressure of the folded papers in my sock. Their presence was so noticeable it was difficult to refrain from reviewing the notes during my morning classes.

When lunch time came, I apologized to my worried friends and ran to the east court, a place I had never visited, since the east side of the school was for advanced track students.

Clark was pacing by a bench. The courtyard was devoid of other students. The sun was not yet high enough over the school to chase away the shadows of the small court, so I pulled my blazer tighter around me as I rushed to him.

"Hey," he said.

"Hey."

"We have to be quiet, it echoes like hell here," he said, motioning to the stone walls around us. "You said Mykail understood the notes?"

I nodded, crouching to extract the notes from my sock. As I unfolded them, I stepped closer, dropping my voice to a whisper. "Apparently, they were written in a code the experiments use among themselves."

"Does he know who wrote them?"

"No. But this is what the notes said."

Clark took the papers from me, glancing at the scribbled annotations.

"Is…is this really…"

"Yes," I said with an excited nod. "An experiment, or maybe even a few experiments, gathered this information for us. Their cell number, testing schedule, Dome time…everything." I watched Clark's expression both pale and become entranced with wonder as he continued to flip through the notes. "If it was another experiment, we could probably narrow it down. There can't be many experiments that are just loose in the back of the Commission that could gather all this."

"…there are quite a few, actually," Clark corrected. "There are a lot of experiments on Dana's personal security detail. Some of Sean's men are former experiments. There are a few who are staffed just to contain the experiments in the back if any of them try to overpower the

262

scientists. But it does mean that at least someone with security access is interested in helping us."

"How many possibilities are there?"

Clark pondered the answer for a moment. "Easily over a dozen. Maybe as many as thirty." He flipped through the notes again. "I think the security codes changed a day or two before I got these, so it has to be one of the experiments staffed in the security detail. But even then, there's a lot of possibilities. And my school stuff was left unattended in the conference room, so it really could be anyone."

"Do you think we can trust the information?" I asked when he did not continue. "If it's someone staffed with security, it could be a trap."

"Or they could be trying to dismantle everything just like us," Clark mused. "Dana has not been kind to the experiments, even those on the security staff. One of them might have become fed up with it."

"Then you trust it?"

"Only because it was so close to the codes changing," Clark said. "That gives us a few months with these codes before they change again, and time to look up information on these experiments."

"Look them up? How?"

"We'll have to get into Commission Records," Clark said, folding the papers slowly. "I don't have clearance to get in. Maybe my mother does…" His distant gaze finally focused on my face, answering the silent question in my eyes. "It's a room filled with records of every person who has ever been brought into the Commission and their charts when they become experiments. The electronic records are high security and can only be accessed on an account that records every chart opened. But I do know that every quarter, they update the hard copy of the experiment's charts. If we could get into the Records room, we could look at their charts without detection."

"Where is the Records room?"

"Next to Dana's office. And I don't know who would have the clearance to open the door. Dana obviously, and probably most of the scientists."

"Could we steal one of the scientist's access cards?"

"Even if we did, I don't know that that would work. I'm pretty sure the Records room also has a fingerprint and retina scan. It's tightly guarded."

"Do you think Sean would have access?"

"…maybe," Clark said hesitantly. "He for sure would know the master override code. That one is only used in emergencies like fire or a cave in or something. But he does control all the override codes and the rotation of security codes every quarter."

"Do you think Sean could have gathered this for us?" I asked, hoping the person closest to Dana would also be interested in removing the dangerous man from such a high position of power.

"It didn't look like his handwriting on the original notes," Clark said. "And Sean is not an experiment, so I don't think he would know that code."

I drew in a deep breath, crossing my arms as I tried not to shiver in the cold shadows of the courtyard.

"I really wish we knew who this was so we could know if we can trust them."

"Me too." He tapped the papers against his palm before handing them back to me. "Memorize the experiment numbers and their cell numbers. Then give these to me and I will do the same. I'll also put together a fake calendar of their schedule so no one in the Commission will recognize it."

I took the papers and nodded quickly. "Then we should burn these."

"Did you burn the originals?"

"No, not yet. Once I have these memorized, I will."

"Good." He pushed his hands into his pockets, his eyes dropping in embarrassment. "Also, I feel it's only fair to warn you, Dana has been getting really pushy about getting you to come to the Commission after school. He's already talked to my mother about carpooling to and from the Commission. He's probably already working on getting you the proper clearance for the building."

I hesitated, needing a moment to draw in a deep breath before I nodded and tried to smile.

"Okay, so that will let me get closer and we can start working together on this every day." I tried to sound like I was eager to be trapped in the Commission every day, but my instincts were screaming at me to not allow myself to get even closer to Dana Christenson.

"Yes, but we cannot take this too fast," Clark reminded me. "Nothing to draw attention to us. We stay quiet, and careful."

"I will be," I said. "But I also want to be sure that I build up a tolerance to Dana's presence so he doesn't overwhelm me so much."

Clark's eyebrows went high. "More power to you..."

"Um, about that..." I said, dropping my gaze to the ground. "I'm sorry, but do you mind if I ask you a pretty personal and...sort of embarrassing question?"

"...sure..."

"You told me that Dana…sometimes…corners you." I refused to raise my gaze. "If he does that to me…should I fight him? Or would that just spur him on and I should just wait for him to get bored."

He cleared his throat, and even though I had not raised my head to check, I knew he was also looking everywhere but at me.

"I try to fight him," he said. "It does tend to spur him on, but I feel like I have to for my own sanity. Just…keep yourself safe, whatever that means for you."

"…do you think it would be possible to steal Dana's access card during something like that?" I murmured, still focused on a very specific weed struggling to grow through the cracks in the concrete.

"I wouldn't try it," Clark said. "You know what his presence can do. If you're not thinking straight, and he catches you trying to steal his access card, he'll know we're snooping around."

I nodded slowly, reluctant to admit that Clark was right and it would take a lot more ingenuity to gain access to the restricted parts of the Commission of the People.

Clark cleared his throat again.

"I'm heading back inside. I'll talk to you later."

"Thanks for everything, Clark," I said, raising my head to give him a sincere smile.

"We have to support one another through this," he said. "If we're really doing this, we can't abandon each other."

Before I could think better of the action, I stepped forward and hugged him tightly. His entire frame stiffened at first, but he then placed his arms around me briefly, patting my shoulder before breaking the hug. Without another word, we returned to our normal lunches, pretending that we were not plotting the downfall of the most powerful organization in the world.

* *** *

Monday and Tuesday night were spent with Mykail trying to memorize the numbers of the experiments denoted by our mysterious helper, noticing that most of the cells were in Ward Eight. When I asked Mykail about it, he told me that Ward Eight was the ward where the experiments were strong, but not uncontrollable like those in Wards Nine and Ten.

I was starting to feel confident with my memorization, running through the numbers randomly in class when my mind wandered. But when Wednesday rolled around, I was thrown for a loop.

I walked out of the school building at the end of the day with Becca, Jill, and Taylor, talking about something silly that had happened in Taylor's last class. I was near the front of the group, half-walking backwards to listen to Taylor's story when she stopped, staring in confusion at what was idling at the bottom of the school's steps.

"What's with the limo?"

I turned and my blood ran cold. A limousine sat at the curb, drawing the attention of all at the front of the building, though none of the students dared to approach. Of course, their hesitation was likely due to the burly man stationed dutifully at the back passenger door, watching me behind his dark glasses, dressed in a pristine black suit.

"Miss Sandover," he greeted with a shallow bow of his head.

"Sean?"

"You know him?" Jill gawked.

I ignored her, watching Sean step away from the car and approach me.

"I have been sent to pick you up," he said, reaching around my back to lightly press into my backpack, guiding me down the final steps toward the car. My feet followed, but it took my brain a few seconds to catch up with the situation.

I turned over my shoulder, stumbling a little as my legs descended the steps.

"I'll...talk to you later," I called to my friends, trying not to commit their confused and concerned expressions to memory.

Sean opened the limo door for me and, too dazed to do anything else, I climbed inside. Once the door closed, my eyes adjusting to the dark interior behind the tinted windows, I was startled to see my parents sat on one side of the limo. They wore somber expressions, but Dana, who was directly across from me, his back to the partition between the driver's seat and the stretch limo, was flashing a cat-like smirk, sitting comfortably in another expensive, immaculate three-piece suit, his dark glasses hooked in his breast pocket, leaving me under full assault of his fiery gaze.

Once the door was closed behind me and Sean had started driving away from the school, my mother slid down the seat and joined me at the back of the limo, hugging me tightly.

"Oh, honey, I'm so sorry," she whispered, running a hand over my hair.

"What are you sorry about? What's going on?" I looked over her shoulder at my father and Dana. "You're scaring me..."

"I'm sorry that you couldn't tell us what happened," my mother continued, pulling away and returning to her seat next to my father.

"Will you tell me what you're talking about?" I asked, confusion causing the words to come out at a squeaky pitch.

"Dana told us about the boys who attacked you outside the club a few weeks ago," my father explained solemnly.

My eyes flew back to Dana. I was too surprised to glare, though I desperately wanted to. His grin only widened.

"Why didn't you say anything to us?" my mother asked.

"I..." My gaze turned to Dana once again, my mind scrambling for the best thing to say, since I did not know what he had already told them about the attack. "I just..."

"Traumatic events lead to behavior that might seem illogical," Dana interjected, his eyes rolling discreetly before he spoke. I felt affronted by the silent scoff—he had no right to be annoyed at my tied tongue. "I'm sure she would have told you in time, but I felt that I needed to explain my growing concerns for her safety."

"What concerns?" I snapped. "The only *concern* should be that you were the one looming outside a club full of teenagers when it happened!"

"Lily!" my mother snapped. "He saved you."

"Dana told us that he often drives to the club to check up on the younger members of the Commission, and that he happened to see you being pulled into the alley as he was leaving," my father elaborated. "He stepped in to save you before they were able to do more harm. You should at least show some respect toward him."

I wanted to tell them what Dana had done to me afterward, remembering too well the shaking fear that had seized my muscles once trapped in the limo with him—for all I knew, I was sitting in the exact same vehicle as that night. But I remained silent. I wanted to know why they had picked me up before I said anything more.

"I also told your parents that this attack was the reason for the announcement to everyone in the Commission concerning their children's behavior," Dana added. "And that I saw these same boys coming on to you again last Saturday, even after the warning."

"Dana is worried that you're not safe from these boys," my mother said. "He has offered to let you come to the Commission after school so that you can be protected."

There was a confusing tug of acceptance and rage in my chest. While I had been preparing myself for going to the Commission after school so I could stage our breakout, I was furious with Dana for using the incident at Club Archangel to sway my parents into agreement, making them think that he was my protector, not a predator.

Dana's smirk growing made me realize my anger was plain on my face, so I quickly schooled my expression, dropping my gaze and staring pointedly at the floor, keeping my mouth firmly shut.

"I think it's a really good idea," my mother continued. My expression may have been more neutral, but the scoff and eye roll happened without my bidding. "Lily, this is a very generous offer from Dana. I want to be sure that you'll be safe."

"What about my friends?" I said. "What if I want to hang out with them instead? You know? Like a normal teenager?" I had to put up a fight. I knew that was part of my game with Dana.

"Sweetheart," my mother said slowly, as if I was five years old again, "until these boys back off, I would rather you be safe. After they start leaving you alone, then maybe we can talk about a different arrangement. For now, I think it would be safest if you were protected and removed from their vicinity."

"But this isn't fair," I whined. "I don't want to be at the Commission all the time. I want to at least *pretend* to have a normal life sometimes."

"I'm sorry, honey, but I have to agree with your mother on this," my father said, though he did not meet my eyes as he spoke. "We need to keep you away from these boys for a while. Dana said that there can be some jealousy between the Commission families and that's likely why you're being targeted. If we can keep them away from you, you will be safer. Besides, you won't be alone. You'll be with Clark."

"What if I just agree to go right home after school and not leave?" I said, pushing back more than I normally would have before becoming part of the Commission.

My mom shot me an exasperated look, appalled that I was resisting Dana's apparent 'generosity' so strongly. My father turned to Dana.

"You know, when we work late, Lily is the one to take care of Mykail," he said. "Maybe staying home would be best. We wouldn't want Mykail to be left unattended late into the night."

I felt a smirk of my own pull my lips upward as I lifted my head and looked at Dana. I could tell he was irritated by the way the muscles in his jaw clenched.

"I don't worry about Mykail as much as Little Lily," Dana said. "But I can see where his care could become problematic. So, we can have Little Lily come stay at the Commission until dinner time, at which point, one of my staff will escort her home, preferably at a time when one of you is home as well."

I could see how Dana was trying to limit my time alone with Mykail, but my parents seemed to like the idea that I would never be out from under adult supervision—supposedly for my safety. I started chewing the insides of my cheeks and bouncing my leg in irritation.

"What do you think about that, Lily? Is that an okay compromise?" my father asked, turning back to me.

I huffed, leaning back in my seat and crossing my arms, not trusting whatever answer might slip out of my mouth.

"We're not trying to be controlling or overbearing," my mother said gently, that irritating, superior parent tone grating my ears. "We're just worried. Dana is, too. Until things calm down a little, let's just try this and see how it works out."

I still did not answer, staring out the tinted windows defiantly.

I could sense my mother's anger at my behavior. I had never acted so petulantly before. But that was exactly what I was doing—acting.

I had been planning to get more access to the Commission as it was so I could do my part in organizing a rebellion to dismantle the institution, but with Dana watching my every blink and sigh, I had to put up a fight to keep him from thinking it was my plan to have him draw me closer.

"This won't be forever," my father said patiently.

"I'm sure she'll get used to it," my mother said to Dana. I rolled my eyes, but continued to stare dutifully out the window.

"I'm sure," Dana agreed. "I do not want either of you worrying yourselves sick. She will be very safe. I will have her brought back home around seven every day. This is merely a precaution until these boys learn their place."

"We appreciate you being so concerned, Dana," my mother said.

"You seem to have taken Lily under your wing," my father said. I perked up at the hint of suspicion in his tone.

"Well, I feel as if we're practically family," Dana said. "I will tell you, Tommy, that most of the parents in the Commission do not raise their children as well as you have raised Little Lily. Most of these parents are self-important brats themselves, and raise their children without regard for the rules. Unfortunately, as leader of the Commission of the People, I am often called upon to step in and set the standard for acceptable behavior." I felt his eyes fall on me, though I dared not meet his gaze. "I feel no such need to do that for Little Lily."

"We are flattered you think so highly of us," my mother laughed demurely.

"I do," Dana said. "But, that being said, I do feel responsible for her safety until the others do learn to behave. There are so few good children in the Commission, and they are the future of this organization.

It is very important to me to keep the good ones safe and get rid of the bad ones."

"Get rid of?" I echoed before I could stop myself. "As in kick them out of the Commission?"

I made the mistake of meeting his gaze, and the molten gold held my attention as he flashed his teeth in a smile.

"Don't be silly," he said. "No one ever gets out of the Commission."

I don't know how long he held my gaze. I was certain it had been for at least an hour, but my parents said nothing to stop our staring, and I was only torn from the spell of his eyes when the car came to a stop. I turned out the window and saw we had already pulled up to the curb in front of our home. There must have been another route from the school to my house, as I had not recognized the streets and houses we passed earlier.

"I know you're not pleased about this arrangement Little Lily," Dana said. "But I know Clark will enjoy the company and you will be far safer. Your parents and I will arrange all the details and I will have someone pick both you and Clark up every day after school."

I huffed and grabbed my backpack, rudely getting out of the car without a word—accidentally hitting Sean with the door as he was approaching to open it for me.

"Sorry," I said quickly before storming toward the house, ignoring the stern way my mother used my full name in scolding.

I was nearly to the front porch when another voice called to me.

"Little Lily."

I stopped in my tracks, debating if I could control my expression or emotions long enough to face him. Drawing in a deep, steadying breath, I turned around, watching Dana wave Sean back as he walked toward me.

"What?" I sneered, crossing my arms to protect myself as his unhurried pace brought him closer.

"Impressive little act in there," he complimented. "It was quite cute, actually."

"What are you talking about?"

"I know you're intrigued by the Commission," he said. "And I know you're actually very curious about what happens down there, aren't you?"

"You wish," I snapped. "I should be asking you why you're so obsessed with having me in the Commission every day."

"I already told you why. I want to keep an eye on you."

Grinding my teeth together, I mustered the courage to take a few steps closer to him, my arms still firmly crossed as I gazed up at him.

"I am getting really sick of being your entertainment," I growled. "You are toying with me and my family. I know you're doing it on purpose, too. But I won't bow to you as easily as them. If you keep this up, I won't stop fighting you until one of us is dead, and if that means I have to take down the entire fucking Commission to get away from you, fine."

Dana's knowing smile only fueled the angry fire within me.

"Quite the temper you've been hiding," he said. "I doubt even your parents know you're capable of this. You've dimmed that fire your entire life, and I cannot stop my fascination at watching what you do when I fan those flames."

"I'm not going to play your game," I sneered.

"But you already are," he whispered, leaning down to pierce my soul with his knowing gaze. "And I am enjoying it *immensely*."

"Well enjoy it while you can," I said. "Because I plan to burn you to the ground."

"I am looking forward to it."

He turned away so quickly I found myself dizzy at his movement. He nodded to Sean standing stoically by the car and the taller man opened the door of the limousine again, waiting for the head of the Commission of the People to disappear inside before he closed the door, nodded once to me, and returned to the driver's seat.

When the car's engine started, I turned and went to the front door, my hands starting to shake and my knees wobbling as I unlocked the door and stepped inside. I slumped against the front door, going to my knees as I pressed my forehead to the door and clenched my fists.

"You stupid, *stupid* girl..." I scolded coldly. "This is fucking *suicide*!"

I remained kneeling at the front door, shaking as though in a blizzard, until I felt the strength enough to stand. I was deliberate with my steps, the adrenaline giving way to fear and understanding as I went to my room just long enough to toss my backpack against the side of my desk and grab the key to Mykail's door.

When I appeared at his door, he was sitting on his bed, waiting for me, clearly having heard me come in.

"What's wrong?" he asked, standing and coming to the door as I unlocked it with trembling fingers. He helped me ease the door open and then took my arm in a tender hold to guide me into the room. I forced a wobbly smile.

"He wants me to go to the Commission after school every day. My parents have agreed."

He sighed, squeezing my arm before lowering his hand to entwine our fingers.

"Okay..." he said. "So, it's happening."

"It's happening."

I followed his guide to the bed, sitting with him and turning my attention to our interlocked fingers. I could not help but think our hands looked good together.

"I want you to be extremely careful," he said gently. "I know this is part of the plan and everything, but...I'd rather stop the plan entirely than risk you being pulled into the lab."

I squeezed his fingers. I could feel the fear sinking deeper into my bones. I had to push it away.

"Are you sure that you're not just jealous?" I asked, smirking at him and lightening my tone so there was no doubt I was teasing him. His eyebrows rose as he smiled to match me.

"Do I have a reason to be jealous?"

"I don't know..." I sang. "I'll be close to Dana." I tried, and hopelessly failed, to keep a straight face.

"Oh, and is he of interest to you in ways that should make me jealous?" he asked, leaning closer, his bright blue eyes taking my breath away.

"That depends," I joked. "What sort of ways would make you jealous?"

"The kind of ways that would make any man jealous when the woman he likes is with another attractive man." His grin was stunning, his hand squeezing mine as his other hand trailed up my neck to cradle my jaw. The muscles in my abdomen fluttered as excitement and heat chased away the last tendrils of fear from my body.

"And what way would make you the most jealous?"

"I would say..." He paused to think, his thumb passing over my face gently. "Not being able to see you right after school. I won't be able to just sit and talk with you about how your day was, or how your classes are going."

"You actually like those conversations?" I asked skeptically. "That's just me prattling on about meaningless teenage stuff."

"It doesn't matter if it's meaningless teenage stuff or rebellion against the government. I just like being with you," he said. "I like listening to you talk. I like seeing you smile. I like the way you follow trains of thought down different paths that makes me think of things differently."

I was certain the embarrassed blush in my face was burning his hand.

"Can I kiss you?" he asked.

The tender words ran up and down my spine like electricity and, before I could answer, I was moving toward him, latching onto his lips as if my life depended on it. My hands went to his shoulders, one snaking around the back of his head to rest in his soft hair, while the other hand drifted down his back until my fingertips brushed the base of his feathered wings. He held me close, his fingers digging into the skin at my waist and neck.

Every touch and movement was exhilarating.

I felt every place where our bodies made contact, as though we were already connected and moving in sync. His breath mingled with mine, our energies entwining while I leaned into him for support.

The kisses made me dizzy, giddy, swaying as I held onto him like a rock in a tumultuous tide. I felt intoxicated by his presence, his very being chasing away all thought until there was nothing left in the world but the two of us.

He was magnetic and I was being drawn closer to him, not caring about the danger, not worried about being caught, desperate to pull him to me even if it was a recipe for disaster.

Chapter Twenty-Eight

Following my unconventional departure from school on Wednesday, Thursday morning was spent explaining to my friends why a limo had picked me up. I had spent the entire bus ride to school coming up with a stupid excuse about having to go to a meeting with my parents that I had completely forgotten about and the driver had picked me up. I could tell they didn't believe me, but the excuse at least stopped the barrage of questions.

For the first half of the day, I thought the tension I could feel in the hallways was my own apprehension at having to spend my afternoons at the Commission soon, but as the feeling grew and persisted, and it was clear there was a lot more whispering than usual, I began to pay attention in earnest to what was happening through the school.

The entire student body seemed anxious, and for the first time I heard the rumors about the Commission of the People starting nationwide Sweeps once again. Even those who had nothing to fear from the Commission were talking to their friends about how unnerving it was to think of the Commission vans patrolling the streets after curfew, waiting for any hint of someone putting a toe out of line.

The tension was thick through the entire school building. Even at Archangel that Friday, people were behaving strangely.

From the moment I walked into the club, I was hearing rumors about people who had not come to the Archangel. Even if they had legitimate excuses, like illnesses or family engagements, most students bathing in the thrumming bass were convinced that the absent students had actually been taken by the Commission of the People never to be seen again. The weather had been getting colder and plenty of students were catching colds or the flu, so I was certain most of the absences could be attributed to illness, but the tension was palpable.

The fear of the Commission of the People held more power than the rational explanations.

I remained close to Clark through our evening at Archangel. Feeling the anxiety among the other students, we dared not speak of the notes or our plans. I had not even had the chance to tell Clark that I would be joining him at the Commission after school starting the following Monday, though something told me he already knew.

The gossip circulating the club that night all centered around concerns that the Commission was going to start conducting Sweeps again. The Commish Kids were somber as well, quietly saying they had not heard of any confirmation that the Sweeps would be happening and

274

wondering who had started the rumor—though they all agreed it had to do with the disappearance of Miranda Jacobs. Even the Jacobs family had been absent at the most recent Commission meeting, which had put the Commish Kids into a quiet state of anxiety, sharing looks with one another that left no doubt about what they worried had happened to Miranda.

That Saturday, the Commission meeting had a very different atmosphere. The adults were acting normally, but the younger members were tense and quiet, glancing at one another suspiciously and jumping every time they looked at the door, hoping to see Miranda walk in and prove that their suspicions were wrong. The usual antics of posturing among the Commish Kids were absent. Everyone was too anxiety-ridden.

I barely knew Miranda, unable to immediately place her features in my mind when her name was mentioned, but I was feeling the same apprehension and fear about her absence and possible fate. I was also scanning the room for her when my family arrived, but she was absent again.

The fear in the Commish Kids tripled when we saw Mr. and Mrs. Jacobs enter the Commission meeting room without Miranda or their younger daughter Julie. With the height of tension among my classmates, I expected some of the teenagers to rush to them and demand to know where Miranda was, but instead, gazes followed them to their seats and the heaviness in the air grew.

The Jacobs family arrived only two minutes before the start of the meeting, so there was not enough time for the parents of the Commish Kids to recognize the anxiety swimming in the air, but when Mrs. Markus stepped up to the podium, her head down and her face somber, they also realized that something was amiss. Seeing her drawn expression, I could feel the direction of the meeting in my gut, twisting my organs until I was fighting curling up in pain. The room fell quiet even before the doors were closed and Clark's mother started the meeting. The few moments she took to stare down at the podium before raising her head to speak to the Commission had my heart pounding angrily.

"Good evening, everyone," she said, her voice quivering. "Our first order of business is a very important matter that Mr. Christenson would like to discuss immediately. Mr. Christenson?"

She stepped away from the podium as I scanned the silent, nervous room for Dana. He rose from a random seat at one table across the room and strode confidently toward the podium. The sense of dread had overtaken the adults, feeding off Mrs. Markus' lowered gaze and

Dana's imposing posture as he stood next to the podium, retrieving his pocket watch, fiddling with it as his head moved in a sweeping motion, eyes scrutinizing everyone in the room behind his glasses.

Mrs. Markus backing to the far corner of the platform brought my attention to Sean, who was standing by the door leading to the back offices of the Commission, his expression equally somber, bordering on looking ill.

"Good evening, ladies and gentlemen," Dana greeted, not bothering to stand at the podium, instead turning the microphone to the side to pick up his voice as he leaned on his elbow, his fingers rubbing over the gold back of the pocket watch. "I have found myself in a very troubling position, and I feel this issue must be resolved with great immediacy."

Out of my periphery, I saw my parents shift uncomfortably, glancing at the others at our table and around the room, worried.

"If you will remember my announcement before, I told you that the rules of this commission must be followed to the letter," Dana continued. "Unfortunately, it seems that despite my efforts to curtail certain behaviors, there are those among you who have not heeded the warning. This is particularly true among the young members of this organization. I understand that youth brings with it a certain arrogance, but my patience with such behaviors has run very thin. Last week, we took Miranda Jacobs into custody. For those of you not acquainted, she is the daughter of Cal and Diana."

He motioned to the parents, both of whom were sitting stiff in their chairs, seeming indifferent to the onslaught of gazes turning to them.

I struggled to draw a full breath, looking at Miranda's parents before urgently looking around the room. The other Commish Kids were wide-eyed with horror at the confirmation of their suspicions regarding Miranda's absence.

"On what charges?" bellowed an angry voice at the back of the room. Dean, Miranda's boyfriend, was standing, glaring hatefully at the head of the Commission of the People.

Dana's head cocked slightly. "Smuggling and ownership of a firearm."

"Impossible!" one of the adults, apparently Dean's mother, said, shaking her head. "Someone must have planted that evidence! Miranda would never—"

"That is what I believed at first," Dana interrupted sharply. "But upon further investigation, we found substantial evidence. We're still investigating *all* the smuggling allegations. But considering that she had already taken several trips to the northern border in the last two months, returning with more money than she departed with, and the secretive route she took to the border, we had substantial evidence to take her into custody for smuggling."

"She would never do that!" Felicity barked, standing.

"Felicity, sit down!" her mother ordered.

"Are you certain you want to insert yourself into this?" Dana asked, looking between Felicity and Dean. "I know she had assistance in her trips north. Are you trying to tell me that you know more about her crimes?" One of Dana's eyebrows arched over his glasses. "Maybe you were involved in some way?"

Felicity's mother snatched her daughter's wrist, pulling her sharply back to her seat.

"Do any other young members wish to speak up?" Dana asked, looking over the room once again. Dean remained standing, leaning on his hands on the table, but no one else stood or spoke. I could feel my parents look at me, but I could not return their gaze, vigilant, terrified about what Dana was going to say next.

Dana turned over his shoulder and nodded once to Sean. Dana's head of security opened the door he was stationed by and through the door, two suit-clad Commission guards guided in a girl a little taller than me. I had only seen her once or twice in school, but she looked like a complete stranger, her head hanging low, her hair in disarray around her face, her bruised arms secured behind her back as the two guards led her by her elbows to the platform. She was dressed in a painfully-bright red jumpsuit, her bare feet barely able to carry her as she was forced to Dana's side on the platform. One guard lifted his leg into the back of her knees and she crumpled, trembling, quiet sobs emanating from behind her curtain of dirty hair.

I had stopped breathing, staring at Miranda as she curled tightly over her knees, crying and trembling. The room had gone very still and silent. I could feel the disgust and horror rolling from those around me. I was certain I was not the only one that wanted to turn away, but it seemed all of us were unable to move, unable to blink, our brains turning to static at the sight before us. I could not even turn to look at Miranda's parents to see their reaction to their daughter's state.

"I do not want to say this again," Dana growled dangerously, entirely ignoring the sobbing teen at his feet. "This commission keeps this country together. This organization is responsible for the peace of this nation. If anything, *anything*, threatens that security, it is our duty to eliminate it. Disregarding the laws of this country will *not* be tolerated!" His voice rattled everyone in the room—even the guards jumped when he suddenly raised his voice.

I heard Dana's words, but my gaze was glued to Miranda. She had started to tilt sideways, her body rocking with sobs as her shoulder touched the platform, her back coming into contact with Dana's shoe.

"P-please…" Miranda's voice was barely audible. "*P-please…*"

"Quiet," Dana ordered, lifting his shoe to push her away as he pocketed the gold watch.

"You can't do this!" Sarah screeched, leaping up and startling everyone in the room. Her parents tried to wrestle her back, mortified at her outburst and worried about turning Dana's anger onto their daughter.

"I most certainly can," Dana said simply.

"What are you going to do with her?" Brian asked, though he remained seated.

"I haven't decided yet," he admitted, looking down at Miranda as she continued to tremble and plead between sobs. "She's still sitting in the docket for testing. Once we have the preliminary labs done, I'll make a decision. Maybe she'll even become a gift for a new Commission family."

I could feel the shift in the room following the statement. While the Commish Kids were still up in arms over Miranda's fate, there was a palpable feeling of uncomfortable guilt that radiated from the adults, many dropping their heads, imagining how they would react if the next new family was gifted the child of one of their colleagues.

"What are you doing? Say something!" Kelly snapped at Miranda's mother, who was seated at her table. Diana remained still, her eyes vacant as she looked in the direction of her collapsed, trembling daughter.

"What is wrong with you?!" Ryan added, standing from the table next to Miranda's family. Like other parents, his father reached forward to grab his son's arm and yank him back to his seat. He jerked away from his father's grasp and stormed around the table toward Diana. Sean had nodded to one of the guards stationed around the room, who leapt into action to restrain the young man as he approached the adult of the Jacob family.

"How can you just sit there?!" Ryan barked. "How can you throw your daughter away?! Fight for her! What if it was Julie?! If he'll take Miranda, he'll take Julie too!"

That was the first time that evening that Diana's face showed a semblance of emotion. Her gaze dropped, her head bowing. While the reaction didn't seem to stop Ryan from pushing against the guard restraining him, continuing his tirade about how Diane should fight for her children, her reaction made me turn to Dana.

Dana still had his dark glasses on, and he was leaning casually against the side of the podium, but I could feel his gaze on me—something about the way he tilted his was evidence of where his attention was focused.

When he smirked and turned his head entirely to the same door that Miranda had been led through, I felt the fear in my gut turn to lead.

The door opening silenced the other Commish Kids that had joined in the fervent demands for Miranda's freedom. Again, the heaviness in the room grew as Sean gently placed his hand against the back of Julie's head and guided her toward the raised platform at the front of the meeting room.

Miranda's younger sister could not have been more than seven years old, and was tripping over the baggy red jumpsuit that, even with the pant legs rolled up, was too large for her tiny frame. Her hands were secured with handcuffs in front of her and her confused, wide eyes searched the room for her parents.

Sean led Julie to stand next to her sister. When tears began to well in her eyes and she started toward Miranda, opening her mouth to speak, Sean's large hand clasped her shoulder and kept her still.

The pulse thudding in my ear was so loud I was certain that everyone in the room could hear it. The other members of the Commission of the People had gone very silent and very still, gazes glued to the tiny, shivering girl in the oversized red jumpsuit with tears streaming down her face.

"How could you?" Ryan's voice was the one to break the deafening silence. I expected him to be glaring at Dana, showing his defiance to the leader of the Commission, but his attention had focused back on Diane and Cal, who had both dropped their gazes to the floor. "How could you let him take them both?!"

"I gave you all fair warning," Dana reminded, his voice halting whatever other arguments the other Commish Kids were about the sling in the direction of the Jacobs family. "I warned everyone in this room that if the behavior of the younger ones did not improve, I would take anyone who was not fit to be part of this Commission."

"On what charges did you take *Julie*?!" Dean barked. "She's six, for fuck's sake!"

"Conspiracy to traffic individuals across the border."

"She's *six*!" Felicity repeated, her voice tight with barely restrained tears. "Even if that was true, she doesn't know better!"

"She knew well enough," Dana corrected. "And even then, she should have been better watched and guided to avoid my interference, but here we are. As I've said, I have no qualms about detaining children.

And I feel it is only fair to show all of you that I will keep good on that promise if I am forced."

My head was swimming, my vision tunneling around Julie and Miranda. I pressed my hand over my mouth as a wave of disgusted nausea threatened to overpower me. I was not the only one fighting the bile rising in my throat. Many of those in the Commission had raised a hand to their mouth.

"Do I have your undivided attention now?" Dana asked coldly. "No one, no matter their age or their position in Central, is exempt from the laws upheld by this commission. Thinking that politicians are exempt from the law just because they are the ones to write it is why the Washington System collapsed, and I refuse to let Central do the same. There is no room here for hurt feelings or second chances. The only rule here is to obey."

"How can you do this, you sick fuck?!" Dean yelled, standing again as his parents tried to contain him. His outburst caused many other Commish Kids to stand, angered into action even as their parents tried to tell them to sit quietly and not draw attention to themselves, the reality of Dana's actions leaving them desperate to keep their own children safe. Several Commish Kids did not join Dean and the others, though only a few seemed to be in agreement with Miranda and Julie being taken by the Commission of the People. Most were wide-eyed, looking rapidly between the restrained prisoners, Dana, and the angry Commish Kids drawing more guards further into the room to be sure they did not get too close to our imprisoned classmate. The youngest kids among the tables were tucking themselves under their parent's protective arms, confused and frightened, not understanding most aspects of the anger in the room, but acutely aware of the severity of the situation.

I was only able to move my head to look between Dana's unperturbed expression and the Commish Kids angrily yelling at Dana that he had taken Miranda and Julie under false allegations. Clark was doing the same, his face even paler than usual.

"Even if you think you have something on Miranda," Dean's angry voice rang out over the din, "Julie did nothing wrong!"

"I have evidence. Photographic proof if that is something you need," Dana said simply, calmly, leaving no doubt that he did have evidence to back up his claims that Miranda's younger sister was involved with some plot to smuggle people across the border. "And I would be very careful how much you question, young man. Do not think for one moment it would take much for me to find the proper evidence against you to bring you in."

"Are you threatening me?" Dean gasped.

"Yes." Dana stood straight again, Miranda flinching as his feet slid closer to her, though she dared not raise her head, her tears continuing to fall on the polished boards of the platform. "I want to make this perfectly clear," he continued. "This is the last warning I will give to all of you. Obey the laws of the Commission and Central, or I will remove you from the general population, as I have a right to do. These latest events occurring within the younger members have told me I have been too lax in reminding all of you the responsibility we have to this country. And if my lack of control over the younger generation has allowed for such blatant disregard for the law, then I must assume it is the same throughout the country. It has made me seriously consider bringing back the Sweeps."

The adults rapidly turned to one another, gasping at Dana's drastic course of action. The teenagers struggling against the guards were being guided back to their worried parents, as the mention of the Sweeps dulled the fire in their eyes. The Sweeps had not been active in over thirty years, and were considered the final notorious Commission practice to be hidden in the shadows of America's post-Second Revolution reformation. If the Sweeps were reinstated, Commission officials would be dispatched to homes suspected of illegal activity to raid their homes in the middle of the night, detaining everyone within the house and turning the house upside down to find any reason to arrest the families within.

Even the prospect of reinstating the Sweeps was extreme, and anyone old enough to remember the times of the Sweeps had started shaking their heads, discussing with other adults at their table about how the American populace would handle the Sweeps becoming commonplace again.

"You may believe I am overreacting, but I will not allow this governing body to become a replica of the Washington System. If that means I must take extreme measures, then I shall do so," Dana said, watching as Dean was finally wrestled back to his table, where his father angrily grabbed his arm and yanked him back into his seat, though the furious teenager was still glaring hatefully at the leader of the Commission of the People. "And the young people need to learn their place. You are a part of the Commission, and the good of the many," his shaded eyes turned to the weeping Miranda and the trembling Julie trying to hold back her tears, "outweigh the needs of the few. And obeying me is certainly for the good of the many, something it seems many of you have yet to learn. So let what you've seen here today be a lesson."

I finally was able to drop my head and let out a shuddering breath when Dana motioned for Miranda and Julie to be taken away. Sean was gently guiding Julie off the stage, and even the guards who went to Miranda and guided her out of the meeting room were gentler than I anticipated, but even as cold dread regarding their fate cooled the rage circulating the room, I felt a shiver of anticipation run down my spine.

I knew my classmates were angry, and I knew Clark and I could use that to our advantage.

Unknowingly, Dana had helped us grow our rebellion against the Commission of the People.

* *** *

It was a silent car ride home. None of us could speak after the horrific scene we had witnessed at the beginning of the Commission meeting. I had been unable to be mentally present for the rest of the meeting—though I was certain I had not been the only one.

Mykail sensed something was wrong when I went to his door after changing into pajamas, but I could not muster the will to tell him what had happened. Even as he continued to ask what was wrong, I could only muster the words: "It was a bad Commission meeting…"

When he finally realized I was not going to disclose specifics, he pulled me into his arms and we found a comfortable position on the bed. He was warm, and smelled of the special lotion Dana had given us for his wings. It was not a strong scent, but I had already come to associate it with comfort—it meant I was close to Mykail.

Within the warmth of his embrace, I drifted into sleep.

I sat upright abruptly when a loud bang sounded downstairs and the thundering footsteps drew close. The paces were heavy, loud, the boots of those rushing into the house making the walls shake.

"Mykail!" I gasped, trying to shake him awake. He did not stir.

Voices joined the cacophony of boots as orders were barked, unintelligible, but deafening.

Fear kicked me in the gut. This was a Sweep.

Once the realization solidified in my mind, the barred door of Mykail's room was violently flung open and several men dressed in black with visors shielding their faces swarmed around us, filling the small space like a heaving, dark shadow.

"That one!" one man ordered, pointing his gun at Mykail.

"No!" I screamed. "Mykail! Mykail! Wake up!!"

He remained frighteningly still, even as I violently shook his shoulder, screaming. Cold, gloved hands took my arms and shoulders,

282

pulling me away from Mykail, yelling nonsensical orders as I kicked and struggled, pleading with Mykail to wake. When they pulled his limp, sleeping form from the bed, I cried and screamed so loud my throat ached, pleading for the Sweep Team to let him go and hoping my parents would hear and investigate the commotion.

"Let him go! You can't do this!" I bellowed, finding my struggles frustratingly weak against the weight of hands on me.

"Yes, he can," my mother's voice said behind me. I tried to crane my neck around to see her, but was only met with the dark shadows that the Sweep Team seemed to embody. But I knew my mother was there, watching, a cold, dead expression on her face.

"It's alright, honey," my father's voice said in the same direction. "This is for the best."

Another realization hit me—my parents had been the ones to call in the Sweep Team. They had learned of our plotting and had turned us over to the Commission of the People. We were about to be used as another example to keep the rest of the Commission in line.

The man who had yanked Mykail from the bed, causing his body to be out of my line of sight, lifted the gun and turned the barrel on him.

"No!"

The gunshot was deafening. I did not see Mykail's wound, nor did the Sweeps Team pick him up to remove him from the room, but I knew he was dead. The fear was making it harder to breathe and harder to struggle against the confines holding me in place.

The man with the gun removed his visor, and the dark smile that painted Dana's face froze all further struggles.

"It's alright, Little Lily," he crooned. "You'll be safer at the Commission with me."

I snapped awake, sweating, my breath stuck painfully in my throat. Disoriented, it took me far too long to realize I was in my own bedroom. It was not the first time Mykail had moved me to my own bed after falling asleep in his room, but it always confused me when I first woke.

Focusing on slowing my breathing, my gaze dropped to my bed spread, the thundering of my heart tripping into a slower pace. Tears began to gather against my will, and before the sobs overcame me, I untangled from my blankets to take a shower, hoping to distract my thoughts from the fear and the flashbacks of seeing Miranda and Julie the previous night.

The images were sharp, making it difficult for me to breathe. I had not felt the same outrage as my other classmates about Miranda's fate—I did not know Miranda well at all and struggled to muster the rage around my fear—but from the way the two Jacobs daughters had acted, as well as the fervent declarations from her friends, I knew the girls were not guilty of the crime for which Dana imprisoned them. That added a new layer of terror to the lingering fear from my dream. Would it be possible for Dana to make up an accusation to imprison me? Would anyone stand up for me if I was paraded in front of the Commission in the red jumpsuit? Would my parents also stare at me blankly, as though I was no longer their daughter?

My desire to take Dana down became stronger, and when we found a way to break out the experiments of the Commission, I vowed we would also free Miranda and Julie.

Remembering that Monday I would be going to the Commission after school for the first time, the determination in my chest was quickly dulled, and I clambered out of the shower. I needed something to distract my brain from the constant waves of fear.

I stepped out of my bedroom with my wet hair in a braid and my most comfortable sweatpants and sweatshirt on my shivering body. Seeing Mykail's barred door open down the hall, I went downstairs to find him helping my mother silently in the kitchen. It had started to become normal to have Mykail help my mother in the kitchen. A few days previous he had silently helped clear the table and started doing the dishes without prompting. My mother had given him certain tasks that would help her in the kitchen, as she had to have him in a place where his large wings would not block the workspaces she needed.

"Good morning, honey," my mother greeted tiredly, buttering some toast for breakfast while Mykail continued scrubbing the frying pan in the sink, briefly glancing back at me with a curious and worried expression.

"Good morning," I answered mechanically. I could tell from the dark bags under my parents' eyes that neither of them had slept well.

The family ate a small, silent breakfast, all of us picking at our food, disinterested. I could see Mykail constantly looking among us, his worry becoming more clear with how little we were speaking.

We were processing the previous night. Even if we had wanted to talk about it, there was nothing that could be said, and we felt a sense of resignation that what had occurred with Miranda and Julie was a harsh reality of the Commission of the People.

I wanted to help clean up after breakfast so I could be close to Mykail and so I could have something to distract my mind, but with Mykail and my mother in the kitchen at the same time, it quickly became too crowded and I was forced to sit uselessly at the table, feeling my fears grow again when there was nothing to deter my thoughts.

Trying not to show how frantic I was feeling, I went upstairs and grabbed my phone, texting Becca and asking her if we could meet up in the park near her house. I brought my phone downstairs, checking the screen constantly, desperate for a reply. By the time I sat at the breakfast table again, she had responded that she would meet me there in a half-hour.

I told my mother I was meeting Becca and would call her to let her know when I would be home. She quietly said "fine" as she pushed the buttons on the dishwasher and began wiping down the counters. Mykail was drying his hands on a towel, his expression clearly communicating how worried he was about the heaviness in the room.

With a short nod that was meant to reassure him, I returned to my room and started to dress, pulling on a few layers to fight what looked like a cold, overcast day. As I pulled on my heavier coat, I heard a small voice from my bedroom door.

"Will you please tell me what's going on?" Mykail whispered.

I spun around, startled. I opened my mouth to answer, but hesitated, walking closer to him and peering around the corner to see if my parents were close. They were seated in the small living room at the bottom of the stairs, just barely out of earshot.

Shaking my head, I pecked a kiss on his lips.

"I'll tell you tonight."

I had to rush to the bus to get to the park on time. Becca was already waiting for me, sitting on a bench further down the walking path from the play area where children were, once again, enjoying a Sunday morning without care for the cold weather.

I ran to join Becca, sitting with her and hugging her briefly in greeting.

"Hope I didn't mess up any plans you had for today," I said when I pulled away from the hug.

"Nope," she said with a smile. "I was just sitting around at home, bored." She turned, folding one leg under her and resting her arm on the back of the bench as her face became creased with concern. "Are you alright?"

"...honestly? Not at all."

"What's going on?"

I drew in a breath of cold air, looking around us as casually as I could to be sure no one was within earshot.

"I really want to talk to someone about the shit that's been happening in the Commission," I started. "I know I'm not supposed to, and if you don't want to hear it, that's fine, just tell me. I just...I don't know, I need someone to talk to."

285

"I'm here," Becca said, rubbing my shoulder comfortingly. "Just tell me what's going on."

"You know Miranda Jacobs?" I whispered. She nodded slowly. "She was taken by the Commission."

"Taken?" Becca gasped. "What happened? What crime did she commit?"

"They said she had a gun and was smuggling things over the border, maybe even smuggling people."

"That's insane. She would never do that!"

"That's what all the Commish Kids were saying. What's worse is they took her little sister because she was somehow involved in it all…"

"Her little sister?" Becca repeated. "Not the six-year-old sister…" When I nodded, her eyes went wide and her face noticeably paled. She turned away, resting her elbows on her knees and covering her mouth with both hands. "I can't believe it…"

I watched her reactions, trying not to feel guilty about upsetting Becca, but also relieved to have told someone about what I had seen the previous night.

"It was a Sweep, wasn't it?" she whispered.

"Not yet," I said. "Dana is talking about starting the Sweeps again, but nothing is official yet."

"Why would he start the Sweeps? What spooked him enough to try and bring that back?"

"I don't think anything really spooked him," I mused. "I think he's doing it just because he's Dana fucking Christenson and he can do whatever he wants."

Becca let out a shuddering breath. I pulled my jacket tighter around me, crossing my arms and sighing.

"Is there anything you can do?" Becca asked. "Is there some way for the rest of the Commission to overturn that decision?"

"I don't think so," I whispered. "Dana scares everyone too much."

"What will happen to Miranda and her sister?" Becca asked. "Imprisonment? Or…they won't be killed, will they?"

"I…" I hesitated. I wanted to tell her about the experiments and that it was likely the two would become test subjects, but I knew that the information would put her at risk. "I can't tell you. I can't put you in that kind of danger."

Becca stared at me, her eyes filled with conflict. She took a slow, measured breath.

"Lily…if the Sweeps really do start again…then I'm already in danger."

The words were carefully spoken, hidden meaning in each long pause and whispered word.

"What do you mean?"

It was her turn to hesitate. "If you tell me what is likely going to happen to Miranda, I'll tell you," she whispered. "I'm afraid to tell you."

"I'm afraid to tell you what will happen to Miranda," I responded. "Telling you about this could land me in the same position." I turned to face her fully, leaning closer to her on the bench. "Are you saying…you would be considered…" I decided not to say the words "Commission criminal" out loud for fear of any nearby ears picking up the words.

She dropped her gaze in silent answer.

My heart picked up pace again, running through every interaction I had ever had with Becca, trying to determine how she would be considered a danger to the stability of America. Unable to think of what it could possibly be, I decided to take a chance.

"Miranda will likely become a type of medical experiment," I murmured, dropping my eyes immediately when I saw her jaw drop. "It happens to a lot of the people they arrest. And it's why…" I drew in a deep breath to steady myself, though I could not strengthen my voice, "I've been trying to come up with some way to expose the Commission to the people and have it dismantled."

The words sat heavy in the air between us, heightening my anxiety the longer Becca did not respond.

"Is this some sort of sick joke?" she asked.

The words struck me like fists and I lifted my head quickly. Her face was even paler than before, her hands shaking in her lap.

"I wish it was, but it's true." I started shaking my head. "I can't even tell you the messed up shit I've seen down there. And Dana Christenson? He's absolutely insane, and even paraded Miranda and Julie in front of everyone to make examples of them to keep the rest of us in line. And so many people just go along with what he says, like he's some kind of god."

"What about Leader Simon?" Becca interjected, interrupting my rambling. "Doesn't he have some control over Mr. Christenson?"

"I don't know, I haven't met Leader Simon. But according to Dana, he knows what goes on in the Commission and doesn't care, or maybe he's also afraid of Dana, just like the rest of us."

My desperation to understand the expression on her face led me to lean forward again, my voice breaking when I spoke.

"Please believe me…"

"I do…" she said, her own fear causing her voice to shrink. She swallowed hard. "But…if you…what do you plan to *do*, then?"

"…I'm still working on that," I said. Her reactions to what I had already told her did not leave me feeling confident that she would handle hearing about our vague plan of breaking out experiments to expose to the people. "But if I found a way to do it…would you help me? Do you want the Commission gone?"

Becca understood my silent cue for her to confess what made her a Commission criminal. While she collected herself, taking a few deep breaths, I tried not to let my panic consume me. I had already broken the rules of the Commission, and if anyone knew what I had told her, we both would be taken down into the cells of the Commission—a reality that was only just hitting me as Becca was preparing to divulge her own secret.

"I guess…if we both know the other's secret, we can't tell anyone else because we'll both get thrown into the Commission…" she whispered, turning to face me. "I could get taken into the Commission…because of Jill."

"Jill? Why?"

Becca drew in a deep breath and looked around her to be sure no one was nearby. She then leaned closer.

"I was thirteen when I met her. I thought it was just some weird, awkward phase…" She closed her eyes, swallowing hard and shaking her head. "But I…never grew out of it…"

"What are you talking about?"

"I…I love her." She lifted a hand to cover her eyes as tears began to gather. "I know I shouldn't…but…"

I felt my mouth drop open, even though I had made a promise to myself not to react to whatever secret Becca held.

She was in love with another woman.

Homosexuality had been considered an illness during the Second Revolution, and the Commission was always on the lookout for anyone who would fit the title of "degenerate" used to describe all the undesirables in the American population. The knowledge of Becca's secret felt uncomfortable, confusing, forcing me to take a few seconds before I responded.

"Is it only Jill?" I asked once I found my voice again. "Or are there other instances?"

"There are other instances," she said, lowering her hand again and sniffing back her tears, being sure not to meet my gaze. She was shaking, petrified at having said her darkest secret out loud knowing it could get her killed, or worse.

I placed a hand on her shoulder and squeezed.

"Thank you for telling me."

She clenched her jaw, swallowing hard.

"That's…the first time I've ever said it…" she choked. "I just…I was…I was always so scared of…"

"I won't say anything to anyone," I promised. "And maybe, if we can get the Commission out of the picture, you'll even be able to tell Jill how you feel."

"No," she said shortly. "No, there's no way."

"You never know."

"I don't want to push her away or scare her," she insisted. "It's better for her to never know. She likes Devon. That's the end of it."

Remembering how Becca had looked when I told her Jill clearly liked Devon, other behaviors clicked into place. Becca had been terrified of having a Commish Kid close enough to suspect her feelings for Jill, and her secret heartbreak had been too hard to hide when she started to realize Jill liked someone else.

"I'm so sorry…" I murmured, rubbing her shoulder, providing as much comfort as I could, now overthinking if it would raise alarms for anyone walking nearby if I were to hug her. "Thank you again for telling me. And I'm going to try to find some way to take this whole thing down."

Becca barked a disbelieving laugh.

"I would certainly sleep easier."

"…would you be willing to help if I found some way to do that?" I felt hope rise in my chest.

She nodded. "As much as I'm able."

Chapter Twenty-Nine

I somehow managed to get through school on Monday even with the butterflies tying my stomach into knots. I was nervous, yet oddly exhilarated. It felt like I was finally setting the first part of my plan into motion, and that once I got down into the Commission, the plan would start coming together. I had to remind myself that I had to take action slowly so as not to tip off Dana to what I was doing.

When the last bell of the school day rang, I made my way to the front of the school with most of the other students. Someone from the Commission had called my father the previous night and told him that I would be carpooling to the Commission with Clark, and I was to meet Clark in the southern parking lot.

I said goodbye to Becca and the others as they turned to walk to the buses. I had told them that I was part of an after school club, and would be going there immediately after school. Becca was the only one who shot me a knowing glance when I turned the other direction at the bottom of the stairs.

"Hey stranger," Devon said as I turned and nearly collided with him walking around the front of the building.

"Hey!" I greeted with a smile.

"Haven't seen you around much. I miss hanging out with you at Archangel," he play-pouted. "I guess the Commish Kids have a pretty tight leash on you."

"You could say that." I rolled my eyes.

"Yeah, I remember what Melissa used to be like. We actually dated for a few months in freshman year."

"No!" I gasped.

"Yep." He groaned, shaking his head. "The Commission was the reason we broke up. She was so damn secretive about everything. And when she wasn't being secretive she was always warning me to be careful. She drove me absolutely nuts!"

"Sounds like her," I agreed.

"Despite how annoying it was, she really thrives in the Commission." His face fell. "Not like you and Clark."

I hesitated, worried about what Devon had seen different about our behaviors.

"What do you mean?"

"I mean…Clark's afraid of his own shadow," he said with a one-shoulder shrug. "He never goes out with anyone, never shows an interest in dating, I think you're the only girl he's shown any interest in at all. And you've changed since being in the Commission too. You used to be just a little shy, but once you loosened up I think you were able to show more of yourself. Now it seems like you're always looking over your shoulder." He shook his head and laughed. "Sorry, this sounds so offensive. I didn't mean to just show up and start offending you."

I laughed, waving the statement away, not at all offended, though I was worried that I was not able to properly control my facial expressions or hide my anxiety. If I was going to be plotting against the government, I needed to cultivate a stronger poker face.

"What I actually came here to tell you was that my band will be doing some songs at Archangel two weeks after the Halloween party. I wanted to know if you could stick around with the commoners that night."

"You're in a band?"

He laughed. "You would know that if you hung around us a little more," he teased. "Yeah, we're doing some of our songs and I want you and the other girls near the stage. You know, to give us support, pretend we're good so people will listen."

"That's amazing," I said. "I'd love to! I'll have to talk to Clark and see if there is some way I can stay on the dance floor that night."

"Great, and we should also dance together at the Halloween party. You're allowed to do that at least, right?"

The awkwardness returned, a thousand flashing images racing through my mind. "Uh..." was all I could manage to say as I thought about the jealousy on Jill's face, the expression I now knew to be heartbreak creasing Becca's features, and the fact that I was far more interested in Mykail than Devon.

"Yeah, that should be fine," I finally managed to force my mouth to say.

"Awesome. I'll see you at Archangel then."

"Hey, Devon," I said, stopping him before he passed me, "you know, you should really ask Jill to dance with you more often."

He smiled sheepishly. "I would...but, between you and me...she doesn't have great rhythm."

"That's unfortunate," I laughed. "But she really likes you. She would love to dance with you more often."

"She likes me?"

"C'mon, surely you've seen that," I said.

"I mean...I guess, but..." He shrugged again. "I just never really thought about her like that." He took a deep breath, puffing out his cheeks as he exhaled. "Thank you for telling me."

"Sure." Obviously, the conversation was dead. "So I owe you a dance at the Halloween party."

"Or two," he teased. "I'll hold you to that. And remember, it's a costume party, so you better dress up!"

"For me, every Friday at Archangel is a costume party."

"Then I love Fridays," he said with an even larger grin. "I gotta go, but I'll see you at Archangel, yeah?"

"I'll be there," I said, turning to watch him pass me and head toward the direction of the buses.

"Popular," another familiar voice said, causing me to jump and turn back around to see Clark approaching.

"I didn't see you," I said, placing a hand on my chest as I let out a huff.

"How could you past Devon's flirting?" he said with a suggestive smile.

"Oh, yeah, he kinda…does that."

"Do you like him?"

"No. Not like that, anyway."

"Maybe you should just tell him that, then," Clark suggested. "Best to just let him know outright. He's a good guy, but he's not great on subtle cues."

"I told him Jill liked him, so hopefully that will take some of his attention." I drew in a deep breath, pulling the straps of my backpack tight as the air between me and Clark changed. "I guess…I just follow you?"

He nodded, turning back the way he had come and leading me around the side of the school to the south parking lot, which was where the teachers parked. There was a black car at the far end of the lot away from the other cars where a man in a simple black suit and sunglasses stood, waiting for us.

As we approached, he opened the back door and waited for both of us to climb into the back seat. My hands were shaking as I fastened the seatbelt, and I jumped when the door shut after Clark took his seat. The driver silently got into the driver's seat, adjusted the mirrors and began driving out of the parking lot.

The reality of where we were going, and that this would become my new routine, hit me in the silence of the car. My head was going light, my stomach doing angry flips, adrenaline coursing through my veins with enough ferocity to nearly make me combust.

"Since this is your first day with this kind of access, we'll be setting up everything needed for your clearance first," Clark explained.

"My mother told me I should show you around the upper levels of the Commission building before we go downstairs."

"I guess I never really thought about those upper levels."

"That's where everyone in the administrative staff has their offices during the day," he elaborated. "Even Dana has an office up there, though I don't think he's up there very often."

"He's down in the basement?"

"Almost always," Clark confirmed. "He breezes in and out without anyone noticing. He does leave the Commission at some point every day, but he's also always down in the basement. It's hard to explain, just always expect that he's nearby." He shook his head. "Anyway, we'll get you a clearance card and your chips and then I'll show you around."

"Okay…" I said with a wobbly smile. I cleared my throat, trying to mask my nervousness, but Clark smiled gently at me.

"Don't worry," he said. "I'll be with you the whole time."

I glanced at the driver and then at Clark again, realizing that our topics for conversation were greatly limited with an employee of the Commission right in front of us. His dark glasses made it impossible to know if he was watching us through the rearview mirror. It seemed everyone on Dana's security staff wore sunglasses.

Clark mimicked my action, looking at the driver before drawing in a deep breath.

"…do you have a lot of homework today?"

I tried to engage in the conversation in order to distract myself from how close we were getting to the Commission building and the dread creeping deeper into my bones. I hardly realized what Clark was saying or what I was asking, but it was some mundane conversation about homework, school, and upcoming university preparations.

The final turn after passing the security gates had me falling silent, watching as the car pulled up to the front doors that had become the beacon of fear in my life. I was struggling to draw a deep enough breath as I leaned down and grabbed my backpack, the driver stepping around the car to open the door for us.

As soon as my foot hit the pavement, a wave of finality washed over me. I was walking into the lion's den intent on finding a way to kill it. That moment before entering the building and getting my clearance was my last chance to turn back on the plan and decide not to fight the Commission of the People or Dana Christenson. I could submit, accept the reality of my country, and do whatever was necessary to make that reality tolerable. But stepping into that building with the thought that I was going to spy meant I was committing to fighting Dana, hoping against all else that my will was stronger than his influence.

The sound of the car door closing behind me surprised me out of my stupor. Clark stepped to my side, holding his backpack over one shoulder.

"Deep breaths," he said. I obeyed, closing my eyes with a long exhale, forcing my heartbeat to slow the spread of adrenaline through my body.

A young man dressed in another simple suit rushed outside and grabbed the keys from our driver. The man who had driven us led us to the lobby door, stepping inside without a glance behind him. I willed my feet to follow, falling into step behind Clark.

The automatic door slid silently aside and closed again behind us. The woman at the reception desk flashed an impossibly-white smile and stood from her desk chair.

"Hello, Clark," she greeted in a shrill voice.

"Hello, Cassie," he said. "This is Lily Sandover." He motioned to me. "Mr. Christenson has given her clearance, so she just needs to finalize everything."

"Oh, right." Cassie rummaged in the drawers of the large reception desk as our driver ran his clearance card over a device near the lowered counter where our jackets and bags were checked for each Commission meeting. Once the card reader beeped, he pressed his hand flat to the screen behind the reader.

Cassie returned in front of us with a folder, opening it.

"Here we are," she declared, handing me a card in a plastic sleeve attached to an expandable lanyard. "Here is your clearance card. It's best to keep it attached to a belt or belt loops." She grabbed two devices and placed them on the counter next to the open folder, typing a few codes into her computer, her long nails clicking on the keys. One device was a large screen and the other had ten, small round metal pads meant for my fingertips.

"Fingertips first, please," Cassie said, nodding to the reader. "Place your fingers here and press down as hard as you can until I tell you to stop."

I did as Cassie instructed, then followed her instructions as my full handprint was also recorded.

"We have your face, profile, and retinal scans..." she mused, her eyes averted to her computer. "Give me just a moment."

She fiddled with more things behind the counter as I shot Clark an exasperated look. He gave a short, understanding nod in response. Our driver had taken station next to the reception desk, his hands folded in front of him and his head bent, his covered eyes unreadable as he waited for us.

"Okay," Cassie said, ducking behind the desk and popping up with a plastic tub filled with meticulously filed cell phones. Each phone had a rubber band, securing a piece of paper with typed names. I saw one with my name on it and my hand instantly pressed into my pocket, feeling the outline of my phone.

"Can I have your cell phone, please?" she asked. I hesitantly extracted it. She took it, transferring the name and rubber band as she handed me the phone from the plastic tub. "You can pick up your phone when you leave," she assured. "This will be your phone while you are on Commission property."

"But what if my parents try to call?" I asked. "How will I be able to tell them I'm on my way home?"

"This is still your phone," Cassie assured. "It's just a device that is friendlier to the machine frequencies in the building."

I glanced at the dark smart phone, suspicious.

"What do you mean?"

"There are jamming signals in some parts of the building," Cassie elaborated. "This phone can work around those signals. It's just for privacy so that no one can use their own phones to spy on the Commission. So don't lose that one."

"What if I do lose it?"

"We shut it down remotely," she said, snapping the lid back on the tub. "If necessary, there is also a means of activating self-destruct."

I almost dropped the phone as if it was going to explode in my hand.

Cassie returned her attention to the computer, clicking around the screen until she grabbed a tiny, plastic bag and copied the number on the bag. The small bag held a piece of paper with three, miniscule specks of black in a line. Once she finished typing, she grabbed a paper from the printer and folded it around the small bag, placing both items in a fabric pouch.

"You'll need these later, so I'm handing them to Mark for safe keeping," she explained, her high heels clicking as she walked to our driver and handed him the pouch, which he took with both hands.

"Alright," Cassie said with a nod as she returned to her computer, "that card I gave you will get you just about everywhere. It might take about ten to twelve hours before all the electronic locks recognize your hand and fingerprints, so just stick with Clark today."

I nodded silently.

Cassie scrambled to get Clark his Commission cell phone once he set his other one on the counter next to the folder.

"Mark will check your bags and then you can head inside," Cassie said, closing the folder and jerking her head to our driver.

"Thank you, Cassie," Clark said, pocketing his Commission-issued phone and ushering me to the side of the desk. We placed our bags on the counter as Cassie turned over her shoulder.

"Mark, check them," she ordered.

The driver obeyed, going through Clark's backpack thoroughly first. Even though I was certain I didn't have anything in my possession that could get me into trouble, I felt nervous. Once Mark finished looking through the backpack, he quickly pat Clark down, much to my surprise. The security checks were tighter than when my family came to the Saturday Commission meetings.

My backpack was also searched and—to my discomfort—I was also patted down by Mark.

Once we were both cleared, Mark picked up the pouch he had been handed and led us to the elevators.

"Are you alright?" Clark asked. My spooked expression must have been obvious.

"Yeah, fine. Just…a little surprised, I guess…"

"Sometimes security is a little tighter than normal. They randomly pick days to thoroughly check everyone," Clark explained. "Today must be one of those days."

The elevator doors opened and Mark ushered us in.

"Four," Clark said. Mark stepped into the elevator after us and pressed the button for level four.

"Floors one and two are call centers," Clark explained. "They're the cubicle workers. Level three is conference rooms and a kitchen. The fourth floor is where my mom's office is, which is where we're going. Most of the Commission-Only staff have their offices on the fourth floor."

"Commission Only?"

"The people who don't hold any other office in Central," Clark clarified. "Your father, for example, is Chief Regulator for the Western Region and he's also in the Commission. My mom is Advisor to the Commission and that's it. She's Commission-Only. Your father isn't."

The elevator doors opened on the fourth floor and Mark stepped out, turning and watching us as we passed.

"We'll be right back," Clark told him. I spared a glance at Mark as we rounded the corner before catching up to Clark and leaning closer to him.

"He's creepy…"

"Mark?" Clark asked, startled. "No, he's not so bad."

He stopped and knocked on the door with a nameplate that read Danielle J. Markus. Clark opened the door without waiting for an answer, leaning in hesitantly.

The elaborate, immaculately-kept office surprised and confused me. It was bright and beautiful with large windows that let in broad rays of sunlight and gave the room a warm, inviting atmosphere. The office was a stark contrast with what I had seen in the lower levels of the Commission, and while it should have eased my heightened anxiety, it only served to unsettle me further.

"Oh, Clark, you brought Lily with you," Mrs. Markus greeted from behind her large desk, sliding her chair away from the computer she had been using. She stood, walking around her desk to approach us. "How are you today, Lily?"

"Alright," I said.

"I'm so thrilled that Clark will finally have someone his age to talk to while he's here," she said lightly, glancing at her embarrassed son. "I'm sure he's been bored out of his mind."

"The others, like Melissa, don't come here?" I asked. I was almost certain it was only Clark that Dana forced to be at the Commission after school, since he had developed such an obsession, but I figured that at least some of the children of the other Commission advisors would also be around the Commission from time to time.

"No," Mrs. Markus said. "Melissa is involved in hunter-jumper activities after school. She's a busy girl."

"What's hunter-jumper?"

"Horseback riding," she clarified. She turned her attention back to Clark. "Are you giving her a tour?"

"A short one," he affirmed. "I'm showing her around up here before we go downstairs and start on homework."

"Sounds good," she said with an approving nod. "I should be down around five." She smiled at me. "Lily, if you ever need anything, you can always come up to my office before five. I'll be in my office in the basement after five if you need me. Don't be shy."

"Thank you, Mrs. Markus."

The interaction with Mrs. Markus confused and angered me. She was clearly caring and had a very maternal aura, but she had allowed Dana to abuse her son and had even been seduced by the leader of the Commission of the People. On top of that, she was fully aware of the experiments being run in the basement and did not seem to have empathy for the test subjects. I felt like I could not trust her simply because I did not understand how she could so easily play the supportive, caring mother and the cold demeanor she would need to stomach what the Commission did below ground.

"You two keep each other company and enjoy having the Commission mostly to yourself," she said with a wink. "Clark, Dana wanted to talk to you when you were settled."

"Why?" he asked, a noticeable tremor in his voice. My heart sank, worried about the paling of his face, also worried why Dana wanted to see him.

"You're not in trouble," she said with a light laugh. "He just wanted to talk to you about something. He didn't say what."

Clark nodded obediently, his gaze falling to the carpet.

"Okay," he murmured. "I'll see you downstairs later."

He turned and walked to the door. I followed, trying not to look too nervous as I glanced between Clark and his mother as we left.

"Alright," she called, returning to the other side of her desk. "Love you."

"Love you, too," he repeated mechanically.

I closed the door behind us as Clark turned toward the elevators.

"Anyway," he muttered, distracted, "that's really all you need to know on this floor. The other advisors also have offices up here, but if you ever need to find a particular office, there is a map of the offices on each floor next to the elevators." As we rounded the corner, prompting Mark to press the call button for the elevator, Clark motioned to the placard on the wall between the elevators.

"The fifth floor is the Records Department. Those are the other workers who file everything into the system about criminals taken in by the Commission."

"They note everything?" I asked, knowing that both of the people with me would understand what I was really asking.

"No," Clark admitted. "They handle the surface level information. Keeping track of families and the names of those apprehended. They do not keep record of what happens to them afterward. Those records are all downstairs."

"But they can access those records from their computers up here, right?"

"If they have the necessary clearance, I would assume so," he said. The elevator doors opened and we walked in, Mark stepping in after us and hovering his hands over the buttons, waiting to hear where we were going. "Seven," Clark told him.

He pressed the button and folded his hands behind his back, watching diligently as the doors closed and the elevator began another ascent. I looked between the back of Mark's head and Clark, uncomfortable with the stranger's presence.

"Floor six has more offices, mostly for the people who live downstairs."

"Live downstairs? Like the scientists?"

"Them, some of the other administrative staff…there's quite a few who live down there," Clark said. "The sixth floor is generally pretty empty. It's sorta just there for show. If someone who knows nothing about the Enterprise projects wants to meet with those people, the sixth floor is where they meet. Those offices help the Commission keep up appearances and keep most of the secrets hidden. We're just going to the seventh floor to show you Dana's and Sean's upper offices. The floor is generally empty, too, but sometimes they have meetings up here."

"You don't need to show me everything," I said gently. "Especially if Dana is never there."

"It's good that you at least know where Dana's office is," he said, dropping his gaze again. I was about to insist that he did not have to go through all the trouble, until I realized he wanted to show me something about the upstairs offices, but could not tell me what with Mark directly in front of us.

Mark stepped out before us, keeping his hands behind his back as he stood to the side of the doors and waited for us to leave. Even though his head was slightly bent, I could feel his eyes following us as we rounded the corner out of sight.

Clark led me down yet another starkly boring hallway. The walls were devoid of anything breaking the sterile, off-white walls.

"Everything up here is too…" I could not come up with the appropriate word.

"Surreal?" Clark guessed. "It's really weird coming up here when you're used to the basement. And really the only people with offices up here are Dana and Sean."

"So I might be able to find Sean up here?"

"Unlikely. He has an office in the basement where you will find him more often than not. Otherwise, he's usually pretty close to Dana."

At the far end of the main, boring hallway was a large, black door with a nameplate across the front reading "Dana Christenson." I hesitated when Clark hit his knuckles quietly against the door.

"Is he in there?" I whispered.

"I highly doubt it," Clark said. "I just always knock."

He opened the door slowly, peering around the edge until he confirmed no one was in the office.

Dana's upstairs office looked like something straight out of a magazine. The large windows let in the sunlight to illuminate the expensive, well-dusted modern furniture that so perfectly adorned the room. The desk had a large computer sitting to one side so as not to obscure the view of the two black chairs where Dana could hold small meetings. There was also a seating area in one corner where a couch and two chairs surrounded a glass coffee table. The walls held large pictures of American landscapes, though there were a few bookshelves lined with almost-identical books.

"Not what I was expecting…" I muttered.

"This is Dana's upstairs office," Clark said. "The reason I wanted to bring you up here is because…" He motioned for me to follow him as he stepped around Dana's desk to the computer, where the screensaver showed the seal of the Commission of the People.

The pristine nature of the desk and computer made me flinch when Clark dared to disturb it by pressing a key on the keyboard. The screensaver clicked off and the screen became filled with a fully-booked calendar of the month, showing the events for the day in a list on one side.

"You can always access his updated schedule from here," Clark explained. "You can access it from any computer in the Commission, because everyone is always updating his schedule. And the reason I suggest coming up here to see his schedule is because you can view it undetected."

"Undetected?"

"See the cameras?" he asked, pointing to the black orbs in the ceiling in each corner of the room. "They're fake."

"How do you know that?"

Clark hesitated, turning his gaze from mine in shame.

"Let's just say that one day I got brave and thought I would find some recorded video of what Dana does to me so I could show her," he mumbled. "So when I asked Sean to show me the security footage for this office he told me there were no live cameras in this office. I even hacked into the security mainframe just to be sure."

"You can hack into the security mainframe?"

"It's not too difficult." Clark shrugged away my surprise. "It's the Records Department that's difficult to get into without being detected." He returned his attention to the screen, reading over Dana's schedule as I spared another glance at the fake security cameras.

"What about his office downstairs? Does that have cameras?"

"Yes, but only two, so there are a lot of blind spots," Clark said distractedly. "Looks like Dana has a meeting with some of the security detail today, so we need to have Mark downstairs in ten minutes," he added. With a sigh, he straightened and turned away from the computer. "Ready for a tour of the basement?"

"As much as I'll ever be."

"I know you've seen a lot of it already, but I also know the first few times down there are confusing, so I'll just give you another tour," he said as he led me out of the office and back to Mark. Once in the elevator, Mark produced his own key from his pocket and took us to the basement level.

We were silent on the descent to the basement, though Clark did remind Mark of the meeting in ten minutes. Mark had only nodded once, still facing the elevator doors. As the elevator continued to descend, Clark took a breath as though he were about to speak, but stopped, sighing and closing his mouth again. Confused, I shot him a worried look. Mark also turned over his shoulder, remaining silent, staring at Clark from behind his glasses.

Clark shook his head with a thin smile.

"I'm fine," he said to Mark, his tone suggesting that Mark was a close, concerned friend and Clark wanted to assuage any worries he might have.

I looked between the two, confused by the warmth in Clark's voice.

Mark did not seem entirely convinced, but he eventually turned back to dutifully staring at the closed elevator doors.

It took us even longer to reach the basement as usual, since we were coming from the top floor of the building above, which also gave my anxiety plenty of time to grow to an unhealthy level. The basement did not appear at all different from all the other times I had been down there, but knowing that this was now to be my daily routine made the shadows in the room appear even darker, more sinister.

Mark bowed his head to us silently before walking out of the elevator and toward the Commission meeting room. Clark and I were slower to leave the elevator, but I rounded on Clark when Mark was out of sight.

"Does he not speak?" I said, exasperated.

"He can't."

"What do you mean?" I asked, following Clark as we also walked toward the meeting room.

"He physically cannot speak," he elaborated. "He's a former experiment. Dana either removed or damaged his larynx so severely that he can't speak. He can't really understand English either."

"He's a former experiment?" I gasped.

"Now you've met the gift Dana gave to my family," Clark said, motioning in the direction Mark had gone as we walked between the empty tables in the meeting room.

"But...he looks so normal," I said. "And he can go outside with you."

"Next time we see him, I'll show you," Clark said vaguely, hooking his thumbs in his backpack straps, uncomfortable. "We'll find a conference room to leave all our stuff in and then I'll show you around a little."

I followed him to the door at the back of the meeting room, the same hallway where Dana had brought Clark and me after I was attacked at Archangel, but my mind was buzzing with the realization that the man who had driven us to the Commission, pat us down as a security measure, and stood silent watch as we went to the various floors of the building, had been an experiment that had suffered under the Commission's cruel experimentation.

"I'm sure you saw that there are three other doors out of the meeting room," Clark explained as we walked. "You always want to take one of the two doors on the right side of the room from when you walk in. Those lead to the offices and cells. The door on the left leads to the living quarters."

"Like where Dana lives?" I asked. "Have you ever been in there?"

"No," Clark said. "I don't really have a reason to go back there. I don't even know what the rooms look like back there."

He opened the door to the dimly-lit hallway and began walking to the door at the other end.

"From here you start running into the doors that need clearance cards," he explained. "You'll need your card to open almost every door." He stopped at the door and motioned to the black pad next to the handle. "Just press your card to the pad."

I did so, not bothering to remove it from the plastic. I heard a soft beep and a click, prompting me to press down on the cold handle and open the door, walking into another hallway that I vaguely remembered.

"And that's all it takes," Clark said, following me. "Some doors will need more verification, but I'll show you what those locks look like if we come across any of them."

Clark took up the lead, taking the first left off the main hallway.

"Down this hall are the conference rooms and a few of the offices," he said. "Generally, we'll be in one of these rooms. We just pick a conference room that has no scheduled meetings and stay in there until we go home."

"That sounds supremely boring," I laughed.

"It generally is," Clark agreed with a roll of his eyes. "Again, I'm sorry you're stuck here, but I will be so happy to have someone to talk to now."

We approached the first conference room door. The conference rooms had a singular black table surrounded by black chairs and a projection screen on the far wall, while next to the door were windows allowing us to peer into the room. Next to the door was a small, square screen that Clark tapped twice to light.

"This is where the schedule is posted for the rooms," he said, tapping his fingernail against the text on the screen. "The office staff will be having a meeting in this room at five-thirty, so not this room."

He turned, walking to the next conference room, though he stopped to point at a door on the opposite side of the hall.

"That's Sarah's office," he said. "She's pretty much in charge of the schedules and paperwork in the Commission. She's really nice, but she gets stressed out really easily and can get a little snappy. But if you ever need any pens or office supplies, just ask her. She has a stock of everything you could ever need."

The office next to Sarah's did not have a name on it, nor did the two doors after that one.

"Are some of these offices empty?"

Clark nodded, turning his attention to the screen next to the door of the next conference room. "At one point people worked in those offices, but I guess they couldn't really handle the Commission. And since everything is so secretive, it's hard to hire for certain positions."

"…what happens to the people who quit the Commission after working down here?" I asked. Based on the sick feeling in the pit of my stomach, I already knew the answer.

"Take a guess," Clark said coldly, walking to the next conference room and looking at the schedule. "I hate Mondays. Every room is always filled," he grumbled, shaking his head and moving down the hall to another conference room.

I had been looking at the office doors with the blank name placards when a tapping sound brought my attention to the conference room we had approached. Dana was standing on the other side of the glass, his glasses hooked into his breast pocket, and a broad smile on his face. All eyes in the crowded conference room were on us.

Clark had frozen, unsure what to do until Dana crooked a finger and invited the two of us into the room.

Sparing an apologetic glance at me, Clark opened the conference room door and waited for me to step inside before he followed.

"Good afternoon, Little Lily," Dana greeted. I tried not to jump when the conference room door closed behind me and Clark. "Allow me to introduce you," he said, turning to everyone seated at the table. "Everyone, this is little Lily Sandover, Tommy Sandover's daughter. She is the reason I've called this meeting today," he said. "She has recently been the target for some of the younger members of the Commission who have nothing better to do with their time. She will be staying down here with us every day after school until the threat abates. She'll mostly be keeping Clark company, but I wanted to be sure everyone was aware of the change in clearance."

Dana turned back to me. "There are a few people you should know," he said, motioning over the table, his hand finally pointing to Sean. "You already know Sean."

I nodded to him and he smiled warmly in response.

"That is Jim," Dana pointed to a man who raised his hand to get my attention. He was a young man with a very soft face and bright blonde hair hanging over his eyes. "He is in command of the security for the cells and wards of the Enterprise labs."

"Do you want her to have clearance into the back?" Jim asked.

"Level B. She can go back and take a look, but she cannot access Ward Ten, the Dome, or the cells themselves." He shot me a challenging look as he spoke and I could not help but shy away.

"Over here is Sarah," Dana continued, apparently not noticing my flinch. "She's in charge of the organization down here." He winked at her and her bright smile and flush accented how pretty she was with curly auburn hair cascading around her freckled face and bright blue eyes. She nodded to me with a short wave, but Dana had already motioned to the three men standing to one side of the conference room, dressed in identical matching suits. I recognized one as Mark.

"These boys over here are a few of the elite security force of the Commission," Dana explained. "Mark, of course, you have already met. He is the Markus family gift."

Mark dropped his head in a shallow bow.

"They don't really speak, and they can't understand almost anything you say, but they do know a few commands. And most importantly, they are dedicated to the security of the Commission," Dana said, walking toward the three men. "As with Clark, I have put Mark in charge of your safety. He is your personal bodyguard. These other two, Sam and Dale, are Mark's backup if I ever need to steal him away for something else. They'll just quietly loom in a corner. You'll get used to ignoring them."

Dana's pace stopped next to Mark, who did not dare to turn and face the leader of the Commission. After a quick glance in my direction, Dana smirked and stepped in front of Mark, reaching both hands to the former experiment's face.

"I'm willing to bet, Little Lily, that you have never seen one of these before."

Dana stepped away, Mark's glasses in his hands, and I understood with one look why Mark had been taken in to the Commission of the People.

He was not like anyone else I had ever seen before. I had not given much thought to his slightly darker skin, but with his eyes revealed, I could see his other Asian features. His eyes were narrow, shaped like almonds above high cheekbones. With the exception of his jaw, the lines of his face were soft, not nearly as angular as Caucasian men. His nose was smaller, flatter against his face, and his lips were narrower.

Mark bowed his head but Dana pressed two fingers to the bottom of chin, pushing his head back up.

"No, no, no," he scolded gently. "Let her get a good look at you."

Mark looked at me, his eyes gentle and mildly frightened. I looked into the almost-black eyes, admittedly fascinated. Dana was right, I had never seen an Asian before, not even on the news. Very rarely were the political tensions in Asia covered on American news, and even then it was a brief note before moving on to something more prevalent in our home country. I had only heard about what Asians looked like by rumor.

I was staring no matter how I wanted to stop. I wanted to stop studying him, knowing that just because he was Asian he was no different from anyone else in the room, but I was shocked at how exaggerated the rumors of the Asian appearance had been and I continued to look over the differences in his features.

"He is quite the specimen, isn't he?" Dana said. "His face was the least-chinky of the batch, which is why he's allowed to go out for very limited times with his glasses. We don't let him out too much, though." Dana took Mark's chin, turning his face as he appraised Mark. "Got him out of a large, hidden society in the Western Region about eight years ago. They had been hiding in a destroyed, quarantined neighborhood ever since the population cleanse of the Second Revolution. Made quite the little society there, which gave us plenty of subjects to turn into our experiment security force."

He dropped Mark's chin, his fingers running down one of the large tendons in Mark's neck. "Unfortunately, most only know the orders we used to train them, so communication can be difficult. And of course, we had to name all of them since their other names were too damn difficult. And some of them we had to use more severe methods of domination…like this one who refused to obey until we took his voice." Dana's cold smile grew when he saw Mark shiver from the hand tracing down the scar that lined the same tendon. "But I couldn't very well let this one be killed. Like any good, stereotypical slant-eye, he can fight. Which is why he is in charge of your security."

Dana's hand left Mark's neck and he smirked.

"You didn't get a word of that, did you?" Dana chortled. The rest of the room also laughed. Only Clark, Sean and I remained silent. I could feel the disgust and discomfort rising in my throat. Dana placed a hand on Mark's head, ruffling his hair roughly as Mark cringed.

Dana's golden eyes turned to me. "Come closer, no need to be afraid," he said. "He's very tame now."

When I did not move, Dana crossed the room and grabbed my wrist, pulling me over until I was standing directly in front of Mark.

"See? Nothing to be afraid of," Dana said. "For the most part, they're dumb as bricks, but they know their orders and the order is to keep you safe." Dana took my wrist again, bringing my hand to lightly slap Mark's cheek. I yanked my hand from Dana's grip, glaring at the leader of the Commission. "You could slap him and he would not retaliate. He's your guard dog. He'll do whatever is necessary to protect you and won't retaliate if you do anything against him."

I stared at Mark, who was looking between Dana, the laughing, jeering people around the conference table, and me as I stared into his dark eyes apologetically.

"Now, with all that out of the way," Dana continued, "I need to have a discussion with Clark. The rest of you are excused. Mark," the experiment flinched when Dana turned to him, "take Little Lily," he pointed to me, "to conference room five." He held up five fingers and jerked his thumb over his shoulder to the hallway. Mark bowed his head shallowly, motioning to the door and guiding me into the hallway.

I spared a glance at the nervous and frightened Clark as I followed Mark's lead out of the room. Clark tried to smile at me, but I could not even muster a quirk of my lips in response.

Mark led me to the dark conference room two doors down the hallway, silent, opening the door for me as the lights automatically clicked on.

I put my backpack in one of the chairs with a heavy sigh, already feeling the stress wearing me down. I turned to Mark as he bowed his head and began to leave.

"Mark!" I hesitated when he turned back, unable to stop staring at his eyes. They were so dark, so different, and I knew I should not have been staring, but I could not stop myself. "I..."

He waited patiently. I wanted to say so much, to ask him questions, to apologize for what had happened to him, but knowing he would be unable to understand me, I found myself uselessly opening and closing my mouth, trying to decide if there was anything I *could* say to him.

"I'm so sorry..." I finally uttered. He cocked his head to the side, confused. My heart broke. I took a hesitant step closer and he retreated, watching me carefully as I lifted both hands peacefully before making a fist with my right hand, placing it against my chest and making a few clockwise motions, wondering if the few sign language words I knew would translate to him. He looked between my hand and my eyes, his expression filled with bewilderment.

"I'm sorry," I repeated, trying to convey with my eyes what I was trying to tell him.

His expression softened, the confusion leaving his face. My heart picked up pace as he opened his mouth, seeing the dilemma in his eyes. His lips closed again and his gaze fell to the floor. A few moments later, he looked up again and opened his mouth.

I could do nothing but blink at him as he tried to communicate.

He reached a hand out to me and I hesitantly placed my hand in his, surprisingly not afraid despite my earlier concerns about the silent man. He brought my hand up to his neck, pressing my fingers to the scars along the tendons in his neck, extending up to his ears and below the collar of his suit. I felt tenderly along the raised skin, feeling the crushing weight in my chest again at realizing how extensive the surgery had been to rob Mark of his voice. Tears were welling in my eyes before I could stop them.

"I'm so sorry..." I whispered yet again.

He pointed at me and nodded, which made me believe he could not understand what I had said at all. He then pointed at his ear, pinching the lobe and dropping his hand.

"What?" I asked.

He hesitated, looking around the room and then motioned for me to come closer, but since I was standing so close already, I did not take another step.

"I'm sorry, what are you trying to say?"

He pointed at me again with a quick nod. I stared at him, but realized that he did understand the apology and was trying to reply. He then pointed at his chest before reaching up and tugging on his earlobe again. I guessed the motion was the experiment sign language for 'thank you' or 'it's alright.'

I laughed awkwardly and nodded, hoping we had shared a short understanding with one another. Mark's face also brightened and he smiled, the sight of which chased away some of the heaviness crushing my ribs. I did not know how old Mark was, but his face had a very bright, innocent look about it for being that of a grown man. His dark eyes were suddenly very expressive and full of light.

When Clark suddenly appeared at the door, I backed away from Mark. Clark looked between us, hesitating half way through the door.

"What's going on in here?" he asked suspiciously.

"I was trying to tell him I was sorry for what happened in the other room. I think he understood me," I said with a nervous laugh, retreating a few steps from Mark.

"Ah, he probably understood the apology, but thankfully, I don't think he understands a lot of what the others said about him in there."

"That doesn't make it any better."

"No, no, it doesn't," Clark agreed. He turned his focus onto Mark. "Eighteen-Thirty."

Mark bowed his head and stepped out of the room, positioning himself outside the door.

"What was that about?" I asked.

"That's the time he's taking us home," Clark explained, dropping his backpack to one of the other chairs and sighing. "Dana says he's sorry that he doesn't have time to chat with you today because he has meetings until ten," Clark added, malice dripping from each word. "I'm going to show you around more of the Commission, and we'll have to go back to the lab before we get too settled to get your tracers put in."

"In the lab? The same lab where we saw Eina that first night?" I asked, the cold fear returning like a splash of ice cold water.

"Yeah, Mark's got the tracer chips. Everyone with our level of clearance or higher has tracer chips in their body."

Each American child was given an identity chip behind the right ear shortly after birth. Central adamantly stated it was not some kind of tracker and it was only used for medical purposes in case of accidents, crimes, or odd complications. I was pleased to realize that the chip behind my ear was not some government tracer, but that did not quell my fear at having three tracers accessible to Dana Christenson and the Commission of the People put in my body.

"Don't worry, it's a simple process. And I'll be there with you."

"You will?"

"Of course," he said strongly. "Come on, I'll show you around a little more."

We stepped outside the conference room and traversed the final distance down the hall to the hallway juncture. Mark trailed behind us silently, his hands clasped behind his back, keeping his distance while still being noticeable out of the corner of my eye. Dana had not returned his glasses, meaning I was able to see the way he kept his eyes mostly averted to our feet, not daring to raise his gaze.

"There are more conference rooms down that hall," Clark said, pointing in one direction at the hallway juncture. "But back this way are the other offices. After we see those, I'll take you to the labs for the tracers."

The hallway we turned down had three open corridors on the right side of the hall, one at the beginning, middle, and very end. Clark would stop at the mouths of the corridors, explaining who worked in the offices that had name plates, including where the advisor's downstairs offices were located. We turned at the last hallway, where Clark's mother's office was located near a door that read "Library of the Commission of the People."

"A library?" I asked, pointing at the door.

"The last two doors in this hall are doors to the library," Clark confirmed. He opened the door, revealing the towering bookshelves illuminated by bright lights in the cavernous room. While the library was not the biggest one I had seen, it was one of the most beautiful. The tall shelves were made of dark wood and each aisle had an old-style rolling ladder. There were large second, and third levels of balconies with beautifully ornate banisters and sweeping spiral staircases.

"I did not expect a library down here," I said, marveling at the room. "Why would the Commission need a library?"

"A lot of these are banned books or law books," Clark answered, looking around the shelves, his eyebrows high. "There are all sorts of documents and books of the Second Revolution, pre-Secondary Revolution things...several things that they have not allowed in the Central Library."

"So, on top of taking in people who were dangerous to the security of America, the books were confiscated, too?"

"Sometimes, the books were more dangerous than the people," Clark said. "I've always wanted to go through all these and see what is in here, but I don't even know where to start."

"There's so many..."

"Come on." Clark jerked his head out the door, where Mark was waiting. The three of us walked to the end of the hallway, turning right and walking to another door that read "Commission of the People – Records."

My heart skipped a beat.

"This is the Records room," Clark noted unnecessarily. "As you can see, this room is completely secure. Card, fingerprint, and retina scans. There is also a camera at every angle pointed at this door." He motioned around the hallway and I looked up, trying to spot the hidden cameras. "No blind spots. No way to get in without the proper clearance."

Clark turned away and was about to say something when the next door on the left, across from the middle corridor, opened and two familiar people stepped out.

"You have been treading a fine line lately, Sean," Dana said dangerously as he stepped out after his head of security.

"You don't need to know everything," Sean groaned, rolling his eyes as he turned to face Dana. "Let me handle some things on my own. If you're always looming over me, I can't do my job properly."

"Why? Do I frighten you?"

"No, I just get sick of putting up with your tantrums when you don't like the way I handle things," Sean said with a bark of laughter. I found fear invading my veins again, startled that Sean would dare talk back to Dana so casually. "I hate putting up with you all the time. Why don't you find someone else to bother and let me do my job?"

Dana laughed and placed a hand against the side of Sean's face— a hand, I noticed, from which Sean did not flinch.

"I love it when you get bossy…" he purred, his voice dripping with honey. I shivered, able to feel the effects of his charisma even down the hallway. "But surely you understand that this is not about me monitoring you as your boss. This is me monitoring you to see if I can trust you, and if I can't trust you, you will be replaced," Dana said as if it was a mere inconvenience.

"Okay," Sean said easily, "but good luck finding someone who will put up with your shit. I'm going to be hard to replace."

"Very true." Dana's hand dropping to Sean's chest. "It will be difficult…but don't think it's not possible," he warned with a dangerous smile and a mischievous glint in his eyes.

To my surprise, Sean seemed completely unbothered that Dana was threatening to replace him, which I was certain meant that Sean would be killed.

"You need to trust me a little more. I have been here for seven years. Name the last employee who was not an experiment to stay with you that long," Sean challenged with a raised eyebrow.

"You know I can't," Dana said. "Why don't you come to my office around midnight and we can discuss this further?" he murmured, running his hand along the lapel of Sean's suit and pretending to straighten it, blinking slowly as he turned his gaze up to the taller man's face. It was fascinating, though uncomfortable, to watch Dana so openly flirt with another man.

Sean just laughed and grabbed Dana's wrist, pulling it away from his chest.

"Don't you have work to do?" he scolded. "You have a meeting in five minutes." Sean turned away from Dana, walking toward us easily.

"Sean!" Dana whined behind him. "Why don't you ever play with me anymore?"

"I'll play with you when you stop being such a spoiled brat," Sean laughed over his shoulder. "I'll talk to you in the morning. Get to work, sir."

Dana's gaze fell on me. He winked once before slipping into his office and closing the door.

"Sorry about all that." Sean rolled his eyes as he stopped in front of us.

"Sean..." I started, "Dana just said he would replace you. You could become an experiment."

"He didn't mean it." Sean shook his head, glancing at the closed office door. "It's taken me years, but I know how to read him pretty well. I can tell when he is serious and when he's just playing. He really enjoys making people squirm, and he's in one of those moods today."

"Isn't it dangerous to talk to him like that, though?"

"He threatens to make me into an experiment at least every other day. He started doing it about two years ago. As you can see, I'm still here," Sean said. "I know when I can push back a bit. He likes keeping people around who don't put up with his shit. He finds it refreshing."

Sean reached into his suit pocket, pulling out a pair of sunglasses as he turned to Mark.

"Mark," he called, extending the sunglasses. The silent man stepped forward, accepting the glasses with both hands and a small bow as Sean placed a comforting hand on Mark's shoulder. The head of security then glanced at Clark and me.

"Have you had your tracer chips put in yet?"

"No..." I murmured, my stomach churning again at the thought of being in the lab with all the needles and sharp objects I had seen my first night in the Commission of the People.

"Just so you know," Sean said, "Dana does not have access to the tracers. Only I do. He will only be able to trace you if I am with him."

I blinked at Sean stupidly, surprised to find the information relieved some of my acute fear. "...thank you..."

"I'll leave you alone now," Sean said with a decisive nod. "Lily, if you ever need me, my office is right here on the corner," he pointed at the left corner office in the middle hall.

"Thank you," I said again. He nodded and said goodbye to Clark before disappearing inside his office.

"Wow..." I breathed. "He's a lot braver than I thought."

"He's probably the only one who can talk to Dana like that," Clark agreed.

"They aren't...like..." I looked at Clark expectantly.

"No idea," he admitted. "I've seen Dana flirt with him a lot, but I've never seen it go beyond that, so who knows?" Clark pointed at Dana's office door. "I shouldn't need to tell you..." he said, raising his eyebrows as he motioned to the nameplate.

The next door we approached, I remembered all too well—it was the door leading into the back labs of the Commission. Clark stopped outside it, turning to me.

"Are you ready?"

Shaking, I forced my head to nod.

Clark stepped aside and let Mark pass. The experiment used his card and fingerprint scans to open the door. I was startled to see that a former experiment like Mark had the clearance to go into the cells of the Commission, but I could not command my voice to ask Clark the questions, the terror at being in the back of the Commission again seizing my voice.

We were stopped at the security desk, where monitors were showing dozens of camera angles of the experiment cells and labs. I tried to take in everything on each little box, but the security officers standing forced my eyes away.

"Clark," one of the men greeted, surprised. "And Lily, the new girl..." His brow creased in confusion before his eyes widened in realization. "Oh, right, tracers."

He reached a hand over his desk to Mark, who extracted the pouch from his jacket pocket, handing it over. Mark seemed to understand quite a bit for knowing limited English. When my quizzical gaze focused on Clark, he gave me a one-shoulder shrug.

"Mark was here when I got my tracers put in a few years ago," he explained. "He knows what to do."

"Alright, you're not entirely in the system, yet..." the man at the desk mused, grabbing something behind the counter. "Hey, Jason, gimme a hand, will ya?" he said to the man behind him.

"What'd you need?"

"Scan Mark."

"Shit, really?" Jason groaned. "I hate doing these freaky fuckers…" I watched Jason grumble as he grabbed something off the desk and walked to Mark. "You," he snapped sharply, pointing at Mark's feet, "shoe off."

The man behind the desk caught my attention again.

"If you could place your right hand against this screen," he nodded to the flat screen he had placed in front of me. I obeyed, the screen scanning my palm and beeping as the guard typed into his computer. I turned again to watch Jason and Mark. Mark placed his right sock in his shoe, leaving his foot bare.

"Do you think he's clean?" Jason said. "I never know with these freaks. Hey Clark," he called, "can he do anything on his own? Do you have to bathe him, or can he do it himself?"

"Damn, what is with you people?" Clark sneered. "He's not an invalid. He can bathe and dress himself. He's perfectly capable."

"Aren't you defensive," Jason teased coldly before smacking the side of Mark's right leg. "Foot."

"What are they doing?" I whispered to Clark.

"All experiments have a microchip in their right foot and a tattoo with their experiment number. Security scans it on high-security days to be sure no one tries to sneak in," Clark explained. "I'll show you," he said in response to my still-puzzled expression.

Jason was mumbling crude things under his breath as he held a screen to the bottom of Mark's foot. I cringed at the words leaving his mouth, flinching at some of the racial slurs I had only heard once or twice before.

The man behind the desk was about to tell me something, but Jason sighed heavily and pushed Mark's foot away, standing straight.

"There, the fucker's been scanned."

"Quit bitching," the other man laughed. "We have to check them, since all the damn slant-eyes look the same."

"Their eyes are dead, I swear. Like there's no soul in them," Jason grumbled as he returned to his position behind the desk.

"Cuz they don't have one," the first one said with a bark of laughter.

"In case you've forgotten, he can snap your neck before you even blink," Clark snapped. "So shut up and do your job. Bullying him is pretty pathetic."

I stared at Clark, stunned he was willing to so boldly defend Mark. I, of course, was uncomfortable with the racism, but I had been unable to command my tongue to form a response.

"Back up, kid," Jason growled. "You keep your freaky fucker in line. That's the only job you need to be worried about, got it?"

The man behind the desk lifted a device in front of my face, telling me to look into the circle and stopping further words from Clark and Jason.

When my retina scan was finished and the man turned to his computer again, Clark tapped me on the shoulder, walking to Mark.

"Turn around," he told the experiment, motioning with his hand. Confused, Mark stood still until Clark placed a hand on his shoulder and turned Mark's back to me. Clark tapped the side of Mark's right calf and the experiment lifted his foot again. I saw the surprisingly large tattoo on Mark's instep that read "80029" in bold, black numbers

"The chip is under the tattoo," Clark explained, releasing Mark's ankle and nodding, silently telling him to put his shoe back on.

"Alright," the man behind the desk sighed, replacing the cardboard with the three chips in the bag. "You can go in. Go straight back until you reach the last door of Ward Six," he instructed. "Go to the hallway on the left and that will take you to Lab One. Clark should know where to go."

When Mark had put his shoe back on, he took the bag with the tracers again and started toward the door leading into the experiment cells.

My mouth was dry, my hands shaking as I followed Clark and Mark to the door. I could feel the cold sweat over my entire body, becoming cold and clammy as Mark pressed his hand against the palm reader next to the first door, granting us access to the first hall with floor-to-ceiling glass doors to the cells.

"These are the termination cells," Clark explained, his voice echoing in the vastness of the hall. Only two of the cells were occupied—one housed a girl about my age who was curled in the back corner, covering her head as she shivered. Clark placed a hand on my back to keep me moving when I stopped to stare at her.

"Maybe it's best if you don't look…"

"I want to." I wanted to see them, I *needed* to. I needed to see who we were fighting to free. I wanted to see them as the people they had been before Dana got his hands on him. Seeing someone my age in a cell that ultimately led to execution made my heart rip into pieces and fanned the fire of determination within my chest.

314

The other occupied cell held someone I could not discern, since he was curled up in the back corner, his back facing the glass.

With the use of Mark's fingerprints we moved into Ward Three. Not as overwhelmed as I had been on my first visit, I was able to fully study my surroundings. Before entering the doors marked with a large "3" we stepped across a hallway extending both directions, leading to doors marked "1" and "2."

"Those are Wards One and Two," Clark nodded to each door. "To get any further into the labs, you have to go through Ward Three and Ward Six. Wards One and Two both lead to dead ends."

I looked around the bright main hall of Ward Three as we walked, vaguely remembering the area from my first tour. I noted the smaller hallways branching from the main one that led to more cells, but I was unable to explore the ward completely, Clark guiding me insistently through the main row of glass doors. One of the experiments ran to the glass, banging her fist against it angrily as we passed. I jumped, startled by the appearance of the young woman with a shaved head and a metal muzzle around her mouth.

"It's alright," Clark said. "That glass is strong enough to withstand even the strongest experiments. She can't reach you."

"What can...I mean...what kind of..." I did not know how to phrase my question.

"I don't know," he admitted. "I don't know most of the experiments. But we are in Ward Three, so she's not as powerful as the ones further back."

"What ward did Mark come from?" I asked as we reached the door on the far side of Ward Three.

"Eight," Clark answered. "Originally, Mykail was in Ward Seven, if I remember correctly."

"I know," I said before I could stop myself. I waited to see if Mark showed any reaction to what we were saying, but he continued a steady pace to the door leading out of Ward Three and into another hallway where the doors at either end were marked with a "4" and a "5" while the one in front of us was decorated with the number six.

"Wards Four and Five are the other two gift wards," Clark explained as Mark placed his hand to the door leading to Ward Six. "They also dead-end, just like Wards One and Two. Ward Six is the first of the weapons, so they might be a little more aggressive. Just keep walking. The lab is just past this ward."

Several of the twelve cells on the main hall of Ward Six were empty. I could not help but hesitate outside the cell of a young black girl, who was sitting in the middle of the cell, staring at us blankly. She looked to be only seven or eight years old, and while a part of me was sickened at seeing such a young girl there, I was also frightened, realizing that she was some kind of weapon. I could see the danger in having a powerful weapon concealed behind such a young, innocent exterior.

When we reached the end of the ward, Mark opened the door once more and led us into a larger hallway with two corridors open on either side. Mark turned to look at Clark, who pointed to the right. Mark led us down the appointed hallway.

"These are the labs," Clark explained. "You went into the other one on your first night here."

As we entered the corridor, the door at the end of the hall that read "Lab One" opened and a man in a suit similar to Mark's stepped out. He was also Asian, but looked younger with a softer, thinner face. As he passed us, he and Mark looked at one another, speaking silently for the briefest moment before the other man walked away. Mark turned his head over his shoulder to watch him leave, but did not miss a step and opened the lab door for us when we approached.

I hesitated before stepping in after Clark.

The lab was bright, much brighter than the lab I remembered from my first night in the Commission. Every table was empty and the curtains were drawn back, making the room look larger and less intimidating, somehow. There was only one man in the lab, diligently studying something on his table. He only looked up when Mark closed the door behind us.

"Hello," he greeted. "You must be Lily Sandover." He clicked his tablet off with a smile and motioned us closer.

I walked on legs made of jelly, noting the locations of the sharp instruments lying around the room. I had always been afraid of needles, but knowing that these needles were in the Commission of the People made them even more menacing, particularly since I knew that I would be getting the tracers put under my skin by what I assumed would be large needles.

The scientist motioned to one of the tables.

"Go ahead and hop up here for me," he said before grabbing one of the many plastic boxes stacked on one of the shelves in the corner. I sat on the very end of the table, wringing my hands in my lap, trying to control my breathing. I looked around anxiously as both Mark and Clark approached, Clark offering me a comforting smile.

The scientist returned with the plastic tub and a device I knew was used for scanning the chip behind my ear for my medical information.

"Alright, I'm going to scan this now," he narrated, setting the plastic tub down and pressing the tip of the pen behind my ear as he glanced down at his tablet once again. He stared at it for a moment and then nodded, moving the pen away.

"Good. So, we're just putting in three tracer chips. They will be placed under the skin of your left ankle, the joint where your thumb meets your hand, and then one next to your right shoulder blade," he explained. He opened the tub and I saw new, plastic-wrapped instruments, including a metal tray and a bottle of solution. The scientist wheeled over a stand and spread everything on the surface before reaching out to Mark for the chips.

"I will numb the areas before putting these in, don't worry." He laughed lightly, clearly seeing the terror in my expression.

He filled the metal tray with the solution and dropped the microchips in to sterilize them before grabbing one of the three syringes he had to unwrap. I cringed and closed my eyes as he ripped off the plastic, trying to keep my stomach from squirming at the sight of the needle.

"Do you have a fear of needles?"

I nodded, my eyes still closed.

"I'll have Clark hold your hand while we do this, alright?" the scientist said gently. I was surprised by his patience and concerned tone, considering his place of employment. "I need you to take off your shoe and sock and roll up your jeans on your left leg," he instructed. "This should work very quickly. Have you ever been numbed by the dentist?" I nodded. "It's going to feel like that."

With shaking hands and a light head, I kicked off my shoe and pulled off my sock. Everyone was waiting patiently, but I felt embarrassed by my shaking hands and frightened by the needle that glinted maliciously in the scientist's hand.

When my leg was exposed, he placed a hand against my knee, using his arm to brace my leg while the scientist positioned the syringe.

"Take Clark's hand. Face away and close your eyes. There will be a pinch and then it will feel cold."

I did as I was told, squeezing Clark's hand tight. I cringed when I felt the pinch, knowing it was the needle going under my skin. It took everything I had in me not to be sick or pass out. Every muscle was clenched tight until the needle was removed, and even then, the nausea lingered.

"Okay, we'll wait a few moments. While we're waiting, I'll also numb your hand," he said, motioning Clark to step to the other side of the table, where he took my other hand. I still kept my eyes shut, not sure if I could handle the way the room was spinning.

The scientist set my hand on the biting cold surface of the stand and steadied my fingers before reminding me of the pinch and pushing the needle into my skin. I wanted to lay on the table, or even on the floor, just to have something solid to support me.

I felt the tingling for a few minutes in both my hand and my ankle. "Can you feel that?" the scientist asked, poking my ankle.

I shook my head.

"Can you feel this?" he pressed, prodding the middle of my calf. I nodded tightly, eyes closed. "Okay, we're ready for the first one. Mark, over here…" he ordered. I heard footsteps and then felt Mark's warm hands brace my knee and rest over the top of my foot. "Okay, Lily, squeeze Clark's hand and keep your eyes closed. You will feel some pressure on your ankle, but you should not feel any pain. If you do, tell me immediately and I'll stop."

I nodded, turning my head to Clark, who wrapped his other hand around the back of my head, guiding me to rest my forehead on his shoulder. I took deep breaths. Because I was so anxious already, I felt the pressure that the scientist warned of and it made me jump. Despite my flinch, Mark's strength held my leg still.

It felt like an eternity that I felt the pressure and the movement of the scientist as he moved around me, placing the first tracer in my ankle. I didn't actually feel anything, but being so tense, I was extremely sensitive to everything I could feel. By the time the bandage was placed over the area on my ankle, I was afraid to move at all for fear of passing out.

"First one done," the scientist announced. Mark's hands moved, my leg falling limply over the edge of the table. The jolt scared me and I had to take slow, even breaths to keep from vomiting.

"Here, drink some water," the scientist said quietly, bumping my hand—which was still clutching Clark's desperately—with what could only have been a plastic bottle. I shook my head, my eyes tightly closed. "It will help a little."

Shakily, I took the bottle, trying to lift it to my lips, though Clark had to help support the bottle so I wouldn't drop it. I managed one big gulp before I pulled the bottle away, exhausted by the simple action.

"Let's just get the next one done and then I'll let you recover while your shoulder numbs."

Once again, I placed my head against Clark's shoulder while Mark steadied my forearm and the pressure was applied to my hand. I was so tired that my body felt as though it was shutting down, numbing my brain a little to what was happening. My hand was carefully wrapped and I was offered water again. If I had not exhausted myself so much, I would have been embarrassed at being so worked up that holding the bottle was such an endeavor.

I was lucky that the others in the room were being so patient with me.

I could not tell how long it was before I was able to open my eyes but when I did, I saw everyone standing calmly around me. Clearly my reaction was not unfamiliar to the scientist. No one spoke or asked if I needed anything, which allowed me to focus on keeping my breathing as slow and steady as possible.

After a few more gulps of water, the scientist nodded to me.

"Ready for the last one?"

I hesitated before nodding, realizing it was a rhetorical question.

"Okay, you need to take off your shirt for this," he said. "Clark, stand over there and turn your back." The scientist nodded to a different area of the room. Clark gave my hand a comforting squeeze before he stepped away and turned his back.

Though I was uncomfortable, I pulled my shirt over my head and let it sit in my lap, feeling exposed and embarrassed clad only in my bra, and even though I did not want Clark to see me half-undressed, I wished I had his hand for support.

The scientist felt along my right shoulder blade, pressing a little harder at one spot, lower on my back than I expected the tracer would be.

"This is where the chip will go." He reached across me to Mark, grabbing his wrist and pulling his hand to rest on my left shoulder, his forearm pressing into my collarbones and giving me something to lean into. "Hold her steady."

Mark's other hand rested just above the scientist's hands, and even though I was dizzy sitting upright, I felt that I had regained my bearings a little as I leaned into Mark's steady hold.

"Okay, you're going to feel a pinch..." the scientist repeated. I lifted both hands to Mark's arm and held onto the fabric of his jacket tightly, my head resting against his bicep. I felt the pinch and gripped tighter onto Mark's arm, cringing. Then, the needle was gone and the scientist moved away. I felt Mark try to move, but I held onto him, refusing to let my support go, knowing I would collapse face first to the concrete floor if he stepped away. I felt his hesitation but then his hands resumed their positions.

I remained with my eyes closed and my head against his bicep, waiting for the ordeal to be over, counting my breathing and praying that time would pass faster.

The scientist asked me if I could feel anything, and when I shook my head, he slipped my bra strap off my shoulder before telling Mark to hold me steady once again, applying pressure to the numbed part of my back.

My final tracer was placed and the bandage was secured over the wound, though it was still several moments before I could release Mark's arm to replace my shirt.

"Okay," the scientist said once I was redressed. "Clark, you can come back now. As for the wounds they should heal in a few days. Try not to scratch them. You can take the bandage off tomorrow morning. Don't shower tonight and just be careful of the bandage around your hand for the rest of the day. If you can wrap it in a regular bandage to keep the wound covered, it should heal faster."

"...thank you..." I choked.

"Go rest," he said. "Take the water also." He placed a hand on my shoulder. "If you have any problems with them, like if they start to hurt or fester, let me know. My name is Randy."

"Thank you..." I said, a little stronger.

I tried to walk out of the lab, but my wobbling legs only supported me with Clark's assistance, and the walk back to our conference room felt incredibly long with my knees knocking together. I continued to apologize to Clark for holding onto him so tightly, though he continued to reassure me that it was no trouble. I was embarrassed at my reaction to the ordeal, but also thankful that Clark was being so supportive despite the dramatics.

Once back in the conference room, I curled up in one of the chairs and felt the exhaustion take hold of me. I wanted to talk to Clark, but stress pulled me into unconsciousness and I was asleep in no time. I was woken by the gentle hand of Mark on my left shoulder. When he pointed to his watch, I realized it was time to go home.

Clark had also fallen asleep with his head on the table, cringing as he rolled his neck when Mark woke him. My body was also sore, but I desperately wanted to curl up again and go to sleep.

I was still half-asleep as we retrieved our phones and drove to my house. I felt a dull pain on all three areas where the tracer chips had been placed, but it was not unbearable and did not help me fight the weight of my eyelids.

What was unbearable was explaining the bandaged hand to Mykail and my mother and father over dinner. While my father was worried, my mother continued to insist that it was a smart idea, insisting that Dana knew what he was doing and was only trying to keep me safe. Mykail just stared at me, silent and sympathetic.

When the time was right and I knew my parents had gone to bed, I crept to Mykail's door, opening it skillfully to avoid the loud noise of the bolt. Mykail immediately pulled me into a hug.

"I'm so sorry."

"Don't be sorry," I assured, hugging him back. "I'm alright."

"Are you sure?" he asked, glancing at my hand, pulling it close and studying it. "You said you have a fear of needles…"

"Yeah…" I said, embarrassed, particularly thinking back on my behavior around the three who had been in the same room when I got the tracers. "It's okay. I'm alright."

He took my bandaged hand in both of his, squeezing gently, relaxing his grip when I flinched a little.

"Sorry, did that hurt?"

"I promise, I'm alright," I said again.

"You said you have one here, one on your foot, and one on your back?" he asked. "Where on your back?"

I hesitated, wondering if I was ready to turn my back to Mykail and take off my shirt to show him the bandage. The muscles in my abdomen clenched, but it was not with anxiety—at least not the same kind of anxiety. With a shy smile and my face burning hot, I turned around and pulled my shirt over my head.

I held tight to the fabric of my baggy pajama top and felt his eyes on the bandage on my back, barely visible above my worn-out sports bra. I waited for him to say something, but he was silent and still. My heart was pounding in my chest, and I could feel my breathing picking up pace again.

His hand touched my shoulder blade, gentle, and he leaned close, his lips finding the top of my shoulder and planting a tender kiss to the skin. My eyes fluttered shut involuntarily and I swayed. His other hand wrapped around my belly to support me, seeing my shaking.

He pressed a few more kisses over my shoulder before I turned my head toward his, inviting him to kiss me fully. His breath fanned over my lips and I closed the space between us, turning and wrapping my arms around his neck as I kissed him full-force, pressing my chest to his and abandoning the baggy t-shirt to the floor.

His arms circled my waist and lifted me, walking me to his bed and using his wings for support as he lowered us both to the mattress. Within the protective cocoon of his wings, there was nothing other than the two of us. I felt his hands drift over my sides and arms as we kissed, chasing away the tension still lingering in my muscles.

With his weight on his wings, both his hands were free to touch me. It was almost too much for my inexperience to feel one hand on my waist, another on my neck, and his lips and tongue against mine all in the same moment.

Like before, Mykail's hips circled down to mine, causing a jolt to rocket through me and Mykail to swallow the noise I made in a deep kiss. I groaned again and my hips moved. I had never felt such intensity, and I was starting to crave further contact, chasing the pleasure my instincts already knew was waiting for me. I didn't care if my desire was the result of teenage hormones. I wanted him.

He broke away from my lips and moved to my neck, kissing and nipping at the skin in a way that made me bite my lip to keep me from making more noise. I didn't know what to do, so I dug my nails into his back and focused on the feeling of his lips moving from my neck to my collarbone and then down my sternum, pressing a kiss to the fabric of the bra as one of his hands slid up my ribcage to palm my breast. I arched my back, pushing into his hand, biting my lip so hard it almost bled.

It was the most intimate we had been. He did not remove my bra and he did not make any further moves toward sex, which was good because even though my body was craving it, I knew we were not ready, particularly with the circumstances of our relationship.

Eventually, my jaw sore from kissing, Mykail rolled to the side, his wings still surrounding us.

"I'm sorry…" he whispered, just as breathless. "I did not mean to move that fast." His fingertips played over my cheek as I tried to gain my bearings and calm the fire in my body. "If I do anything that you don't want me to, I want you to say something. I promise, we won't go any further than you're comfortable with."

"If that ever happens, I'll let you know."

He kissed me gently once on the lips before kissing my cheeks, nose, and even my ears, making me giggle. When he backed away, a beautiful smile adorned his features.

"Hey, Mykail? The experiments have a way to speak through gestures, right? The sign language?"

"Yes."

"What does this mean?" I pinched my earlobe, mimicking Mark's earlier actions.

"What?"

I repeated the action and he laughed, grabbing my wrist.

"No, that action asks the question 'what?'" he explained.

"Oh…" I said, confused. Thinking back on the conversation Mark and I had struggled through, it didn't make sense for him to ask such a question when he was the one explaining things to me.

"You seem confused," Mykail chuckled.

"It's nothing."

"Which ear was it?"

I thought about it, pointing to my left ear.

"That's different, then. That means 'I'm sorry.'"

Chapter Thirty

The biggest dilemma I faced Tuesday morning was not the quiz in biology class or the fact that I had not read the assigned chapters of *An Angel Without Wings*—it was that Mykail had left a hickey on my right collar bone and I was failing miserably at trying to cover it with makeup.

I resorted to finding a shirt to cover it, pulling a turtleneck from the bottom of my dresser drawer. I hated turtlenecks, but it was my only option that morning—at least the colder weather gave me an excuse to wear it.

The turtleneck dilemma seemed pointless compared to the problem presented to me at lunch.

I was sitting with Becca, Taylor, and Jill, trying not to think about my first after-school day at the Commission, when Felicity and seven other Commish Kids, including Dean and Ryan, approached us. I hoped they would pass by, but I knew from their purposeful stride that they were on a mission to talk to me.

Becca had fallen silent when she saw my staring and her silence caught the others' attention.

"Lily," Felicity said sharply as she approached, "we need to talk."

"About what?"

"Miranda," Dean growled. My heart began pounding. I saw Becca turn to me while the other two looked on, confused and put off by the abrupt approach.

I stood, glancing apologetically at my friends.

"Sorry, I'll be back."

I followed the group of Commish Kids though every part of me was wary of the impending discussion. A part of my brain reminded me that I could use the situation to see if any Commish Kids were ready to take down Dana after the ordeal with Miranda and Julie, but I did not want to reveal too much about my own plans and risk getting exposed to Dana.

I was led to the back of the school, stepping out of one of the smaller side doors onto the grassy hill leading down to the football field. When I walked through the door, the other Commish Kids rounded on me. I retreated a step, bumping into Ryan as he closed the door, frightened by the angry faces surrounding me.

"Who the hell called the Commission on Miranda?" Samantha, a girl I had only met once, asked around her clenched teeth.

"I don't know."

"Is there any truth behind the accusations?" Matt pressed.

"Of course not, you moron!" Dean snapped, shoving the boy in the shoulder.

"I'm just asking…"

"Why are you asking *me*?"

"You're Mr. Christenson's new favorite, right?" Felicity sneered. "You're even going there after school like Clark, now."

"…how do you know about that?" I asked suspiciously. They groaned and rolled their eyes, which did nothing more than aggravate me.

"Everyone knows. Everyone can see how fascinated he is by you and your family," Ryan snorted.

"So, you're going to get Miranda and Julie out of there," Dean demanded.

"*What*?" I gasped, my eyes shooting wide. "What makes you think I can get her out?" My heart raced as terror ran through my whole body, worried that the others knew of our premature plans to infiltrate the Commission and had already tried to take matters into their own hands.

"You're Dana's new little slut, right?" Dean snarled. "Find a way to convince him. Beg, cry, fucking suck his cock, it doesn't matter. Just find a way and get them out."

"Fuck you!" I barked. "You really think that I can convince Dana to do *anything*? If you want her out, *you* convince him!"

"You don't care about Miranda or Julie?"

"I'm saying that you should do something about it rather than use me as a shield like a fucking coward!"

"Dana is more willing to listen to you than any of us," Kelly said. "You have a better chance."

"I can't get her out. Dana will be set on keeping her, particularly because everyone is so insistent that she should be released. If he didn't listen to anyone at the meeting, what makes you think I will have better luck?"

"Because you're the new favorite," Ryan repeated simply, as if a child would understand the concept. "We would ask Clark, but he's been Dana's favorite for years now, and since Dana is now interested in you, seems like he's not as into Clark anymore. You can get his attention."

"Dana won't let her go," I said strongly.

"What will happen to them?" Kayla whispered, her voice weak. Everyone fell silent, the words sitting heavy in the air, dulling the anger in the group and replacing the feeling with fear.

"If I had to take a guess...she'll be tested on and turned into a gift experiment. I mean, think about it. All the experiments we have were taken as criminals just like her, and when we see her again being given to a family...it'll be like Dana throwing it in our face that he owns us."

Make them approach it. Don't implicate yourself... I told myself.

"The fuck Dana *owns* us," Ryan grumbled.

"He certainly seems to think so with the way he runs our lives."

"Then we're just going to have to remind him that he can't do whatever he wants just because he's the head of the fucking Commission of the People," Dean snapped. "If we have to go all the way to Leader Simon, we will. We can show Dana that he can't push people around like that."

"Damn right. He's losing his damn mind," Ryan agreed with a strong nod. "Reinstating Sweeps? Believing false accusations against teens? It's the Post-Revolution Cleanse all over again. There's no reason for it!"

"You're saying he doesn't have a reason to believe accusations against teens, but now you're talking about overthrowing him, which means his paranoia is justified. He'll be ready for rebellions," Matt groaned, exasperated. "He's Dana fucking Christenson! He's got the entire military of America at his disposal and night-raid Sweeps teams that will crush any revolution brewing. You'll be taken in like Miranda and Julie if you try anything."

"Then we can work from the inside!" Dean growled. He approached Matt, angrily grabbing his blazer collar with both hands and pulling him close. "You know Miranda never smuggled anything over the border, and you know for a fact that six-year-old Julie didn't *help* her, so Dana brought in both of them under false allegations and made an example of them in order to scare us into line. Those are the fear tactics that the Washington System used before the revolution."

"No, those are the fear tactics the Commission of the People use today," Matt retaliated. "Christ, Dana is Leader Simon's attack dog, and you want to stick your hand in his cage and piss him off?"

"If I have to, I will put him down like a dog," Dean sneered. "The Commission of the People might need a new leader anyway. Dana's still acting like we're in the revolution. The population is clean. We don't need the Commission anymore."

"And how exactly do you plan to do anything about that?" Matt challenged. "You're forgetting the entire American military he has at his disposal."

"My uncle is the Chair of Warfare. If word doesn't actually get to the military, no one will act on it."

I watched, listening carefully. The aspect of military retaliation had been keeping me up at night. I had no idea how we were going to stand up against a man who could call the nation's armed forces to his aid when needed. Hearing that Dean's uncle was the Chair of Warfare gave me a glimmer of hope that a solution had presented itself. We didn't have to defeat the military, we just had to keep the officers uninformed until we had the people's attention and support.

"This is treason," Matt whispered. "I want Miranda and Julie out too, but going up against Dana? The Commission? It's like tackling the government all over again, and all it will do is lead to bloodshed, and probably an even worse system, regardless of whether you fail or succeed."

"You've been reading *An Angel Without Wings*. Thomas Ankell didn't know if he was going to live or die, or succeed, or fail, but he could not stand what was happening around him, and he would have rather died than sit back and pretend to *not* see what was going on. I'm going to do the same," Dean declared. He looked around the group of teenagers. "I refuse to let Dana get away with this. I don't care if he takes me, too. I'll fight him until he relinquishes his title as head of the Commission of the People, or until I'm dead."

Everyone was quiet, sharing worried glances, not sure how to respond.

Dean looked exasperated.

"Aren't you *pissed*?!" he bellowed. "Someone accused Miranda falsely and she was taken into the Commission. Who's to say that the same won't happen to you? The Commission is stepping out of its bounds! Dana's stepping out of his bounds and disregarding the rules he's supposed to enforce! Are you really going to stand by and let him do that?!"

"No," was the general, albeit hesitant, consensus.

"Fine. Saturday at the meeting we're speaking up, in front of our parents, Dana, *everyone*. We still have our right of speech. We are within our rights to voice discontent."

I was pleased that I had not put myself in the position of leader of the angry group. It was safer to let the others take action first, until I knew how to use my close proximity to Dana to my advantage.

The others were finally thinking of rebelling, but like a coward, I had not stated anything about the revolution I had been planning with Mykail and Clark.

I didn't want to put myself in direct danger just yet.

* *** *

Mark was waiting by the car after school. Since I was earlier than Clark, I felt a little awkward standing in silence with the former experiment.

"Good afternoon, Mark," I said as I approached. He bowed his head. "How are you?" I asked on reflex.

He lifted his head, but did not move otherwise until he cocked his head to the left, confused.

"How are you?" I repeated, enunciating all syllables. I was sure he had been asked before, since it was a common courtesy question.

Mark's mouth opened and he nodded in realization before becoming flustered about how to respond. He lifted his hand and gave me a hesitant thumbs up with a smile. The action was so awkward that, before I could help it, I laughed. His smile widened and he dropped his hand, his shoulders shaking as he chuckled silently, embarrassed.

"What's so funny?" Clark asked as he approached.

"Nothing really," I said. "I asked him how he was doing and he gave me a thumbs up. It was kind of adorable."

"Like I said, he's actually a really good guy," Clark agreed. He nodded to my hand. "How are your battle wounds?" I glanced at my bandages.

"Okay. They itch but they don't hurt."

"That's good. Are you ready to go?" he asked, looking between me and Mark.

Mark opened the door to the backseat.

He drove us to the Commission of the People and we checked in before going to the basement and finding a conference room to complete our homework. I was already less nervous than the previous day, and settled into the conference room without thinking too much about what I was doing—which was easiest to do having not seen Dana that day.

"How was school?" Clark asked casually as he pulled out his laptop.

I hesitated in pulling out my e-reader. I wanted to tell him about the confrontation at lunch, but I knew I could not discuss the treasonous feeling within the Commish Kids while lingering in the belly of the beast.

"Oh, it was really tough, particularly Lit class," I said. "We had a quiz on *An Angel Without Wings,* and I am just not seeing what Mr. Dermott is talking about. Maybe you can help me?"

The confusion was clear on his face, but I knew he had heard the hidden meaning in the request.

"Sure," he said, standing so he could occupy the seat next to me. I saw his eyes flick to Mark as he moved. The experiment was standing by the door to the conference room, his back to us. "What do you need help with?"

I faltered, still unsure how to hold the conversation discreetly. I drummed my fingers along my e-reader when an idea presented itself. I unclicked the note-taking pen from my e-reader and clicked the screen to life.

"I don't really know," I mused, rapidly scanning the page of a different book I was reading for something that would tell Clark about what had happened at lunch. "I mean, we're here," I underlined a partial sentence line in red.

"People who want to help..."

"Oh...okay..." He did not lift his head, but his tone conveyed the question he was unable to ask aloud.

"I just can't seem to grasp the context. You know, how the symbolism applies to real life and all."

The gears clicked.

"Okay." He grabbed his laptop and opened a new document. "Here are my notes," he said, typing a simple question.

"Who?"

"But Dean said that this section applied specifically to modern times as well as pre-revolution American history."

"Dean?" Clark repeated. "He's not the best student. Maybe he misheard."

"Maybe."

"Have you read the newest assigned chapter?"

"No."

"Tell you what," he said, his voice shaking as he tried to keep up the façade, well aware of the cameras that could be listening to our every word, "we'll read the chapter and make different notes on it, then compare." He grabbed his own electronic reader from his backpack and resumed his seat next to me, shifting as he clicked the screen to life and pulled up a different book.

I caught on quickly. I shifted in my seat so I could glance at his screen without moving my head, being sure he could do the same for mine.

Our silent conversation began.

He wants to help? Clark underlined the words in the order he wanted to say them as he found them on the page. I did the same.

He's very angry.

About the last meeting?

Yes.

He would be a strong ally, Clark admitted. *He knows powerful people. What did you tell him?*

Nothing, I assured. *I let him talk to the others.*

Others?

There is a group.

Who?

Annoyed that Clark had asked me for specific names, I wrote them in the margin.

Felicity. Samantha. Ryan. Kayla. Kelly. Dean. Karmen. Trevor.

What did they say?

They were angry. They didn't want to be controlled.

What do you want to do?

Maybe you can talk to them. You know them better.

I glanced up at the sight of movement in the corner of my eye and I let out a startled yelp, dropping my e-reader to my lap, the note-taking pen falling to the floor. Dana was crouched outside the conference room, only his nose and eyes visible through the window as he watched us.

Clark also jumped when he saw the unnaturally bright eyes studying us. Mark was still at his post by the door, and seemed not to notice the leader of the Commission lurking like a child outside the conference room.

For several moments, no one moved.

When the initial shock passed I became confused.

"Is he going to come in here?"

"Who knows?" Clark grumbled.

"What do we do?"

"Ignore him. He'll get bored and either leave or come in."

Even though Clark said to ignore Dana, both of us were unable to tear our eyes away from the leader of the Commission of the People. When I was finally uncomfortable enough, I glanced between Dana and Clark a few times before turning back to my e-reader, trying to ignore the needles prickling over my skin at Dana's continued scrutiny.

I tried to quickly—but nonchalantly—delete the notes I had made in the margins, hoping the actions did not look suspicious to the sharp eyes of Dana Christenson.

Clark had also returned his attention to the book, clearing his notes and underlines as he moved his gaze back and forth, though I was certain he was not actively reading, waiting to see if Dana would come in or leave.

I dared not turn to confirm that Dana was still peering through the window.

The door did finally open and I looked up. Dana stepped inside, closing the door behind him.

"Hey, kids," he greeted with a smile. "How was school today?"

Neither of us could respond, so we glanced at one another before staring blankly at Dana. He stepped casually to the other side of the table and placed his forearms over the back of one of the chairs, leaning toward us with a smile.

"Why do you two seem so nervous? I'm not interrupting anything, am I?" He looked suggestively over the two of us but there was a dangerous edge in his voice.

"What would you be interrupting?" Clark took the task of answering out of my hands.

"Oh, I don't know." Dana sighed, pulling the chair back and sitting gracefully, turning the chair so he could put his shiny shoes on the glossy table's surface. "You can never trust what goes through the mind of a young man when he's left alone with a young woman, especially a particularly beautiful young woman like Little Lily."

Dana studied his nails, disinterested.

"For instance, it might start with a simple observation of how pretty her eyes are, or her lips, and before he can help it, that young man is thinking of how her features would look during a slew of lewd and perverted acts." He pointed at Clark with a devilish smile. "See? Like just now."

"I was not thinking of anything like that!" Clark defended sharply.

"Yes, you were."

"Dana, we're not alone," I snapped, pointing to Mark. He glanced in the direction of the experiment and shrugged.

"He's a man like any other, Little Lily," he told me. "Even though I fix all the experiments, they still have instinctive urges."

I rolled my eyes, which made him chuckle.

"You don't approve."

"I don't approve of most of the things you do."

"Why?"

"Why *would* I approve?" I challenged.

"Because I am making the world safer," Dana answered. "I am giving those people who live out there," he motioned his hand in the air to symbolize the American people, "a chance to live that old American Dream people used to rave about before the government began selling the bastardized version."

"By bringing in some of the people who are trying to achieve that same dream and mutilating them?" I snarled. "What makes their dreams any less important?"

"Little Lily, you are so young and idealistic," Dana said, shaking his head. "Everyone's dream is important to them. And that's the only person they care about when achieving their dreams."

"That's not true."

"No?"

"Friends and family care."

"Oh, they do?" Dana challenged, taking his feet off the table and leaning on his arms, his bright eyes dancing as they locked with my gaze. "So your parents picking you up and moving you here was part of your dream? They were just trying to support you?"

"It wasn't my dream, it was my father's dream, and because I love him I was willing to make that sacrifice," I explained.

"Then you had to sacrifice your dream for your father's because you love him? Because half of him is inside you? Because he raised and protected you?"

"Yes."

"But you don't think he protected you well enough, do you?" Dana smirked. "Or you wouldn't be here right now, is that correct?"

I hesitated. It was no secret to Dana that I did not want to be in the Commission of the People, or anywhere near its leader. And since I was still a minor, it was legally my parents' job to protect me, rather than walk me into the arms of a predator like Dana Christenson.

"I feel like no one could stop you if you want something, Dana," I said. "And I know you wanted my family here."

"You flatter me," Dana said, leaning back in his seat once again. "But I have a question for you, Little Lily. When you sacrificed for your father's dream of coming to Central, doesn't that mean that you feel your own dream is substandard in comparison to your father's? That you believed his ambitions were more important because of some abstract bond of familial obligation?"

Again, I faltered. When he saw I was struggling, he continued.

"Why did he not care about *your* dream?"

"It wasn't like that..."

"Then explain how it was."

I stuttered, opening and closing my mouth uselessly, my tongue tripping over my teeth.

"You can't even answer."

"It's not as though he completely disregarded what I wanted," I defended. "He was elected."

"So, the people are using him as a means to an end for their own dreams, then," Dana declared. "Electing someone who will give them what they ask for, something that will make the struggle of life a little easier. Are their dreams more important than yours?"

"How should I know? Maybe," I admitted, getting angry with the debate I was obviously losing. Dana snapped his fingers and pointed at me with a smile.

"There you go," he said. "You now realize that everyone's dreams are not equal, even if it is of great or equal importance to each individual."

"It's not my place to take anything from anyone," I said, my voice raising. "If our dreams are all equal, then I have to work just as hard for it. I can't cheat and steal from other people just for my own gain."

"But people have no problem doing that anyway," Dana pointed out. "That's all the government used to do. Give, give…give everyone their rewards without the work, and what happened? America became a land with a lazy, entitled population that screwed the other half of the population who would rather be given what others must work for."

"What if they *are* willing to work?"

"If they were, I would have no need to take them in," Dana said simply, his eyes wandering around the room—I could see he was getting bored.

"So people who come from other countries don't even have the option to work hard? They are denied the dream that used to make America the best country in the world?"

"They have their own countries," Dana groaned. He glanced at me sideways. "The world is a much smaller place than it used to be. Why do you think Gregory Altereye and his men are trying to find other planets to live on? We need to expand. But, until that point, people must work within their own country. It's no longer the time where people can lead a country one direction, fuck it up, and then go to another one because it's too difficult to fix their own. America did it with the Second Revolution. It's messy, and it's bloody, but it needs to be done for a country and its people to function properly."

"So, you're saying that the Central System is better? Taking people under cover of darkness? Mutilating them? Turning them into monsters? Killing them when they don't turn out as expected?"

"Look around next time you're outside," Dana said. "Look at the poverty line, and how low the crime rate is. Look at the rate of people unemployed, homeless, starving…we are leading the world with the happiest, healthiest population. We have not seen war since the Second Revolution. Overall, I would say this system is *much* better."

"So, the fact that the population doesn't know what happens to the people the Commission captures is not a factor?"

"Oh, Little Lily, they know," Dana chuckled brokenly. "Maybe not the specifics, but it is not difficult to figure out. Why don't they say anything? They don't *want* to know. It's too much on their conscience. They turn a blind eye because it's a dark spot on their otherwise-perfect world, and that moral conflict interferes with achieving their own dreams."

"I think the people of America would like to know that the subjects of the Commission are being turned into weapons. If we're not at war, why create human weapons?"

"Preparedness." Dana shrugged the question off. "And curiosity," he added with a malicious grin.

"Then that's *your* dream? Make an ultimate weapon out of humans? And that's important enough that you can justify killing all these people?"

Dana smiled wider.

"There is nothing to justify," he said coldly. "But you are starting to understand."

"Then what you're saying is that *you* should be taken into the Commission? You said that no one was an exception to the rules, so that would also include you, right?" I could feel pride bubbling in my chest.

"I'm also working toward my dreams, yes." Dana leaned forward once more. "I'm curious, Little Lily, what keeps you from taking what you want? What stops you from standing up for yourself? Telling your parents that you refuse to move here?"

"They're my parents…"

"No, forget societal influences and obligations. What stops you? You can ignore society, so why don't you?"

"Because it would hurt the people I care about and who care about me."

"Oh, those people," Dana groaned. "They don't see you as anything other than an obligation and a means to an end."

"That's not true," I replied. "If I took everything I wanted, I might have it, but then I wouldn't have anyone, and it wouldn't be worth it in the end. As I got older I realized that there has to be a compromise."

Dana smiled and pointed at me again.

"Exactly. That is why the Commission exists. People would take what they wanted without regard for the people around them, causing harm to plenty of good citizens. The Commission took them and now everyone can work collectively to the benefit of the good citizens rather than trying to figure out what to do with the criminals and people who cause others pain. *We* handle the societal compromise so the populace doesn't have to." Dana drummed his fingers along the arm of the chair. "You can't make an argument against the existence of the Commission. You said yourself that those people hurt others because they take what they want without regard."

"That doesn't answer the question about you, though," I growled. "You take what you want from people—from *society*—without regard."

"No," Dana said, shaking his head, "people give me what I want. I don't take it. I just make people want to give it to me."

"Then...doesn't that make you much worse?"

He shrugged. "No one has complained so far."

His phone buzzed and he groaned in annoyance, fetching his phone from his pocket. He stared at the screen for a moment before collapsing in the chair, his head rolling back and his hands falling uselessly to his lap.

"Emergency meeting, kids," he sighed, though he made no effort to move. "I must leave."

"What happened?" Clark asked, speaking for the first time since the debate started.

"Leader Simon..." Dana grumbled, getting out of his chair with the lack of enthusiasm a child had when throwing a tantrum. "We'll talk tomorrow...maybe."

He left. It was so abrupt and bizarre that I stayed still while my brain continued to spin, needing some time to collect myself before I turned to Clark and smacked his arm.

"Ow! What the—"

"Why did you just sit there through that whole thing?!"

"I'm sorry, I didn't know what to say," he mumbled. "I just...kinda freeze up when he's around and he's in that playful mood."

I sighed and closed my eyes, slumping back in my seat, exhausted.

* *** *

Clark and I were supposed to be working on homework, but after Dana left, we spent our time underlining words in our books to communicate. I told Clark more about Dean and how angry the other Commish Kids were during the gathering at lunch. He told me that he would have to keep a close eye on Dana's calendar and plan a time around his meetings to break into the records room and look up the experiments that had been denoted on our mysterious notes.

There was a level of excitement that I could not deny at our plans slowly starting to take shape. Even though being at the Commission after school was not something I was enjoying, there was a level of exhilaration at plotting right under Dana's nose.

I went home turning over too many thoughts in my head.

When I walked in the front door, my mother and father were waiting for me at the dining table. I stopped in my tracks when I looked over their stern expressions, instinctive fear seeping into me.

"What's wrong?"

"We got a message from your school today," my mother started.

"You've failed two consecutive tests," my father added. I sighed, walking to the table and sitting, realizing I was in for an immediate lecture. "Do you want to tell us what's going on?"

"Dad," I started, "I'm trying really hard to adjust to all this...I mean...the Commission and everything..."

"I know it's hard, honey, but you are part of the Commission of the People and you need to be conscious of the image the Commission has as a whole, which means you need to be the best you can be."

"What do my grades have to do with the image of the Commission?" I snapped.

"Honey, calm down," my mother said.

"No, don't tell me to calm down!"

"Lily Grace Sandover, sit yourself down and do not talk back to me!" my mother ordered, pointing at the chair that I had vacated in preparation of storming to my room.

"No, *Mother*!" It was the first time in my life I had rebelled so openly. "How can you expect me to be fine when I know that the Commission of the People mutilates people and turns them into weapons?! *I'm* the one that has to be there every day and see these people! I would think my own parents would understand that that is difficult for me!"

"We've been over this, Lily," my mother said. "They are *criminals*. It's for the greater good that the Commission takes them off the streets."

"Dad, how can you be okay with this?" I gasped, turning to him. "The Commission took in your own brother, for God's sake!"

My father hesitated before sighing. I felt my heart fall and my jaw drop at the way his shoulders slumped.

"You don't care?" I hissed. "Aren't you...are you even *angry*?"

"Lily," he started tenderly, "you're young...and when I was your age, I was angry. I was angry at my father for calling in my brother, but I was also angry at my brother. Now, I know that you think what the

Commission does is wrong, but as I've gotten older...I've come to realize that people like my brother are dangerous. You can't fight against something as powerful as the good of the nation's people, and that's what the Commission seeks to protect."

"I can't believe I'm hearing this!"

"Lily, you're only seventeen. How do you expect to know everything about the world and how it should be?" my mother said. I hated when she used the age card.

"Sweetheart," my father started, trying to divert my attention, "I know that you care, and I know that you're upset about what you see in the Commission. But something that you'll come to realize is that not everyone is equal. There are some people that are dangerous to the delicate balance of society. I know it's a tough pill to swallow, but what Dana and the Commission does is the best thing for American society. It keeps things balanced and safe."

"But...all those people...people like Mykail..." The gathering tears stopped my words. How was I expected to just shut off my feelings about all those who had been taken from their families and had their lives destroyed?

"You're going to have to learn how to stop looking at them like that," my mother said. "They're not people anymore."

Her words left me dumbfounded.

"And you're going to have to get your grades up," she added. "No more failing tests. If you do, we will have to ask Dana if there is someone in the Commission who can tutor you through your classes until you get the grades you used to pull."

My blood ran cold at the thought. I couldn't have someone looming over my shoulder. It would make planning the revolution impossible. I went quiet and bowed my head, nodding.

"Okay..."

"Alright, dinner is in the oven. Go ahead and set your stuff down and wash up," my mother said, standing and going into the kitchen.

I was furious at my mother and father for being so accepting of the Commission, even after seeing all that happened there, even after seeing the way Dana treated Miranda and Julie in front of everyone, and seeing the way Eina screamed when he was on the table...They were still somehow able to accept the Commission of the People.

I stormed to my room, passing Mykail's door. I was sure he had heard everything but I was so angry that I could not face him. I threw my bag angrily against the side of my desk and shrugged off my coat, my tunneled vision turning red.

A few minutes later, after I had taken off my shoes and flopped on my bed, there was a knock at my door. My father poked his head into my room.

"I know you're pissed," he said. "But I just wanted to let you know that, regardless of the grades and everything else, I really appreciate how good you've been about the move and the Commission and everything." He stepped into my room, closing the door behind him. "You're mother...I think she's just trying to process everything, and I think that she says what she does because she wants to believe it herself."

I groaned and sat up.

"She never used to think like that."

"Oh, your mother's always been steadfast," my father laughed, sitting next to me on the bed. I huffed again, rage still fiery in my veins. He reached an arm around me, hugging me as I rested my head against his shoulder. He smelled the same way he always had—a hint of cinnamon and aftershave. It was comforting to realize that, even after everything, *that* had not changed.

"Your mother's been a little difficult lately," my father admitted. "We've had our disagreements about the Commission. It's hitting everyone hard."

"Then you don't agree with the Commission?" I asked, hopeful. He hesitated and then sighed heavily, causing my heart to fall.

"I agree that the Commission is essential in maintaining the balance of current American society," he said carefully. "What I don't agree with is Dana. There is something about him that...worries me."

"Only something? Not *everything*?"

My father laughed.

"Alright, I admit that Dana is not entirely right in the head. But...I also think that he might have been raised in that environment. He said that he worked with Bryant Morris, he must have only been a boy at that time. Imagine if you were raised with that horror around you all the time. I think that has the potential to screw anyone up."

"I agree with that..." I said slowly. "But Dana is in a really powerful position of the government, and he doesn't seem to be in a fit mental state to be making rulings on people's lives."

My father rubbed my shoulder, pulling me into a tighter hug. We sat in silence, not sure what to say, knowing that, at the moment, we were powerless.

"Are the kids still upset about Miranda and Julie?" he whispered.

"They're really upset."

"I don't blame them. If they needed to be taken in, that's the Commission's ruling, but Dana didn't need to make such an extreme example of them at the meeting. I guess the problems with the Commission children have been pretty bad." He turned to me and rested his head on mine. "Are those boys still giving you trouble?"

"No."

"Good," he said, kissing my forehead. "I'm sorry about your mother today. I'll talk to her. She should have been more understanding of how hard this has been on you." My father kissed my head again and hugged me tight before standing. "Alright, I'm getting Mykail for dinner. Come down whenever you're ready."

"Okay."

"I love you."

"I love you, too, Dad."

* *** *

My father did try to talk to my mother that night. Mykail and I both listened to them in the living room, but the discussion quickly turned into a heated argument where my mother accused my father of not supporting her in raising me as a proper Commission child. My father tried to remind her that they had always told me it was my choice if I wanted to go into politics, but now I was stuck and it was going to take time for me to adjust.

The fight got ugly, and by the time it was over and my mother stormed away, I was close to tears and Mykail had to hold onto me while I cried into his chest, replaying the horrible words my parents were spitting at one another.

Wednesday I walked around in a haze. I was tired and stressed about the fight between my parents. Becca asked me what was wrong, but I assured her that it had nothing to do with the Commission. I asked if she would be willing to come to my house on Sunday. I wasn't sure if I was allowed to invite people over, but I knew that my mother and father had a charity event for the whole day on Sunday, so they would be out and I would be able to talk openly with Becca.

I wasn't sure, either, if I was going to show Mykail to Becca or not—it was something I planned to discuss with Clark.

The day went by without incident. After school, I walked to the side parking lot and found Mark standing next to the car. He smiled and bowed his head when I approached. I smiled and bowed my head a little as well, hoping I was able to hide my bad mood from him.

I tried to smile when he straightened, but I saw his face fall. Since we were alone in the parking lot, I knew he had seen my drawn expression.

"I'm alright, I'm alright," I said quickly, giving him two thumbs up with a wobbly smile. He shook his head and carefully put his hands on top of mine, pushing them down.

He knew I was lying.

I allowed my hands to drop to my sides, not knowing what to say, averting my eyes to my shoes. I had no way to communicate with him and he had no way to communicate with me, but we both knew that the other was worried.

A thought clicked. I raised my head, pinching my left earlobe to tell Mark I was sorry. He hesitated and then rubbed his nose once before biting his lower lip.

I sighed. He was trying to tell me something, but Mykail had only taught me a few of the signs. I used another one I knew. I ran my hand through my hair and closed my eyes, tilting my head to the side tiredly. That meant I didn't understand. He nodded, reaching up and pinching his left ear.

"You don't need to be sorry, Mark," I said. "I'm alright."

He shook his head again. Reaching out, he pointed at my face with both pointer fingers and pushed them into my cheeks. I backed away at first, but when he moved his fingers to make me smile, the action made me break out laughing.

Mark chuckled silently.

When the laughing abated, we stood in silence, waiting for Clark. Mark was relatively relaxed, standing next to the car, but when he started to glance at his wrist watch more and more frequently, I started to notice just how long Clark was taking.

I pulled my phone from my pocket to check the time. I had a text message from Clark.

Hey. I will be a little late. Long story. Tell Mark that I am okay. He gets frantic when I'm not on time and he will come looking for me. Make sure he knows that I'm okay.

I turned to Mark quickly, who had turned his covered eyes toward the school, his fingers tapping nervously against his leg.

"Mark?" I jumped at how quickly he turned to look at me. "Clark is okay," I said slowly and clearly so he could understand. "He will be here soon."

Mark just stared at me through his sunglasses. I groaned in frustration.

"I really need to figure out the best way to communicate with you…" I repeated very clearly and slowly that Clark was okay and Mark nodded, his shoulders dropping as some of the tension left his frame.

We waited for twenty long minutes before Clark appeared. After fifteen minutes, Mark was pacing anxiously no matter how many times I tried to tell him that Clark was alright. I even tried to show him the text message, but realized that it was unlikely Mark could read English. I was also concerned about Clark's continued delay, not sure what to expect from the 'long story' he had to explain why he was late. I spent the last five minutes of our wait trying to calm Mark. I had to resort to grabbing his arm and telling him Clark was alright again and again, his pacing heightening my own anxiety.

When he did see Clark half-running across the parking lot, Mark darted to him.

"Mark, I'm alright," Clark said, lifting his hands and walking with Mark back to the car. "I promise. I'm sorry that took so long. I'm okay. I'm alright."

"Where were you?" I asked. "Mark was going to go postal any second."

"Sorry. Yeah, he gets a bit frantic," Clark said. "Saved me my teeth once, though, so I'm grateful he does worry."

"What do you mean?"

"I'm bullied a lot, and one time I was jumped by some guys after school. Mark came looking for me when I was late and he gave those guys some black eyes and kept the beating from getting worse." Mark opened the car door for us and Clark smiled as he climbed in the backseat behind me. "So it's really good that he gets worried. But, since he can't read English, it's really difficult for me to send him a text message to tell him I'm going to be late. Thankfully, you were there today."

"Then what kept you?" I pressed as Mark got into the driver's seat and started the car.

He turned in the seat to face me fully. "I need to tell you this before we get to the Commission. Mark, radio."

Mark turned on the radio.

"Up," Clark said, motioning his hand. Mark turned the volume up so that the songs on the radio were loud enough to drown out our voices. Clark motioned me closer and I leaned in so that his mouth was next to my ear, but he still had to talk loud to be heard over the music. "What I'm about to tell you cannot leave this car. We will talk as we did yesterday as soon as we get to the Commission. Mark, if you can understand or hear any of this, radio down."

I turned to see if Mark did anything, but he was focused on driving.

"Okay, good." Clark leaned back to my ear. "Dean and the others came up to me and told me that they were going to get Miranda out regardless of anything Dana said. They are going to try talking to Dana at the Saturday meeting, but they said that if that doesn't work, they are going to break her out."

My jaw dropped open in surprise, but I could feel myself smiling.

"We decided that we would see how things go on Saturday, and if Dana still refuses, we will meet to figure out how to take Dana down and break out Miranda and Julie," Clark continued. "We'll see how many people we can get behind us by the Halloween party at Archangel."

My grin grew. There were more of us. I could not believe our luck at how our plan was coming together on its own. Clark and I were able to gather information and supporters without outright stating that we were planning to tear down the Commission of the People.

I could not say anything for several long moments as I processed my excitement.

"I know," Clark agreed with a knowing smile.

The rest of the car ride was silent save for the loud radio. I was in shock. Even the blaring car radio could not cut through the racing thoughts of the innumerable possibilities that were opening to us with other Commish Kids to help with our rebellion.

Chapter Thirty-One

It was the first Friday where I was expected to get ready for Archangel at the Commission of the People. Clark told me to bring everything I would need to school and, therefore, to the Commission. Annoyed, I hauled another bag around containing my dress, shoes, and makeup, which I barely managed to stuff in my locker around my books.

But once at the Commission, the bag sat ominously on the table. I had not thought about how uncomfortable I would be undressing and redressing when Dana could appear at any moment. There were bathrooms throughout the Commission offices, but I still did not trust that Dana would not barge in while I was undressing.

When I had finished my homework, agonizing over the question most of the day, I finally turned to Clark.

"Hey...where's the best place to get dressed?" I asked. Clark hesitated, also glancing at the bag on the table.

"You can use my mother's office," he suggested. "She's got a private bathroom there."

"What about you?"

"I just need to change my shirt. I'll stay in here." He glanced at his phone. "We have about an hour, if you want to go ahead and get ready now."

I started to reach for the bag on the table when movement outside the conference room caught my attention. Sean knocked lightly on the door before stepping in.

"Hello Clark, Lily." He nodded to both of us. "I just wanted to let you know that Dana doesn't want you to ride the bus home tonight, Lily. Mark and Josh will drive you and stay outside the club in the car until you're ready to go home."

"Why?" Clark asked. "It's dangerous for them to be out like that. What if either one of them gets seen without their glasses? And why both of them?"

"It's a team day, and Dana is willing to chance them being seen," Sean answered. "I don't like the idea, either, but Dana insisted." He looked at me. "You've probably seen Josh before, but I don't think you've actually met him. He came from the same hidden society as Mark."

"Oh..." I said, not sure how else to respond.

"Don't worry, they're just there for protection, considering what happened a few weeks ago." Sean looked between us once more before giving a single nod. "Just let Mark know when you're ready to go."

As Sean left, Clark let out an exasperated groan and shook his head.

"I don't like this..." He turned to me. "Go ahead and use my mother's office. I'm going to try and find Dana. I don't want Mark and Josh sitting in a car where any of our classmates could see them. It's too dangerous to leave them exposed."

"Yeah, but do you really want to confront Dana?"

"No," Clark admitted. "But it's dangerous enough to have Mark driving me everywhere in the day. If two of them are looming outside Archangel, people will get curious. It's not worth the risk."

Clark stood and started toward the door, prompting me to grab my bag and also leave to go to Mrs. Markus' basement office. I wanted to get dressed as quickly as possible, taking advantage of Clark distracting the leader of the Commission of the People.

I curled my hair quickly and put on some makeup in the bathroom mirror before grabbing my dress. With the dress slung over the side of the sink, I shed my blazer and started to unbutton my school uniform skirt as I kicked off my shoes. When my second sneaker hit the wall, I shimmied out of my skirt. As I placed it on top of my blazer, I glanced in the mirror and saw a tall figure leaning against the doorframe, watching me undress.

I screamed and spun around, backing into the sink clad in my socks, panties, and button-up shirt, my hand pressed over my chest as I tried to contain my thundering heart.

"What the hell are you doing?!" I snapped at Dana, pulling my shirt down to hide as much of my underwear as possible.

"Watching you," he said simply. "And no need to be shy. You have nothing I haven't seen before." He stood straight, stalking toward me as I tried to plan my escape from the bathroom, fear consuming me. My body began to grow hot under his intense gaze and I found my breath becoming shorter and faster.

He stopped only a pace in front of me, staring down at me with a look of dominating confidence that forced a red-hot blush to my face. I felt my legs trembling, and though I wanted to say it was only from fear, I knew there were other reasons my body was shivering. His gaze was gentle, adoring, but his aura and frame were overpowering, promising that Dana would take whatever he wanted.

The combination of his powerful eyes and overwhelming charisma was more of a turn-on than I wanted to admit.

He tucked some hair behind my ear, his fingers tracing along the edge of my jaw.

"You look beautiful, Little Lily," he purred, his voice dripping with nectar. My eyelids fluttered and my breath shuddered out of me.

His fingers traced down my neck to rest over the exposed collarbone under my collar, pushing the fabric aside to trace over the ridge. His finger then pressed into the dip between my clavicles, slowly descending down my sternum until he could deftly unbutton the next button of my shirt. I shuddered, wanting to slap his hand away, though both my hand over my breasts and the one holding the bottom of the shirt refused my brain's command to move. I felt disgusted by myself, knowing that I should move to push him away, though the growing fire in my abdomen demanded more attention from him, finding sparks of pleasure following the wake of his fingers as they undid another button.

Dana's presence felt like a drug for my inner, animal instincts. His very being, the severity of his stare, the heat of his finger taking my wrist and pulling my hand away from my breasts all made me want to bow to carnal desires I had never explored before.

My hand went limp in his grip, coming away from my chest with ease, following his guide to rest against the front of the sink. His touch ghosted along the inside of my wrist, trailing over the loose fabric of my shirt as it ran up my arm, over my shoulder and down the middle of my chest again, returning to the task of unbuttoning my shirt until he reached my other hand, prying the last of the fabric from my grip.

With both my hands clasping the front of the sink as though it was the only port in a storm, I felt my skin grow hot, shivering as both his hands stole inside the shirt, skirting up my sides in a tantalizing dance until they passed over my bra, to my shoulders, and hooked in the shirt, removing it in an agonizing pace as he closed the space between us and dropped his head until his lips were hovering over my bare shoulder.

My eyes slid shut, drawing in a sharp breath in anticipation of his kiss. Internally, I was fighting a battle, screaming at myself to push him away, to not give in to his touch, to his warmth, to his power that begged to be worshiped. I needed to stay strong. I needed to never surrender to his seductive powers.

Every sensation of my body was amplified around him, though. I could feel the brushing of his unbuttoned suit jacket as he leaned closer. I could smell the clinging cologne as though I had doused myself in the scent. I could hear his gentle inhale and exhale. And as his fingers moved the fabric down my arms until it pooled around my wrists, I was certain I could even count the number of threads drifting over my skin.

He did not kiss my shoulder, instead tilting his head so his nose barely touched the top of my shoulder, dragging closer to my neck, up to my ear, and finally pressing into my hair as his cheek rested against my temple.

As he drew in a deep breath, his fingers tightened around both my wrists. He stepped even closer, one of his legs slipping between mine as his thigh pressed into my pelvis. I gasped, my hips pressing forward before I could stop the action.

The bolt of pleasure that rocketed along my nerves terrified me. I knew what kind of man Dana was. I knew how dangerous he was. And I knew that he would do whatever he wanted to me no matter how much I fought. To feel pleasure from his touch was horrifying and to feel my hips moving to meet his touch felt like a betrayal of the worst kind.

He chuckled. "Are you afraid, Little Lily?"

I closed my eyes tight, nodding against his shoulder.

"Are you afraid of me? Or how I make you feel?"

There was no way I could form the sentences to explain all the ways I was afraid in that moment. I was terrified that his charismatic power would draw out my secrets about Mykail and our rebellion. I was petrified that Dana would rape me in that bathroom. I was scared that my hips were gently pressing and releasing against Dana's thigh, seeking an instinctive pleasure I hated myself for craving. I was mortified that the danger of that moment was exciting me so intensely.

"You already know..." I mumbled.

His lips dropped to my ear. "I want to hear you admit it."

I let out a shuddered breath, shaking my head.

"I won't."

"Pity," he whispered. "It's far more pleasurable when you surrender to the feelings. I want you to admit how you really feel around me. I want you to give me control over your fear."

"I won't give in to you like everyone else..." Even I knew it was a pathetic statement with my voice trembling so severely.

"I can feel how your body gets hot when I touch you. I can feel your hips moving against me. You're already starting to seek the pleasure you know I can give you. All you need to do is surrender to me. Believe me, in the end that will be safer for everyone, including you."

"I don't care," I said, moving my head away from him as I felt his lips move to kiss my temple. "I won't give in to you."

I felt Dana smile even wider.

"Do not think I am easily fooled, Little Lily," he said. "I am sure you and Mykail have been sharing glances at the very least."

346

I turned to look at him quickly, yanking my wrists away from him, intending to pull my shirt back on, but his hands took the fabric, causing it to come away completely when I slipped from his grip and began slowly backing out of the bathroom clad only in my bra, panties, and socks.

"Did you think I would not notice?" Dana said, following me, dropping the shirt to the bathroom floor as he stalked after me. "I am pleased to see that your body appears unexplored. But perhaps I should perform a more thorough examination, just to be sure."

"Don't you dare touch me," I snapped, fear bolting through my limbs again when I felt my hips collide with Mrs. Markus' desk.

"Little Lily," he tutted, shaking his head as his hands went to either side of my hips on the desk, pinning me, "he's not even human."

"And what? You are?" I challenged.

He smiled wickedly. "Touché."

I fumbled with my response, not expecting his answer. One of his eyebrows arched high, smirking as he watched me try to process what he had said.

"You're...not human?"

"There's not much human left in here."

"What are you then?" I asked. "Are you one of the Machines of Neutralization?"

He laughed richly. "Of course not."

"Are you saying you're one of the other experiments?"

"And if I were?"

For some reason, even though the thought had occurred to me before, I was not prepared to believe that it was actually possible for Dana to be a former experiment of the Commission of the People. My mouth was open, trying to think of something to say in response, but no words could be found. He smirked again.

"What? You can't put the pieces together?" he taunted.

"You said you worked under Bryant Morris."

"I did," he said. "There might have been some things that happened in the lab that weren't put on record, but certain novel ideas had to be tested."

"...you *opted* to be an experiment?" I gawked. "And even after all that, you're running the same experiments on other people? Whatever Bryant Morris did to you really fucked you up."

"You flatter me," Dana said. "But enough small talk. You do not have long before Mark and Josh will drive you to Archangel. You best get dressed."

"I will when you leave."

His smirk grew, somehow both teasing and menacing.

"You would rather stay naked in my presence? Perhaps I've misjudged how resistant you are to me."

Embarrassment turned into anger. I shoved him away, giving myself the opening to walk around him and return to the bathroom where I snatched my dress from the side of the sink and pulled it on with as little care as I could manage, enraged at his teasing. My anger even stopped me from removing my bra once my dress was on, despite the fact that the dress had a low back and was meant to be worn without the undergarment.

As I was straightening my face in the mirror, messing with my hair and desperate for some movement that would dispel the anxiety in my body, I spotted Dana walking slowly back to the bathroom, stopping directly behind me and pressing his fingers into the bra band. I froze, my fingers still tangled in my hair, watching him carefully.

With a simple flick of his fingers, he unhooked the bra and my anger turned back into terror.

But he did not move further.

"You are very beautiful, Little Lily," he murmured, catching my gaze in the mirror. "And I cannot wait for the moment when you realize your beauty, and learn to wield it as a weapon."

More than the fear of having Dana so close to me, more than the worry that he would pin me to the sink and try to use his seductive powers on me once more, the fact that my heart skipped a beat and affection spread through my chest at the words terrified me. Some part of me, the primal part that he awoke whenever he was close, was reveling in the praise, in the thought that Dana saw me as powerful in my own right despite how powerless he made me feel.

Being sure to maneuver my arms to take off the bra without unzipping my dress, I shoved my school clothes into the bag with my makeup, hoping Dana was unable to read the conflict in my expression.

"Be careful tonight, Little Lily," Dana told me, stepping back as I snatched my bag from the floor and began storming out of the office.

I returned to the conference room, wanting to throw things and scream to dispel the energy in my body and express my frustration at my reactions to Dana, when Clark's pale and confused face made me stop.

"What's wrong?" I asked quickly, dropping my bag to a chair and approaching him.

Clark did not speak, instead turning his eyes to the folded pieces of paper that lay on his open textbook.

"When?" I demanded.

"Sometime when both of us were out of the room," Clark said.

"…was it Mark?" I whispered, turning my eyes to the figure just outside the conference room door.

"I don't think so," Clark said. "He followed me to find Dana."

Clark and I were both frozen apart from looking between each other and the folded notes on his textbook. The hair on the back of my neck rose, certain eyes were on us in that moment, reading our reactions, waiting for us to either show that we were up to something or that we had found the helpful notes.

As if reading my mind, Clark lifted his gaze to fall on the security cameras around the conference room. There were two in opposing corners, likely leaving no section of the room as a blind spot.

"Are those real?" I asked, following his gaze.

"I thought they were," he said. "But now I'm not so sure."

Mark turning away from the door and walking into the conference room startled both of us, but he bowed his head, unaware why we were so on-edge. Clark glanced at his watch.

"Shit, we have to go," he muttered, snatching up the folded papers and putting them in his pocket as he hurriedly shoved his books into his backpack. I hurried to do the same, having to dig my heels out of the bottom of my bag and then running to Mrs. Markus' office to retrieve the sneakers I had abandoned in my haste to get away from Dana.

When I stepped out of the office, Clark and Mark were waiting for me, joined by Dana and a man I had never met before. The man was dressed in the same suit as Mark, though his frame was far thinner, and his hair was cropped shorter. He was also shorter than Mark, and standing next to Dana, he looked even smaller.

"There you are," Dana said. "This is Josh. He will be joining Mark tonight and driving you to Archangel. I'm sure Sean already told you that I do not want either of you riding the Commission bus home tonight."

"Why not?" Clark asked.

"Because that is my order."

"But what if someone notices them?" Clark insisted. "It's dangerous enough to have Mark drive me as often as he does. I don't want to put Mark, Josh, or the Commission in a difficult position if they're spotted by our classmates."

"You seem to have no faith in Mark," Dana noted. "They won't be standing at the front doors. They will park around the back of the club after they drop you off and then you can leave through the side door to meet up with them."

"Why are you so worried about us?" I asked suspiciously.

"I've angered a lot of young people with that fiasco concerning Miranda and Julie," he explained, looking at his nails, disinterested. "And since you two are my favorites, I must be certain you are safe. I wouldn't want you two swept up in some failed coup against me."

"I thought you had control over everyone in the Commission," I challenged.

"Maybe I do, maybe I don't," he said, bored. "Who's to say? But you two better get going. Wouldn't want you to miss out on the teenage revelry."

Clark turned to me and nodded, telling me to follow him as we walked away from Dana. Mark fell into pace behind us and Josh joined him, just as silent and stoic.

Once Clark had angrily prodded the button for the elevators, he shook his head.

"I can't believe he's doing this," he grumbled. "He was the one who always told me not to put Mark in any unnecessary danger by taking him out in public, and now he does this."

We went through the process of grabbing our phones from the reception desk as the car was pulled to the front of the building.

It was a short, awkward drive to Archangel with Josh and Mark in the two front seats. Josh made a motion to Mark in the first few minutes of the drive, but Mark shook his head and completed some motion I could not see. After that the two did not even look at one another, both focused out the windshield as they chauffeured us to Archangel. I seemed to be the only one curious about the silent conversation, as Clark just shrugged when I shot him a questioning look.

Club Archangel was as loud and bright as ever with teens filing in excitedly, eager to get out of the cold, autumn night.

"When we're doing our rounds, we'll look over the notes," Clark whispered as we stepped through the open front doors.

Since I was able to leave my bags in the car with Mark and Josh, we were able to pass the line of people checking their items and have our IDs scanned before entering the flashing lights. As usual, we stopped at the table where Becca, Jill, Taylor, and the others were waiting.

"There they are! *Finally*!" Devon declared when he saw us. "How are you two?"

"Good," I answered tiredly.

"Are you ready for the Halloween party next week?" Jill grinned, an excited light playing in her eyes.

"Already wanting tonight to be over?" Becca teased.

"Of course!" Jill gasped. "The Halloween party is the best one of the year!"

The group chatted about previous Halloween parties and their costumes for the upcoming event, but I was hardly paying attention, waiting for the moment when Clark and I could slip away and go over the notes in his pocket.

Clark was far more skilled at finding an opening, and he jumped in on a lull in the conversation and told the others we were going to do our rounds, guiding me away from the table and into the sea of dancing students. He took my elbow and leaned in so I could hear him over the thrumming bass.

"Maybe we should actually do our rounds and see if anyone is talking about the rebellion of the Commish Kids," he suggested. Agreeing quickly, we started our shuffled wandering to hear the gossip of the evening.

I was not sure whether to be disappointed or happy when I did not hear anything about our rebellion among the other students.

After rounding the room once, I took Clark's wrist and pulled him behind one of the raised platforms on the dance floor, being sure we were shielded from view of the balcony. He dug his hand into his pocket, looking over each shoulder before keeping his hands low and unfolding the notes.

"Have you already looked at these?"

"No," he said. "I didn't want to risk it."

We both leaned close, trying to catch a clearer view of the scribbled letters and numbers in the flashing lights.

S18Q1B009E1-1**
S12Q5B118E0-3
S4Q19B787E12-0
S23Q2B107E6-9*
S10Q1B027E8-1
S9Q4B423E7-2

I squinted at the strange code, seeing they were different from the first notes but no less discernible.

"What is that?" I asked.

"...they're addresses," Clark whispered, his eyes darting across the page.

"Addresses?" I repeated.

"When Central was being established during the post-war radical uprisings, they created a new system of identifying buildings in the city so that uprisings would not know which buildings to target," Clark explained. "These are in that code."

"How do you know that?"

"I saw the information in one of the books I read in the Commission's library when I was bored one summer," Clark explained. "I don't exactly know how to read them, but I remember this is what the codes looked like. I bet if I could find that book again, we could figure out which buildings they are."

"What do you think this person would want us to know addresses for?" I asked.

Clark flipped the page, seeing a crudely drawn outline of a room with several lines through the middle of it. Below the drawing was the scribbled title of a book.

"Looks like they've also told you which book to look in," I noted.

"Maybe, but I'm pretty sure the book I saw this in had a different title. Maybe there's more notes in this book." He smiled as he lifted his gaze to meet mine. "Looks like we're studying in the library on Monday."

With only two pages, Clark replaced them in his pocket and nodded once.

"We know what we're doing on Monday, then," he said. "So let's go to the balcony and see what the other Commish Kids are talking about tonight."

The balcony radiated with a sense of tension. There was a lot of anxiety bouncing around the Commish Kids and whispered theories attached to Miranda's name. But most clearly, the other teens on the balcony seemed unsure how they should interact with one another, overanalyzing every conversation, greeting nod, or lingered glance.

Worried that the other Commish Kids would immediately pick up on the idea that Clark and I were scheming against the Commission of the People, we made our way to a deserted corner, occupying two chairs. I leaned close to Clark.

"I meant to tell you," I whispered, "I invited Becca to my house on Sunday, is that allowed?"

"What?!" Clark gasped. "Of course that's not allowed. You've got Mykail there!"

"I know...but..." I stopped. I realized that even though we had spent so much time together over the last week, I had not told Clark that Becca knew of our intent to overthrow Dana and the Commission of the People. My argument for having Becca come over died on my tongue, knowing Clark would be heavily against the idea of looking for help outside the Commish Kids.

"But nothing," Clark snapped. "What are you going to do if she catches a glimpse of him? Do you really think you can explain that?"

"Well…" I refused to meet his eyes. He was silent for several long seconds and then he groaned, pinching the bridge of his nose.

"Please, please, *please* tell me you didn't do what I think you did…"

I did not respond. He groaned again, hiding his face in his hands. "Lily…" he moaned, sounding as though I was physically hurting him.

"I'm sorry, but she knew something was wrong and I needed someone outside the Commission to talk to…"

"You just put her life in danger," he told me sharply. "I can't believe you would risk her safety like that."

"She wants to help."

"No, absolutely not."

"Why not?" I challenged. I knew we could trust Becca even though she was outside the Commission. I thought that Clark would know her well enough to understand that she would not say anything to endanger us or herself, and the fact that he was so opposed to her knowing the truth irritated me more than frightened me.

"We can't trust people outside the Commission," Clark said strongly. "When you were first introduced to the Commission, and you saw everything that happened there, you were frightened, weren't you?"

"Yes."

"And if Dana had taken Miranda in the same night, or even one week later, you would not have said anything in protest because you were still processing. You were trying to figure out the situation and what the boundaries were. If Becca becomes a part of this, she's a weak link. She will not be in the Commission every day. She will be the weakest against Dana's influence. She's not with him every day, she doesn't have to face him, and as soon as he puts a little pressure on her, she will fold."

"How can you say that?" I growled. "Becca is your friend as well."

"Of course she is," Clark sighed. "But she's now in danger, as we all are if she exposes us."

"Alright, alright," I groaned. "For now, we'll keep her on the outside of the plan, but she already knows about it, so it wouldn't be fair if we just leave her out in the cold."

"It might not be fair, but it will be safer," Clark said. I glared at him, not liking his reaction. He glanced at me and sighed heavily. "Fine. She can come over to your house and meet Mykail, but that's all. Until we really know what's going on, it's probably better that that's as much as she knows."

"Thank you, Clark."

"I'll be over there as well," he declared strongly.

I huffed, but was secretly pleased that he would be there—it saved me from explaining everything and telling Becca something I shouldn't. Since Clark was more in tune with what was safe for other people to know, he would be able to stop me from saying anything that would put us in even more danger.

The night wore on as all other Fridays had. The Commish Kids were so tense most did not leave the balcony, watching for any out of place movement or suspicious glance. They even patrolled the balcony more than watching the dancers below, scrutinizing one another, unsure who to trust. Clark and I watched from our spot, sensing the apprehension. Though I did not want to admit it, I was thrilled to see the anxiety. It was more likely we could get others to join our cause if they were riddled with fear about the Commission and Dana Christenson.

When the club was closing and others were leaving, the nervous ball in my stomach grew. The Commish Kids gathered, waiting for the meeting to begin with dark and angry looks.

"Alright," Melissa said, calling the meeting to order. She went through the procedure of recording her voice as she opened the meeting. "Who has anything they would like to share?"

For the first time since I had been part of the Commish Kids, no one spoke. Melissa looked around, annoyed rather than surprised.

"No one?" she groaned. "Come on, everyone. Pull it together."

"Let's face it," Dean growled. "No one actually went around the club tonight to hear the gossip because we were too busy gossiping among ourselves about last week."

Many Commish Kids murmured in agreement. Melissa stopped the recording with a heavy sigh.

"You mean this whole thing with Miranda?"

"What else?" Dean snapped.

"Are we just supposed to pretend nothing happened?" Samantha hissed. "Just go on like everything's alright?"

"People get taken into the Commission every day. Why should Miranda be treated any differently?" Melissa challenged.

"It's not the same thing," Brent said. "Miranda wasn't a criminal. And Julie sure as hell wasn't a criminal. Dana's doing God only knows what to both of them and they haven't even done anything wrong!"

Again, most of the kids in the Commission agreed. Melissa studied the faces around her, her attention finally focusing on Clark.

"Clark?" she asked. "What do you think?"

I felt my heartbeat pick up and a nervous sweat formed on my palms as I wrung my hands together. Clark took a deep breath and lowered his eyes, feeling the same anxiety.

"Why ask *him*?" Gracie groaned. "He's Dana's pet. He's going to favor what Dana does more than what happens to any of us."

"Shows how little you know about me," Clark growled. "I don't agree with what Dana did with Miranda and Julie, but if I'm honest with myself, I know I can't do anything to change it."

"Why not?" Dean challenged angrily.

"Dana is the second most powerful man in the world. What he says is law, particularly when it comes to the Commission and who gets taken," Clark said. "If you want to say something about what he's doing, you have to make a deal more appealing to him rather than just order him to undo what he's done."

"Make him a deal? No, we just need to argue on Miranda's behalf," Dean said. "If her parents won't, we have to step in."

"Why do you keep underestimating Dana?" Clark asked incredulously. "It's the fact that he had something on Miranda that her parents *didn't* argue for her. And the more that we fight against Dana, the more anger we show, the more likely he is to turn even our own parents against us. So he's trying to scare us into backing down by making an example of Miranda and Julie. That also will turn our parents' attention on to us and they will be sure we are following Dana's word so that we don't get into the same trouble as Miranda."

"I don't give a shit about that," Ryan snapped. "If Dana is doing something we find corrupt, we have a duty to stop it. He said it himself. No one in the Commission is above the law, not even him."

Several Commish Kids who had not shown support for opposing Dana started nodding and voicing their agreement. My hair stood on end and my pulse began thudding through my veins, reacting to the angry energy building within the circle of teenagers. The feeling was exhilarating, the anger becoming so powerful I could almost taste it in the air.

"Look," Melissa said, raising her hands and shifting in her seat as she tried to take control of the meeting again. "For all we know, there is legitimate evidence against Miranda, and if there is, then Dana is not doing anything corrupt or illegal."

"But she's innocent!" Dean snapped.

"Of course you think that she's innocent. You love her."

"No, I think that because it's *true*!" Dean barked, standing. "Dana is doing this just to scare us. He's using fear tactics just like the Washington System did. I don't know what we did, or which one of you fucks did whatever stupid shit you did to catch his attention, but Dana cannot just take someone innocent to use as an example. He thinks that will make us more obedient? Fuck that! I'm fucking *pissed*! And I'm going to make sure Dana knows that."

His declaration was met with a chorus of agreement from a majority of the Commish Kids.

"Anyone else?"

"You bet I'm in," Ryan said. "I'm sick of this fear-mongering shit."

"What are you going to do if you fail?" Melissa challenged. "If Dana doesn't listen? Are you going to try and take down the whole Commission?"

My heart had stopped, my breath stuck in my throat, hanging on every millisecond that passed before Dean answered.

"If I have to. Look, maybe all of you are alright with just accepting what Dana's doing, but I'm sure as hell not gonna lay down and take it."

"Then you could be the next one paraded in front of the meeting," Matt said with a slow shake of his head.

"Fine," Dean retaliated. "Then I'll just work from the inside. This is not fair. It's not fair to us, it's not fair to Miranda, and it's sure as hell not fair to Julie. So if I have to rip that place apart even as a prisoner, you better fucking believe I'll do it."

A powerful shiver ran down my spine. We were gathering our forces to go to war with Dana Christenson, and I was eager to move forward with our rebellion.

Chapter Thirty-Two

My insides were in knots Saturday night. I took a few deep breaths as quietly as I could without calling my parents' attention while we descended in the elevator. That night would be the first act in rebellion against the Commission of the People. Even though my heart was thrumming in exhilaration, my mind could not stop obsessing over all the ways things could go horribly wrong.

None of the Commish Kids, including me and Clark, knew Dana well enough to predict how he would react, and for all I knew, one wrong word would sentence all the angry teenagers in the Commission to a life of imprisonment and experimentation. For all Dean said about working from the inside to dismantle the Commission, should things go wrong, I remembered all too well the fog that invaded my brain whenever I traversed the cells. I could only assume that being imprisoned made the brain fog much, much worse.

I knew the only way we would ever stand a chance at effecting change in the Commission of the People, was to expose the cruelty publicly.

My parents took their normal seats in the meeting room, socializing with the others at our table easily. I ignored the conversation, casting my gaze around the room to scan the other Commish Kids. There were a lot of younger kids in the room, more than I remembered actively noticing before. What would happen to the younger children if their older brothers and sisters started rebelling against Dana? Would they follow? Would Dana imprison them in revenge? Would they stay loyal to the Commission and turn on their own siblings?

Clark tapped my shoulder, causing me to whirl around with a soft gasp. He smiled apologetically.

"Sorry."

"It's fine." I pressed my hand to my chest and drew in a deep breath. "What's up?"

"Not much at the moment," Clark admitted. "But..." He looked around slowly. "You mentioned Mykail said we needed to do something before Eina was finished?"

My heart fell. "He's done?"

"No, no, I don't think so," Clark said quickly. "But...something big happened. The entire security staff was anxious and many came back with bruises and cuts after Eina was pulled out of his cell, even Mark."

"What does that mean?"

"I don't know, but considering how happy Dana is, I would think it's something we need to worry about."

"Eina's not that dangerous," a familiar cold voice said behind Clark. We both turned to face Dana's shaded eyes.

"Damn it!" I snapped. "Do you have to sneak up on people?!"

"I do nothing of the sort," he said. "You're just painfully oblivious to your surroundings. If you are scheming, that could prove detrimental to your plans."

"Like we would be stupid enough to scheme here," I growled.

"Why are you worried about Eina's completion?" Dana asked, looking between the two of us.

"Mark came back with claw marks across his face," Clark said angrily. "What the hell happened in the lab?"

"Oh, Eina got a little testy and broke his restraints. Took all of the chinks to hold him down and sedate him. It was quite the scuffle."

"Eina...broke his restraints?" Clark gawked. "Didn't you just replace those with triple restraints?"

"For him, yes," Dana affirmed. "The cuffs, the chains, and The Teeth. We even sedated him, but he's grown too strong for that. We'll have to up the security and his dosage, for his safety as well as our own." Dana's body shuddered as his smile grew. "It's really quite exciting!"

"Hardly," Clark snapped. "Dana, he is now getting powerful enough to break out of the cells and if he gets out to the people...I can't even imagine the chaos."

"He won't get out." Dana waved the question away.

"Maybe not out of the Commission, but he can get out of his cell," Clark repeated.

"And the first person he's going to go after is *you*," I said, smiling thinly at Dana.

"You think so?"

"Of course," I scoffed. "You've tortured and mutilated him. I'm sure he hates you more than anyone else."

"So be it, then." He shrugged.

"That's it? So be it? That's all you think?"

"Yes," he stated. "Everything is fleeting. Nothing is permanent. Eina is my favorite experiment we've done in the Commission so far. Bryant Morris was killed by his favorite. It would only be fitting that I be killed by mine. Keep the tradition going."

"Oh, Dana, what on earth are you talking about?" my mother said with a nervous laugh, stepping up to our conversation and breaking his concentration. I ground my teeth together, angry that she would interrupt. What made her intrusion worse was her obvious flirtation. It made me sick, particularly when I could feel the charisma ooze out of Dana in response to her fluttering eyelashes and coy laugh.

"Nothing of consequence," Dana assured, reaching a hand to take hers, kissing her knuckles before his fingers began dancing with hers in the space between them teasingly. "It has been a long time since we have really spoken, Karen. Your husband has been so helpful with the transportation routes, but I do fear that means I am monopolizing his time."

I blinked in surprise, not recalling my father ever saying that he had been regularly meeting with Dana.

"No, I understand," my mother said as Dana's hand, still wrapped around her fingers loosely, dropped. I expected my mother to pull her hand away, but instead, she allowed him to hold it loosely, her face blushing.

I felt my mother slipping away, being swept up in the powerful aura of Dana Christenson. Even her fingers seemed to be squeezing his, being sure he did not let go. She was falling under his spell. I had to do something quickly before she was lost like so many others in the Commission of the People.

"I'll make you a deal," Dana started. "I'll look at my schedule and coordinate a time where we can meet and catch up. After all, I have had Little Lily here with me after school and Tommy here for work, there is no reason that you shouldn't come visit every now and then, as well."

"Thank you, Dana." My mother smiled, turning her face away demurely. "Lily, your father would like to introduce you to someone."

"Fine," I said shortly, eager to no longer bear witness to the flirtation. I did not bother to hide my disgust as I walked away. I wasn't sure if I wanted to throw up or cry as both my throat and eyes were stinging. Clark stayed with my mother and Dana as I walked around the table toward my father.

"Ah, Lily," my father called. I stepped to his side, studying the group of suits with my father. "Paul, this is my daughter Lily," he said before motioning to one of the men who had gray hair and deep lines on his face. I extended my hand reflexively. "Lily, this is Paul Matthews, the Chair of Internal Affairs for Leader Simon."

"It's a pleasure to meet you."

"You, as well," I said instinctively, though I was caught off-guard by his high position. "You're a member of the Commission?"

"Since I was a boy," he affirmed. "My mother was brought into the Commission when I was six. Bryant Morris was still alive, then, of course, but I remember seeing Mr. Christenson when he was only Mr. Morris' assistant. That was a long time ago, back when I was still young."

"Dana was Bryant Morris' assistant?"

"That was how Mr. Morris always introduced him," Mr. Matthews told me. "I may be the oldest Legacy in the Commission, but the other Legacy members also remember."

"Like who?"

"Lily," my father said cautiously, warning me against asking more questions.

"Sorry…" I said quickly, lowering my head, not really registering how well my father had me trained. "I didn't mean to pry."

"It's alright," Mr. Matthews said. "I can understand being curious about Mr. Christenson. He is quite the man, isn't he?" The other four men in the group that I should have known by name laughed. "If you were wondering, Mr. Christenson has not changed at all in the time I've known him."

"He's always acted this way? *Always*?"

"I'm not *that* old," he chuckled. "I'm actually younger than your father," he teased. "As long as I've seen him, yes, he has been the same."

"How old was he when you first met him?" My father asked the question that time.

"Oh…he said he was about twenty-two or twenty-three…I can't rightly remember."

"So he's…well, a lot older than he looks," my father said with a nervous laugh.

"No kidding," another man interjected. "My wife always talks about how, when she's his age, she wants to look as good as he does."

The conversation diverted as I studied Mr. Matthews. He looked older than my father, but I understood that most people in the Leader's Cabinet aged quickly due to the stress of the job. I memorized his features. He was a small link into Dana's past, and if I could figure out where he came from, I might be able to find some weakness that could help me bring down the leader of the Commission of the People.

I remained at my father's side through the next conversation about the stock market, but a gentle tap on my shoulder diverted my already-wandering attention. I turned to see Mark behind me. He had his glasses on, which made him blend in with the rest of the security detail filing into the room.

"Mark," I greeted brightly, though my heart fell when I saw the three large but shallow gashes across his left cheek. He smiled at me and lifted his hand, wiggling his fingers in a silent greeting that made me grin wider. "Hello," I said. "Are you alright?"

"Lily? Who is this?" my father asked.

"This is...uh, Mark," I said, suddenly very nervous about introducing the former experiment to my father. "He's...sort of, in charge of my security when I'm here."

"He's part of Dana's security detail?" my father tried to clarify.

"Not only that," Mr. Matthews interjected, "these guys are the internal security. They're experiments themselves. Most of them can't understand much English past their commands. They're all...what's the politically correct way to say this? Of East-Asian origin."

"You're kidding," my father gasped, turning to Mark again. "What happened to his face?"

"Probably a scuffle in the back. They're pretty frequent."

"But if this is Mark, this is the one that the Markus family owns," another man added.

"No kidding, this is the one?" another chortled. "He's shorter than I thought. Sean's praised his skills to the high heavens."

I turned to Mark again and smiled apologetically, hoping he could not understand and becoming uncomfortable with the conversation between the older men. His expression seemed as relaxed as ever, though I was certain the wounds in his face had to be hurting him.

"Are you okay?" I asked, pointing to my own cheek. His hand lifted to his face and he gingerly touched the wounds before glancing at the blood on his fingertips. He lowered his hand and turned to me again before lifting his hand to his left ear and pulling on it discreetly.

I'm sorry.

I wondered why he was always apologizing.

The doors closing startled me. I was not the only one who jumped out of their skin. Most of the room was scrambling to take their seats, having not paid attention to the time, feeding off an energy in the room that I had barely noticed until I was also rushing to my seat. Mark walked toward the front of the room, motioning to a few of the others in the security detail. Those in suits and glasses spread through the room, stationing themselves around the entire room and amplifying just how many men and women made up the internal security of the Commission. And not all of them were Asian like Mark—several were black. Sean was standing near the platform, whispering something to Dana as Mrs. Markus called the meeting to order.

She had barely opened the meeting when she turned the microphone over the excited Dana.

"Today's meeting is going to be unconventional," he started. "Recently, there has been immense progress on the Machine of Neutralization Project. As you might have noticed, or even heard if you were here earlier, there was a bit of a struggle because Eina broke free of his restraints and caused havoc in Ward Six. That being said, I would like to bring him before this commission and show the progress that has been made. We will do this very quickly before his sedatives wear off."

A tremor went through the room, but it was not just from the members of the Commission. The apprehension was clear in the stiff posture of the security detail.

"Bring him in." Dana motioned to two men by the door next to the stage, one of whom was Mark. Mark opened the door and reached through, grabbing the chains that were handed to him and guiding the experiment through the door as the man opposite Mark grabbed the second set of chains so the four people who had led the experiment to the meeting room could come forward.

Everyone was silent as the Machine of Neutralization prototype stumbled and fell to his knees. He was dressed only in baggy shorts and chains. There were two cuffs around his wrists and ankles and one large one around his chest attached to four guiding chains. The cuff around his neck was connected to three guiding chains and the iron looked like it was weighing too heavily for him to stand.

I did not fully remember what Eina looked like, so I felt as if I was seeing him for the first time. He looked to be in his late twenties, his light brown hair dirty and knotted. His pale skin was dotted with bruises and cuts where the cuffs bit into his flesh. Blood was dripping down his body in thin rivulets, bringing my attention to the sharp points on the inside of the cuffs around his chest and neck, puncturing his skin whenever he moved, preventing excessive motion.

His body shuddered as the chains were separated between the four security agents charged with guiding him. Mark and the other man stationed on each side of the door stepped back. One of the men holding Eina tugged on the chain attached to his chest and I cringed with the experiment as the points lining the inside of the restraints sliced into his skin. One of the men turned to Sean, who stepped up behind Eina, hooking his arms under Eina's and pulling him upright so he could walk.

"Be careful, Sean..." Mrs. Markus said nervously from her position next to the podium.

"Don't worry everyone, he'll be safe for ten minutes or so," Dana explained to the worried room. "We pumped a lot of sedatives into him. He's only running at ten percent."

Sean brought Eina next to the podium, where his legs folded under him, his head bent low in drug-induced fatigue. Sean took up station between Dana and his favorite experiment.

"I know he doesn't look like it now, but his DNA has been successfully altered to the specifications we hoped, using certain strands of animal DNA," Dana explained. "His strength, speed, and reflexes are at phenomenal levels, almost to the point where we cannot record them without assistance from our computers. Even some of our best cameras cannot capture his movement correctly."

The room filled with excited murmuring. Conversely, I remained skeptical, certain that Dana was exaggerating.

Dana walked to Eina and lifted the experiment's arm. Even sedated, he growled and flinched away from the touch, though Dana only grinned at the sound.

"He's got enough tranquilizers in him to put down an elephant, yet he can still growl and react to me," he explained. He lifted the experiment's arm high and wrapped his other hand around Eina's bicep. "His muscles have not grown at all, but they have not atrophied, either. He is currently able to lift nearly five times his own body weight. You can see the results of those tests on the fifth slide of your presentations."

I wanted to study the results as most members of the Commission eagerly did, but I could not tear my gaze from Eina. His shaggy hair was hiding his face, his head bent low, swaying with the effort to not collapse entirely, his thin, pale frame nearly glowing under the lights of the platform.

Even though I could not see his eyes, I could feel the power radiating from him, albeit barely, due to the sedatives. I tried to convince myself that Dana was working everyone up to believe that Eina was more dangerous than any other experiment, but there was a part of me, an instinctive part, that understood the experiment was exceptionally deadly.

"For now, his testing will be halted and we will wait for him to fall into a normal routine before we start again. Once we are certain he has completely stabilized, we will do one more set of treatments, which will hopefully lead to us training him for the program itself," Dana explained, dropping Eina's arm carelessly. He walked behind Eina and wrapped a hand around his neck, lifting his chin so we could see his face.

His eyes were mostly closed and his mouth was open as he breathed heavily. His face was even paler than his body but his cheeks were flushed bright red, a side-effect of the sedatives in his system.

"Take a good look, everyone. He's the first experiment of the Machine of Neutralization program to reach this stage," Dana announced. "Within a few years, we should be able to mass-produce these weapons. They will be more devastating than any WMD created so far."

"What do you plan to do with them?" a member of the Commission asked. "We're not at war."

"Not now, no," Dana admitted. "But who knows what's brewing in the dark depths of the world? It pays to be prepared."

He moved his hand away from Eina's face and the experiment let out a growl, opening his teeth to bite. Dana's reflexes were also fast, able to pull his hand away as the rest of the room gasped at the sudden movement.

Eina's eyes rolled in their sockets and his head dropped again, labored breaths rocking his entire frame.

"You know the rules," Dana said with a challenging smirk. "If you bite me, I bite you." His attention turned back to the members of the Commission. "I would like to put forth a proposal to the Commission of the People," he called. "Given that Eina is likely to be the first success of the Machine of Neutralization project, I would like to see if the changes we have made to his physiology could be passed through breeding. I have found Eina's sister in the holding cells and I would like to use her as the first female Machine of Neutralization and test the possibility of procreation."

"Are you not worried about the effects of inbreeding?"

"At the moment, no," Dana said. "We understand Eina's physiological reaction to this testing. It would be easier to attempt replicating the testing on someone from the same bloodline. If she is a success, we can try breeding and see the results we get from the resulting child," Dana explained. "I am putting this proposal in front of the Commission of the People. Will anyone second?"

I prayed silently that everyone would remain silent.

"I'll second," one of the men at a table on the far right of the room called.

"With the second, will all in agreement stand?"

The sounds of chair legs scraping the floor and people standing were much louder than normal. I dared not to look. I did not want to see the people standing in agreement for the plan—I just prayed it was not the majority.

"Very well, as soon as we process her paperwork, we'll transfer her into the lab and begin her testing," Dana announced. "You may be seated."

Eina growled loudly and lunged behind him toward Dana. The leader of the Commission stepped back easily, and the experiment fell to the ground, letting out a choked cry as the chest cuff punctured his skin from the fall.

"Looks like we better get him back into his cell before he hurts himself more," Dana declared, turning to the security detail tightening the slack in the chains securing Eina. "Take him back and be sure he does not get loose again. The drugs are obviously wearing off, so move quickly."

The security detail that had been stationed around the room funneled toward the door, surrounding Eina as he was led to the same door Mark was guarding. It took quite some time to get them out of the room, the mass of black suits slowly diminishing as the Machine of Neutralization was taken back to the cells.

"Exciting, isn't it?" Dana said, ignoring the security filing from the room. "Unfortunately the excitement cannot last. I have another item I wish to discuss with everyone tonight." He extracted his pocket watch, tossing the gold back and forth between his palms as he stepped away from the podium and began pacing the platform. "We have a problem."

I could feel my heart choking me, trying to climb into my throat.

"The Commission of the People juggles many responsibilities and, as you are all aware, I have come to realize that our younger members have been acting outside of what would be expected for members of this commission." He looked over his captive audience, changing direction on the platform. "Recently, you will remember, I took Miranda and Julie Jacobs under charges for illegal drug trafficking and firearm possession. Apparently, this has not been well received by the younger generations."

I was certain that his eyes were picking out every teenager among the tables behind his shaded glasses.

"I would like to hear what the young people in this room have to say to me regarding what happened with Miranda and Julie Jacobs."

Three seconds of deafening silence passed before Dean stood.

"Dean, what the hell are you doing?" his father hissed.

"I have something to say," he called across the room, ignoring his frantic parents trying to get him to resume his seat.

"Young Mr. Owens."

"Miranda and Julie are innocent," Dean said strongly. "We all discussed it and agreed that you were wrong in taking them into custody. We demand that you set them free."

"Who is we?" Dana chuckled. "Your group at Archangel?"

"You are trying to scare us into obedience by taking her and making an example of her," Dean accused. "But all you did was make us angry."

"Dean, sit down," his mother snapped, grabbing his wrist.

"I don't see anyone standing to support you," Dana noted, looking around the room. "I truly do wish to hear the concerns of our younger members, so if you are in agreement with Mr. Owens, please stand."

No one moved.

"Looks like we'll have to try this another way..." Dana mused, wrapping the chain of his pocket watch around his fist. "Everyone under the age of twenty, stand," he ordered. Still, no one moved. He groaned, motioning with his hands. "Come on, up, up, up."

Hesitant, my classmates and their younger siblings stood from their seats. I also rose, seeing the nervous expressions of my parents match the other parents around the room.

"Now," Dana started, "Miranda was a friend to you, so naturally you would be upset. But this seems to be more about your fears that I took her under false pretenses. That tells me that you are frightened I might also snatch any of you out of your beds in the middle of the night." Dana began pacing again, dragging his heels in exaggerated, slow steps, his hands clasped behind his back around the pocket watch.

"Let me make this perfectly clear," Dana continued, his voice lined with ice. "If I listened to every complaint about the people I apprehend, thousands upon thousands of very dangerous criminals would be released back into the population. There is a reason we have the policy of never being able to leave the Commission once you're inside."

"Miranda was already in the Commission!" Dean snapped. "Why would she risk doing anything stupid like smuggling? She knew the risks. She's not that stupid!"

"Clearly she was, and she was stupid enough to tell her younger sister all about what made her a Commission criminal. And since Julie did not report her..." Dana lifted his hands to punctuate the statement. "However, young Mister Owens, perhaps you know something that my own intelligence offers do not? Is there something that you would like to disclose?"

Dean remained silent, though I could see even from across the room that his fists were clenched at his sides and shaking with restraint.

Dana's mouth quirked upward in a smirk before he raised his voice to address everyone in the Commission meeting. "Heed what I say, young Commission members," he continued, taking the same slow, deliberate steps until he reached the center of the stage, "you are not invincible. I understand you are young, and young people tend to let their foolish idealism get the best of them. But you are still liable for your actions, and there will be consequences if you decide to test my patience. There will be no further warnings or lectures. I will be forced into action if any of you decide to test my mercy."

"So you think it would be foolish idealism to break Miranda and Julie out?" Dean challenged darkly.

Everyone in the room was so shocked by the statement that most couldn't help but bark a laugh of disbelief, including me. Dana just smiled.

"Good luck with that."

"Dean, sit down, now!" his father ordered.

"I'll do it if I have to," Dean barked, starting toward Dana, away from his father's grabbing hand. The tension in the room rapidly escalated. I watched, trying to think if there was anything I could do to turn the situation around. I knew, at that point, one of two things could happen and only one was favorable. Dean was either going to upset Dana to the point of being taken into the cells, effectively scaring off others who were thinking of rebelling, or Dana would just laugh it off and enrage Dean further, which would put more fuel on the fire of our rebellion.

"You'll do what?" Dana asked, his stance firm as he watched Dean approach. Sean stepped to Dana's side but the leader of the Commission, not removing his eyes from Dean, put his hand on Sean's chest and pushed him backward. "You'll break into the holding cells and take her and Julie? And then what?"

"I'll be sure to destroy everything I can on the way in and out," Dean snarled, finally clearing the tables and stepping up to the front of the platform. "And if you try to stop me, I'll kill you."

"*You*? Kill me?"

"Mr. Christenson, I'm so sorry, please—" Dean's mother had cleared the tables and was rushing to claim her son's wrist and pull him away from the platform. Dana held up his hand to her, stopping her apology, his gaze still locked on Dean. Dean's mother reluctantly released her son's arm, retreating a few steps, shaking with fear about what Dana would do to her son.

"You think you're ready to play with the big boys, kiddo?" Dana asked, an eyebrow arching over the top of his dark glasses.

Dean stood in front of the platform and stared at Dana for what seemed to be an eternity. The entire room held its breath, waiting to see who would be the first to back down.

When Dana stepped off the front of the platform and approached Dean, I was certain I was about to watch Dean be hauled into the cells of the Commission. Dean retreated, his mother rushing forward to interfere. Dana's hand took Dean's shoulder, turning him around and shoving him hard in the back so he stumbled into his mother's waiting arms.

"You're adorable, but you don't stand a chance against me, and that doesn't make this any fun," Dana said with a condescending laugh. "So return to your seat like a good boy and remember your place."

As Dana spun on his heel and returned to the platform, Dean's face fell into a mask of fury, but he did not speak or move to approach Dana again, guided back to his seat by his pale and shivering mother. I felt the tension leave my body, realizing the confrontation was back in safer territory.

Dana returned to the podium, his amplified voice startling everyone. "If I hear of any of the Commission children getting any ideas about being brave and sneaking into the back, you will find yourselves permanent residents of the holding cells. Be sure you think about that long and hard before you concoct any half-baked plans."

I felt Dana's gaze focus on me, but I schooled my expression. I stared defiantly back and, even though he smirked and turned away to start the meeting, I managed to keep my expression from faltering.

Once again, Dana had unknowingly helped stoke the fires of my rebellion.

Chapter Thirty-Three

Clark came to my house surprisingly early Sunday morning. My parents had me up at six—three hours after we had gotten home from the Commission—to tell me that they were heading out for their charity event and that I would be in charge of Mykail all day, so I was also awake earlier than I wanted with a fuzzy mind and heavy eyelids.

Mykail was still asleep when I rolled out of bed again at seven so I left him alone. I prepared a simple breakfast for both of us and then went into his room, sitting on the bed and watching him sleep. He had waited for us to come home from the Commission, but with the distractions during the meeting, we were later than usual, and he had fallen asleep before we returned. I had missed our late night conversation, but I had not had the heart to wake him.

I didn't have long to wait before he stirred and woke, his eyes blinking slowly.

"Good morning."

"Good morning," he murmured, his voice thick with sleep. "Sorry I didn't see you last night," he said, his face creased from slumber as he closed his eyes again, his head falling back to the pillow.

"It's fine," I said, my heart stopping when his hand groped around on the blankets until it found mine. "I made you some breakfast. My parents are going to be out until late, so you're stuck with me."

"How horrible..." he joked. He pulled himself upright and leaned forward, kissing my cheek as I furiously wished I didn't blush so easily.

To hide my embarrassment, I grabbed the plate of toast and bacon I had brought for him, which he took before asking sweetly, "Is it okay to eat up here?"

We enjoyed the morning without a care, eating our breakfast in his room and talking lightly about anything other than the Commission of the People. It was as though the world around us faded away, nothing existing beyond that room. The illusion was shattered when, half-way through our breakfast, the doorbell resounded through the house.

"Who's here?" Mykail asked, surprised. I stared at the doorway of his room, confused, trying to think of who would be at our house that early.

"Stay up here," I said, abandoning my plate and running down the stairs to the front door, not caring about being in my pajamas. I looked out the window next to the front door before I answered.

"Clark?" I gasped as I opened the door. "What are you doing here so early?"

"I wanted to make sure I was here before Becca."

"Who brought you?" I asked, seeing no one nearby.

"Mark," Clark answered. "Sorry, it looks like I woke you up…"

"No, no," I said quickly. "I was already awake, I just…obviously haven't bothered to get dressed, yet." My embarrassment surprised me. I had not been doing anything untoward when Clark arrived, but I felt as though Clark had interrupted something very intimate between me and Mykail. "Sorry, come in."

I closed the door behind Clark, spinning around to be met with a suspicious stare.

"Am I interrupting something?"

"What? No," I said far too quickly. I closed my eyes and sighed heavily. "Clark, you showed up at my house at seven-thirty in the morning and I am in my pajamas…I'm just a little surprised."

Clark relaxed and hung his head with a chuckle.

"Yeah…sorry about that…" he laughed, also embarrassed.

"Let me get dressed," I said. "Do you want anything to eat? I can make you something."

"No, thanks. Do you have anything to drink, though?"

"Yeah, help yourself to whatever is in the fridge," I said, leading him into the kitchen before making my way to the back stairs.

I ascended the stairs two at a time and rounded the corner, poking my head into Mykail's room.

"Who's here?" he whispered.

"Clark," I answered. "You can come downstairs. But…um, we weren't doing anything before he showed up, okay?"

"Nope, not at all," he agreed with a rapid shake of his head. It was clear he had already tried to make things look as innocent as possible— our plates were nowhere to be seen, likely hidden in the bathroom.

I ducked into my room and pulled on the first comfortable clothes I snatched from my drawers, throwing my hair into a ponytail to avoid taming it. Not wanting to leave Clark alone too long, I returned as quickly as I could to the kitchen while Mykail lingered in his room. I guessed it would have been awkward to be downstairs with Clark on his own.

"Sorry about that," I said, walking into the kitchen and leaning against the table in the breakfast nook where Clark was sitting. "Are you sure you don't want anything else?"

"No, thank you. Where's Mykail?"

"Upstairs."

"What time is Becca coming over?"

"Ten."

"Oh," Clark murmured. "I guess I did come over pretty early…"

"I know that you're worried, it's alright," I said, though there was annoyance lining my voice. "I don't really know what I'm going to do, either. I told her that the Commission does experiments on the people they take in, but…not anything specific."

"It's hard for people to really understand until they see one for themselves," Clark completed with a knowing nod. "If you want to desensitize her so that she will be able to handle the truths of the Commission, you need to show Mykail to her."

"You think so?"

"Yes, I do," he said. He looked at his hands nervously. "I thought a lot about what you said…and after what happened in the meeting last night, I realized that we *will* need help from outside the Commission to accomplish this."

"I was thinking about that," I agreed. "Maybe this is a horrible thing to say…but…I want to see Becca's reaction so I can try and understand how the people would react if they were to see one of the experiments."

"It would be different, though," Clark noted. "There's really no way to know how the people will react. It all comes down to how it's presented."

I sat in the seat I was next to, picking at the wood grain of the table with my nail.

"I've been thinking…"

"About?"

"Thomas Ankell used the college campus of Stanford to kick-start the revolution, right?"

"Yes."

"Well…he was really far away from the government. I mean all the way across the country. So, he had some time to act and then hide, but we're *in* Central. We have no time to hide if we start rallying people. So maybe we need to do things a little differently than Thomas Ankell."

"How so?"

"Use the internet," I suggested.

"Dana can track the source easily."

"You've hacked into the system of the Commission before, though, right?" I said. "You're good at stuff like that. There has to be a way."

"That really depends on what you want to do."

"Mass emails, pop-ups on random sites, things that grab people's attention and make them curious," I elaborated. "Like…something with a picture of one of the people in the Commission—not anyone of racial minority—so that way people can start to think about it without scaring them. Maybe with something that says: 'What is the Commission of the People doing to people?' just to promote thought."

"Something like that…" I could see the gears turning in his head. "Social media would be the best way to get our message to people our age…but it's so easy to track those. A mass, simultaneous attack would be the best way to cover our tracks."

"How could we do that?"

"That's the tough part…unless you wanted to get the IP addresses of all the computers in the country—" He stopped and his eyes went wide.

"What?"

"Oh my God, it's possible…"

"What? What's possible? To get a list of all computers?"

"Every computer that accesses the internet registers on a list that is monitored by the Censor Board. Those IP addresses and the sites that these computers visit are recorded and cross checked to be sure that illegal sites are not being accessed. The central computers for this process could potentially be turned around to send the same thing to all computers across the country in mass."

"*Really?*"

"It's possible, but it wouldn't be easy. That place is heavily guarded and security would be hell on earth…not to mention I would have to know what kind of system they run in order to reverse the signals to send something…"

"But just once wouldn't be enough," I said. "It would have to be sent multiple times. The more times the message is sent, the more likely the people will question."

"I guess…it could be a virus," Clark mused. "The best way to do this without it shutting down is to program it right into the main computers of the Censor Board, rather than hack in and do it from another computer."

"Is it even possible to do that? Get into the Censor Board computers?"

"I don't know," Clark admitted. "I think the first thing would be to decide the message we want to send the people and program something to send the message continuously at random periods to be sure that no pattern is traced."

"But just that might not be enough," I said. "We should try and find a way to get on the national news with something, or even use good old-fashioned paper fliers."

"The paper fliers might be difficult…"

"Mykail had an interesting idea," I added. "At parades, you know how people generally spread coupons? What if we were to send these fliers to people who were spreading the coupons and they spread them at the parades?"

"That would be dangerous for the people spreading the fliers." Clark's face scrunched in contemplation. "And what parades? There are so many different parades around this time of year."

"Exactly. We send our fliers to the committees that are preparing the parades that happen close together and then it's harder to track where the fliers come from, particularly if we send them all over the country."

"Except that there is a return address when you send something," Clark pointed out.

"Who says that we send it?" I said. "There are truckers and transport companies going all over the country all the time. We find someone going that direction and say that the Commission demands these be sent to where they're going."

"We would probably have to wait until the electronic messages have been going around for a while so that people are more likely to recognize the message on the fliers."

I smiled, feeling adrenaline coursing through me as we brainstormed the plot of our rebellion.

"We would have to be very careful, though," he added. "We have to make sure that very angry people, like Dean, are not causing too much of an obvious scene to undermine the whole operation."

"Yeah..."

"Maybe Dean could be Dana's distraction," Clark concluded. "If he's keeping Dana busy by poking him like he did last night, then *we* could work without him breathing down our necks as much."

"That might work."

"Okay, so tomorrow, we should do three things," he said. "We should see what that book in the Commission library says, I should look up those addresses, and we should see what kind of system the Censor Board is running to plan the message for the people."

"Sounds like a plan."

For another fifteen minutes, we discussed our list of tasks for Monday, both of us clearly feeling exhilarated by our plans as we were gesticulating emphatically and our words were becoming faster and louder as we continued to scheme. But eventually, we circled back to the three tasks for Monday and conversation trailed off. Clark nodded and drummed his fingers on the table, his face becoming confused.

"Um...shouldn't you let Mykail out of his room for this?"

I mentally kicked myself as hard as I could. Of course Clark thought that Mykail was still locked up. Mykail obviously understood that enough to stay where he was until I came to get him.

"Oh, right," I gasped, trying not to overact, even though I knew I was failing horribly. "I'll be right back."

Following my hurried declaration, I jogged up the stairs to Mykail's room. I reached his door and saw him laughing into his hand, having heard us downstairs when I realized I had forgotten to "let him out."

"It's not funny!" I snapped quietly, though I was grinning, flushed with embarrassment. He took a deep breath to calm his laughter as I tried to open the door as loudly as possible. Mykail took my hand as he stepped out.

"Take a deep breath and calm down," he said. "You're going to have to learn how to hide when you're flustered."

Agreeing, I took a deep breath and schooled my expression as we both started down the back stairs.

"Are you hungry?" I asked over my shoulder, surprised at how natural I sounded.

"No, thank you," he said, playing along.

We crossed the small living room and entered the kitchen, where Clark stood to greet Mykail.

"Mykail."

"Clark," he greeted in similar fashion. "How are you?"

"I'm well, thank you," Clark said, his tone also stiff and uncomfortable. "You?"

"I'm well."

"Okay," I said to try and break the tension, "are you sure neither one of you are hungry?" I asked, realizing it was going to be extremely awkward waiting for Becca with the two of them barely trusting one another and looking one another over suspiciously.

The time was indeed uncomfortable and slow, but Clark and I took our time filling in Mykail on what we had discussed, also showing him the new notes with the addresses listed, telling him what we knew. He was curious if we had figured out who was helping, and unfortunately he had no idea who it could be, either.

When Becca finally did arrive, I told Mykail to wait in his room so we could prepare Becca as best we could before she saw him.

I opened the door and invited her in, trying not to let my nervousness show in my smile.

"Hey."

"Hey there," she greeted back. When she saw Clark, she blinked and hesitated in her step. "Clark," she said, shocked. "I didn't expect to see you here…"

"You don't need to be worried," he said, immediately understanding her apprehension. "I'm on Lily's side. I'm just here for moral support."

Becca breathed a sigh of relief, grinning widely. "I'm sorry, I didn't mean to imply—I mean, it's just—"

"I know, we're both in the Commission. You have every right to be anxious," Clark said, understanding.

"So…then I take it this is a study session?"

"Yeah," I said, walking with both of them into the kitchen and sitting down. "Do you want anything? Something to drink or eat?"

"No, I'm alright, thank you," she said. "Actually, it was really lucky you picked today for me to come over. Turns out our parents are going to the same event today."

I chuckled. "Small town…"

"So…before I forget," Clark said, turning to Becca. "I trust you, but I want you to understand that you do not know the Commission like we do, so…I'm hesitant to include you."

"Geez, Clark, way to break the ice," I groaned.

"No, I understand," she said. "I mean, I'm really nervous about the Commission, and I'm sure my fear is not a good thing in this kind of situation. But if the Commission is taken out of the picture, I will feel a lot better about our country."

"Do you really mean that?" Clark asked. "Do you have a secret that would cause you to be taken into the Commission?"

"Maybe," she said shortly, her tone clipped to tell him not to press the matter. He sighed and folded his hands together, squeezing his fingers nervously.

"Alright," he murmured. "Then can I ask that you do one thing for now until we know how this will progress?"

"What's that?"

"Will you keep your ears open for the rumors about kids taking down the Commission? Let us know what the general sentiment is, if people are supportive, indifferent…"

"I can do that," Becca agreed. "No one has been talking about the Commission being taken down, but people around school have been noticing how tense the Commish Kids have become. I guess it was the whole thing with Miranda, huh?"

"It's gotten ugly, yes," Clark said.

"Also, we need to find a way to gather everyone who is dedicated to taking down the Commission," I told her. "We need to start looking up meeting places and then figure out how to weed out the ones who are really serious from the ones who might turn around and tell Dana what we're doing, which could get us all killed."

"That will be difficult regardless," Clark added. "Dana is terrifying, and if he scares the right person enough..." He trailed off. "We will have to think very carefully about what we want to tell everyone. The less people know, the more likely we are to win."

Becca barked a laugh and we both turned to her.

"What?"

"It's just kind of ironic, if you think about it," she said. "You want to lead a revolution against the Commission because people don't know what happens inside, but you don't want the people within your revolution to know too much." She sighed and shook her head. "It's just funny how the only way to change things is to do the same thing as the institution you want to change."

An awkward five second pause passed before I turned to Clark with a purposeful gaze. He sighed heavily again.

"Speaking of knowledge," he said, standing, "it's time you understand a little more about the Commission."

"What do you mean?" Becca asked, fear clear in her voice.

"Don't worry, we're not taking you there," he said with a nervous laugh. I offered Becca a weak smile.

"Remember how I told you that the Commission runs tests on people?" She nodded hesitantly. "We're going to show you one of them."

Becca's eyes went wide and her mouth dropped open, but she made no moves to stand.

"Where?" she croaked.

"Here," I told her. "He's in the house. He lives with my family."

"Why?"

"It's...kind of difficult to explain," I told her. "Once you see him and your shock wears off, we'll tell you more."

Becca still hesitated before standing and walking slowly around the table, following me while Clark trailed behind. My stomach was knotted and I found it hard to draw in a full breath. It wasn't until we were ascending the stairs that I wondered if I was more nervous than Becca.

We reached the top of the stairs, but rather than going to my room to do my hair and makeup for Archangel as we had done in the past, I led Becca in the other direction and stepped up to the still-open cage door of Mykail's room.

"Becca, promise me you won't scream," I hissed.

"Okay…" she said meekly, clearly not confident in her oath and noticing the barred door with mortified eyes.

I stepped into the room and smiled apologetically at Mykail who was sitting on his bed, his wings resting behind him, his fingers fidgeting in his lap, showcasing his own anxiety.

Becca hesitated before turning into the room, looking over the open barred door in confusion and worry. But when she finally turned into the room, she jumped and gasped, nearly bumping into Clark as she backpedaled.

"Oh my God…"

"It's alright," I told her, motioning her closer.

"But, h-he…he looks…what *are* those?" she asked, her voice thin.

"Take deep breaths," I advised, wrapping my arm around her shoulders to steady her, though she seemed not to notice. Her gaze remained locked on Mykail, nodding weakly as she tried to draw in deep, albeit shaky, breaths. "This is Mykail. He's a part of my family."

"Hello…" he said meekly.

Becca froze. "He can speak?"

"Yes," I tried not to chuckle. "He's perfectly safe. I promise."

"Are those…" Becca turned to me, her eyes wide as she pointed. "They look like w-wings…"

"They are."

"But that's…no, no, this can't be real. You're teasing me and it's not funny," Becca said quickly, retreating a step. Remembering my own near-hysterical confusion when I first saw Mykail, I tried to be understanding of Becca's behavior, but I still felt a twinge of embarrassment and irritation at her reaction.

"The wings are real," Clark said behind her, startling her as she suddenly remembered he was there, "and they work. The Commission created him like that."

"Created him?"

"Well, changed him after they imprisoned him for being a Commission criminal," Clark corrected, his own gaze dropping to the floor.

"They turn people i-into…angels?" she asked, looking between me and Clark.

"No," Clark answered, stepping into the room to stand next to Becca and me. "Mykail was given wings. Some are given other abilities or changed in other ways."

"Those wings…are real?" Becca whispered to me in disbelief. I smiled and motioned to Mykail.

"Go see for yourself."

"No…" She shook her head, laughing nervously and trying to retreat again.

"It's alright," Mykail said, standing slowly so as not to startle Becca further. "I don't mind."

I pushed Becca closer, feeling my own heart race as I watched her nervously approach Mykail.

I let her process what she was seeing, allowing her to walk around Mykail and touch his wings and ask him to move them. I was certain she was handling the situation very well—or at least far better than I anticipated. Judging from the small smile on Clark's face, I assumed he was thinking the same.

A few minutes later, when she had sated her initial curiosity, Mykail offered for her to sit on the bed with him and her questions began. Becca asked about the experiments of the Commission of the People and what we knew of the genetic testing. We told her that every Commission family had one experiment living with them, and that we were planning on breaking others out to reveal to the public as a way to bring light to the atrocities committed by the Commission of the People.

The remainder of the afternoon was spent watching Becca process all the new information she had received that day, answering the lingering questions as they arose. We told her it was understandable that it would be a while before she would want to talk to us because of everything we dumped on her, but she promised wholeheartedly that she would keep quiet about what she had learned, knowing the danger she was in if she said anything.

I was nervous about sending her home, but I knew I had to give her space. I remembered all too well the time it took for me to process the reality of the Commission experiments.

An hour after she left, Mark came to pick up Clark. We had agreed to start working diligently the following day, meaning that that day was our last of *talking* about our revolution. We had to take steps toward making it happen.

The sun was setting in the autumn sky when I finally closed the door behind Clark and locked it. I sighed and leaned my head back. There was no backing out now. I could not take back having shown Mykail to Becca.

My course was set, and now I had to navigate it.

I returned to the small living room at the bottom of the back stairs, watching as Mykail stood at the back patio doors, staring out into the backyard.

"I think that went well," I said, stepping up to his side.

"I do, too," Mykail said, continuing to study the colors of the sunset. "I think she'll keep her ground. She might be shaken up, but she didn't scream or faint, and that's always a good sign."

I laughed lightly. "I guess that's true."

My smile faded a little as I saw the look of longing painted across his features. He was staring into the backyard with the same desire as a starving man would look at a full meal, one of such deep desire that it spoke to a primal part of his being.

"How long has it been since you've been outside?" I asked quietly.

"I don't remember," he murmured. "Even the time I had in the Commission wasn't the real outdoors. The Dome is entirely artificial. I just..." He sighed heavily and dropped his chin. "I'm sorry."

I looked outside and then opened the door.

"Come on," I said, grabbing his hand. He smiled, but stayed put, his fingers tightening around mine to keep me from moving too far.

"I can't, Lily," he whispered. "The tracers in my body will tell Dana immediately that I went outside."

"Just one step," I insisted. "Just over the threshold. No further. Just so you can get a breath of fresh air."

"No, Lily."

"Please?" I said. "Unless he has sensors placed in the thresholds, Dana won't know unless you step away from the house a few feet. Just over the threshold won't do anything."

I actually did not know to what extent Dana would know Mykail's actions, but I was certain that one step would not hurt, and I desperately wanted to do something that could chase away the sadness lingering around Mykail's eyes. We were making moves against Dana as it was, and if Mykail could not even step over the threshold, then we would always be bowing to Dana's commands even when he was nowhere near us.

Mykail looked at the metal strip of the threshold, nervous. I squeezed his hand in reassurance and pulled the sliding door open. I wanted to see him smile when he felt the air of the outdoors again. I knew it would provide him with relief, and perhaps even renew his fighting spirit, giving him something to strive for—the day when Dana was gone and could no longer dictate if Mykail could step outside.

"I'm right here with you," I told him gently.

Tentatively, he lifted his foot and stepped over the threshold, flinching at the cold stone of the patio on his bare feet, but the smile that spread across his face was more than worth the danger. His entire body rocked forward with the exhale he released, his shoulder dropping and the wings relaxing as his gaze filled with wonder and happiness at the simple task. I was certain I even saw tears in his eyes as he stepped out, his head bent to stare at his bare feet on the slate porch in disbelief, his toes wiggling and flexing.

Stepping beside him, I squeezed his hand even tighter. He turned to me, his eyes dancing with elation.

"Just look for a minute," I whispered, turning to the setting sun over our tall backyard fence. We remained for an indeterminable amount of time, holding hands, standing in the cool autumn air, watching the oranges of the sunset permeate into reds and deep purples and finally fade to the navy of the night sky.

"We should go inside," Mykail whispered when he felt me shiver. "It's been far more than a minute."

I nodded, stepping back, trying not to notice my frozen toes and fingers. He walked in after me, his hand still linked with mine, and closed the door.

"Thank you," he whispered sincerely. He closed the space between us, kissing me tenderly, chasing away the lingering chill in my body and replacing the feeling with warm bliss.

He pulled away and ran the back of his fingers over my cheek.

"Can you do me a favor?"

"What's that?"

"Can you undo the cuffs on my wings so I can have a bath?"

For some reason—probably hormones—my heart raced and I felt myself blush hotly at the words.

"O-oh..." I breathed, unable to get my brain to think of anything better to say.

"Sorry to ask," he said. "I didn't mean to make you uncomfortable...it's just...I feel gross and I want to bathe, but..."

"No, no, it's fine." I cleared my throat, scolding myself for not being able to keep a cool demeanor following the question. "Can-can you, you know...do that on your own?"

We stood in awkward silence, both looking anywhere but at one another. Mykail let out a long exhale and I laughed quietly, biting my nail nervously.

"Okay, this is awkward." he chuckled brokenly.

"I guess it really shouldn't be," I said. "I mean...we've..."

"We've never done anything remotely close to bathing," Mykail said with a laugh. "It's okay, I'll just—"

"No," I interrupted. My cheeks felt like they were going to catch fire from blushing so fiercely. "I mean…I can…"

"You don't have to."

"I want to," I told him, finally meeting his eyes. I wanted him to know that I was not merely saying things to make him feel better about his embarrassing predicament.

When he did not move or speak, I squeezed his hand and turned, guiding him to his room. Even though I was acting brave, my heart was fluttering and my stomach was twisted tight with apprehension, excitement, and adrenaline. My hormones were taking control, but in that moment I did not care.

"I'll start the bath," I offered, breaking my hold on his hand as we stepped into the bedroom. I flew into the bathroom faster than I ever knew I could move and rapidly turned on the water before turning to the sink drawer where I knew my mother kept the keys to his cuffs. Mykail could not unlock the cuffs himself, so my mother did not worry about keeping the keys in the only place she really needed them, despite Dana's warnings when Mykail first arrived.

As I was checking the water temperature, I saw movement out of the corner of my eye. Mykail stood in the doorway, wearing his boxers.

He shrugged. "I think it's probably best if I wear these…"

I smiled and nodded in agreement, trying to keep calm at seeing so much of his skin, stepping away and motioning to the tub.

"Is this the right temperature?"

The room got smaller when he walked closer, but I did not feel claustrophobic. My heart was dancing in my ribcage, my skin growing hot, reacting the same way I did whenever Mykail kissed me. It was a warm, secure feeling of being surrounded by tenderness and affection. He gently dipped his fingers in the water while I desperately tried to stop myself from looking him over hungrily.

Maybe I *did* need to worry about my hormones taking over…

"It's perfect."

To distract myself from staring, I removed the surprisingly heavy cuffs from his wings and set them on the counter before turning to his back again. I found myself scrutinizing the creases of muscle in his shoulders and the dip of his spine into his lower back. The white of his wings outlined the area so perfectly, I could not stop the wandering of my gaze.

"Are you alright?" he asked, turning his head over his shoulder, the tendons in his neck protruding in a way that made my heart race. I never knew such a simple movement could be so arousing.

"Y-yeah," I stuttered. "How does this usually work?"

He fell silent, shaking his head.

"I feel like it would be more embarrassing if I told you how your mother bathes me," he said. I made a face at the beautiful lines of his back.

"Yeah, you're right, it would."

Mykail took a step forward, which was for his benefit as I could feel my muscles bidding the will of my hormones, ready to jump at his back and kiss every ridge. He gently put one foot in the water before stepping in completely and sinking into the water, which gently lapped at his belly as the tub continued to fill. He had to sit with his knees almost to his chest as his wings rested against the tile behind him, taking up most of the space in the bath.

I was still for several long moments before I cleared my throat and grabbed a washcloth and the shower gel, kneeling next to the tub and squeezing some gel onto the rag, more than eager to touch his beautiful skin.

"I can do that," he said, reaching for the cloth as I pulled it away.

"Not your back, and around your wings you will need help," I pointed out. There was no way I was going to pass up the opportunity to touch him. He chuckled and his hand dropped into the water.

"Alright..."

I dipped the rag into the water and rubbed it together to get the suds forming before placing one hand against the front of his shoulder and pressing the rag to the skin around his wing. I gently started rubbing the rag back and forth, watching his skin move at my touch. I moved over the main joint of the wing to the middle of his back and neck. He lifted his wing and extended it so I could duck under and get to the center of his back. I was touching the beautiful lines and curves around his spine, admiring them at the close proximity. I moved my hand back and forth across his skin with the cloth, my eyes followed his spine down and then back up to his shoulder blades, admiring his muscles, strong and taught from the weight of the wings.

"Uh...I think that spot is clean..." he whispered.

I quickly moved to scrub the rest of his back, feeling my cheeks flush again.

I finished cleaning his back far too soon for my liking and had to hand the rag to him so he could wash himself. He took it with a shy smile and I ducked behind his back again to rinse off the soap bubbles, splashing water onto his skin and entertaining myself by watching the droplets race down his back.

When I no longer had a realistic excuse to be behind him, I straightened and turned off the water, the tub three-fourths full of warm water. I remained by his side, watching him scrub down his arms and chest, effortlessly graceful. Watching him wash was almost too much stimulation for me. I was beginning to worry I would burn a hole in his skin with how intensely I was following his every move.

Unfortunately, he was so devoted to the task that he was finished far too soon, and rinsed himself off before wringing out the rag and sighing.

"Now, the really embarrassing part…"

"What do you mean?" There was no stopping the various directions my brain went with the statement.

"I can't wash my hair…"

I smiled, looking for a means to rinse his hair. He cleared his throat and pointed at a bowl my mother had in the corner by the bathtub. Using the bowl, I gathered a little bit of warm weather and gently poured it over his blonde hair.

Reaching for the shampoo, my mischievous side reared its head. With more boldness than I ever knew I had, I took advantage of Mykail's closed eyes to stand and slip out of my jeans and peel off my shirt so I was just in my bra and panties. I tried to tell myself it was no different than wearing a swimsuit. I climbed into the tub, sitting atop his legs.

"What are you—" He stopped immediately when he saw that I had partially stripped. He was too shocked to speak at first, so I used his stupor to snatch the shampoo, squirting some into my palm and rubbing my hands together before threading my fingers through his hair.

His hands settled at my waist. The bath felt much hotter than before, my attention focused almost entirely on the feeling of his fingers pressing into my waist and the feeling of his hair passing through my fingers. His eyes were closed against the suds, but seeing the expression and feeling the way his grip flexed and loosened against my skin made the situation feel far more intimate.

The shampoo foamed around his hair as I worked my fingers over his scalp, loving the closeness. I worked over the sides of his head above his ears before lifting myself up to work my fingers through the hair at the back of his head. I did not miss how this positioned my chest close to his face.

Even though his eyes were closed, he must have known, because he leaned forward and his lips pressed to my sternum just above the lace flower in the middle of my bra. I could feel his breath over my sensitized skin, fanning between my breasts. Electricity seared my entire body, amplified by the water, causing us both to be hit by the charge.

He ran his nose up my sternum as I wrapped my fingers in his hair, though not for the purposes of washing. It was to keep steady as my body reacted to him. I closed my eyes and let out a shaky breath as his lips moved over my skin. One of his hands skirted up my skin to the back of my bra. I felt my blood turn to lava in my veins, thinking he would undo the bra, but he instead fisted it tightly. His other hand wrapped around my lower back to pull me even closer so my hips were pressing close to his.

His lips moved over to the swell of my breast exposed above the bra, sucking a mark to life. I gasped and my hips instinctively pushed further forward at the sensation, my fingers tightening in his hair.

With agonizing slowness, his hand released the back of my bra and ran down to my hip as his body shivered with the attempt to restrain himself.

"This is dangerous…" he whispered.

"I know," I breathed weakly, scraping together the coordination to untangle my fingers from his hair.

I grabbed the bowl to splash water over his head and rinse out the shampoo.

"You should…probably…"

"No, you need conditioner now," I protested weakly. "I'll behave."

"I won't," he chuckled weakly.

"Try?" In truth, I did not *want* him to behave. I was perfectly fine with continuing our dangerous flirtation with how far we could go before losing control of ourselves.

He laughed, his eyes still closed, shaking his head.

"Do you have any idea…how difficult that is right now?" His fingers tightened on my skin. "You drive me crazy."

"I know the feeling," I breathed heavily, feeling my blood pump furiously through me.

"Please…you should go…"

I did not listen. I grabbed the conditioner, massaging it through the wet tendrils of hair, concentrating very hard on not making the act sexual. As soon as I could, I rinsed his hair and pressed my forehead to his, both of our mouths open and our heady breaths mixing in the air between us, mounting the palpable tension once again.

"I'll go…" I murmured.

But I could not move immediately. Every cell inside me was crying to stay put, but I knew we weren't ready to jump that far in our relationship, particularly in the dangerous circumstance that *was* our relationship. I begrudgingly pulled away from him and stood, stepping out of the bath and bending to pick up my clothes.

"I, um, I'm going to change and make dinner," I said quickly. "Just…find me when you're ready."

I scampered out of the bathroom, thankful my skin started to cool the further I got from the bathroom.

Chapter Thirty-Four

The rest of the evening had been awkward for both me and Mykail. There was something powerful and heavy between us and the taste of it lingered on our tongues long after we had redressed after the bath. I knew that we had both come dangerously close to losing control of ourselves, and there was a sliver of disappointment in me that we had not gone further.

My hormones refused to be silenced. All through the night and at the most inconvenient times during school on Monday, I replayed what had happened in the tub and my entire body ignited faster than dry timber. Even refastening Mykail's cuffs in the kitchen before dinner had me hot and bothered because I got to admire his muscles in different lighting.

"Miss Sandover," Mr. McDermott called on me when I was daydreaming about the muscles on Mykail.

"Yes?" I said, snapping back to the present.

"What do you think?"

I looked around the class, noting the eyes turned to me. I laughed and cleared my throat.

"I'm sorry, what was the question?"

"Did you do the reading?" Mr. McDermott asked, holding up the book for example.

"Yes, I did," I told him truthfully.

"Okay, then come back from your estate in LaLa Land," he teased. "I asked what kind of reasoning Thomas Ankell gave for his behavior toward the revolution and his son."

"Well, his son was just a baby, and a lot of people gave Ankell a hard time for being a teen parent, especially since Janice came from such low roots and her own mother was a teen parent. But Ankell used his son as a metaphor in his speech for the future that he wanted for America. He wanted to give every child of America the life they deserved because the past was not what defined us, but what we did with our future."

"So you *did* do the reading," Mr. McDermott complimented. "Good. Why do you think he used this technique? It seemed to work, didn't it? Riled the people up, got them ready to march at the Stanford campus…"

"Well, it made Thomas Ankell seem more human," I said a little quieter, not as sure of my answer. "He loved his son and it proved that he had a personal connection to a better future."

"Exactly," Mr. McDermott said. "He appealed to the hearts of everyone. He didn't speak to their wallets or their school careers, or anything like that. He spoke to the hearts of people, to wanting to be happy and have what made one happy because that was what the founding fathers based this country on—bettering oneself."

He turned to look at the clock and sighed.

"Alright, you have two minutes before class ends, so get out of here," he laughed. "Don't forget your papers tomorrow!" he yelled over the din of students packing up their books.

As I walked out of class, Taylor and Jill caught up to me.

"Hey, where were you in class?" Taylor laughed. "You were completely out in space."

"I'm just tired…" I said lamely. "Where's Becca?"

"She had a dentist appointment," Jill answered. "She'll be here by lunch."

I was not only zoning out in class, but also at lunch. Even the awkward stare I shared with Becca couldn't stop me from fantasizing about Mykail. In fact, it made me think about him even more, since the events of yesterday would play in my head all the way up to our time in the bathtub.

I watched the asphalt pass under my feet as I approached the car where Mark was waiting. He greeted me in his usual sweet, silent way, and I smiled. Somehow, facing him made me more embarrassed about the dirty thoughts that had been playing through my mind all day, as if he could see right through me and see what I had been obsessing over.

Clark arrived only a few minutes after me and in near-silence we were driven to the Commission. After a few minutes of quiet, Clark casually asked how my day had been to strike up conversation, though the topics were general and light, hiding the fact that we both knew that we would be starting our path to treason that afternoon.

After the now-routine process of checking in, we descended into the depths of the Commission of the People, sharing silent looks behind Mark's back.

We found an open conference room, where we set our bags down and looked at one another awkwardly, not sure how to begin.

"So, what do you want to do?" I said stupidly.

"I actually wanted to look some things up in the library," he said, trying to sound casual, though the sentence was forced. "Would you like to join?"

"Sure," I said too quickly to be natural. We smiled awkwardly, silently agreeing that we needed to work on our acting skills.

Clark told Mark to stay put and that we would be in the library, but neither of us were sure he understood the command. He remained where he was, though, as we walked away.

I was worried about running into Dana on the way to the library, that somehow he would know what we were starting, stop us, and then throw us into the holding cells that very day. But the hallways were empty and quiet, darker than usual with the mood in which I was walking them.

We went into the library as naturally as we could manage and Clark locked the door behind us.

"So," he started, reaching into his pocket and pulling out the most recent notes, "do you want to find this book and I'll go dig up the city plans for the addresses?"

"Sure."

"I don't know what use that book will be, but maybe there's something between the pages," he said. "From what I could guess with this really bad map, the book should be along that wall," he said, pointing. "The numbers are on the shelves, so you should be able to find it with that."

"Okay."

"I'll meet you at the middle tables," he pointed to the spacious center of the room filled with several large, heavy-looking tables. With a nod, he left me to search.

I walked along the wall, scanning the numbers to see if I was anywhere close when it suddenly occurred to me that there were likely cameras all over the library. I tried to casually glance around, spotting one of the dark orbs above one of the shelves, though I was certain that there had to be several that were carefully-hidden to document every move in the library.

Getting nervous, I continued to look for cameras more than the book I was trying to find. I hoped that the book was not a suspicious title, and that the cameras would be unable to read the title of the book the mysterious notes had suggested we find.

I ran my fingers along the spines of the books as I walked, looking down at the piece of paper again, double-checking the number to make sure I had not already passed it while searching for cameras.

Even in such tense moments, my thoughts drifted to Mykail, my pondering about what he would say about our plotting leading to more lustful imaginings. I mentally slapped myself for letting my daydreaming get out of hand yet again—the situation was far too dangerous to let my hormones get the best of me.

As I neared the section of numbers where the book would be, I slowed and scanned carefully until I came across the black spine that read History of the American Banking System: A Comprehensive Study.

"How the hell is this supposed to help?" I grumbled, grabbing the book and kicking myself for getting so worked up about the cameras. I opened the heavy book and leafed through the pages but the text looked normal and there were no notes written in the margins or envelopes tucked in the pages. I flipped through it a few times, a little slower each time just to be sure, more and more disappointed when nothing magically appeared in the pages.

I sighed and looked at the shelf it came from, seeing the other books on banking systems on either side of the empty spot. I was about to return to the center tables, the book tucked under my arm, hoping Clark found something more interesting than I had, but I stopped, staring at the empty space on the shelf.

Nervous about being spotted by the cameras, I bent down to peer into the gap. There was a black bar jutting out parallel to the wall that was set into a recessed area of the wall. I carefully put the book I was holding on the floor and reached back to touch the cold, metal bar. I pulled on it, feeling it turn, though it stopped at a quarter turn, catching on something. I tried to rotate the handle further, my mind already deciding that the bar was the way to open a secret door behind the bookcase.

I prayed I was in a blind spot of the security cameras.

Taking a deep breath and shaking off the feeling that I was being watched, I tried to turn the bar again, trying to use two hands in my struggle to turn the bar.

"Clark?" I called quietly, even though my voice echoed through the bookshelves.

"Yeah?"

"Can you come here and help me?"

"Can't find it?" I heard his footsteps coming down the stairs from the second floor and, a minute later, he was by my side, looking puzzled as to why I had my hands between the books.

"There's a handle," I whispered.

"You're kidding…" Once I stepped back, he reached between the books to confirm before he backed away, his eyes wide with surprise. "Where to?"

"Don't know," I said. "I can't turn it by myself."

"I really hope we're in a blind spot," he murmured, glancing around before motioning me to reach for the handle again, both of us grasping what we could of the bar. "One, two, three."

We both pulled hard on the handle and, with some strain, managed to turn it. I heard a click and a hiss followed by silence. The door didn't open.

Confused, I pushed on the back of the shelf and felt it give a little, but then fall back into place.

"Is there another one on the other side?" I asked. We both moved to the other end of the bookshelf, removing the books to reveal a second handle. After turning that one to a perpendicular position, I motioned for Clark to go to the other end and push, my heart in my throat, threatening to come out of my mouth if I dared to speak.

There was no need to push hard on the shelf, it moved away easily, wheeling itself on a track into the wall. We were able to peek around the half-hidden shelf into the passage it hid. There was a dark hallway with one light that flickered to life when the shelf had opened, though the bulb struggled to fight the sheer darkness beyond. I carefully stepped into the short hallway, staring at the single door at the other end.

"Stay here," Clark whispered, stepping forward delicately, as if worried the floor would give out from under him.

He moved carefully and quietly, reaching the other door without problem as I held my breath, excitement and adrenaline keeping me from moving as I watched him pass under the single light and reach the other door. I watched with my heart racing as he opened the other door slowly, pressing his ear to the crack in the door to listen for noise before peering into the other room.

"Holy shit…" he gasped, closing the door quickly, but quietly. He shuffled back down the hall, motioning for me to back away, which I did, fear rocketing through me that we had been caught.

"Close it, close it," he whispered, slipping through the narrow opening and helping me pull the bookshelf closed, hearing it click into place again.

"What is it?" I barely managed to choke out.

"It's the records room," he whispered. My eyes shot wide. "We can sneak into the records room from here."

"No way…"

He nodded and took a deep breath, swallowing hard, trying to calm his own adrenaline.

"I've looked over the blueprints of the Commission before, but I never saw anything about a passage connecting Records to the library," he hissed. "Now I wonder how many other secret passages there are."

"How did this person know about it?" I asked, motioning the shelf over.

"I have no idea," he said. "But I'm starting to realize that whoever is sending us these notes is serious about this. That's something...I mean, *sneaking* into Records..."

"We should go in there and look around," I declared.

"No, not yet," he said, grabbing my elbow to stop me from pushing the shelf open again. "We need to check the camera feeds and make sure we're in a blind spot before we go snooping."

"Good point."

"Come on, grab the note. I'll show you the city maps I found."

I replaced the banking book and grabbed the piece of paper, putting it in my pocket as Clark watched.

"When you get home, burn that note."

"Done."

I followed Clark to the tables in the middle of the library where he had pulled out some massive, thin papers of the city of Central, held together by wooden boards. I stared at the thin, blue lines across the map, feeling completely overwhelmed by the small print. He chuckled, seeing the startled look on my face.

"It's alright," he assured. "This is actually fairly easy to use." He grabbed the book sitting at one corner of the map and opened it, flipping to a page and turning to show me a table explaining the new address system.

"The city is divided into sections, which are labeled...here," he pointed to one area of the map, where a darker outline marked a section labeled '12'. "That's what the 'S' stands for in these..." he motioned to the note with the addresses. "And all of these sections are divided into four quadrants..." he motioned to the small numbers in each corner of the square. "Which is 'Q'... 'B' is for block...all of these little squares..."

"That is not going to be fun," I groaned, watching warily as the blocks became smaller and smaller.

"That's why I have this," he picked up a circular magnifying glass and set it on the map, which pulled a smile out of me, even though I was still overwhelmed.

"And 'E' is for establishment, which is the actual address," he nodded. "Okay, so," he handed me the note, "I decided that the two with the stars are ones we should pay attention to, but we'll find them all and see what this person wants us to know about these places."

"Where is the Commission on this map?" I asked, looking over the large paper. It took Clark a few seconds before he found the outer government district where the Commission of the People was located.

"So, there really is nothing behind the Commission, just open fields leading to the reservoir?"

"No one can build here. It's where the Commission extends underground," he explained.

"That would make breaking out difficult...nowhere to hide people in open space."

"We will cross that bridge when we get to it." He waved the thought away. "Right now, I'm just thinking about figuring out these notes."

"Okay, so the one with the two stars is S18," I read for him, "Q1...B009...E1-1..."

Clark followed my instructions with the magnifying glass until he found what we were looking for.

"Here?" he said, not sounding sure of himself.

"You don't know?" I teased.

"It's not that," he said. "This is the address you told me. But, why the old Mackay Power Plant?"

"The what?"

"It's been abandoned since the Second Revolution...at least, that's what I think this is. It's out in the middle of nowhere."

"Why star that address?" I mused, glancing back at the address to be sure I had read it right.

"What's the next one?"

We went down the list of six addresses and while Clark didn't know many of the exact places, he told me the addresses were all in areas where there were few people and were, most likely, abandoned buildings. One of them was quite far outside of the city limits, and another one was very close to the center of the city, so the pattern was impossible to figure out.

"They're all abandoned areas."

"Big abandoned areas," Clark concurred. He stopped and slowly turned to me, surprised. "Oh my God..."

"Meeting places?"

"Meeting places and big buildings to hide people."

I stared at the map before picking up the note with the scribbled addresses once again.

"Holy shit...who *is* this person?"

That afternoon, we cross-checked the large map with smaller maps to double check the buildings noted so that we would explore the right places. Clark jotted down the areas on the back of the note and turned to me.

"Feel like exploring on Sunday?" he asked with a mischievous grin.

We figured the person who had given us the note favored the Mackay Power Plant on the far side of the reservoir, a good distance from the Commission, but I was unsure how we would be able to get escaped Commission prisoners to the power plant without being spotted.

With our Sunday excursion set, Tuesday was devoted to figuring out if we could use our newly-found secret passage to the records room. Clark set up his computer in the conference room while I waited anxiously. He hacked into the security system and found a live feed from the cameras, clarifying his request by going into the area dedicated to the library.

"How do you know how to do this?"

"I learned how to do it so I could watch for Dana," he said distractedly. "Okay." He backed away, showing me the screen with the twelve panels of camera feeds. "Here is the library's main floor, you can watch me from here. I also set up the alarm system right here," he motioned to his computer's task bar. "If moving the shelf or opening the door alerts anyone on the security system, it will flash red, so keep an eye on that, too. It will tell us if there's a sensor in the door."

"What if someone walks in?" I asked, looking at Mark standing by the closed door of the conference room.

"Hit escape. It will shut it down automatically. And don't move the computer from this spot. I have no idea if these cameras are live or not, but your body should block the screen from the cameras behind you," he explained. I took his seat as he stood. "I'll call you."

He tapped the phone in his pocket and I nodded, being sure my phone was right next to the computer to answer his call.

When he left, I took a deep breath to settle myself. I prayed our secret passage was secure enough to be used without detection. We had been so concerned about triggering alarms that we debated locking it again the previous day. But when we decided that we would check the security mainframe the following day, we chose to leave the shelf in place, but not locked, so that Clark could check the passage without fighting with the weight of the locks.

I waited quietly, my stomach tumbling anxiously as I watched the camera feeds. It still took Clark a while to get to the library, and I found my mind wandering back to Mykail despite the severity of our situation.

The previous night we had been very careful around one another, not touching other than holding hands, worried that we would both lose control completely.

The more I thought about actually having sex with Mykail, the more appealing the idea became. If Mykail hadn't been so careful about our relationship, we might have had sex in the bathtub that night. While I was sure I would not have minded, I knew our relationship was dangerous enough, and I had to be sure that I could handle it before we added sex into the mix.

My mind was torn off of Mykail when my phone buzzed on the table. I quickly answered.

"Hello?"

"Hey, can you see me?" Clark's voice asked.

I looked around on the twelve panels of the screen, spotting him by the door, his phone to his ear.

"Yep."

"Okay, follow me and I'll let you know when I'm standing in front of the bookshelf."

I watched his figure move out of one frame and into another, eyeing his steps carefully to see where he would stop. He disappeared completely for several seconds twice before reappearing in the next frame.

"There are a lot of blind spots…" I breathed, unable to keep the hope out of my voice.

"It makes sense," Clark murmured. "This place is large and the shelves make it difficult for everything to be visible. This place would be loaded with too many cameras to watch if they wanted to catch every inch."

"Are you close?" I asked, watching him walk into one frame.

"Almost." I watched him disappear from frame. "Can you see me?"

I scrutinized each frame closely.

"No," I said, a smile spreading over my face as I double-checked each panel.

"I'm standing in front of it," he said, his voice filled with the same disbelief and intense relief I felt. "You really can't see me?"

I looked over the frames once again, checking each edge and corner before I laughed.

"No, I can't."

"Okay, I'm going to go into the hallway. Tell me if any alerts pop up on the screen."

I heard him push the shelf and a series of soft clicks as the passageway was opened. I watched the security alert system Clark had set up, but nothing happened.

"Nothing."

"Good," he breathed. "I'm going to try the door to Records, now."

I had to hold my breath yet again.

After what seemed like an eternity, Clark's voice came over the phone again.

"Anything?"

"Nothing," I breathed, my lungs finally working again.

"I'm going to look around here for a little bit. I'll look for some places to hide, too, just in case we ever get walked in on."

"Sounds g—" I stopped and jumped when Dana opened the door to the conference room. I was so caught off-guard that, for two seconds, all I could do was stare at him. He smiled at me as he closed the door behind him.

"Lily?" Clark's voice hissed in my ear. "What is it?"

"I said, sounds good, Mom," I said carefully. I measured my speech, being sure not to speak too quickly. I glanced at the computer screen and sighed as if bored, carefully hitting the escape key to close the camera feed and pull up Clark's English essay as Dana walked around the table, patiently waiting for me to finish my conversation. "I'll see you when I get home." Clark had gone very silent, understanding immediately that someone else was in the conference room. "Okay, bye."

I hung up the phone and sighed, turning to Dana as he sat on the table next to me, one leg swinging carelessly, the other still touching the ground. His glasses were off, leaving me under the full assault of his molten-gold gaze.

"How's your mother?"

"Off limits," I snapped. He straightened, his grin growing wider.

"Ooh, there's some bite in you today," he chuckled. "I was just trying to be polite."

"I saw you being polite with her at the meeting on Saturday."

"Oh, that was just a little flirting," he said. "Are you jealous?" He gently placed a hand on my hair, looking at me with his seductive power. "Would you rather I pay attention to you?"

My hormones had already been out of control due to Mykail, so the touch was more electric than it should have been. I wanted to blame my hormones more, but his eyes held me in their captivating power, and I knew there was a part of me, some animal instinct inside me, that was jealous and craving his attention.

"No," I snapped, pulling my head out of his reach, trying to put it out of my mind that I found Dana attractive at all.

He leaned over, looking at Clark's essay on the computer.

"Where's Clark?" he asked, straightening when he was satisfied knowing what was on the screen.

"Bathroom," I said a lot more naturally than I expected.

"I came to tell you that I will be at your house Thursday evening."

"What? Why?" I asked, terrified.

"Mykail needs his shots," Dana said. "I'll come over around nine in the evening. If you could pass that information on to your parents, I would appreciate it."

"Do you have to do that for all the experiments you give away? Is it your way of checking up on what the families are doing?"

"That is a good idea, but no," Dana corrected, his rich voice rolling easily from his lips. "Just Mykail. He's a special case."

"Of course," I groaned. "You and your special cases..."

"Speaking of, you seemed pretty fascinated in Eina at the meeting," he noted. "He's amazing, isn't he?"

"What do you plan to *do* with him?" I pressed. "Or any of the experiments for that matter? You can't give them all away, so what do you do with the others?"

"A lot are sold to other countries as elite soldiers or intelligence personnel. The rest are kept in the back."

"You're not worried about those other countries exposing the Commission or using the experiments to attack America?"

"The contracts are very specific," Dana explained vaguely. "It's all very peaceful, I assure you."

I rolled my eyes, leaning back in my chair with a sigh.

"You really do just live in your own little world down here, don't you? Controlling everything perfectly like a god?"

"You're part of that world now. Do I control *you*?"

"No."

"Are you sure?" he pressed. "Because I see fear in your eyes and hear the tremble in your voice. I see the way you react whenever I am near you."

"You don't control me," I said. "And fear seems to be a response you want in people, so you search for it."

"Don't assume to know what I look for in people, Little Lily," Dana said in a condescending tone.

"How often are you in the back of the Commission?" I asked. "Obviously you resurface every now and then, but how often are you back there with the experiments? Do you even know what real people are like anymore?"

Dana laughed.

"What?"

"You amuse me," he said. "*Real* people? This is a far cry from your previous arguments about how I needed to treat people fairly, even if they were criminals."

Open mouth and insert foot... I ground my teeth together, embarrassment gripping my chest.

"Actually, it is a valid point to make," he admitted. "I likely know *real* people better than anyone. The purest cases of humanity are in the back of the Commission right now. It's true that humans are all the same at their core, but there is always a variation in each individual. And after all the experiments I have run, I can look at anyone in the population and know exactly how to break them on the table."

"You have a heightened sense of your own importance, don't you?" I finally managed to say after the five seconds I took to shake off the shiver that ran through my body at his bold declaration.

"No, I know exactly how important I am," Dana said. "And I know how to read people. For instance, you are a rare case, Little Lily. You would be like that eighteen-year-old who became the thing that killed Bryant Morris. It would take forever to break you, and everything would have to be timed just perfectly, but you would break just like he did."

While I should have been mortified at the promise in his words, my mind focused more on how likening me to Mr. Morris' favorite experiment meant that Dana thought I could get close enough to Dana, fascinate him enough, to get a shot at killing him.

"Take a walk with me," Dana said, standing straight and offering his hand. I accepted without hesitation, only questioning my compliance after my hand was in his. I hardly remembered standing and placing my hand in his, which scared me more than following Dana to wherever he was leading me.

I walked in silence, struggling to keep up with his long stride.

I wasn't expecting to walk to the security station that led us into the Enterprise labs. Dana simply flashed his card to the security desk and they nodded, letting him through with me in tow. We stepped into the termination cells without speaking to one another.

"You want to know about humanity? Look at the experiments back here," Dana said as we started to walk the hallway between the cells of failed experiments. "We don't change humans, we amplify what is inside them. Well, with the exception of Eina, of course. We added to him."

I did look at those in the termination cells, but mostly for the purpose of examining the cell layouts and devising a way to break out the experiments. The cells were barren and bland, a small wall barely concealing a tankless toilet. A thin gutter ran through the middle of the room, but otherwise there was nothing adorning the walls, cement floors, or high ceiling. I stopped without meaning to in front of one cell where an older man, laying on the floor, did not even bother to lift his head. I studied every corner and cranny of the cell.

Dana's hand found my shoulder, and his mouth came close to my ear.

"Come, let me show you the experiments that I give away."

I followed Dana obediently, scanning the hallways for ventilation shafts or drains in the floor. The grates covering the ventilation system were too small for a person, and the drains in the middle of the floor were the same, thin gutters covered with slatted metal.

Dana led me through the termination cells and past the first large hallway into Ward Three.

"I've wondered something," I said, gathering all my courage. Dana stopped and turned to face me, leaning against the cell next to us and waving at the experiment inside that stared at him frightened.

"Ask away."

"Why do you give away experiments? Aren't you worried someone will find out about the Commission's deeds by seeing a loose experiment?" I asked, still looking around the ward so I did not meet his piercing gaze.

"As I've said before, people already know that the Commission is not the textbook-clean operation they would like it to be, but it's still a more honest operation than almost every major American company that ever came into being."

"You really believe that?"

"I do. We don't pretend that what we're doing is for a different cause. Yes, we are making weapons out of humans, and almost everyone knows that we fund the training of our military soldiers, they just don't know that we're trying to build an even better soldier." Dana sighed and also looked around the bright hallway, smiling thinly. "As for the Commission members and their gifts, most of them can pass as regular humans without much difficulty, so there's not as much need to hide them. There are only three or four I can think of where special care must be taken to keep them hidden. But I only entrust those gifts to members I know to be loyal, or those to which I hold a particular fondness."

I crossed the hall to the opposing cell, counting how many steps it took to cross the hall, before casually walking in front of the cell, pretending to ponder what Dana had said as I counted seven steps from one side of the cell to the other.

"Little Lily, do you really believe that we take people without reason? There are laws. We only take criminals who have broken the laws of Central. By the time they're in one of these cells," he tapped his knuckle against the thick glass, "they're no longer human. We can do what we want with them. The law says so."

"They are still human," I snapped. "They all feel the same pain and joy as we do. They may have different life experiences but that does not make them less than human. If anything, we're *worse* than anyone in these cells because we *think* that they're below us."

"You think so?" Dana challenged. "You think pain defines a human being?"

"I think it's what connects us to one another, if we can empathize with it."

"That's a very interesting point you raise," he said. "Some would argue that the pain humans feel is what makes us closer to animals, whereas what makes us human is our ability to rationalize and move through that pain. And as far as empathy is concerned, every human cares for one another differently. Most can empathize with only a select group of individuals but not others. But I am in agreement with you, Little Lily. The only thing that spans the species is instinct—pure, simple animal instinct. Fear, hunger, lust…"

Dana stood straight, stepping across the hall toward me with the measured steps I recognized all too well. I stood my ground, both hanging on every word and intently watching how close he drew.

"Society is what changes those instincts. Rules and regulations touting the ideals about equality give people the false idea that everyone is equal, but the fact is, we're not equal, not when society says we are, and not when society represses basic instincts in hopes for creating equality. All human instinct knows is survival. Society and politics can put whatever spin they want on it, but in the end, the struggle every human goes through is simply to sate the animal instincts inside. Humans in power, those who are not equal to the others but are the first to say all humans are the same, first used religion to keep those below them in line. And the backbone of most religions is the human struggle to ignore those animal instincts in the hopes of achieving some higher purpose in life. And as religion, society, and humans grew and evolved, everyone became so focused on their goals, those greater purposes, working toward something that you can conceptualize somewhere in the future, rather than how they feel in the moment."

"Then humans aren't controlled by their instincts," I said, amazed I had kept my stance as he stopped with only a single stride between us. "They're controlled by purpose."

"Every animal has a sense of purpose—survival," he corrected. "Humans have warped and perverted the idea. The reason people are so horrible to each other is because we have to be in order to get ahead. We're all animals, even though society and religion and politics and talking heads on television try to convince everyone otherwise. Humans are horrible because of the repression of that beast within, that selfish, wonton creature that we all pretend we don't have inside us comes out in horrific, manipulative ways when humans use rational thought to translate its desires."

"I don't see you pretending."

"I'm beyond that," he said. "The only thing I will give to all that bullshit about humans being unique is that they are. So drastically different from one another in the way they handle that beast within. There is no such thing as equality, Little Lily. Unless you mass-produce humans on a conveyor belt, they will never be exactly the same."

"That's why we *teach* people," I said. "We don't lock them up and mutilate them because they're not the same as us."

"Can you see Mykail as your equal? Even though he has wings?" Dana asked. I nodded, though my head felt wobbly on my neck. "Do you think he sees *you* as his equal? He knows he could kill you with one strike of those wings. Do you think he doesn't think about that? What about Mark? Do you see him as your equal, even though he could snap your neck before your body even registered that he had touched you?"

"But you created them like that."

"And nature created humans black, white, tall, short, fat, thin, strong, weak, from one area of the globe or another," Dana continued. "The only thing that is equal about them is the fact that they feel fear. You may see someone as an equal, and you might be lucky enough to have them see you as an equal, but with society breathing down people's necks, someone is bound to notice you're not on the same level as one another."

"Then what would you have humans do?" I challenged. "Not try at all? Hurt and kill people further?"

"You're advocating the very same by wanting to free these people." He motioned to the ward around us.

"And I guess I'm advocating it by being a part of the Commission as well, so I can't win."

Dana grinned. "Now you're understanding."

"Understanding what?"

"The concept of survival and purpose," he answered. "You know you can't win either way, but you are using your rational mind to weigh which is the lesser discomfort to your moral compass. And it's that rationalization that will lead us to have fun little debates like this until you can no longer try to convince me otherwise."

"I'm never going to believe that you do good by doing this," I declared.

"And that's what I love about you." His fingers lifted, dancing over my cheek as I tried to back away, my back hitting the cold glass of the cell behind me. "You have a power inside of you, Little Lily, and it is growing with every passing day. I want to nurture that power." He started to lean closer, but I wiggled away and stepped to the side, trying to keep my heart from beating too fast as the hormones and adrenaline pumped through my veins. "I can hardly wait to see where it takes you."

"Are you going to show me around, or not?"

Dana bowed his head in a nod, turning to lead me through Ward Three as I tried to calm down.

"So, does this do it for you?" I said, feeling bolder from the adrenaline following our previous conversation. "Turning people into these creatures? Does it get you off or something?"

"I love your adorable attempt to be crude," he teased, "but it *is* exhilarating. You can't even imagine." Dana walked through the far doors of Ward Three into the hallway that led us to Wards Four, Five, and Six. He led me toward Ward Five, which had two guards standing outside the door. "Watching them react to the tests, seeing the results for yourself, feeling the power you're giving them…"

His voice was doing that thing again—that seductive, honey-laced tone that made me shudder. I desperately wanted my body to stop reacting to the husky tones of his voice.

"You can become the god of their lives," he continued, swiping his card over the pad next to the door, the two guards bowing their heads to him as we entered the ward.

"You are really full of yourself, aren't you?"

"I wish," Dana said. "There are certain areas of myself that I just can't fill the same way…I'm sure you understand."

His hand pressed to my lower back and I became acutely aware of every cell on my body, sure I could even feel the molecules of air moving over my skin, cooling me from the fire that raced through my veins at his warm touch. I trembled as we walked down the center hall of Ward Five, following Dana's guide as he walked down the brightly-lit hallway. It only occurred to me after passing two cells that we were in the ward where Mykail had been imprisoned. The knowledge that I was seeing the same sight Mykail saw every day made my heart break into pieces.

"This is the strongest of the gift wards," Dana explained as we walked. "These are the gifts I give to those I really like in the Commission." He turned a corner and we stepped out of the main hallway to another collection of glass cells. He stopped at an empty cell, which still shone bright and bland under the harsh glow of the lights. "This was dear Mykail's home when he was here."

I blinked, not expecting to be confronted with Mykail's exact cell. I could feel my chest constricting, my heart threatening to break as I thought about Mykail sitting in the cell, his wings on the floor, dressed in the same red jumpsuit. I could hardly imagine the pain and anger and boredom Mykail endured in his cell.

While I was lost in the painful emotions, Dana stepped to my back, leaning down to whisper in my ear.

"Do you want to meet his brother?"

I spun around, my eyes wide. I could feel myself slipping into the fog again, becoming overwhelmed and frightened as I was confronted with my best look at the Commission cells. I thought I had hallucinated Dana asking if I wanted to meet Mykail's brother, but my heart was still thrumming nervously, reacting to the dangerous light playing in his golden eyes. A thousand thoughts flickered through my head, wondering if we would be able to break out Mykail's brother when we stormed the Commission, though I knew that it would implicate me if I were to let my feelings for Mykail change our plan to include his brother.

Dana's smile grew as he stepped aside and motioned across the hall gracefully.

My breath caught in my throat.

There was another man in the cell across from Mykail's with wings just as white and pristine. However, he had a bar clenched between his teeth and a heavily buckled straightjacket holding his arms around him. His eyes were covered with a black blindfold and his legs were buckled to one another to keep him completely immobile as he lay flat on the cell floor.

I was frozen, staring at Mykail's brother.

"I thought it would be nice for Mykail to see his brothers again, so I made sure to always put them across from one another." Dana smiled, his arm securing itself around my shoulders as he moved to stand behind me. "You should have seen the way he screamed and called to his brother, but…he's no longer Mykail's brother. He's become a very dangerous and deadly creature…which is why we must keep him like this. Poor thing lost his grip on reality entirely the more his testing continued."

The fog of the Commission of the People had invaded my mind entirely. I could not think.

I could feel Dana's grin behind me. His fingers danced across my collarbone and up my neck until he could cover my eyes, his mouth dropping to my ear. I gasped and fell back against him before going very still, startled and weak.

"It's incredible, running these experiments," Dana whispered as his other hand positioned itself at my diaphragm. "You can make all the assumptions you want, run tests that you know work…but you never know how they will turn out. The human spirit always finds a way to effect the experiment. We can only assume that the reason Mykail was a success was because he was stronger than his siblings in some way."

I could not move, frightened and stunned, but there was a thrumming in my body that overpowered my rational thinking, reacting to his words which seemed even more potent now that I could not see.

"Is he strong, Little Lily?" Dana whispered. "Does he hold you tight when he kisses you?"

My rising fear finally emboldened me to back away from him, turning in his grip and blinking against the harsh light of the hallway as I faced Dana.

"Does he?"

"We…we haven't…"

"No?" Dana challenged, an eyebrow raising. He began closing the space between us again. I tried not to back away, to hold my ground, but I took two steps backward when his hand went to my shoulder. He followed, pulling the collar of my school uniform to the side and popping the top button off, exposing the top of my breast, where the telling bruise painted my skin. My face flushed crimson and I angrily righted my uniform.

"He thinks he can mark you?" Dana said. "Let me show you what it really means to be claimed."

In three steps, he had me pushed against the cell of Mykail's brother, his head ducking to my neck and his lips closing around the skin. I half-screamed, half-gasped, my back arching, my hips pushing against his leg as he kissed my neck hard, pinning my body to the cold glass. I tried to push him away, but he pulled away from my neck only for the time it took to capture both my wrists in his hand and pin them above my head.

His other hand skirted down my body and wrapped around the back of my thigh as his mouth returned to my neck. As I tried to struggle against his grip, he lifted my leg and hooked it over his hip.

I gasped, startled. I felt the familiar fire rage within me. Overwhelmed by the charge of electricity that shot along my nerves, I could not find the strength to continue my struggles. The more rational part of my brain was kicking myself for succumbing to the feeling, for not fighting even harder when his hands came in contact with my body, but there was something so intoxicating about Dana's very presence that I was unsure I'd ever be able to resist him completely.

His hips pushed upward and my eyes rolled into the back of my head as I let out a shuddered sigh. It felt like my entire body was on fire, pleasure consuming every inch, even with the slight pain where Dana had brought a bruise to life on my neck.

He pulled away, dropping my leg as his fingers took my chin, turning me to face him. His eyes were seductive, powerful, dangerous, and I felt my body shiver in excitement.

"How does that feel, Little Lily? Anything like that little angel of yours?"

I bit my lip to stop the moan that threatened to bubble out of me. It was that damn voice again...

"Oh...there we go..." Dana chuckled. "Seems you have tasted some pleasure but have yet to be fully sated."

Drawing in the deepest breath I could muster, I lifted my knee and pressed it against his hip, pushing him away and finally getting him to release my wrists. I did not want his touch, and I sure as hell did not want to seek the pleasure it gave me. I wanted only to feel those feelings with Mykail. I did not want to ponder why the adrenaline and fear I felt in Dana's presence brought me so much pleasure.

"Don't you know that no means no," I growled, hoping Dana could not see how my legs were shaking.

"If you want to keep fighting this, that's fine by me," he said. "I love the chase most. One day, you'll seek me out."

"Like hell I will," I sneered. I straightened my school uniform as indignantly as I could muster. "Now if you're just going to mess with me rather than show me around, I'll go back and do my homework."

"Pity," Dana said, smirking. "If you want to be boring, fine. I was going to take you to see one of the experiments in progress."

"I will definitely pass on that," I snapped, turning to walk the way we had come into the ward. Dana stayed where he was, watching me leave on quivering legs. I was so eager to get away from him that I almost broke into a run as I rounded the corner and started toward the door leading out of the ward.

"Little Lily," Dana called behind me. I stopped, but I did not turn, hearing his footsteps approach me. He came into view, pressing his key card to the door leading out of Ward Five. I quickly fished my clearance card out of my pocket and stormed through the door, Dana's voice following me. "Don't get lost."

I fled the experimentation cells. I knew I should have been petrified. I should have been running away from the dangerous predator behind me, but there was something more terrifying than Dana that I could not run from—a part of me that was enthralled by the danger, enraptured in the powerful presence and commanding voice. There was a part of me that wanted to surrender to him, I wanted to see how much more pleasure he could bring me.

That feeling within me was more terrifying than Dana himself.

I practically ran past the security office after clearing the wards, trying to find enough oxygen to breathe as a panic attack grabbed at my chest. I hurried past Sean, who seemed worried, but did not follow me.

As soon as I was in the main office area again, I leaned against the nearest wall, hyperventilating and kicking myself as hard as I could for nearly succumbing to Dana's powers of seduction. I clasped my hands over my mouth to slow my breathing, shaking, my knees wobbling even with the wall supporting me.

Once I felt able, and noticed that Dana had not followed me, I straightened myself up and turned to the left hallway, intending to return to the conference room so I could process my thoughts, but I stopped, realizing that Dana was in the back of the Commission and, therefore, out of his office. For three long seconds, I contemplated the bad decision I was about to make.

I walked quietly down the hall, scanning for anyone walking by and listening for voices as I approached the office of the leader of the Commission of the People.

Taking a deep breath, I opened the door and slipped inside, keeping my hand on the doorknob as I closed the door, contemplating leaving before I was discovered. I gathered my courage, turning away from the door to face Dana's office.

His table and desk were littered with open files, books, and papers, even the floor was scattered with piles of documents. The shelves were untidy, as if Dana had torn apart his office looking for something earlier that day.

I stepped up to his large table.

I glanced at the nearest file folder, flicking it open to find that it was the file for an experiment. I glanced over the information before sifting through the papers and looking at another experiment's file. A book opened on one large stack of files was turned to a page about Thomas Ankell's diplomacy when he came into power, another book nearby was turned to a page on the proteins of the human body. There were five or six files opened to different areas of experiments' testing and, as I looked through them, I came across one file with a large red stamp on the front that read "TO BE TAKEN OFF RECORD," laying over what appeared to be a journal. Curiously, I picked up the journal and glanced at the cover before opening the first page to see the name written inside.

Scrawled in nearly-illegible cursive at the bottom of the inside cover was the name Bryant J. Morris.

I turned to the off-record file and opened it. What I saw almost made me collapse in surprise.

Subject #41141
Testing Start: October 8
Presiding: Dr. Sam Pullman

*The Commission of the People maintains the right to apprehend all individuals who threaten the peace and security of the nation of America. Individuals residing illegally or harboring individuals who are in violation of the laws set by the Cabinet of the Leader will be brought into custody by the Commission of the People. (The Code of the Commission of the People: 13-9).

Accounts for Charge:

-Harboring Illegal Residents
-Harboring Individuals Deemed Dangerous
-Assisting Criminals
-Anarchist Activities
-Risking the Safety and Security of the Nation of America

-Sedition
-Domestic Terrorism

Name: William Kaden Sandover

William Kaden Sandover.
Experiment 41141.
My uncle. My uncle had been the experiment that killed Bryant Morris—his favorite experiment.

Chapter Thirty-Five

It was a stupid idea to take the file from Dana's office, but I felt compelled.

I had to learn more about my uncle—the man who had killed Bryant Morris. It was probably best not to know what had happened, what horrible experimentations he endured, but I needed to know why he was Bryant Morris' favorite. If I knew what had been so fascinating about him, I could understand what Dana found so interesting in Eina—and me.

I did not tell Clark or even Mykail that I had taken the file, and for the rest of the afternoon and evening, I was too terrified to open it. When I got home, I took it out of my backpack and put it under my mattress, though all I could do was think about the file, pondering its contents.

I went to talk to Mykail that night, though we kept our distance from one another again.

"Mykail…" I said slowly after we had spoken mundanely about my day. "Do you think Dana was an experiment by choice?"

"What do you mean?"

"I mean…" I sighed and lowered my head. "He said he was an experiment and that there were some things that happened off-record. Do you think he opted to be an experiment in some way?"

"As far as I know, Dana's been there forever," Mykail said. "Of course, there were always rumors among the experiments about where he came from. I wasn't around when Bryant Morris ran the Commission, but one or two of the experiments I knew had been around since the year before Bryant Morris died, and they always had theories about where Dana came from."

"What theories?"

"None of them were true, I'm sure," Mykail laughed. "Some of them were really out there…"

"Just tell me," I chuckled.

"One of them was that Dana was Mr. Morris' bastard son from one of the experiments," Mykail said skeptically with a smile.

"Can't rule it out. He's crazy enough to be, and he did say he worked under Mr. Morris at a young age."

"There was another rumor that he was taken into the Commission when he was a child and Mr. Morris adopted him to be his son and taught him about the Commission so he could take over when Mr. Morris died." Mykail sighed and his eyebrows went high. "Of course, there were the rumors that he was an alien, or even the devil incarnate on earth…"

"Still not ruling that out," I chuckled. I looked at his bedspread and picked at some of the lint, thinking carefully about how to ask my next question. "…did…did the other experiments, the older ones, ever say anything about Mr. Morris' favorite experiment? The one that killed him?"

Mykail went silent, his eyes wide. I blinked at him, surprised by his reaction. When I was about to ask what had him so worried, he spoke.

"Four-eleven forty-one is a myth."

The words felt like a slap across the face. He had to be real—I had his file under my mattress. I opened my mouth to tell him about the file, but there was something about his reaction that made me hesitant. Instead, I said,

"Why do you say that?"

"Because there is no way he could have existed. He's a bedtime story the older experiments tell the younger ones to make them think that they can be strong like him. But…everyone breaks on the table, Lily. *Everyone.*"

"I don't understand…"

"He's the superhero of the experiments, the fictional character that everyone wants to be. No test worked on him, he was immune. He never changed, he just got angrier, and stronger, and then he killed Mr. Morris and liberated the experiments…which is obviously not true."

"You don't believe he was real?"

"No," Mykail said. "None of the older experiments ever recall seeing him. Mr. Morris died of a heart attack, not by an experiment."

"Dana said he was killed by that experiment," I said.

"Dana isn't exactly a reliable source," he said. "Like I said, there is only so much the human body can take. Everyone breaks eventually. If the tests didn't do what they were supposed to do, then the tests would kill him, plain and simple."

We switched subjects, talking about the records room and how Clark and I would divide our research tomorrow. Mykail had been worried about the notes leading us further away from our goal, or even into a trap, but when he heard about the way we could sneak into the records room undetected and the meeting spots that had been pointed out, he started to feel that the mysterious note-giver truly wanted to help, which not only relieved him, but seemed to surprise him.

"Lily, I wanted to talk to you about something," Mykail said, taking my hand. I could not stop the worry and confusion that invaded my body at the tone of his voice. "I've been thinking a lot about last Sunday…"

I blushed, turning away, not wanting to tell him how much I had been thinking about that night as well.

"I want to go outside. But…as long as the tracers are under my skin, I can't," he said. "You said that Dana was coming on Thursday for my shots. Soon after that, I want to take out my tracers."

"*What?*"

"I know where they are and, if we're careful, we could remove them," Mykail said with a confident nod.

"Are you crazy?" I gasped, my brain spiraling out of control as I thought about all the things that could go wrong, particularly with my inability to handle being near sharp objects. "I can't."

"I can take out the ones in my ankles, and maybe the one in my left wrist…but the ones in my wings…I can't take those ones out on my own," he shook his head. "If we're going to be working against Dana, we're going to need to remove everyone's chips when we break them out. I'm gonna be one of those experiments."

"But…Mykail, I can't…" I hissed. "I…"

He squeezed my hand.

"I know it will be tough for you, but we need to do this…and I'm going to need to take yours out as well, to be sure that we won't be noticed when this starts moving quickly."

My stomach turned and I closed my eyes.

"I don't want to hear this," I said rapidly, my words mixing into one blurred sound.

"Lily," he said gently, "I'm not telling you that we have to do it tonight. We will have to remove mine tactfully, so that your parents don't see the wounds."

"How do you even plan to?"

"All I need is a small knife, tweezers, alcohol, and bandages," he said. "The tracers are not set deep, it doesn't take much and I'll heal quickly."

"Oh, God, I can't…" I shook my head, trying to keep my stomach from turning at the consideration of slicing into his flawless skin.

"Alright," he said, "I'll stop talking about it, but I wanted to tell you now, because I will need help. You can prepare yourself however you want."

I could not think about it at all—I didn't care how necessary it was. But my anxiety melted away when Mykail placed a hand on my hair, trying to ease me. His hand was so warm and soft and it made me melt every time he touched me.

"I'm sorry, I didn't mean to upset you," he whispered. He leaned forward and gently pressed his lips to my forehead. Even though the action was gentle and tender, it rekindled that fire within me that quickly turned into a raging bonfire. I shivered and let out a shaky breath as he pulled away.

"I...I should go..." I said weakly.

"Probably wise."

"Mykail?" I asked before I turned away. "When are we going to be able to control this thing between us?"

Mykail stared at me for a moment before he asked quietly, "Do you want to?"

"No, but I miss falling asleep in your arms," I admitted, embarrassed at how cheesy I sounded.

"I miss it, too." He took a deep breath, puffing out his cheeks. "But...I don't believe I can handle that again quite yet," he murmured. "Maybe in a few days..."

"Okay," I agreed, content with the answer for the time-being.

* *** *

I was in a gray room, looking at my chalky, pale skin in the mirror. My eyes were dark, surrounded by black circles, the cracked, dry skin of my face making me look inches from death. My hair was matted and dirty, hanging limply around my cheeks.

I was hideous, sick, worn down by life, *tired*...

I started to cry at my hideous reflection, in so much pain I wanted to break in half. I closed my eyes, tears streaming down my cheeks. When I looked back into the mirror, my tears had left black streaks down my face, darkening the appearance of my blank, exhausted eyes.

I didn't want this...I wanted more...

I closed my eyes again, willing the image in the mirror to change. Upon opening them again, I still appeared sick, tired, the cracks in my face even deeper, my skin peeling off of my body to reveal worn bones.

I closed my eyes again. Opened them again.

No change.

I drew in a breath, feeling the oxygen reach a deeper part of me than ever before, unlocking something in my diaphragm that stretched through my body, warm, powerful, and all-encompassing. I sighed as the feeling washed over me, my eyes sliding shut again. The feeling coiled around each rib, moving up my ribcage like ivy, tracing patterns over bone and flesh as it spread. The blouse I was wearing interrupted the flow of heat. Groaning in frustration, I undid the buttons on the constricting clothing, allowing my skin to breathe and the heat to move through me once again, wrapping my lungs in a protective cocoon.

I opened my eyes.

My skin was peeling off my face, the dark circles under my eyes still present, but the color of my eyes was very different—gold, vibrant, full of power that reflected back on myself. I was completely in control and yet under the spell of the vibrant color.

I felt my breathing quicken looking at the amazing color in the mirror. I touched the dark bag under my eye, trying to get a closer look at the irises when my skin flaked away at the touch, falling into the sink I was leaning over, filling the porcelain with dull, gray liquid as I scraped my fingers over my cheekbone. Yellow warmth invaded as my skin flaked, moving down my jaw and into my neck.

The soft, smooth skin of perfection surfaced under the gray. I moved my fingers over my face, peeling the dead away, watching the gray in the sink become darker and darker with the impurities that had made me so sick and tired.

My skin turned vibrant, nearly glowing, my eyelashes long and soft and my lips turning healthily red. I parted my lips to see my white teeth, barely parted, begging to bite into something.

The warmth that had spread through my body was curling around to my back, pulling me closer to the mirror, embracing me as I shed my gray.

Both hands went to my hairline, pressing my palms to my temples and pulling my hair away from my face. The hair with the texture of straw fell away, crumbling at my touch as soft, full curls, shiny and delicate, took over, framing my face as the grungy hair I had been unable to care for any longer fell to the ground.

I was beautiful, powerful, and no one would stand in my way.

The gentle press of fingers on my cheek caused me to close my eyes and my lips to part in a contented sigh. The fingers moved down my cheek to my nape, wrapping around my frail jugular securely. He was in control, and I willingly surrendered. I rolled my head back and found his shoulder as he stood behind me, strong and steady…

His hand moved from my neck to the side of my head and he pushed me upright, turning my face to the mirror again.

I opened my eyes and looked at the two of us. I matched his eyes perfectly, both of us staring at the perfection of the other. There was communication. There was understanding. He was training me to be perfect, to be what I needed to be. His hand on my head steadied me, making me stare into my reflection, seeing the creature reflected back, beautiful, raw, so full of life and desire that I wanted to fall into her spell.

He was my master, showing me what lay ahead.

His hands went to my shoulders, sliding under the blouse and pushing it from my shoulders to fall with the gray skin that had cocooned the creature. She had been wrapped in illness and banality for too long and it was time for her to unleash her power on the world, to shed the skin of society and show her truest form.

The mirror did not merely show two people with similar needs and powers. We were one creature, moving as one entity in two vessels, at our most powerful when we were together, silent, communicating in a way that never required words.

We were the completed beast.

His head dropped to my neck as we stared at our reflection, reveling in the power we possessed. We would unleash it on the world, of course, but for the moment, we needed to revel in it, to feel that warmth encompass us in a tender embrace. That embrace was not of comfort, nor peace, it was power in its purest, raw form, sparking around the edges and causing every hair to stand on end.

It was electric.

Nothing could touch us. We were above it all, on a higher level where peace was not something to chase. Peace could not compare to that feeling. It was beyond comprehension, beyond the *need* for comprehension. It simply was.

My hand moved upward to his face, slow, staring at our reflection as I pressed my hand to the curve of his warm cheek. The touch caused me to feel a sensation that made me want to moan but was too overpowering to risk breaking the moment with uttered noise. The coiling ivy of heat sparked at my fingertips and wrapped around my arm, traveling veins and transferring at nerve endings with golden power that I could see radiating off my unveiled skin.

His hand moved to my cheek as well, the same spark starting at his fingers, traveling his veins as I watched our collective energy sync together, spiraling, circling, creating something bigger, more powerful, hotter and brighter than the sun, growing with every heartbeat...

I woke with a start, my eyes shooting open, my heart racing. My brain took several seconds to catch up and realize that what had happened was nothing more than an extremely vivid dream.

Or nightmare.

I sat up and ran my hand through my hair, closing my eyes again and sighing heavily. While my mind tried to analyze the dream, I pushed the thoughts away. I did not need to think too long to figure out what had been the cause of the dream.

Dex, who had been disturbed by my sudden jump to consciousness, rubbed against my knee, rolling onto his side. I smiled and picked him up, pulling him close and hugging him as he purred against me.

"I'm in big trouble, Dex…" I breathed into his fur. Somewhere in the back of my mind, I knew where my game with Dana was going to end. I had to keep telling myself that I couldn't let doubt enter my mind, not when Dana Christenson was my opponent—but the doubt was already deeply seated.

I went to school as if nothing was bothering me, though I was constantly mulling over that Clark and I were to meet at lunch. I was unsure if Becca sensed something was wrong, as she kept looking over at me as though she wanted to say something. I wanted to talk to her as well, to confide in her, but we were never alone long enough.

When lunch rolled around, I went to the east courtyard where Clark was waiting for me.

"Hey."

"Hey."

"How are you?"

"Fine," I lied. "How about you?"

"Okay," he said, lying right along with me. "You were a little out of it yesterday. What happened with Dana?"

"He just…he got under my skin a little, that's all." I rolled my eyes. "He showed me some of the experiments."

"Oh." He nodded in understanding. "I'm sorry."

"It's fine," I lied again, shrugging it off. "So, what about the records room? Anything?"

"There are all kinds of places we could hide, and the cameras in the room are not live."

"They're not?"

"No, I searched every area of the security network and they're just in there for show."

"Why would Dana put cameras in one of the most important areas of the Commission just for show?" I said suspiciously.

"Maybe he didn't," Clark suggested. "They might have been live when Bryant Morris was in charge of the Commission, but I think only Dana, Sean, and maybe a few of the leading scientists have access to that room right now, so there's little point. Dana just has to make the scientists believe they're real and they won't try anything."

"Do you think Dana knows about the passage between the records room and the library?"

"I don't know," he admitted. "Maybe, but maybe not. Who knows if Bryant Morris kept secrets from Dana or not…"

"Some of the Legacy Commission members remember Dana was working under Bryant Morris," I said. "They remember before Dana was leader of the Commission."

"And?" Clark asked, confused.

"Aren't you at all curious about where the hell Dana came from? How he got to be the way he is? Maybe even a little about that experiment that killed Bryant Morris?"

"How do you expect to find any of that out?" Clark asked. "I mean, if you want, we can look for the experiment's file in Records, but I've looked through the documents of the Commission when Bryant Morris was in charge and, as far as I could tell, Dana was introduced to the Commission as Bryant's assistant two years before he was killed."

"Only two years?"

"He might have been there longer, but that's when the other members of the Commission met him," Clark elaborated. "I can't find any record of a "Dana" in the experiment archives or doctors' lists of Bryant Morris' time, so the records were either destroyed, or Bryant was doing things to Dana that he didn't want on file."

"We should still try and find out," I said strongly. "It could give us insight into his weaknesses."

"We'll see what we can find in Records, but I don't think Dana would leave anything incriminating in existence," he said. "I do have something I need to tell you. Dean is a few levels beyond pissed off after Saturday."

"I bet."

"So, I took the initiative and told him that I wanted to help him take down Dana, and that I had received a note from someone saying that there will be a few people at the Halloween party wearing a red scarf with a blue stripe and they will be handing out the address for where to meet to discuss taking down Dana."

"What? You got another note?"

"No," Clark answered. "The Halloween party will be our best chance to get people to show up without putting ourselves in danger of being caught. We will be in costume, as will everyone else, and everyone can feel a little easier about approaching the plan of taking Dana down if no one can figure out who they are at first. We decide on a place to meet and then we hand out pieces of paper that tell others where and tell them it is being held under the guise of an *An Angel Without Wings* study session."

"But we don't know where we want to meet," I reminded him.

"I know, but until we can figure out who we can trust, we meet somewhere else, somewhere innocent, like a park. The thing is, we can also say that we got the note from the people at the Halloween party and then no one will know that we're behind this. We can weed out the people who might turn against us, and then move to a real meeting location."

"But there's still so much to figure out," I said, my head starting to spin. "We have to find the blueprints of the Commission, find a way to break out experiments, find some place to put them—"

"We can organize it with the resources we have at the Commission, but there is no way we can execute an escape without help, so we need to figure out who is on our side and finalize any plans when we know how many people we have helping us. We need to start working faster so that Eina is not finished when we try this."

I took a deep breath. It was moving faster than I wanted, but I understood we were running on a clock. It was even worse realizing we did not know when Eina was going to be done, so we had no idea how much time we really had. I was worried that if we moved fast, we would make a mistake and our rebellion would come crashing down around us. However, if we worked fast, and enough luck was on our side, we could make even more of an impact and keep the world from finding out about the weaponized humans the Commission was creating.

"Today," Clark started, "we should discuss what we want our email messages to be. I found the type of system the Censor Board uses, but I still need time to figure out how we're going to hack into it."

I nodded.

"Starting next week, we can start sneaking into Records," he continued. "We have more than enough to keep us busy until then."

* *** *

Dana did not bother us at all on Wednesday, but the thought of him coming to my house Thursday night terrified me enough to make me feel like he was lurking around every corner. I had already made the decision to stay in my room, with the door locked, until he left, worried he would corner me yet again.

A buzzing had started around school, like a swarm of bees invading all conversations in the hallways. Nothing could be made out from the din, but something had sparked energy that engulfed the

416

school. The dull ruckus was obvious to the Commish Kids—people were angry. The Commish Kids were furious, and news of the mysterious people expected at the Halloween party seemed to be written all over their faces as they walked to and from their classes, deep in thought.

I was on a constant adrenaline high. Around every corner could be Dana with a Sweep team sent to imprison us for treason. While I was jumping at every out-of-place sound and movement, it was also an exhilarating feeling. I was never relieved when the adrenaline wore off. As soon as I found myself not nervous, I realized I had let my guard down and my adrenaline spiked again, keeping me in a constant state of hypervigilance, knowing that the time I least expected it would be the time Dana would turn up around the corner.

After school on Thursday, Clark and I worked in peace in our conference room away from Dana, discussing in very vague and coded terms how the Censor Board had their computers set up and how we could design our email message. We decided we had to send the email from the Commission of the People's Awareness Bulletin email so that everyone was guaranteed to open it.

The design for the email was simple—just a picture of an experiment—it would be a different picture for each email that we could obtain from Records—and the words "What is the Commission of the People doing to the people of America?" would be posted atop the image.

I was not nearly smart enough with computers to help Clark, so I decided that, when Monday came around, I would spend my time researching the experiments denoted in the first set of notes while Clark worked on the email.

About three hours before Mark was going to take me home on Thursday, I started looking at the clock with dread. I did not want Dana in our home, already certain he would stay past his welcome.

But when Mark pulled up in front of our house, my parents were the ones that sparked my mortification. They were waiting for me and both walked up to the car as I got out.

"What's wrong?" I asked quickly.

"Nothing," my father assured. "Clark," he motioned for him. Clark was startled, but also got out of the car. "I am really sorry to bother you, but I was wondering if you could explain to my wife the gift that your family received from the Commission."

"Oh…"

"*Dad.*"

"Lily, your mother has never seen...someone like him," my father said, acting as if it was completely normal to gawk over another human being. "Neither have I. I'm curious." My father turned back to Clark, who looked nervous, but could not find reason to deny my parents' request.

"Sure." He ducked into the car and called to Mark, motioning for him to join us outside the car. Mark turned off the vehicle before stepping out and walking to Clark's side. I had already gotten used to seeing Mark without his dark glasses, and I was exceptionally embarrassed by my parents' behavior. Mark looked between my parents and Clark, not sure what was expected of him.

"It's really not a good idea to show you out here," Clark said.

"Right, of course," my mother gasped, scurrying inside as we followed. I looked at Clark, mouthing an apology as he shrugged, understanding that there was no way to avoid my parents' curiosity.

Once we were inside the house, my father turned to Mark, staring at him as if trying to figure out what he looked like under the glasses.

"Paul said that they don't understand English..."

"He understands simple words," Clark corrected.

"Is he safe?" my mother asked.

"*Mom*," I groaned, rolling my eyes, "Mykail's safe, why wouldn't Mark be?"

"Don't snap at me, young lady."

"He's very safe," Clark assured. "If you were to pull a gun or a knife on him, though, he's lethal." He turned to Mark and motioned for him to take off his sunglasses. Mark pointed at the glasses and, when he got the approving nod, he stepped back once and shook his head, nervous.

"It's alright," Clark said. He turned back to my parents. "He always gets a little shy with members of the Commission that he hasn't met yet." He turned back to Mark and pushed him forward, once again motioning for him to remove the glasses.

Slowly, Mark took off his glasses, keeping his head bent until Clark told him that it was alright. My mother gasped and a smile came across her lips while my father studied Mark's face carefully. Seeing their scrutiny, Mark dropped his head again, uncomfortable.

"No, get him to lift his head again," my mother said, stepping closer to study him. I bit back the nasty comment threatening to bubble out of me, though I could not contain my exasperated glaring. Clark tapped Mark's arm and the experiment lifted his head, though his eyes remained focused on the ground.

418

"Wow, he looks so different," my mother said, her eyes bright with wonder. "I thought they were supposed to have darker skin."

"He stays inside mostly, so he's pale," Clark answered her indirect question. "Since he's part of the internal security team, he always makes sure to stay out of the sunlight so he doesn't get darker than the others."

"It's incredible." My mother grinned, reaching out to touch Mark's face. The experiment back-pedaled, startled by her sudden touch. My mother chuckled, her voice changing as if she was talking to an animal. "It's okay, I'm not going to hurt you."

"He's kind of shy." Clark tried to laugh away the awkwardness.

"What language does he speak?" my father asked.

"Actually, he can't speak anymore," Clark said slowly. "Dana took care of that."

"Why?" my father asked, surprised. "He could be taught English, I'm sure."

"Well…according to Dana, Mark would always yell at him in his own language. He was worried about a plot forming behind his back, so he made it so Mark couldn't speak."

"So that's what these scars are for," my mother mused, her fingers pressing to the underside of Mark's jaw and along the tendons in his neck. "That's too bad. It would be interesting to hear him speak."

Mark looked at me and Clark, trying to understand what was happening, but I could only glance back apologetically, which appeared to make him even more nervous.

My mother, smiling like a fascinated child, backed away.

"I'm sorry, I didn't mean to stare," she said with a broad grin, continuing to stare. Clark forced a smile.

"It's alright."

"You seem to like him, Clark," my father noted. "And Lily seems to be fond of him, as well."

"He's a good man," Clark said strongly. My mother barked a laugh that made my anger flare.

"Man? He's not exactly a man any more, is he?"

"What do you mean?"

"Never mind, just something that Dana said…" she said, smiling mysteriously about her gossiping.

"Oh…" Clark said quietly. "No, I think that what Dana meant was—at least what Dana believes—that Mark is no longer human. Not since they completed his testing."

"I guess you have to take care of him the same way that we take care of Mykail," my mother mused. "Bathe him and everything."

"No," Clark corrected. "He's perfectly capable of taking care of himself. He's more like the family bodyguard."

"It's so fascinating," my mother said, still rudely scrutinizing Mark. "Are there a lot of them?"

"Um…I don't actually know," Clark admitted.

"We should ask Dana," my mother said. "He must be very good at protecting you," she nodded to Clark. "With everything that's been going on, Lily, maybe we should get one for you."

"He's not some guard dog, Mom," I groaned. "Clark needs to get home soon for dinner, right?"

"Yes," he said with a nod, relieved to be getting out of the house. "I'm sorry, but my dad will be expecting me."

"Oh, of course," my mother agreed. "Thank you for indulging us, Clark. We appreciate it."

"No problem." He tapped Mark's hand to tell him to replace his glasses. "I'm sorry, I have to go."

"You are welcome here any time, Clark," my father said. "Drive safely. Can he see in the dark with those glasses?" he asked, pointing at Mark.

"They're special lenses. He can see," Clark said, ushering Mark out the door and turning back to me. "I'll see you tomorrow."

"Okay," I waved to him. "Have a good night."

"Thanks. You, too. Thank you, Mr. and Mrs. Sandover."

"Have a good night, Clark," my mother called as he walked to the car, where Mark opened the door for him before getting in the driver's seat.

As soon as the engine started, my mother closed the front door and rounded on me, her face hard and angry.

"I don't know what has been up with you lately, but I do not like this new attitude, Lily Sandover."

"What new attitude?"

"You know exactly what I'm talking about," my mother near-growled. "You do not snap back at me, young lady, and you certainly do not talk down to me, particularly just to look good in front of a boy."

"Oh, *please*. Clark and I are not like that."

"I said enough with the attitude, Lily Grace Sandover!"

"Just because I'm not acting like Dana's good little pet and drooling over every experiment that comes out of the Commission, I have an attitude? I'm sorry for looking at these people as if they're *humans*!"

"Lily, we are not drooling over every experiment Dana creates," my father said, his voice calmer than my mother's, cutting her off. "But we can be fascinated with an experiment, particularly one that we have never seen before."

"You're acting like he's some kind of animal!" I growled. "Mark is sweet and he genuinely cares about Clark and me. He gets worried whenever he doesn't know where Clark is. Isn't that a human reaction?"

"Not exclusively," my mother disagreed. "Dogs also get nervous when they do not know where their master is. Whatever changes Dana made to Mark have turned him from a human into an experiment of the Commission. He is meant to be whatever Dana made him to be, nothing more."

"Then, by that logic, I'm not supposed to be anything more than what you and the Commission *let* me be?" I asked, stunned. "I'm not my own person? I have no say in this?"

"It's not like that for you," my father disagreed.

"Why not?" I snapped. "What makes me so different from Mark and Mykail?!"

"You're so young..." my mother murmured.

"For the love of God, stop saying that!" I groaned. "Stop using my age as a means to escape explaining something that you don't understand yourself."

"Mark was not allowed to be in this country," my mother said strongly, choosing to ignore my previous statements. "That was clear from the laws set by Central. As for Mykail, Dana told us that he was a criminal and a homosexual. You know that this is—"

"Has it ever occurred to you that Dana *lied*?!" I bellowed.

"Don't you dare take that tone with me!" my mother yelled back.

"How can you be so accepting of what Dana does? Weren't you the one who wanted to get out of the Commission because you couldn't stand what Dana did to people? Now you're playing along with him and his games like there's nothing wrong with what he does!"

"There is nothing wrong with what the Commission does!" my mother snapped. "You have been spoiled with the safety and security of this country, but my grandmother told me what it was like before the revolution, before the Commission cleaned up the country. This compassion for the people who were doing such intense harm to the country was a poison that undermined *everyone*. We don't live in a perfect world, Lily. Humans are cruel beings. Nothing will ever change that. The Commission exists to take the most dangerous humans out of society so that the rest of us can live."

"Wow..." I barely managed to force the word from my constricted lungs. It sounded like a sob, and it might have been with the tears forming in my eyes. "You deserve the Commission, Mom."

I ran to my room, the tears cascading down my cheeks. I slammed my door and fell against it, crying into my hands. I wasn't even entirely sure why I was crying other than due to my confusion. The world was spinning in the opposite direction. How could my mother say those things? How could the same woman who raised me to respect everyone and love those who were less fortunate turn off the part of her brain that told her the people in the Commission were human?

There was no way to know how long I was crying, but when I realized I had stopped, I was surprised to find myself staring at the mattress of my bed, remembering the file under it that I had been too afraid to touch. I stared at the line where my mattress met my bed frame, pondering whether or not I should pull it out and read.

My thought was interrupted by the doorbell echoing through the house. A glance at the clock confirmed it was already nine.

Dana was there.

I rapidly locked my door, but remained sitting where I had been during my crying spell, listening carefully. I could not hear the door open, but I started to hear voices from the kitchen. I could not distinguish what they were saying, but I didn't have to wait long until the voices were close enough to understand.

"Are you sure you don't want something to eat or drink?"

"I'm sure, Karen. Thank you, though," Dana said, ascending the stairs. "We can't stay long, I'm afraid."

"Is there anything wrong?"

"No, no, nothing wrong," Dana said, a seductive smile in his voice. "Leader Simon is getting in contact with Altereye and his team, and I would like to be there as well."

"That's so exciting," my mother giggled as she topped the stairs. My heart sped up, realizing how close they were.

"Where is Little Lily?"

"Oh, she got a little upset when she came home today, so she's locked herself in her room, throwing a tantrum," my mother said, sounding annoyed, which hurt me more than I should have let it.

"Teenagers will be teenagers."

"What did she get upset about?" Sean's voice asked.

"Oh…she's having some difficulty grasping the importance of the Commission," my mother said, downplaying the main issue. "Clark introduced us to Mark, and she didn't like the way we spoke to him."

"Ah, Mark," Dana said, his voice right outside my door. "He came out very well. Really had to make some changes to get him to calm down, but he finally came around…with some heavy persuasion."

"He's fascinating," my mother said as I heard her mess with the lock on Mykail's door. "I've never seen an Asian before."

Mykail's door opened. I turned my head and pressed my ear close.

"Mykail, Dana's here to give you your shots," my mother said, speaking to Mykail like a small child. I rolled my eyes, sickened. "I hope he doesn't give you too much trouble…"

"No, he should be fine," Dana said. "Keep the discipline remote handy, though, if he decides he wants to play. Sean, will you hold his shoulders?"

There was no sound for quite some time and then Dana started speaking again.

"How have you been, Karen?"

"Can't complain," my mother said. "How about you?"

"I've been very well, thank you," he answered. "I am sorry to hear that Little Lily has hit her rebellious teenage phase."

"I just don't know what to do with her," my mother groaned. "And Tom has been absolutely no help at all. He keeps telling me that I'm not being considerate of the changes she's had to endure. He's obviously thinking that I could adjust right away to everything and that *I* didn't need to endure any changes."

"He's just trying to keep the peace in the house," he said gently, his voice turning sweet. "Who can blame him?"

"But we're supposed to raise her as a team. When we agreed that we wanted a child, he told me that we would never be at odds with one another as parents," my mother said. "Lately, it's like he doesn't care about her at all…or me."

Dana was quiet for a moment before he spoke again.

"Are you feeling neglected?" The seductive power of his voice made me shiver even from another room. "I apologize, I have been demanding a great deal of your husband lately."

"No, it's not anything like that," my mother said quickly. "I don't know…you're not married, so you don't understand what it's like. Sometimes…you just wonder…"

"If you made the right choice?"

"If…I could have been something more than what I am," my mother admitted. "If I could have accomplished something else."

"I am sorry to hear that you feel as though you have not accomplished anything," Dana said. "But you're wrong. You have raised a beautiful, intelligent daughter and that is more than I can say for most."

"I wish Lily would see that. What about your mother? Did you realize how hard she worked to raise you when you were Lily's age?"

Dana chuckled. "We never appreciate our mother's when we're younger. But I wish I had a mother like you when I was Little Lily's age. My mother never thought of my well-being in the same way you think of hers. She was more interested in pleasing my father than raising me."

"I am so sorry to hear that…"

"Little Lily is very fortunate," Dana breathed. There was another extended silence as I tried to keep my heart from breaking apart in my chest from the pain of my mother's words. "Sean, will you excuse Karen and me for a moment?"

There were footsteps, but they did not go far down the stairs, which told me that Sean was eavesdropping with me.

"Karen," Dana started, "Little Lily is growing up. There is no need to blame yourself or feel as though you are a bad mother."

"I just…I feel like I'm all alone. My daughter seems to hate me…and Tom won't even look at me. We haven't even…" She trailed off.

"That's his loss," Dana said tenderly. "Because any man should treasure you. You truly are a one of a kind woman."

I felt my stomach turn over. He was lying. He had seduced everyone in the Commission before—I was listening to the way he did it.

"It seems like Tom's forgotten." My mother's voice actually sounded pained. That did nothing more than anger me. I did not feel sorry for her. As far as I was concerned, she was no longer my mother. She was just another person infatuated with Dana, wrapped up in his spell and bowing to his whim without thought.

"Do you want to come to the Commission and talk to me about it?" Dana suggested gently.

There it was. That was the end for my mother.

"I'd like that."

"I'm pretty busy this weekend, and I have meetings on Monday, but you are more than welcome to come to the Commission any time Tuesday," he told her. "I'll be there."

"Thank you."

"I am sorry that I have to leave now," he whispered. "Are you going to be alright?"

"I'll be fine," my mother assured. It sounded as though she was close to crying.

"I'll see you Tuesday?" Dana pressed, his voice getting closer to my door as he left Mykail's room.

"Tuesday," my mother agreed.

424

"I'm sorry I'm missing seeing Little Lily," he said close to my door. I resisted punching my door as hard as I could to answer him.

"Don't take it personally." My mother brushed it off. "Is there anything else I need to do for Mykail?"

"No, just make sure he drinks enough water. He might feel a little weird the next few days, but that should not last any longer than the weekend. If it does, just let me know on Tuesday," he said as their voices descended the stairs. I listened to Dana leave the house, but I did not leave my room, even when my mother called me down for dinner. Even though my stupid, immature rebellion led to me going the entire night without a meal, I was too nauseous after the conversation my mother had had with Dana to think of food.

I had lost her.

End of Part 1

To be continued in:

Inside
Part 2

More Works by K.J. Amidon

Inside
(Written as Kyra Anderson)
Inside – Pt. 1
Inside – Pt. 2
Inside – Pt. 3
Inside – Alternate Part 3
Inside the Commission

The Coalition Trilogy
(Written as Kyra Anderson)
Forged Under Fire
The Rising Tide
With Banners Raised

The Significant
(Written as Kyra Anderson)

The Significant Expanded Story
(Written as Kyra Anderson)
The Degenerates
The Deserted

The Faith
(Written as Kyra Anderson)
The Faith
The Sacred

The Dimension Guardian Series:
The Realm of Beasts – The Guardian Tournament
The Realm of Darkness – Blind Ambitions
The Realm of Humans – Fate
The Realm of Light – Imbalance
The Realm of Demons – Scars in Time
The Realm of Exile – Continuum

The Roadside Paradise Series:
Into Oblivion
Wander the Lost
Until Dawn Breaks
Hiding from Sight
For Fools
Challenge Gods